SPILL ZONE

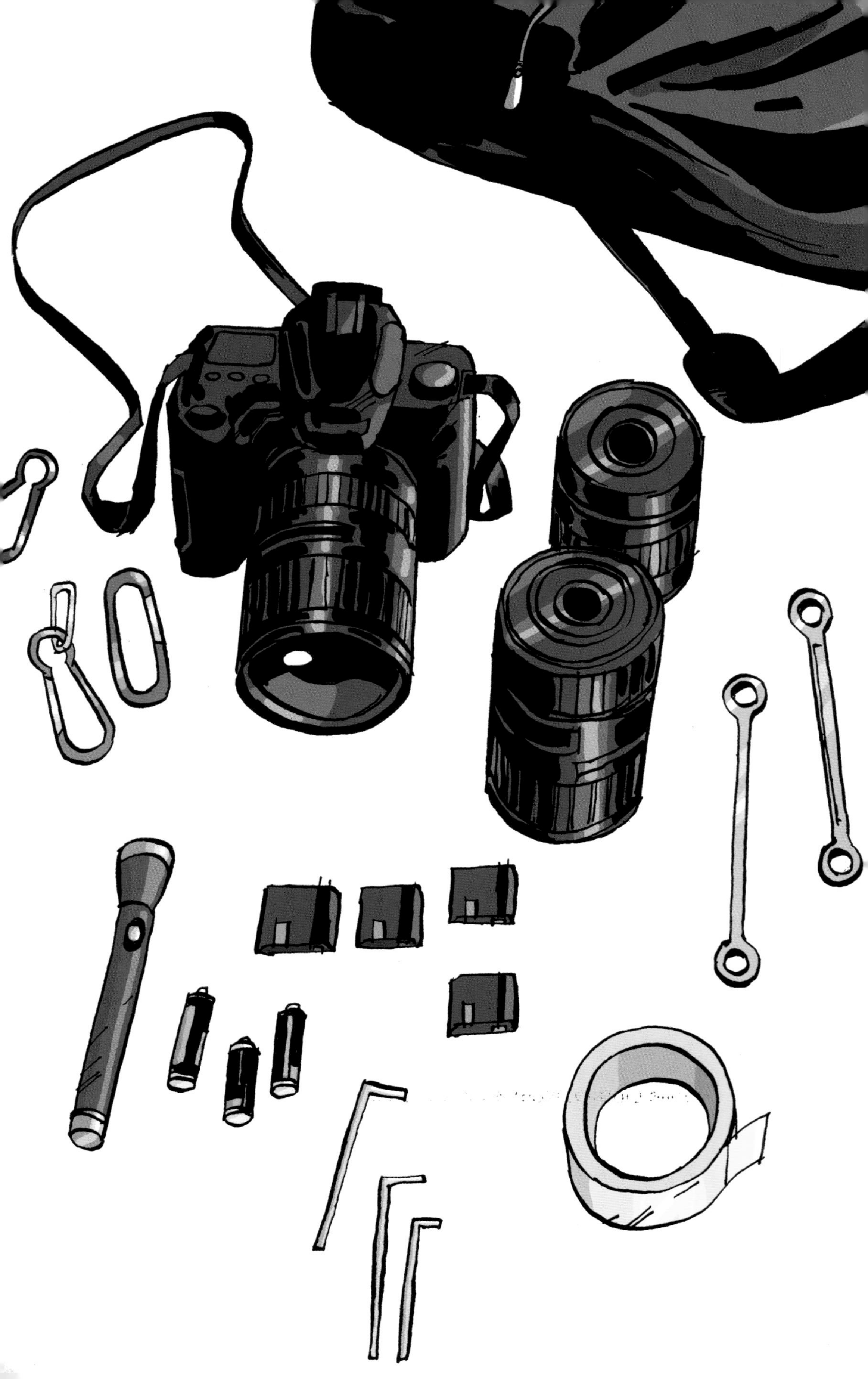

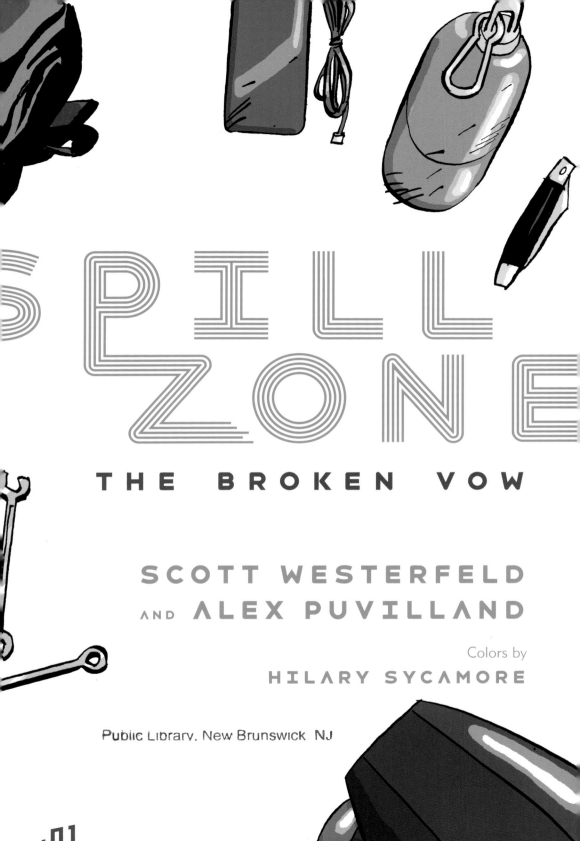

SPILL ZONE

THE BROKEN VOW

SCOTT WESTERFELD
AND ALEX PUVILLAND

Colors by
HILARY SYCAMORE

First Second
NEW YORK

Thanks to everyone in the indie
comics world for welcoming me in
— S.W.

To Leo and Adrien
— A.P.

SPILL ZONE

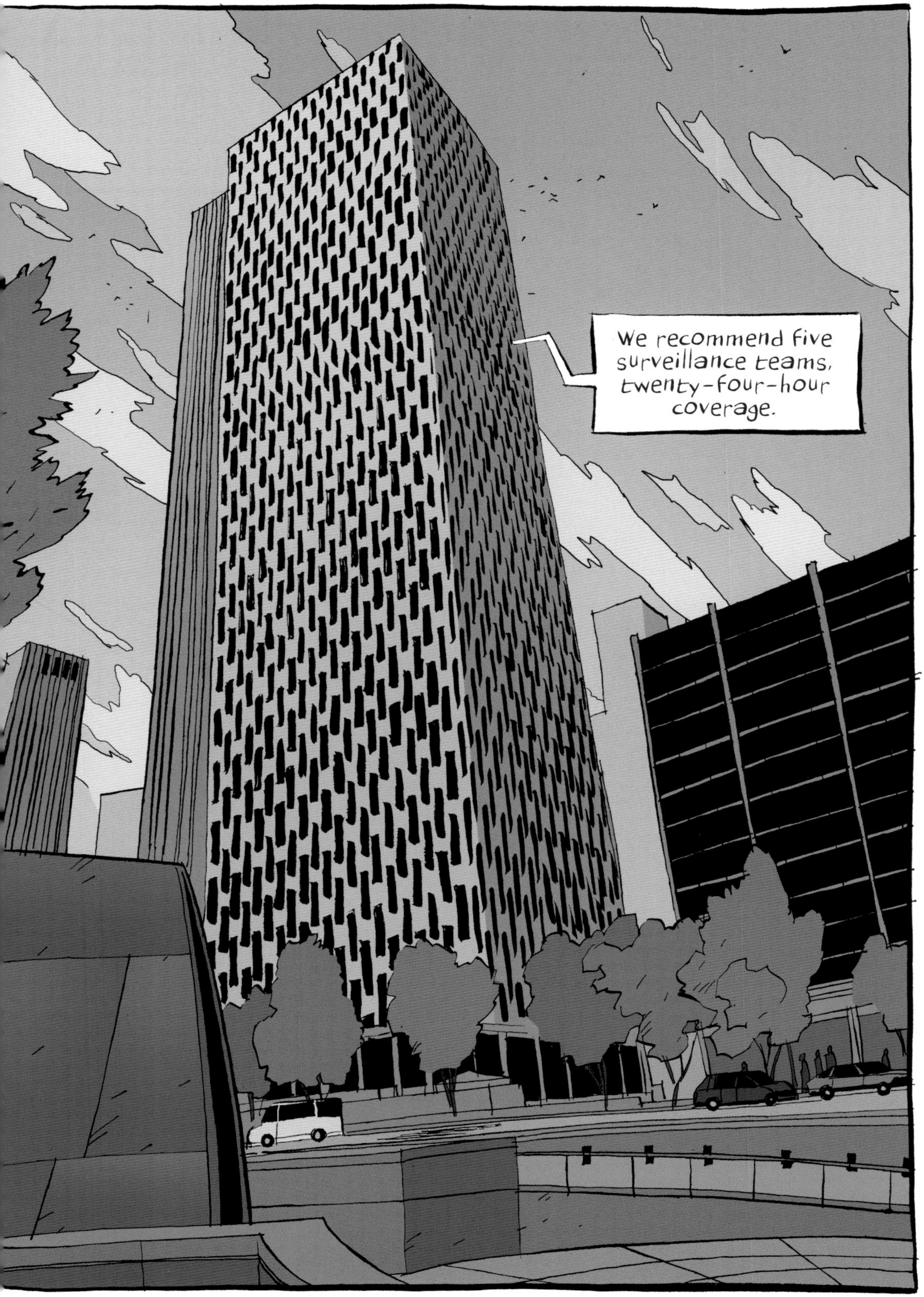
We recommend five surveillance teams, twenty-four-hour coverage.

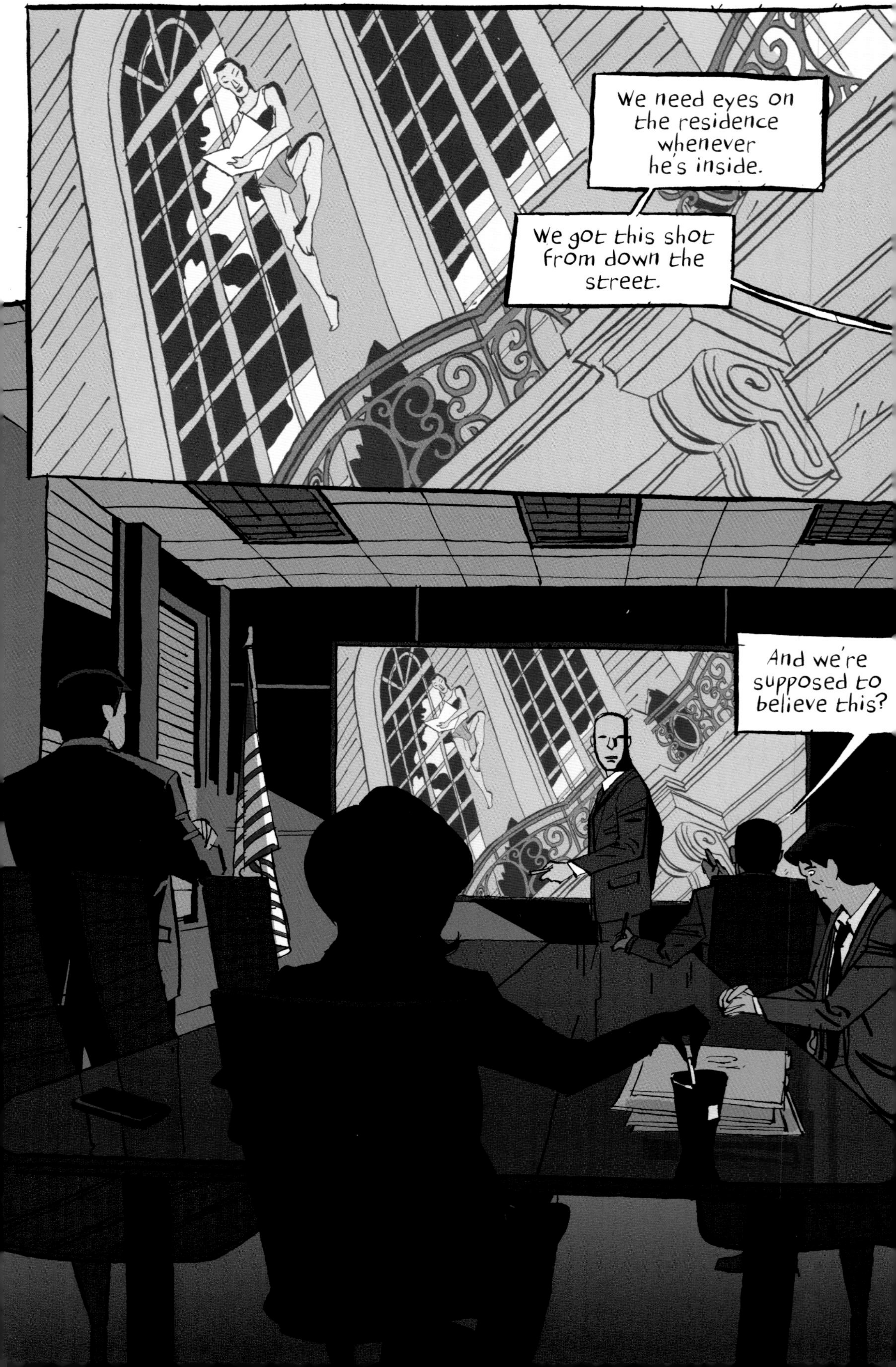
We need eyes on the residence whenever he's inside.
We got this shot from down the street.
And we're supposed to believe this?

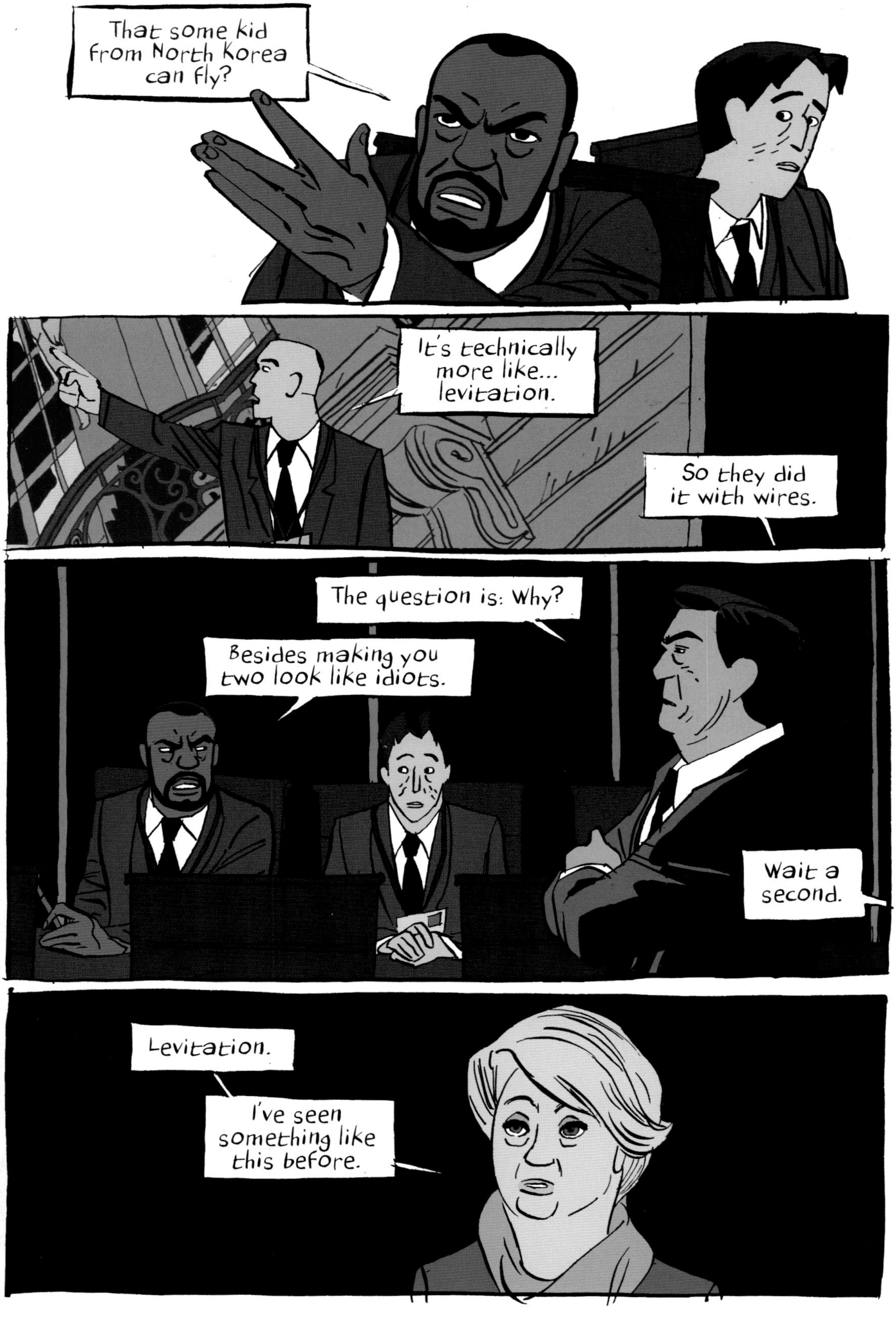
That some kid from North Korea can fly?
It's technically more like... levitation.
So they did it with wires.
The question is: Why?
Besides making you two look like idiots.
Wait a second.
Levitation.
I've seen something like this before.

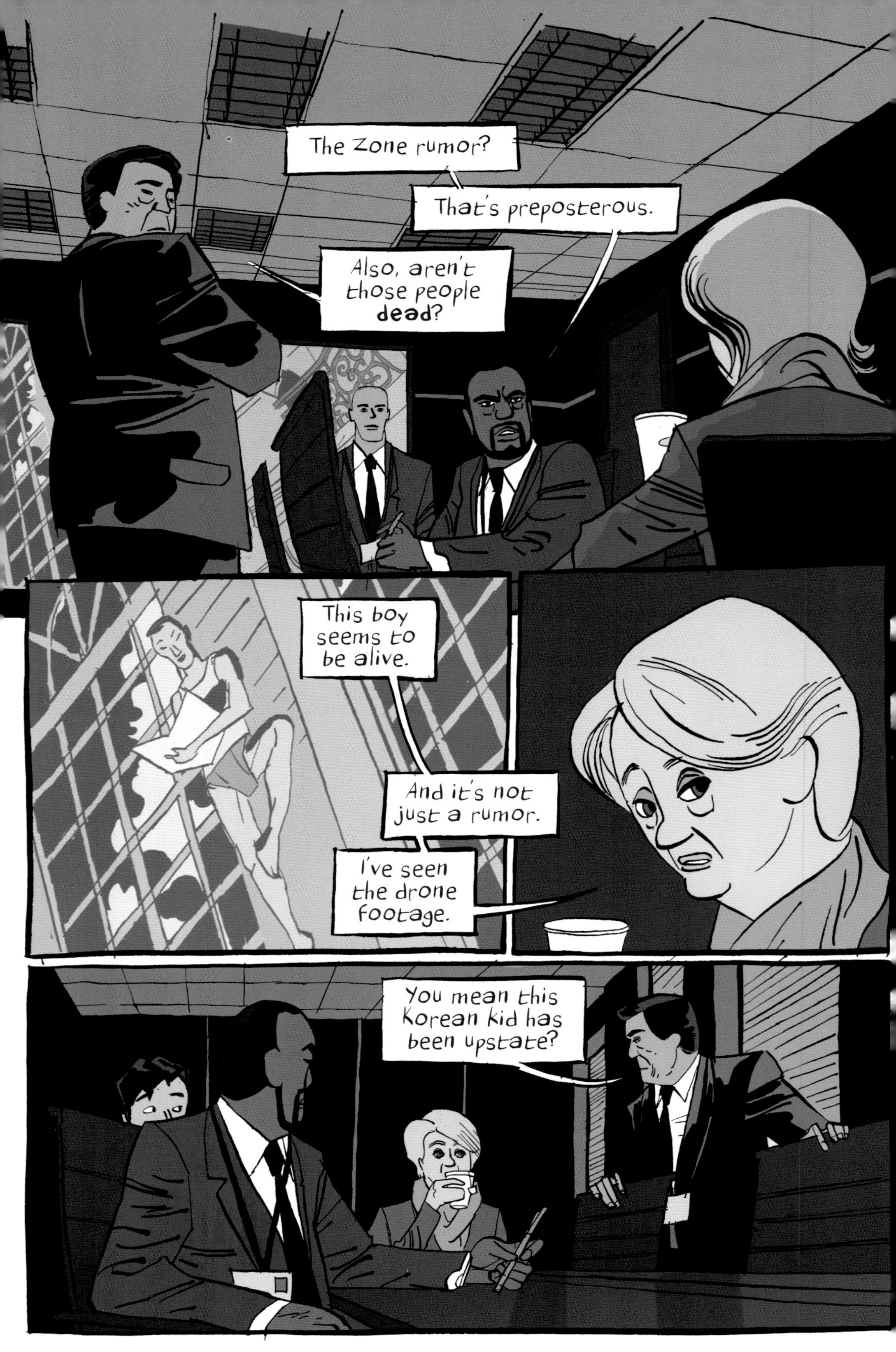
The Zone rumor?
That's preposterous.
Also, aren't those people **dead**?
This boy seems to be alive.
And it's not just a rumor.
I've seen the drone footage.
You mean this Korean kid has been upstate?

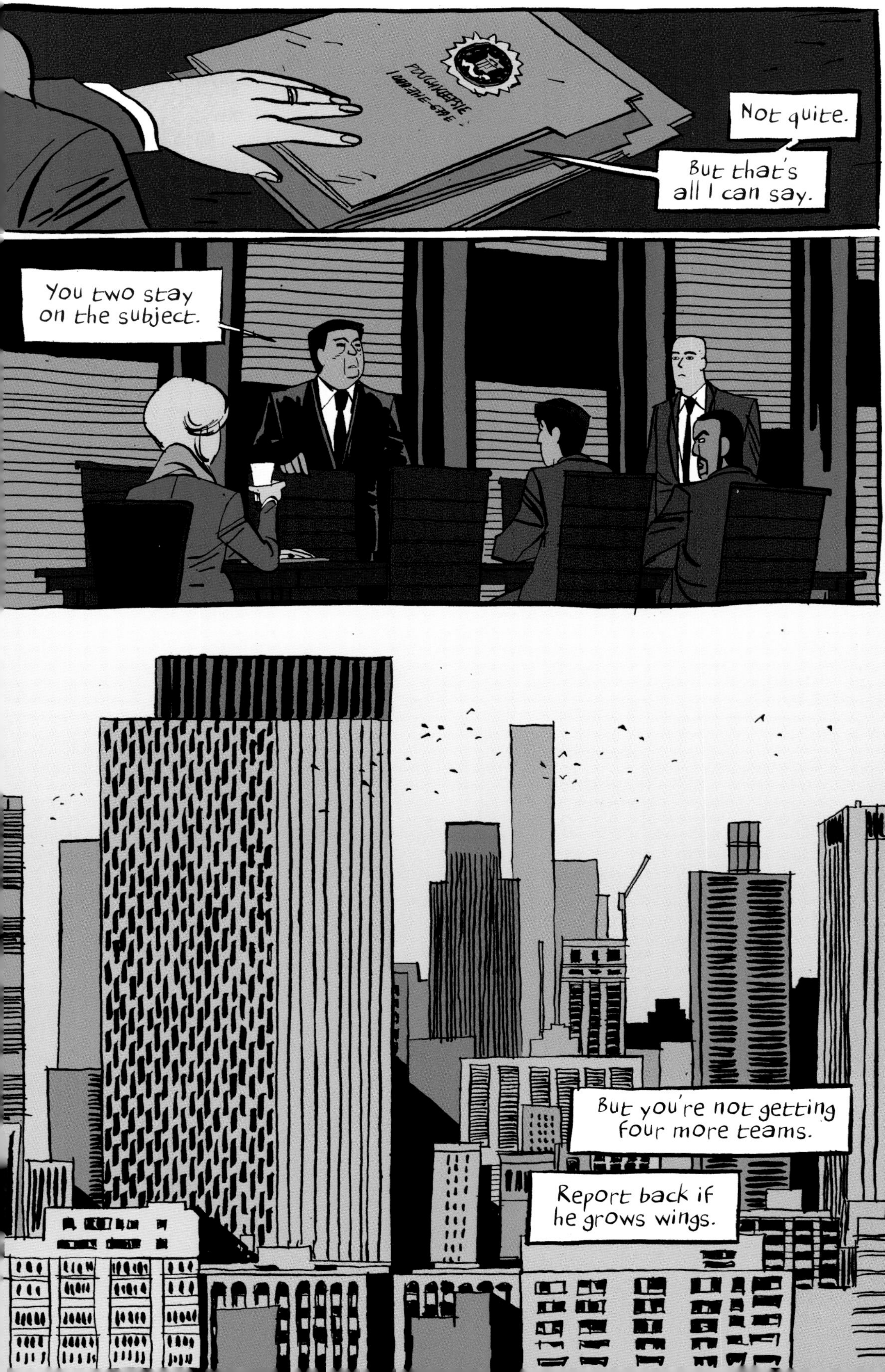
Not quite.
But that's all I can say.
You two stay on the subject.
But you're not getting four more teams.
Report back if he grows wings.

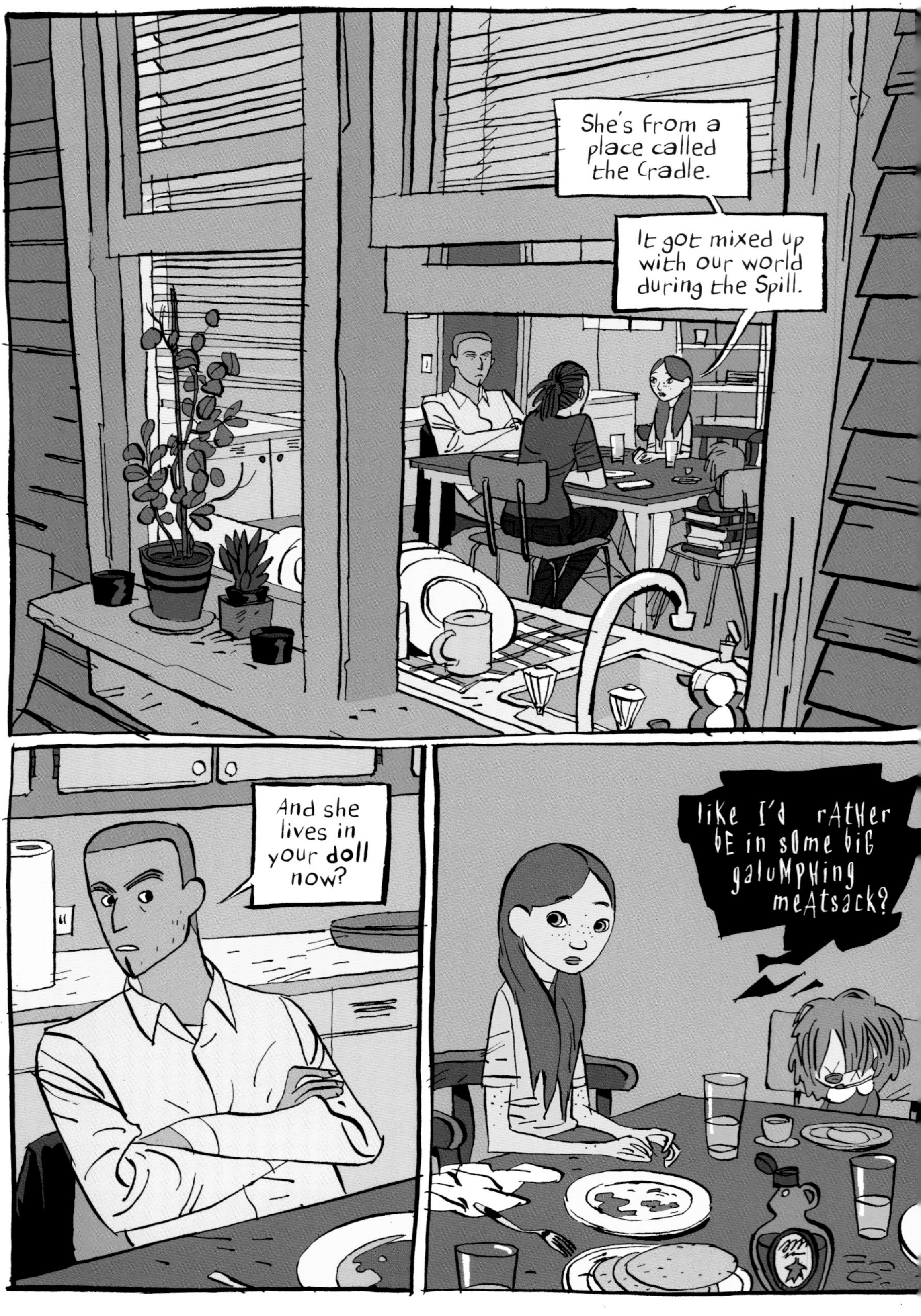
She's from a place called the Cradle.
It got mixed up with our world during the Spill.
And she lives in your **doll** now?
like I'd rather be in some big galumphing meatsack?

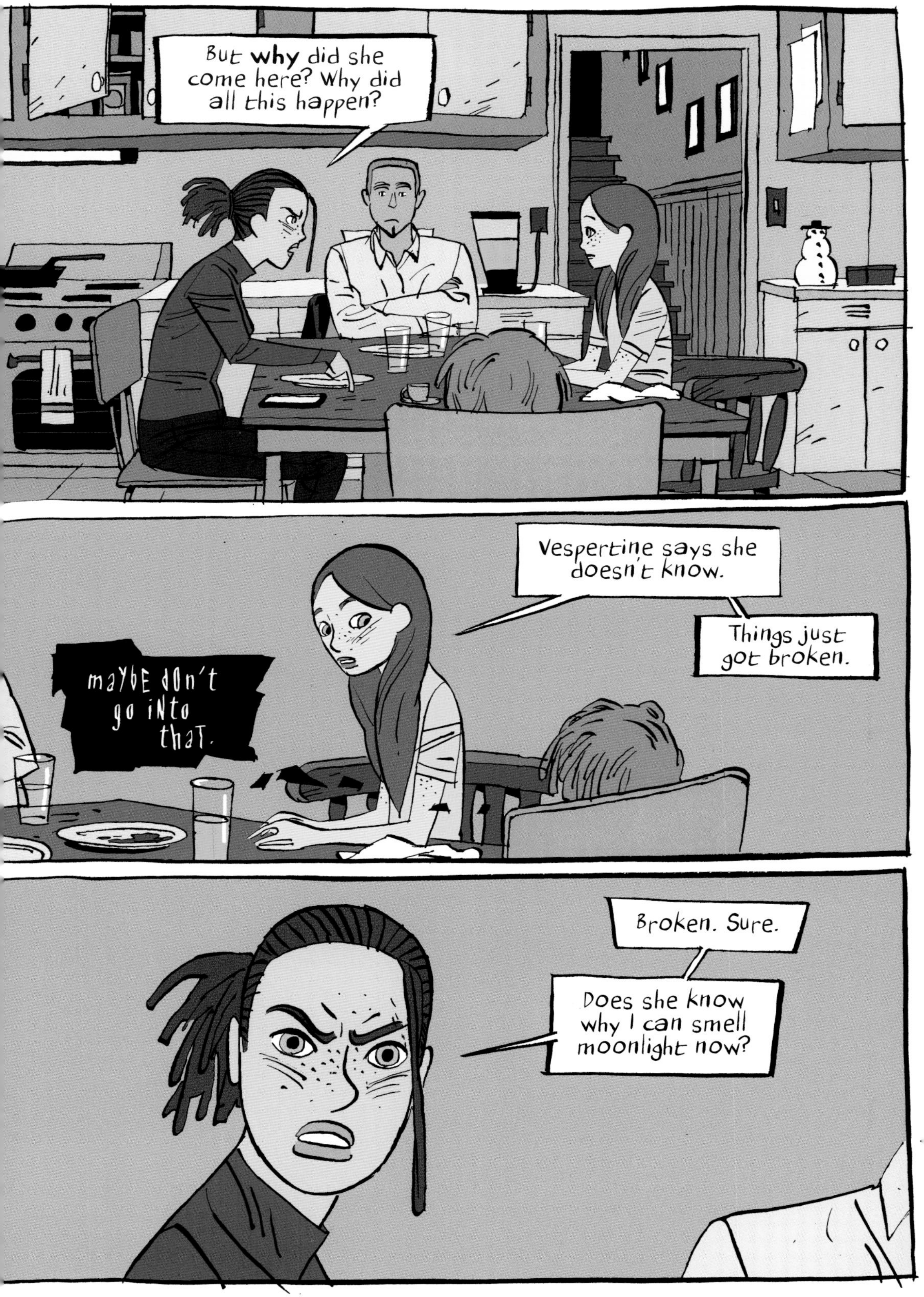
But why did she come here? Why did all this happen?
Vespertine says she doesn't know.
Things just got broken.
maybe don't go into that.
Broken. Sure.
Does she know why I can smell moonlight now?

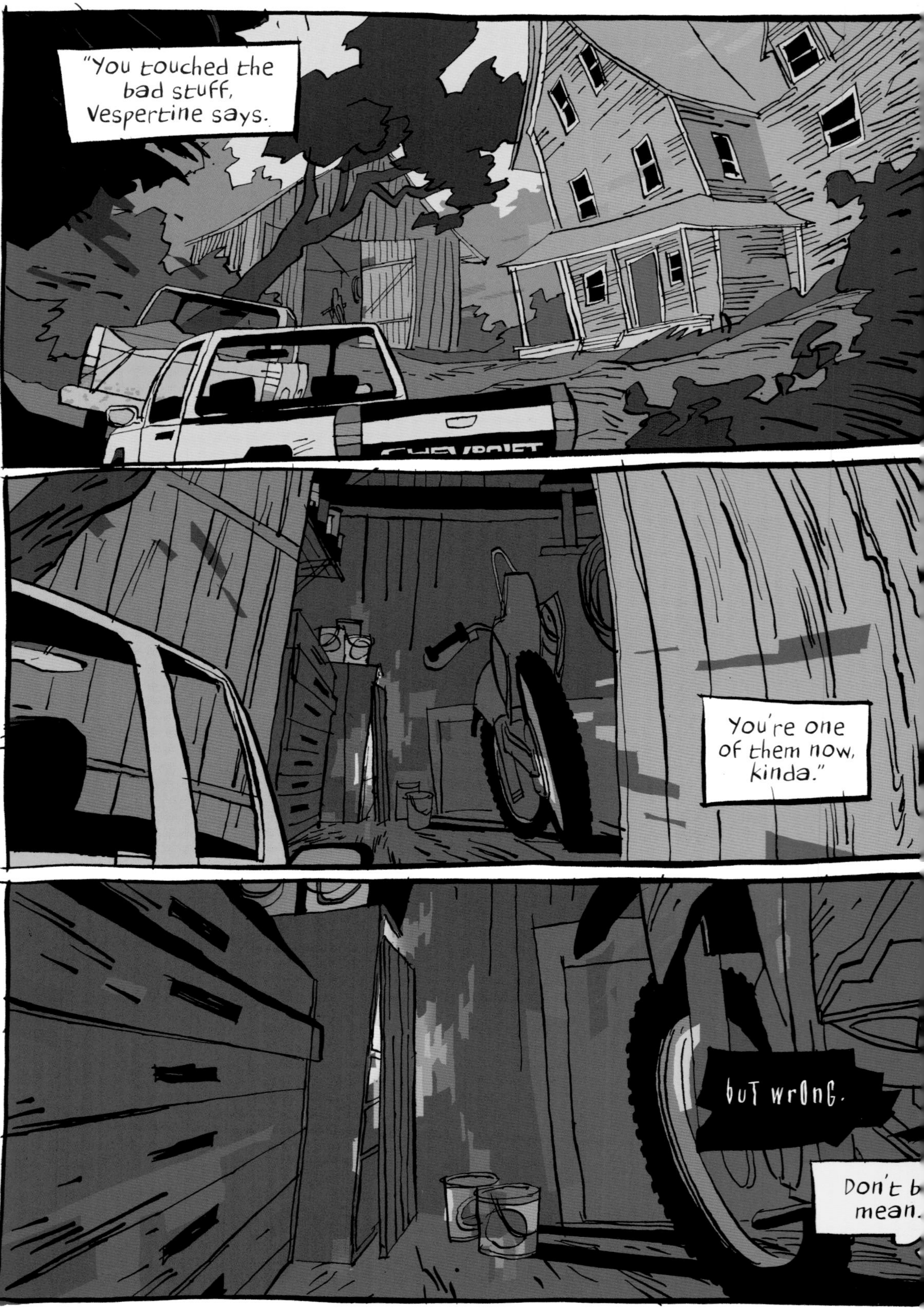
"You touched the bad stuff, Vespertine says.
You're one of them now, kinda."
but wrong.
Don't b
mean.

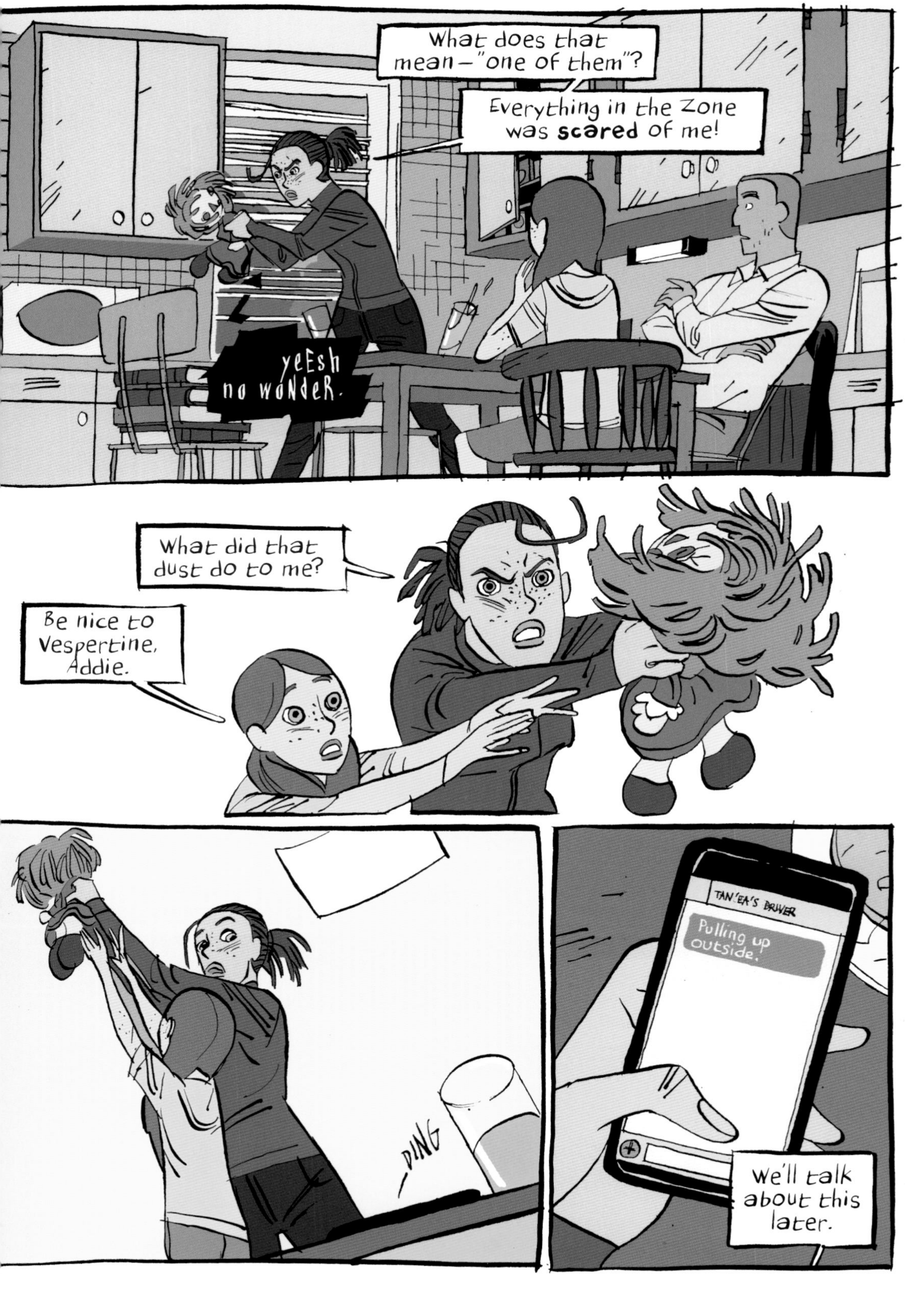
What does that mean—"one of them"?
Everything in the Zone was **scared** of me!
yeEsh no wONdeR.
What did that dust do to me?
Be nice to Vespertine, Addie.
DING
TAN'EA'S DRIVER
Pulling up outside.
We'll talk about this later.

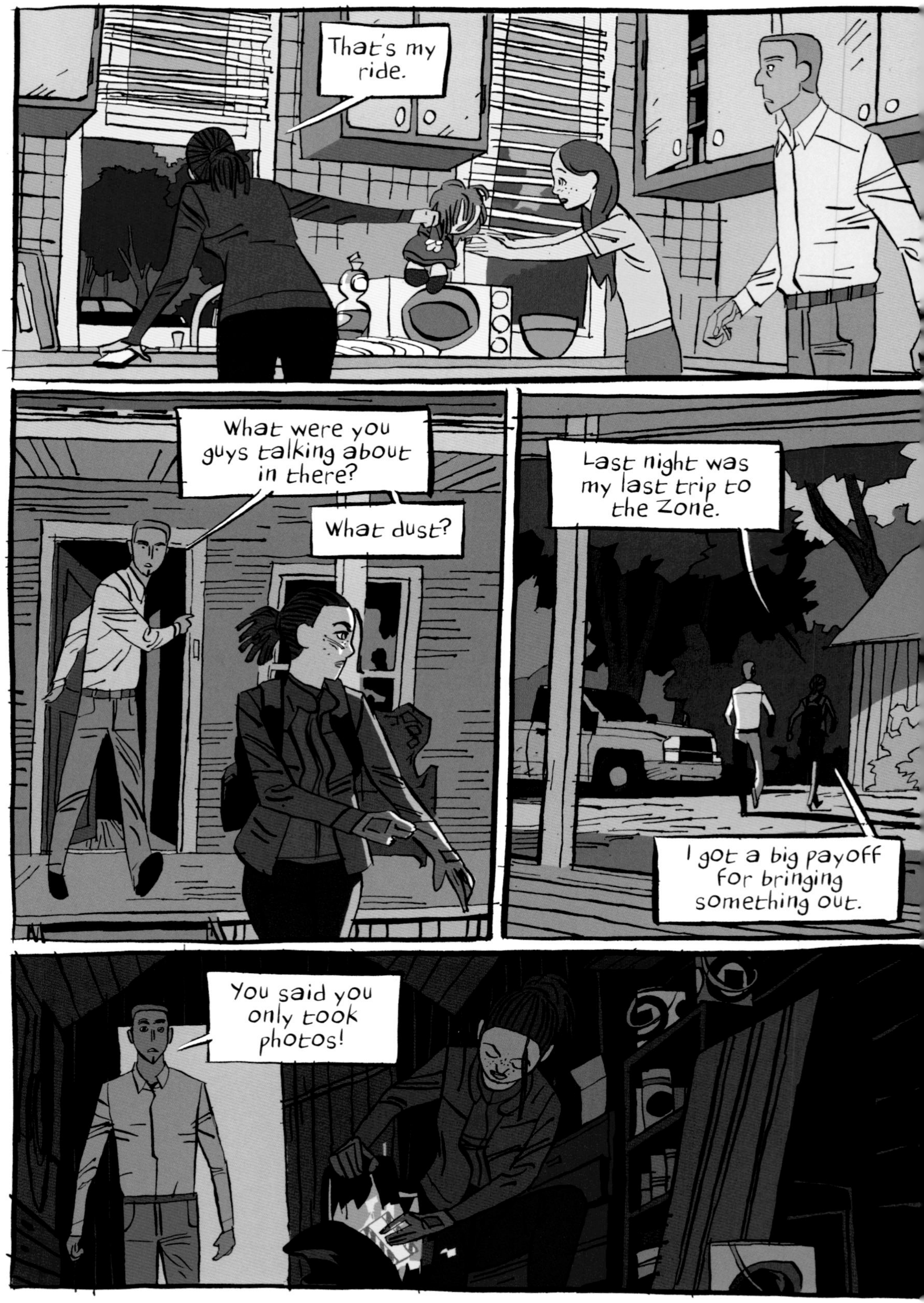
That's my ride.
What were you guys talking about in there?
What dust?
Last night was my last trip to the Zone.
I got a big payoff for bringing something out.
You said you only took photos!

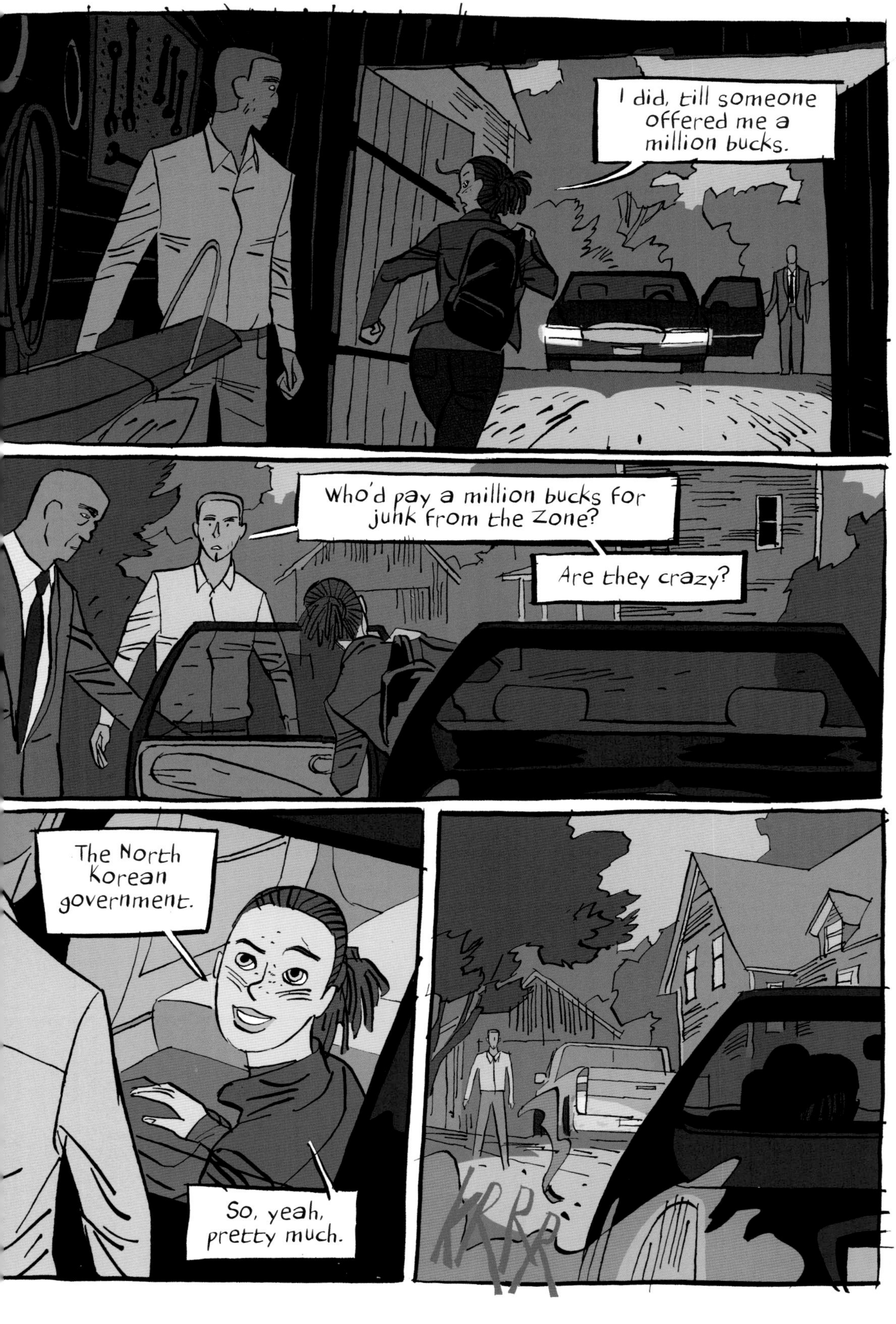
I did, till someone offered me a million bucks.
Who'd pay a million bucks for junk from the Zone?
Are they crazy?
The North Korean government.
So, yeah, pretty much.
KRRR

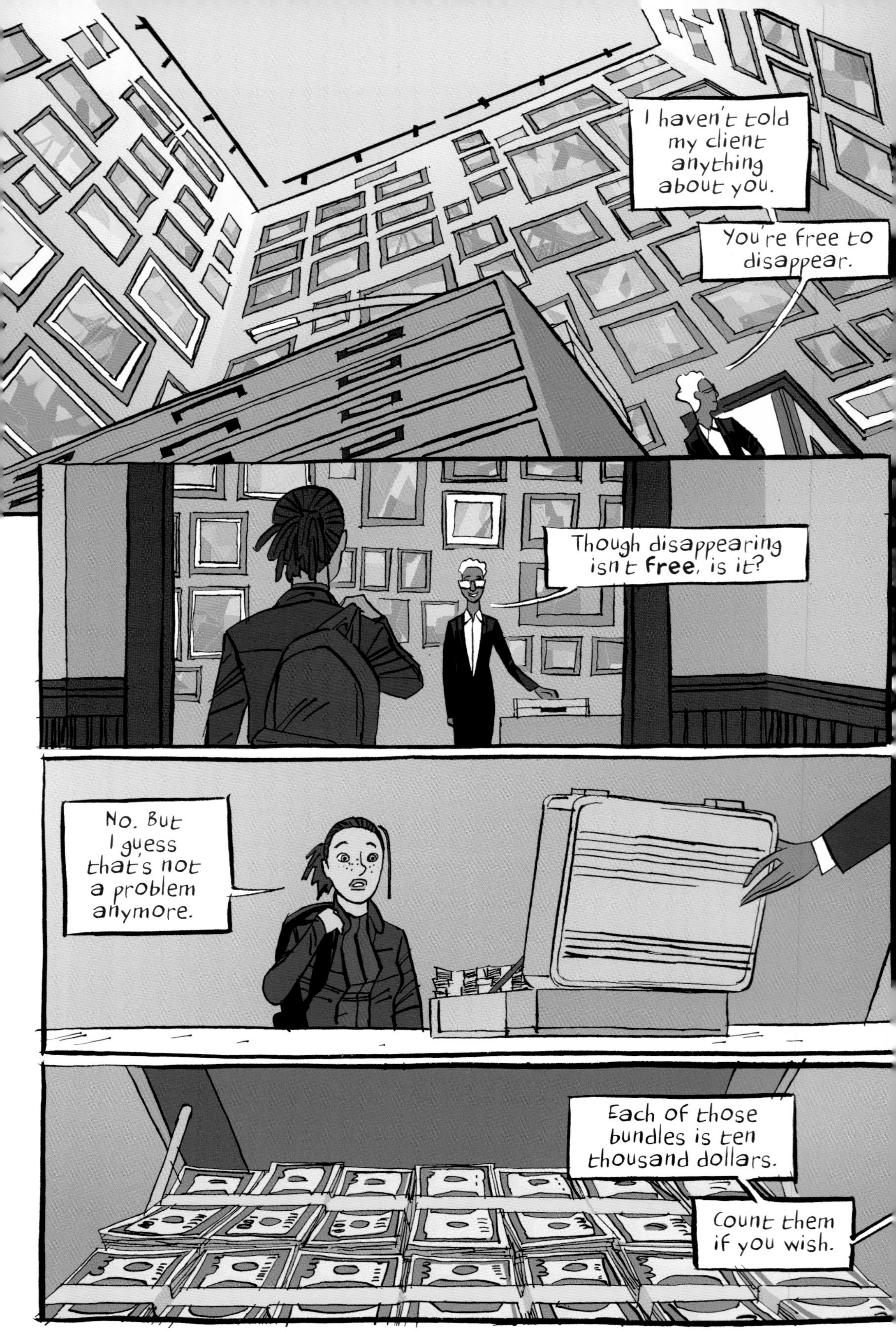
I haven't told my client anything about you.
You're free to disappear.
Though disappearing isn't **free**, is it?
No. But I guess that's not a problem anymore.
Each of those bundles is ten thousand dollars.
Count them if you wish.

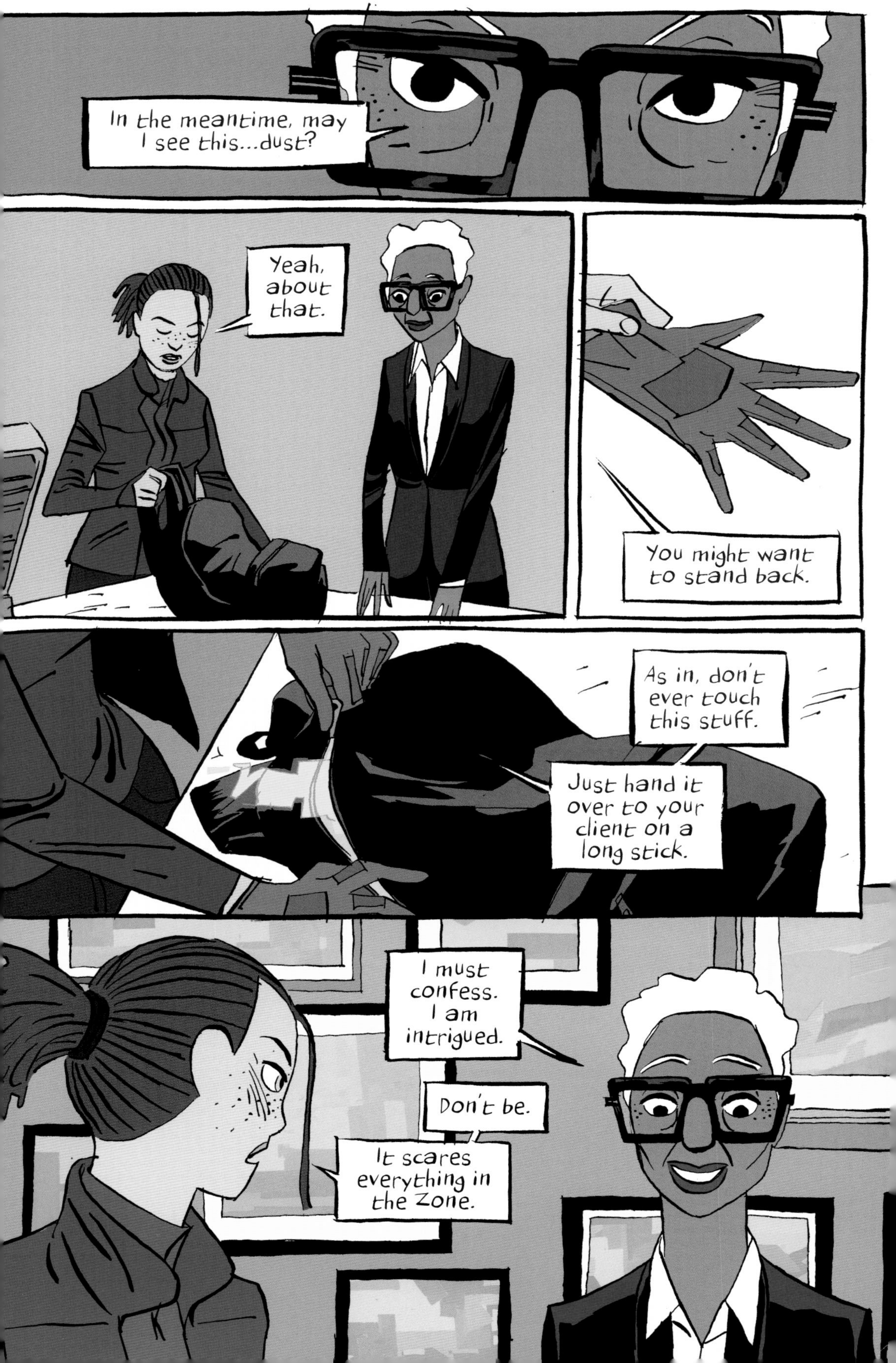

In the meantime, may I see this...dust?
Yeah, about that.
You might want to stand back.
As in, don't ever touch this stuff.
Just hand it over to your client on a long stick.
I must confess. I am intrigued.
Don't be.
It scares everything in the Zone.

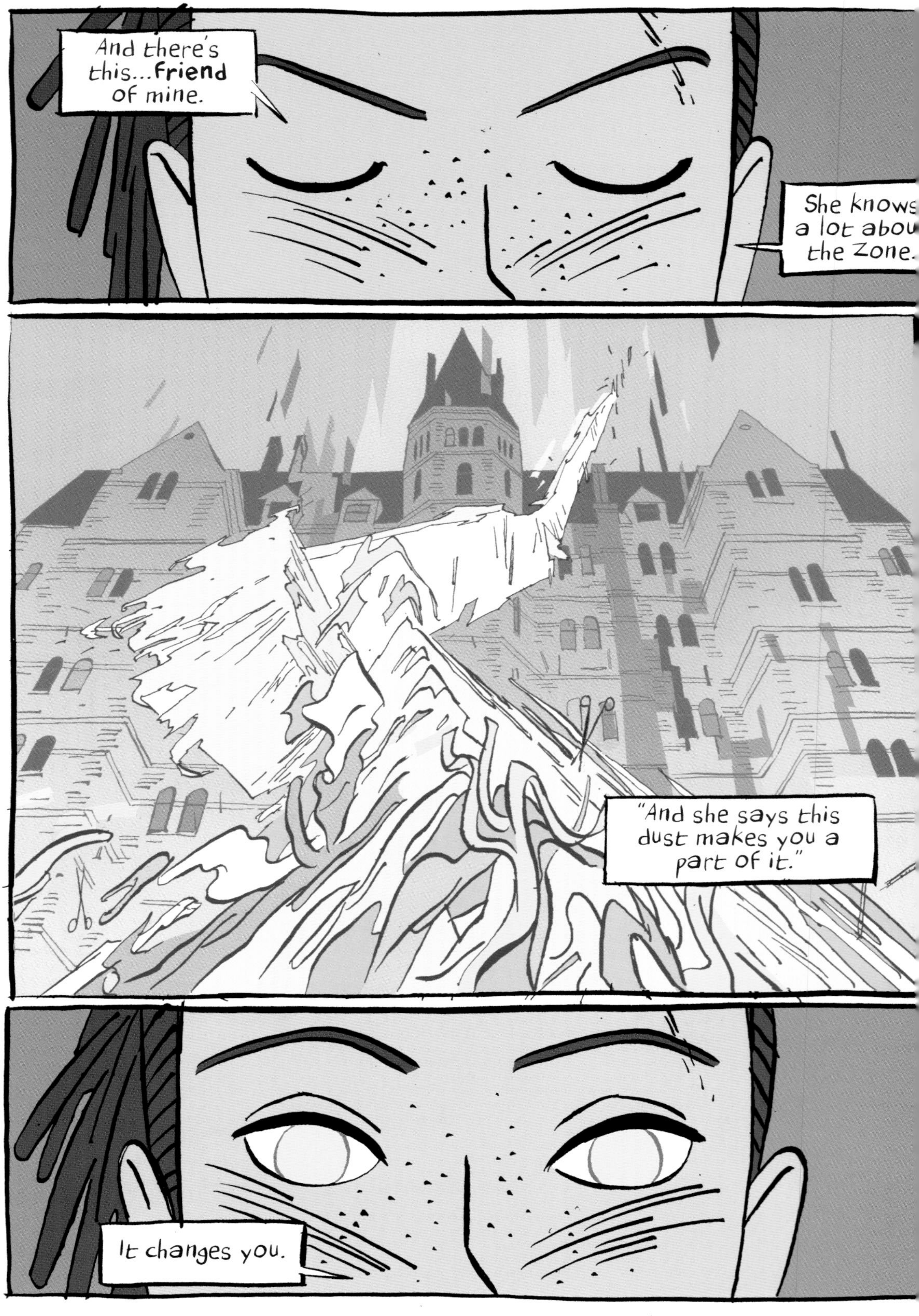
And there's this...**friend** of mine.
She knows a lot about the Zone.
"And she says this dust makes you a part of it."
It changes you.

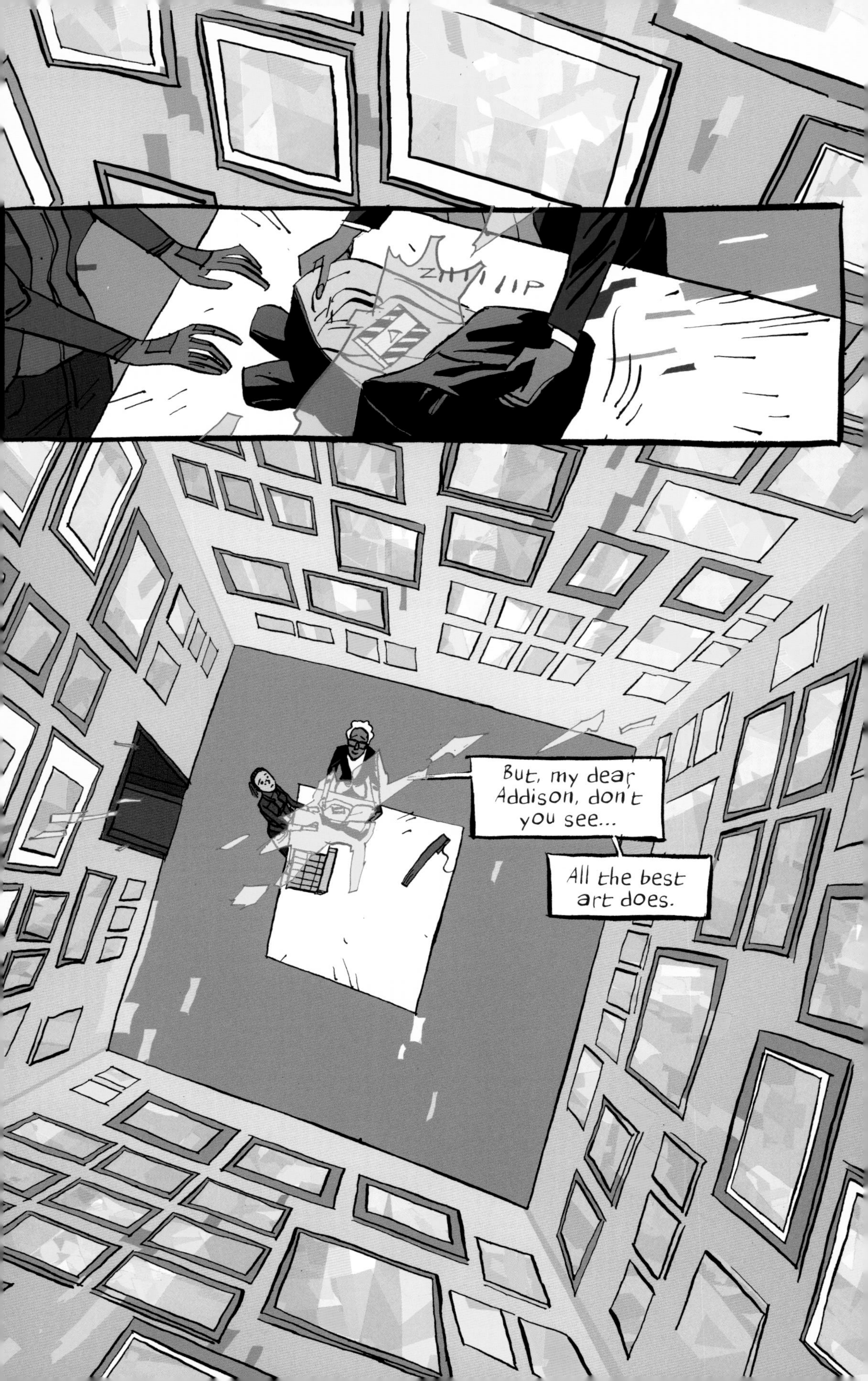
ZHHIIP
But, my dear Addison, don't you see...
All the best art does.

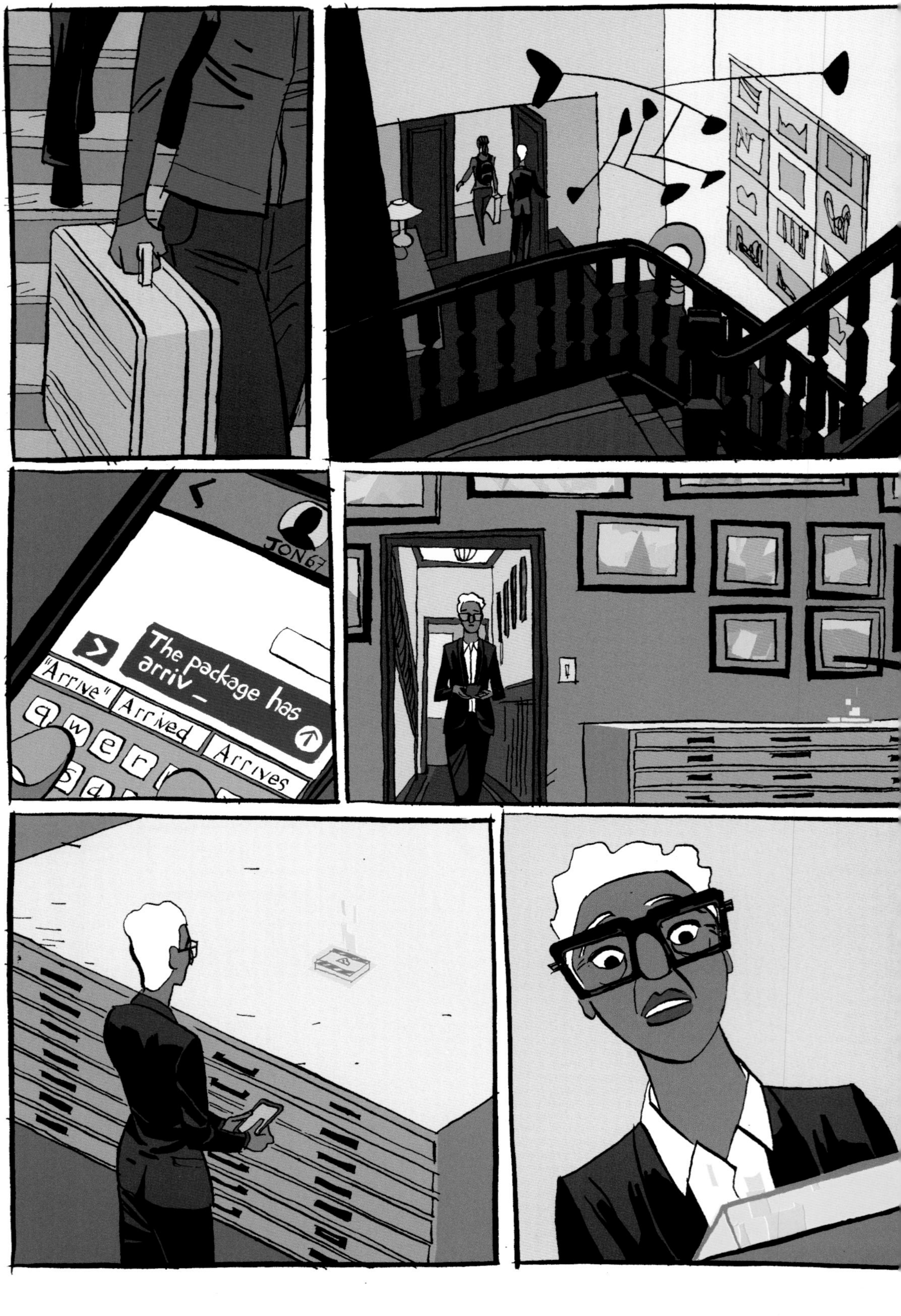
JON67
The package has arriv_
"Arrive"
Arrived
Arrives

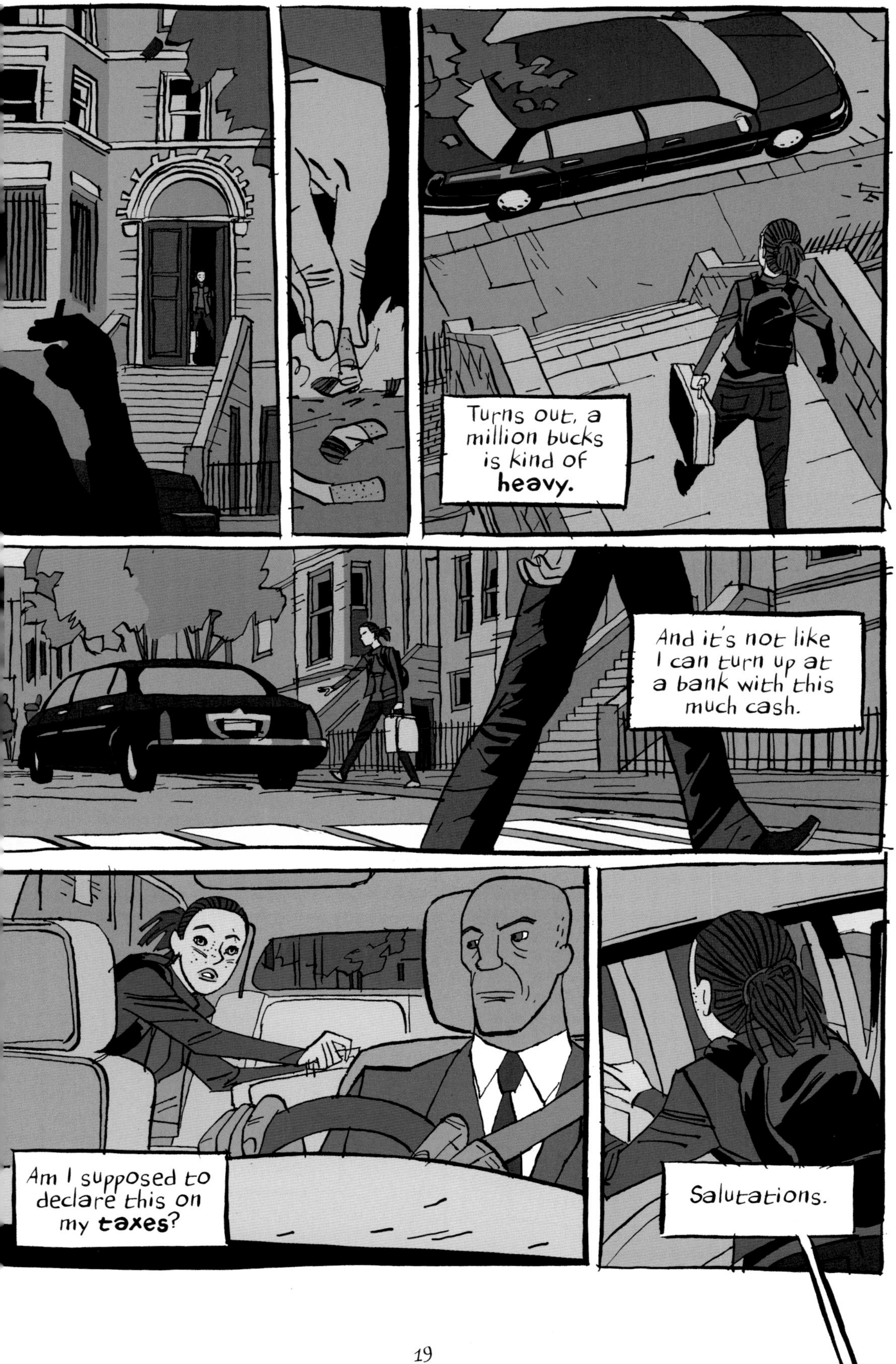
Turns out, a million bucks is kind of **heavy.**
And it's not like I can turn up at a bank with this much cash.
Am I supposed to declare this on my **taxes**?
Salutations.

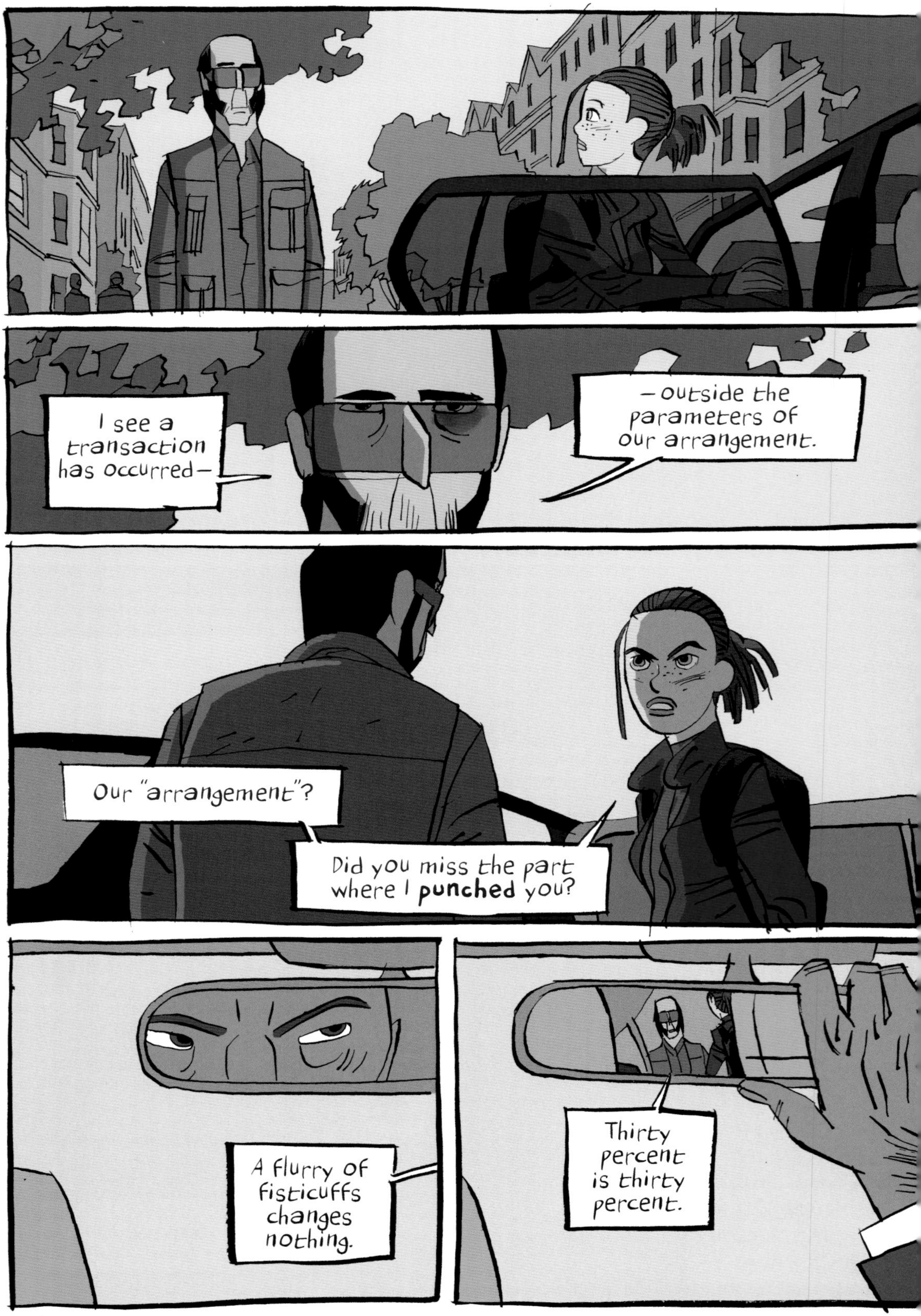
I see a transaction has occurred—
—outside the parameters of our arrangement.
Our "arrangement"?
Did you miss the part where I **punched** you?
A flurry of fisticuffs changes nothing.
Thirty percent is thirty percent.

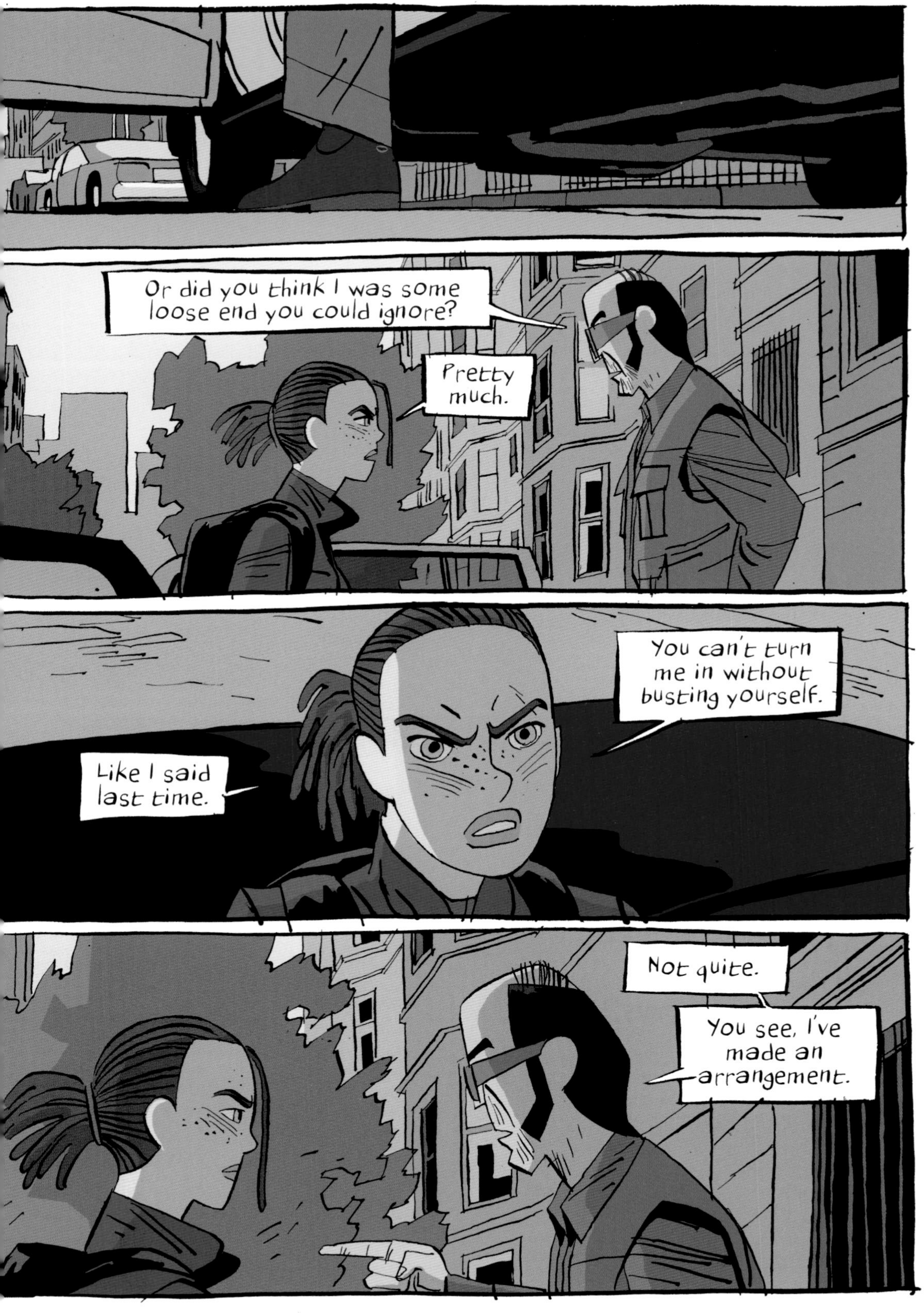
Or did you think I was some loose end you could ignore?
Pretty much.
You can't turn me in without busting yourself.
Like I said last time.
Not quite.
You see, I've made an arrangement.

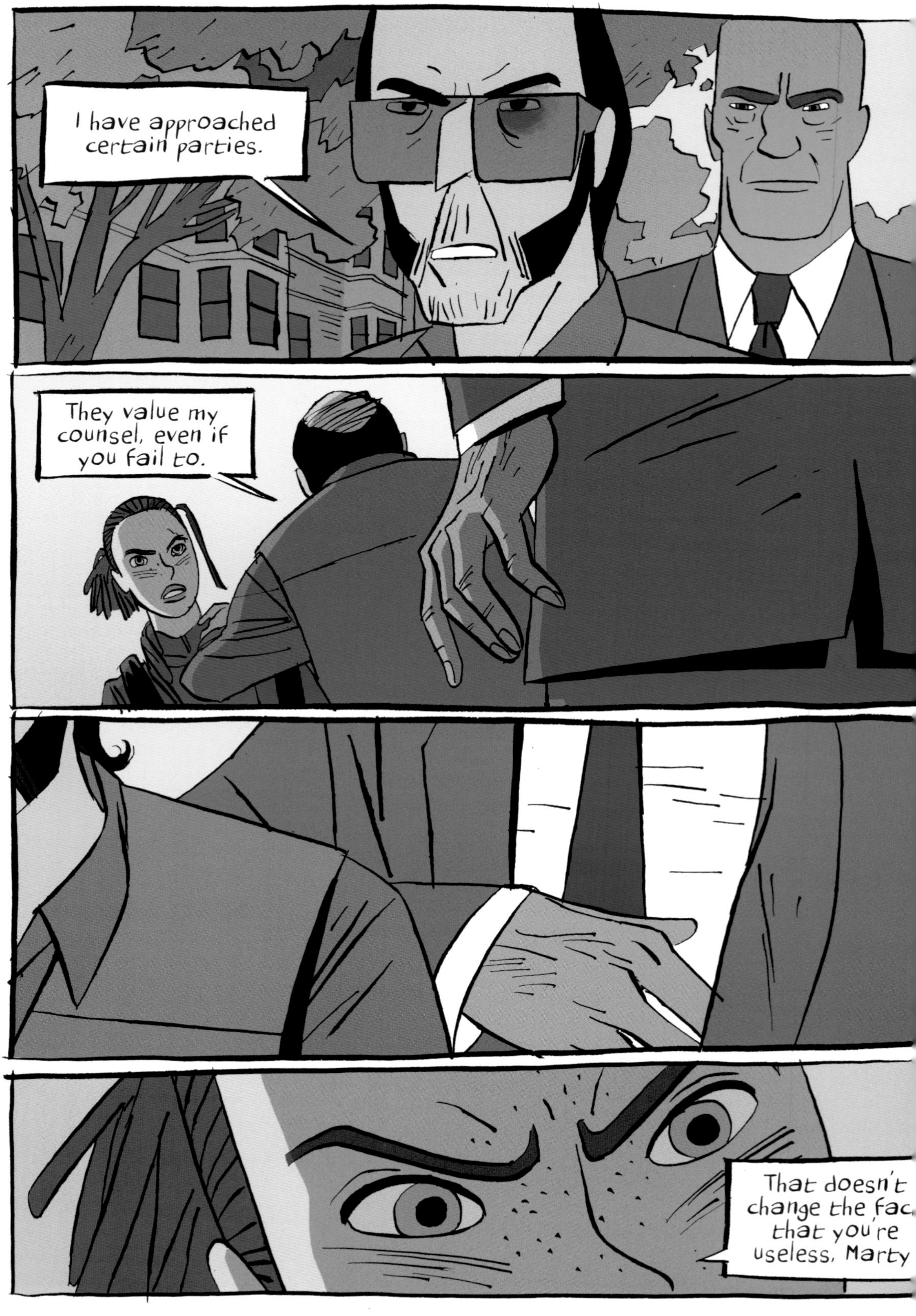
I have approached certain parties.
They value my counsel, even if you fail to.
That doesn't change the fac that you're useless, Marty

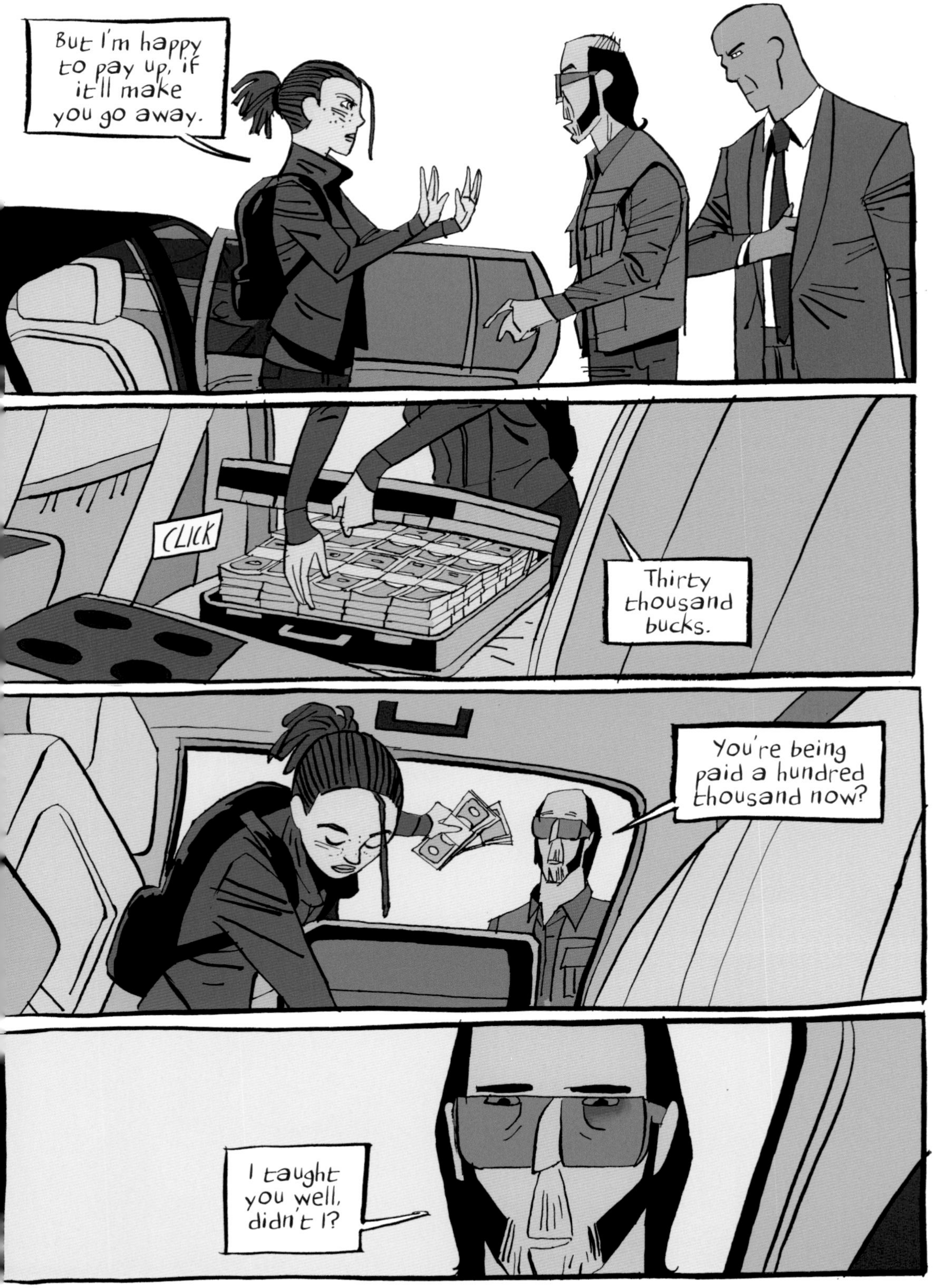
But I'm happy to pay up, if it'll make you go away.
CLICK
Thirty thousand bucks.
You're being paid a hundred thousand now?
I taught you well, didn't I?

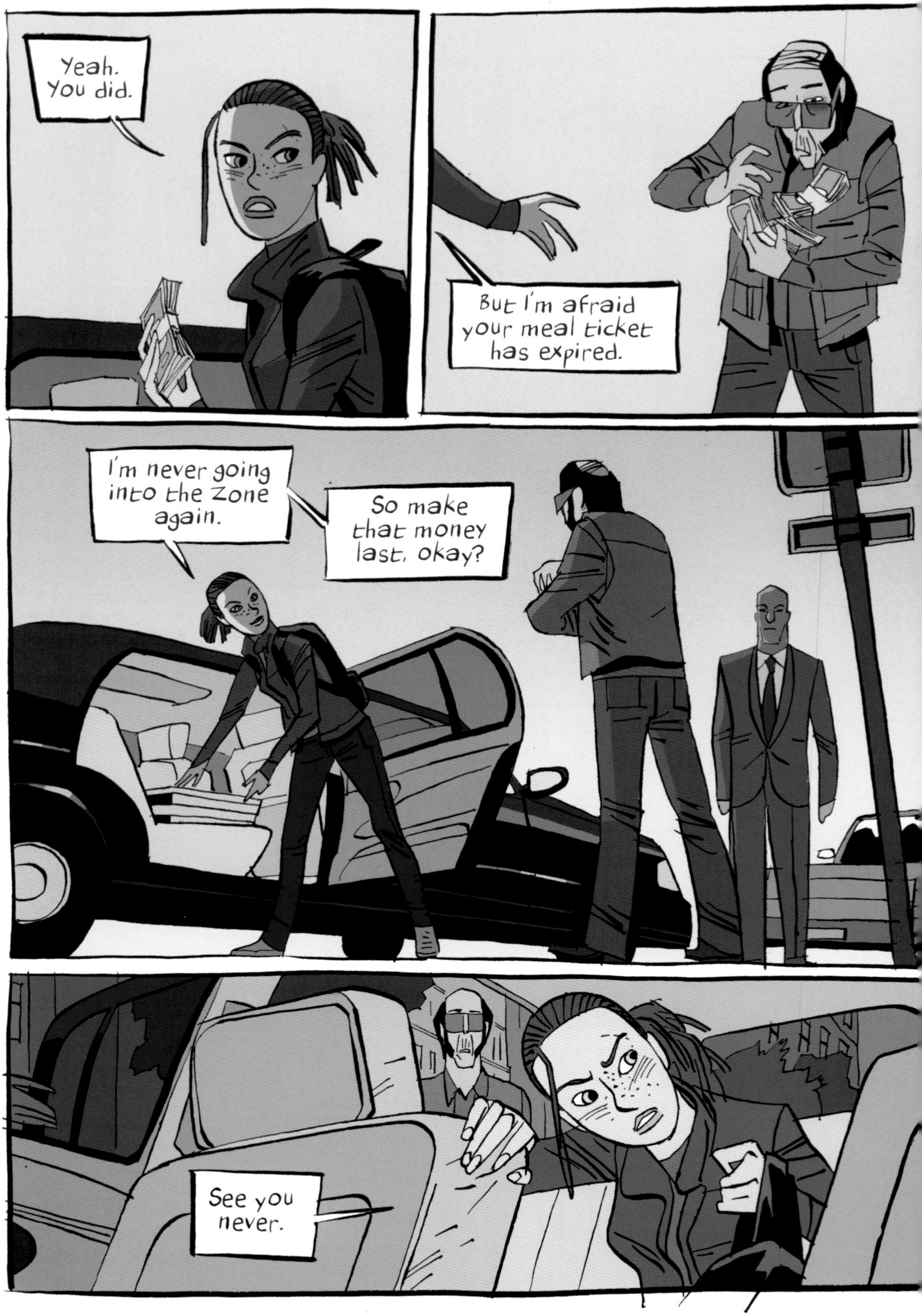
Yeah. You did.
But I'm afraid your meal ticket has expired.
I'm never going into the Zone again.
So make that money last, okay?
See you never.

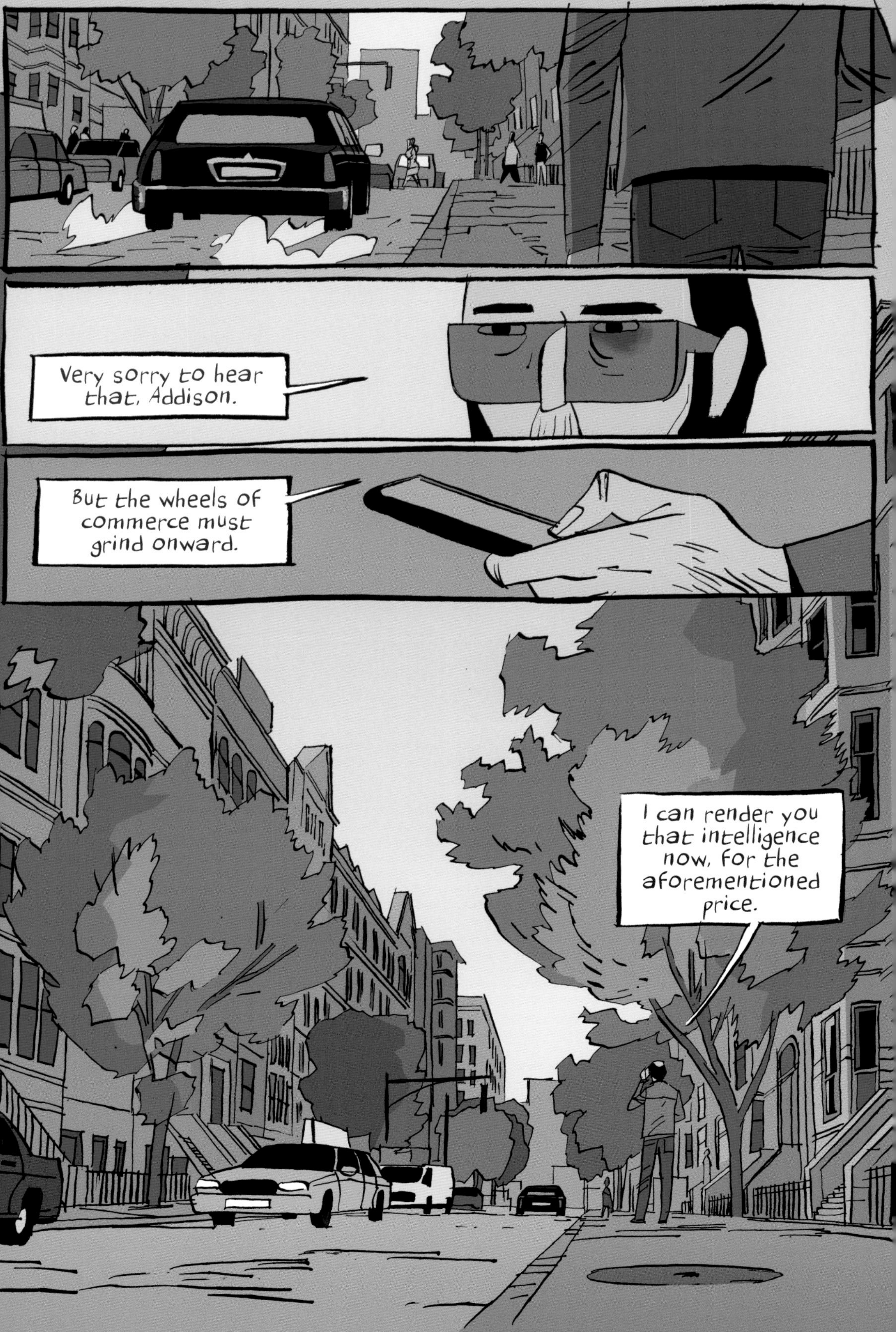
Very sorry to hear that, Addison.
But the wheels of commerce must grind onward.
I can render you that intelligence now, for the aforementioned price.

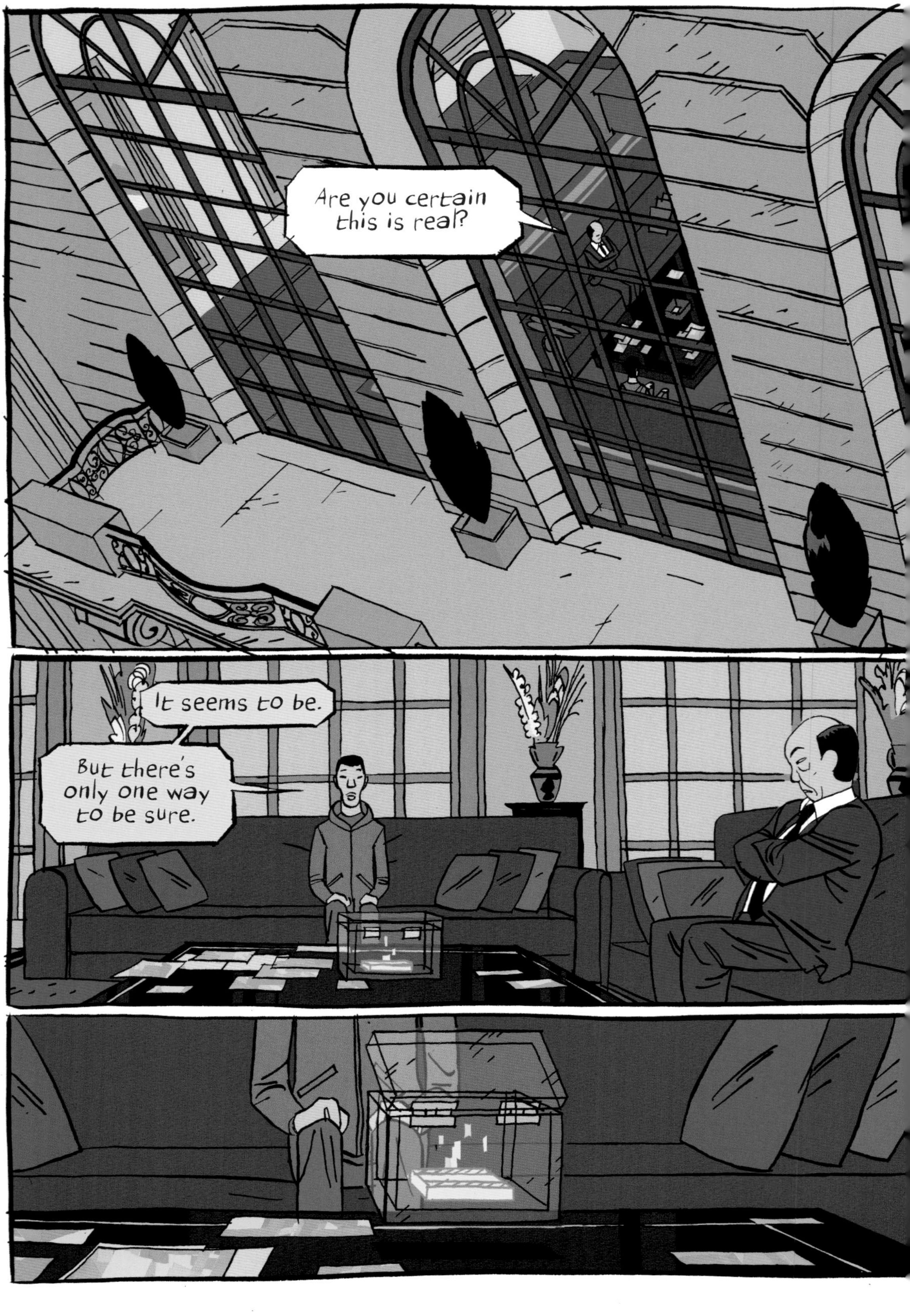
Are you certain this is real?
It seems to be.
But there's only one way to be sure.

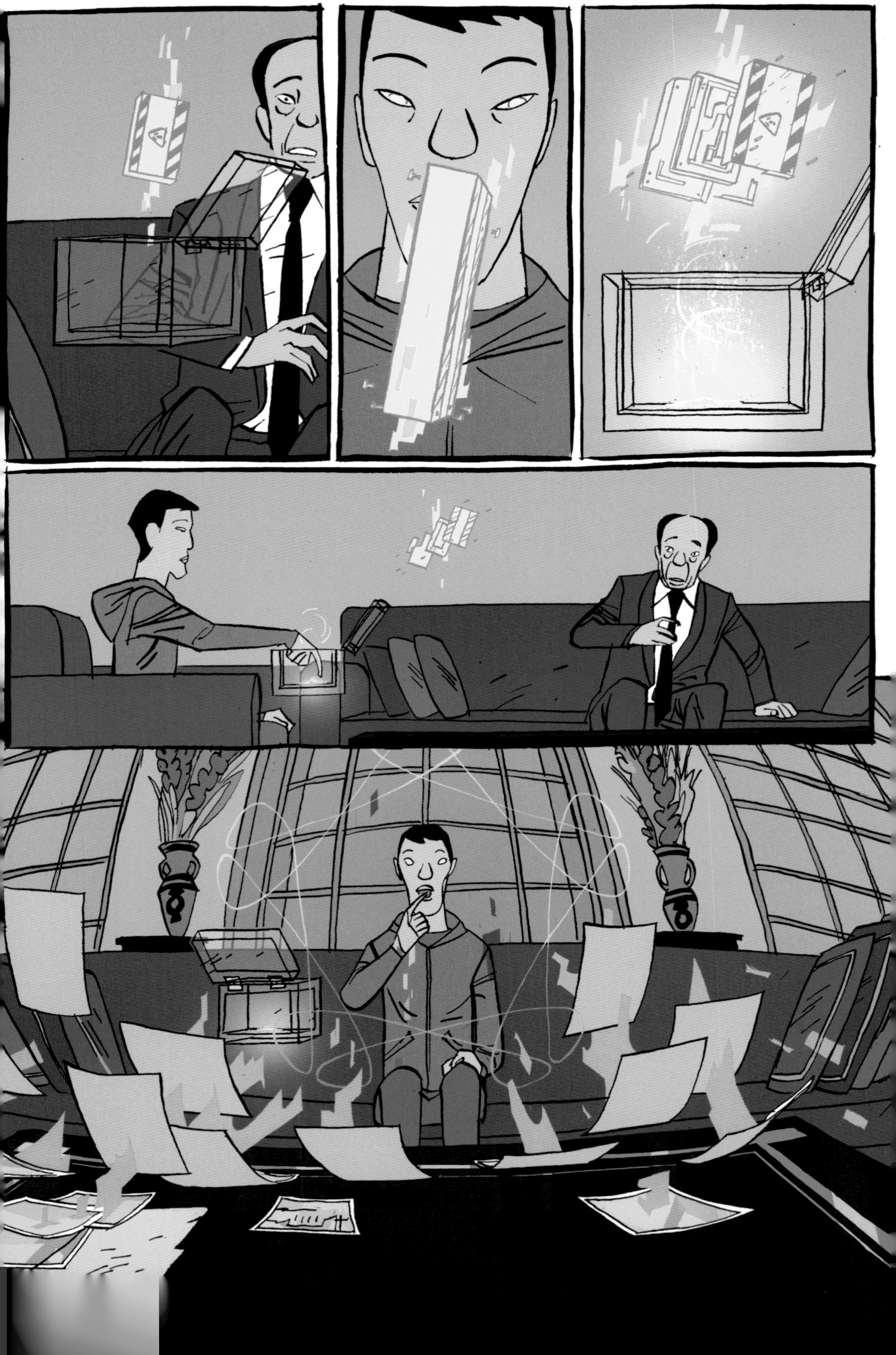

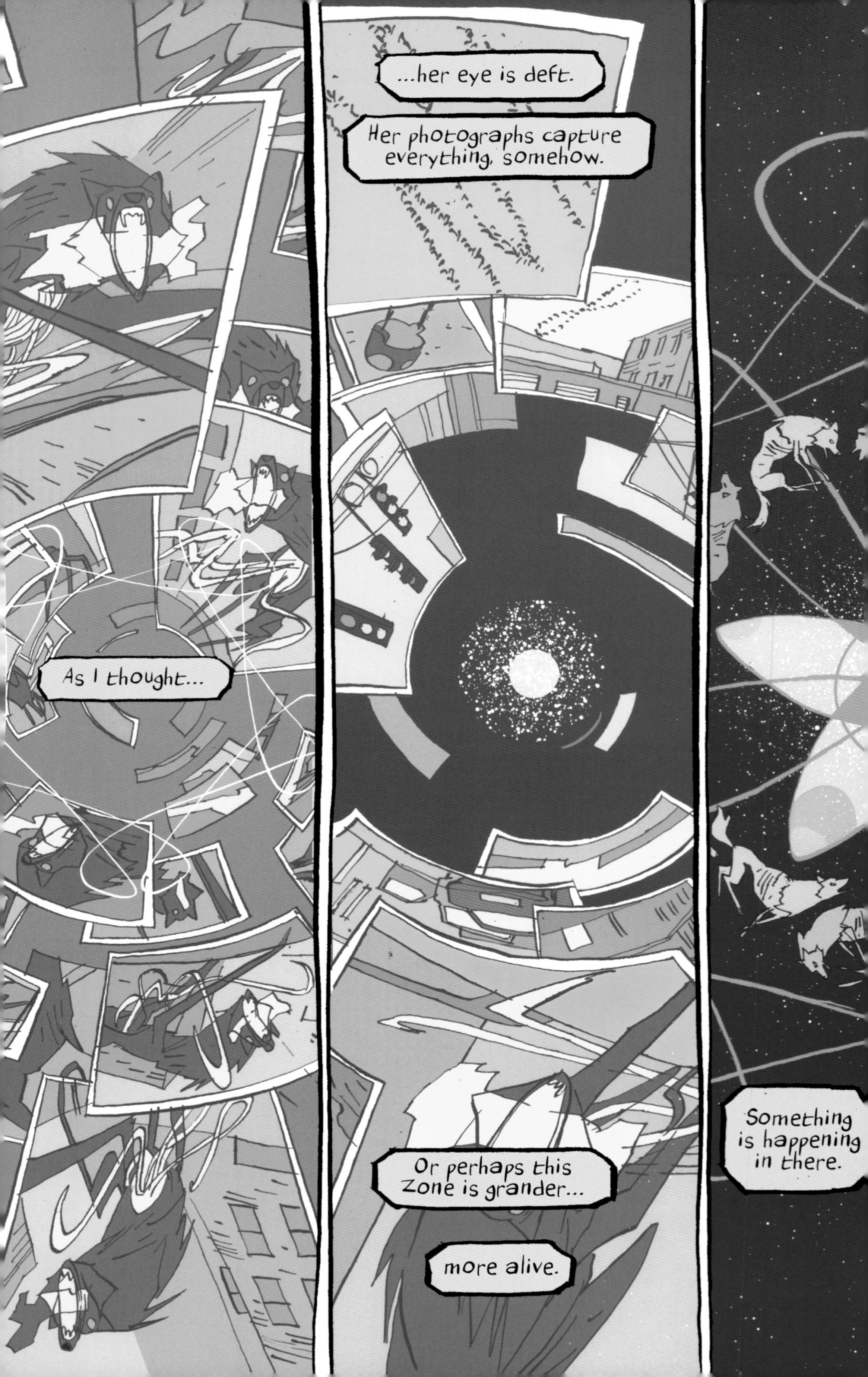
As I thought...
...her eye is deft.
Her photographs capture everything, somehow.
Or perhaps this Zone is grander...
more alive.
Something is happening in there.

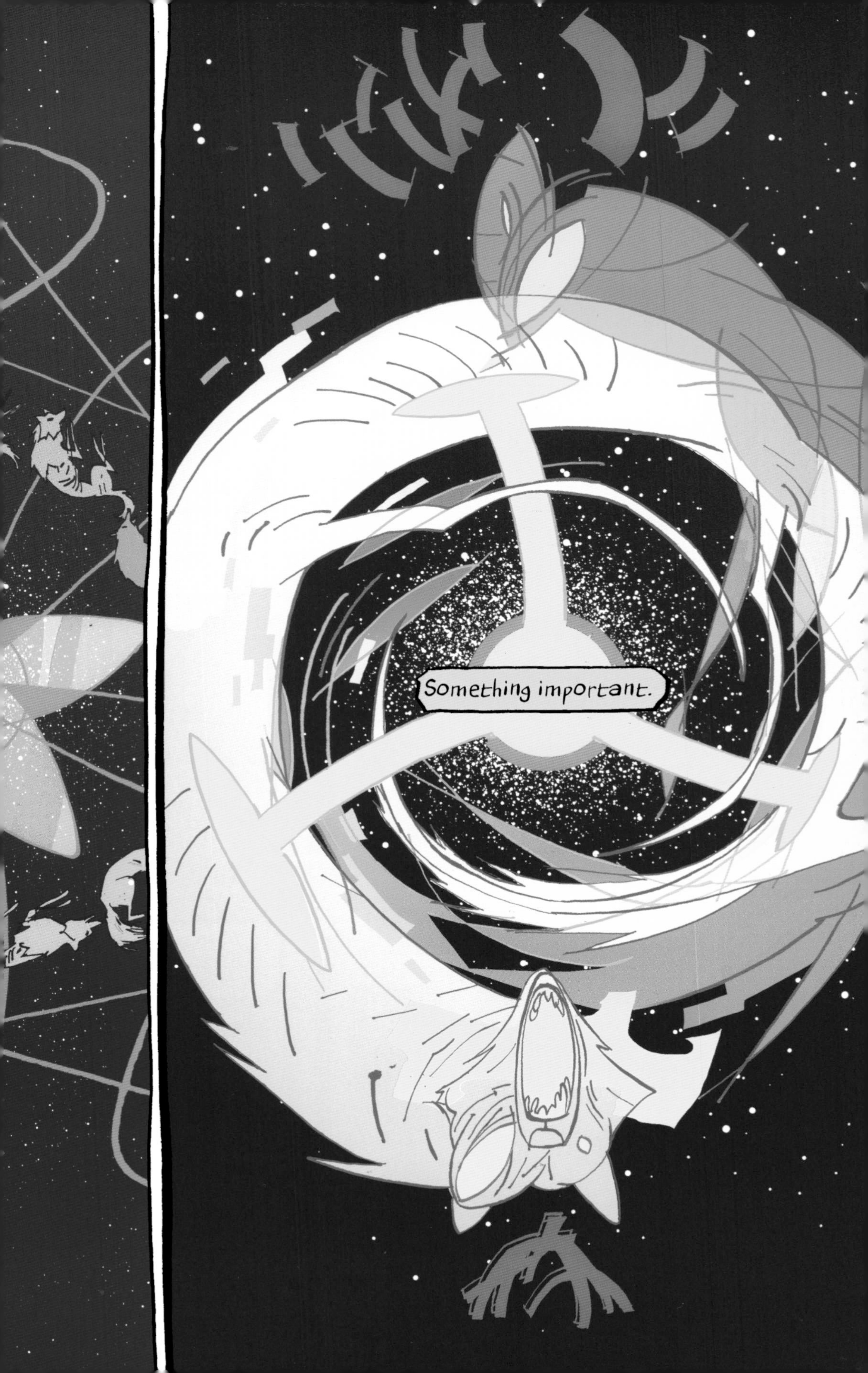
Something important.

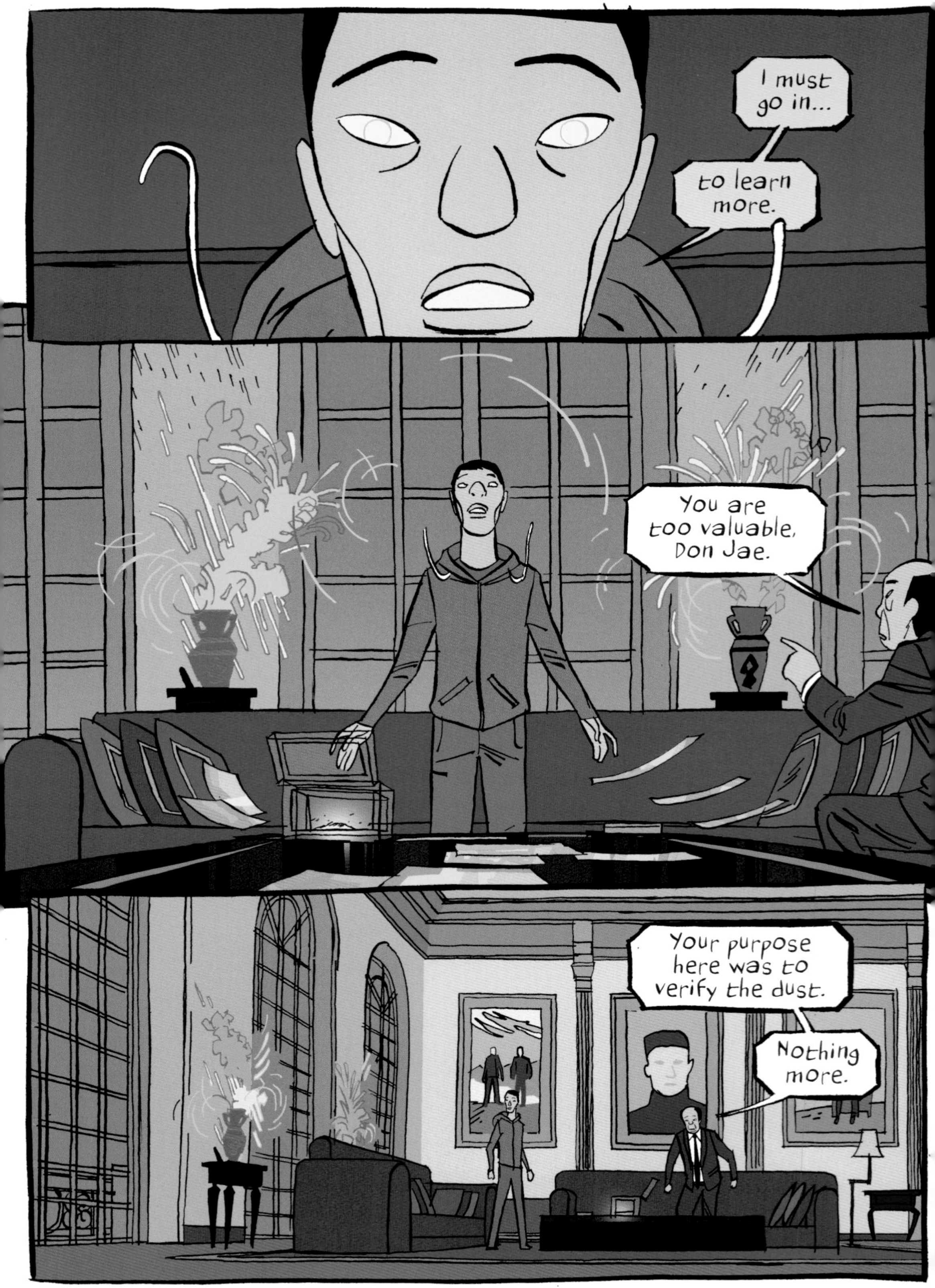
I must go in...
to learn more.
You are too valuable, Don Jae.
Your purpose here was to verify the dust.
Nothing more.

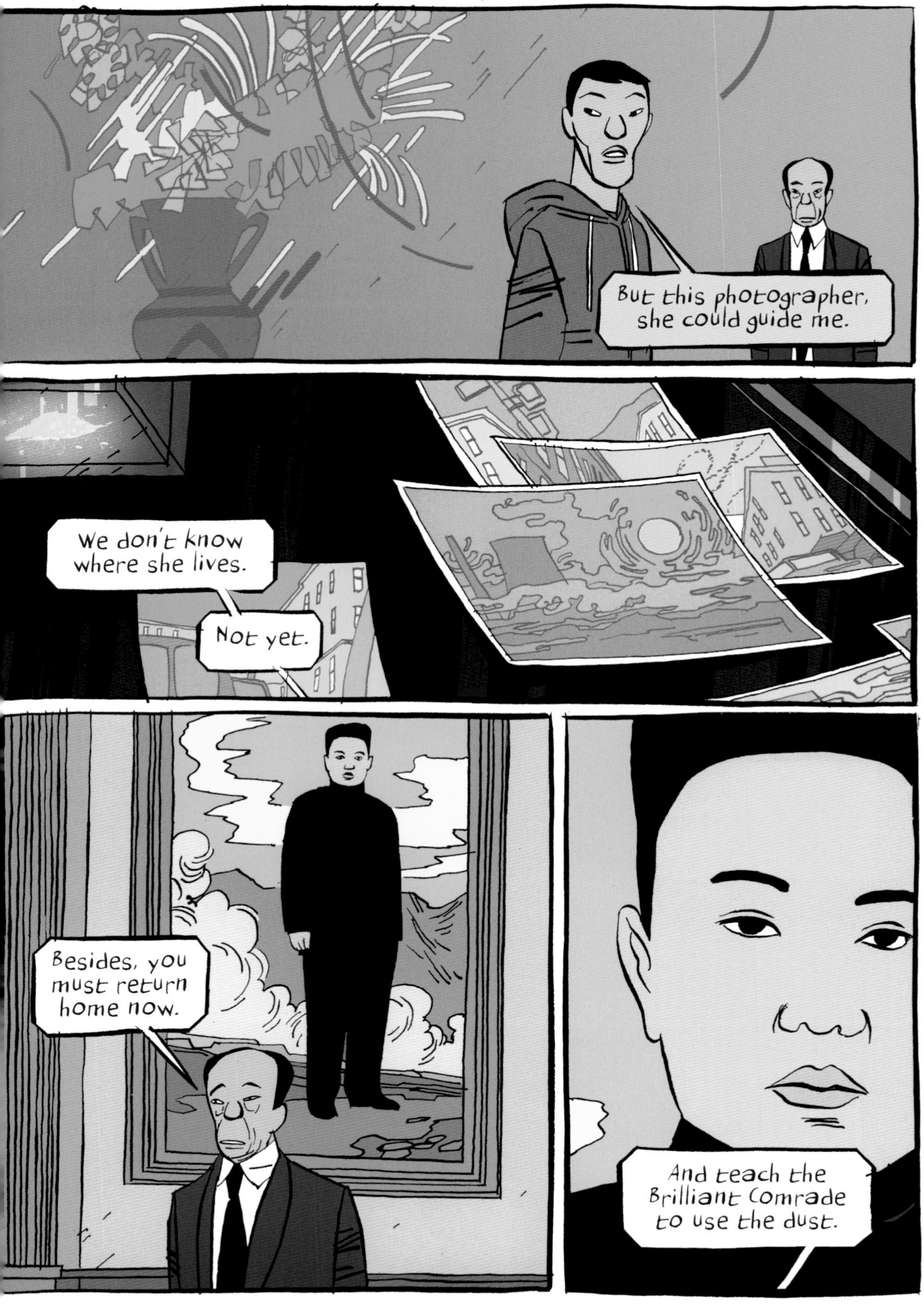
But this photographer, she could guide me.
We don't know where she lives.
Not yet.
Besides, you must return home now.
And teach the Brilliant Comrade to use the dust.

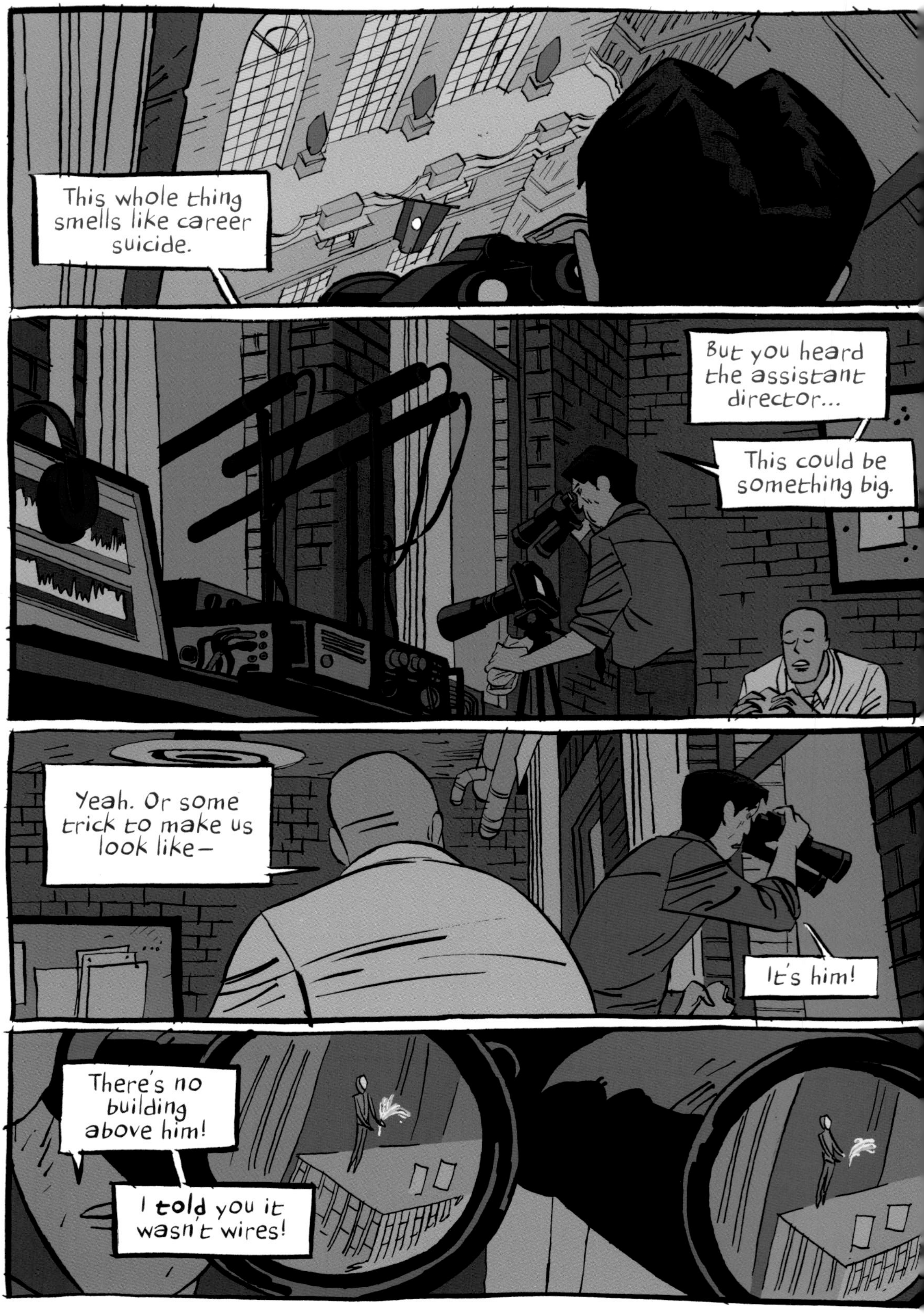
This whole thing smells like career suicide.
But you heard the assistant director...
This could be something big.
Yeah. Or some trick to make us look like–
It's him!
There's no building above him!
I **told** you it wasn't wires!

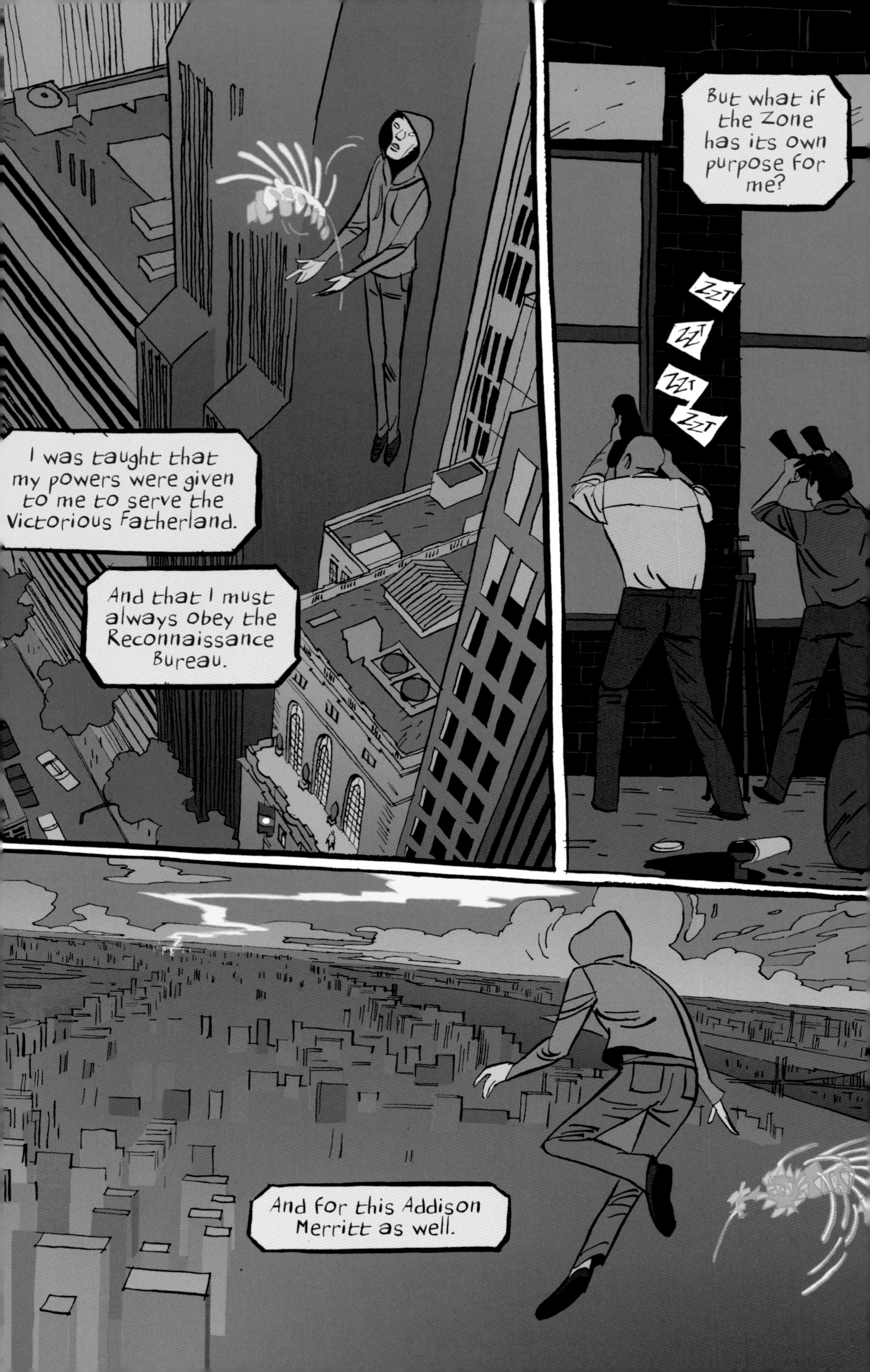
I was taught that my powers were given to me to serve the Victorious Fatherland.
And that I must always obey the Reconnaissance Bureau.
But what if the Zone has its own purpose for me?
ZZT
ZZT
ZZT
ZZT
And for this Addison Merritt as well.

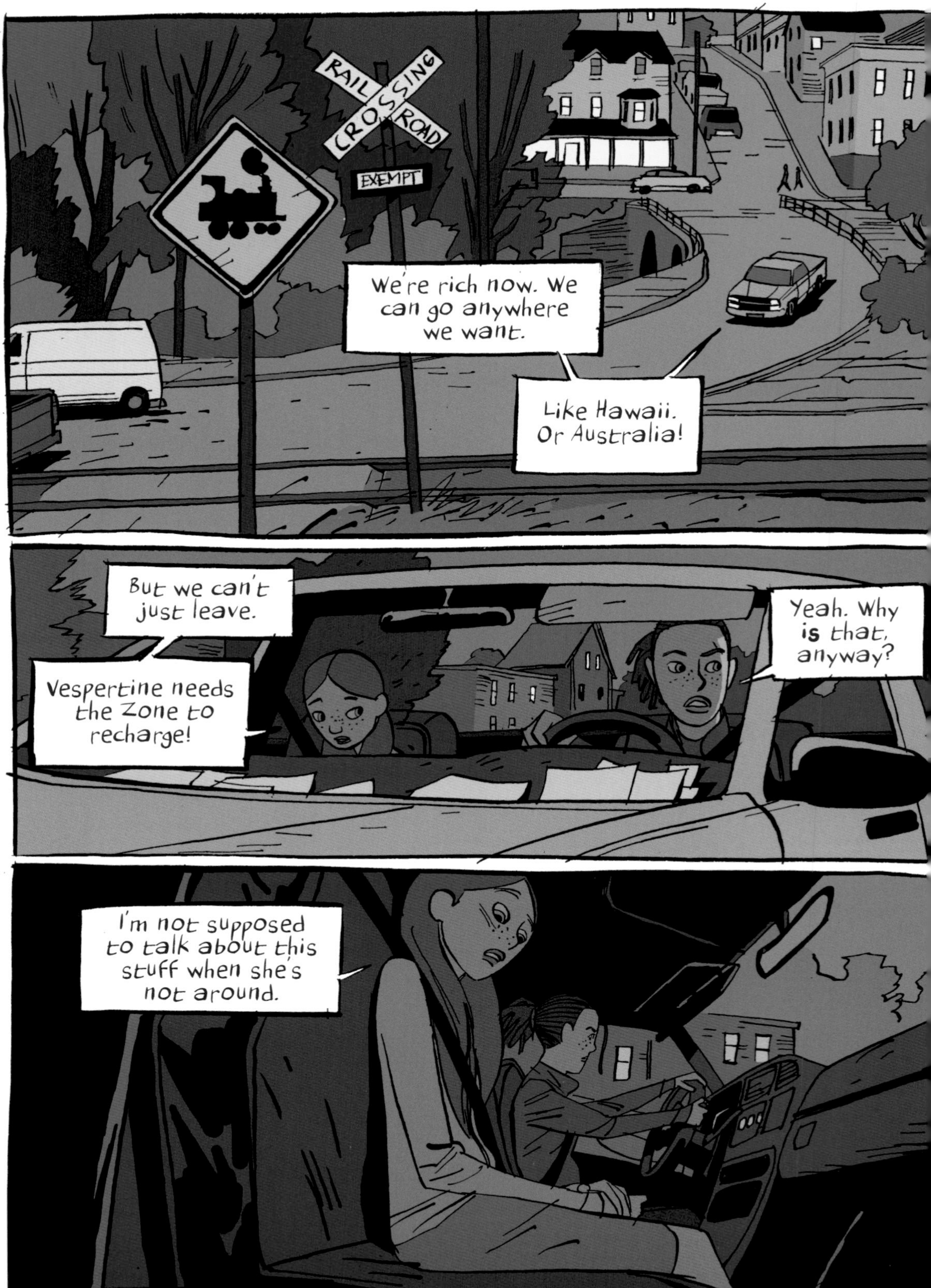

RAIL ROAD
CROSSING
EXEMPT
We're rich now. We can go anywhere we want.
Like Hawaii. Or Australia!
But we can't just leave.
Vespertine needs the Zone to recharge!
Yeah. Why **is** that, anyway?
I'm not supposed to talk about this stuff when she's not around.

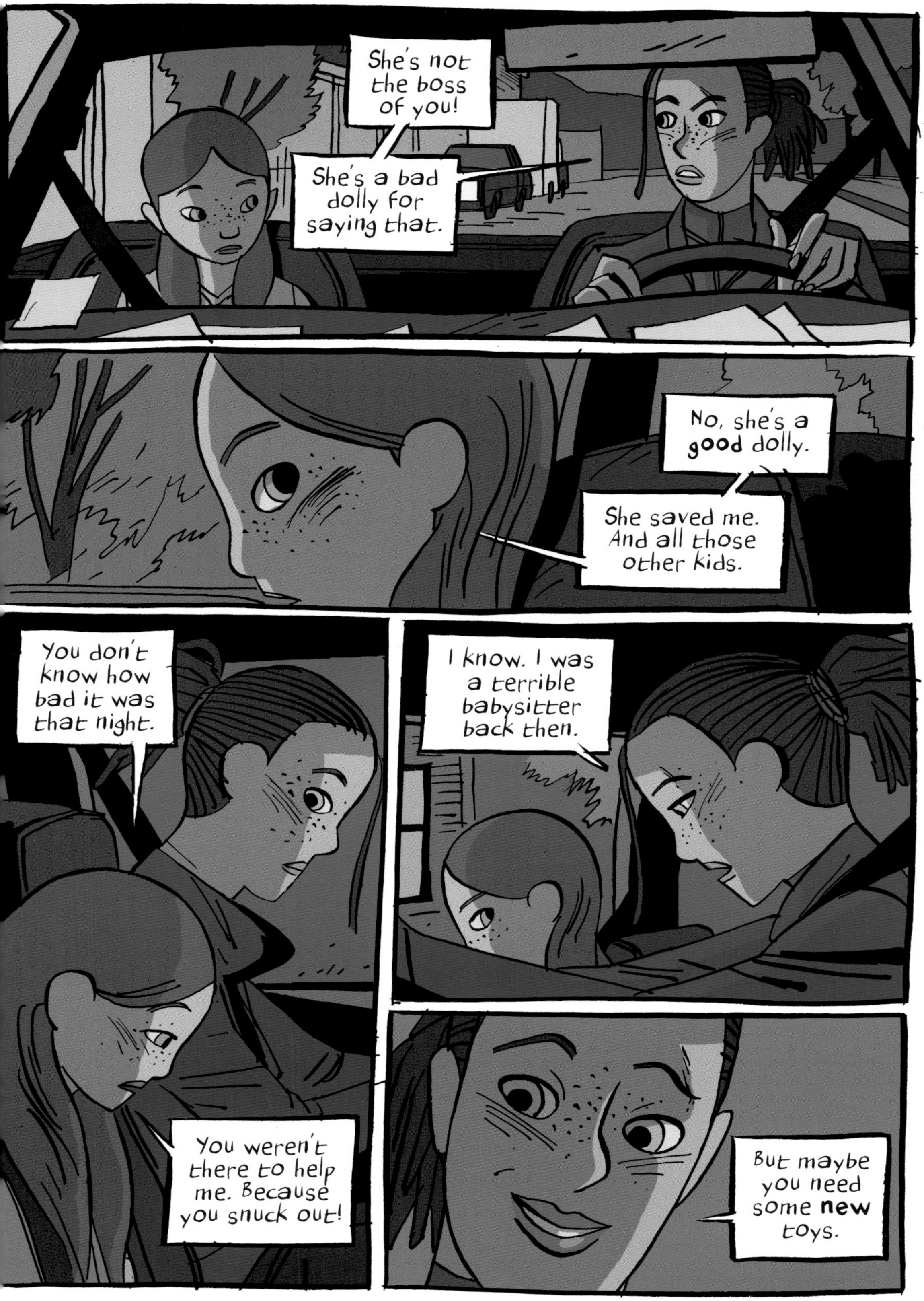
She's not the boss of you!
She's a bad dolly for saying that.
No, she's a **good** dolly.
She saved me. And all those other kids.
You don't know how bad it was that night.
I know. I was a terrible babysitter back then.
You weren't there to help me. Because you snuck out!
But maybe you need some **new** toys.

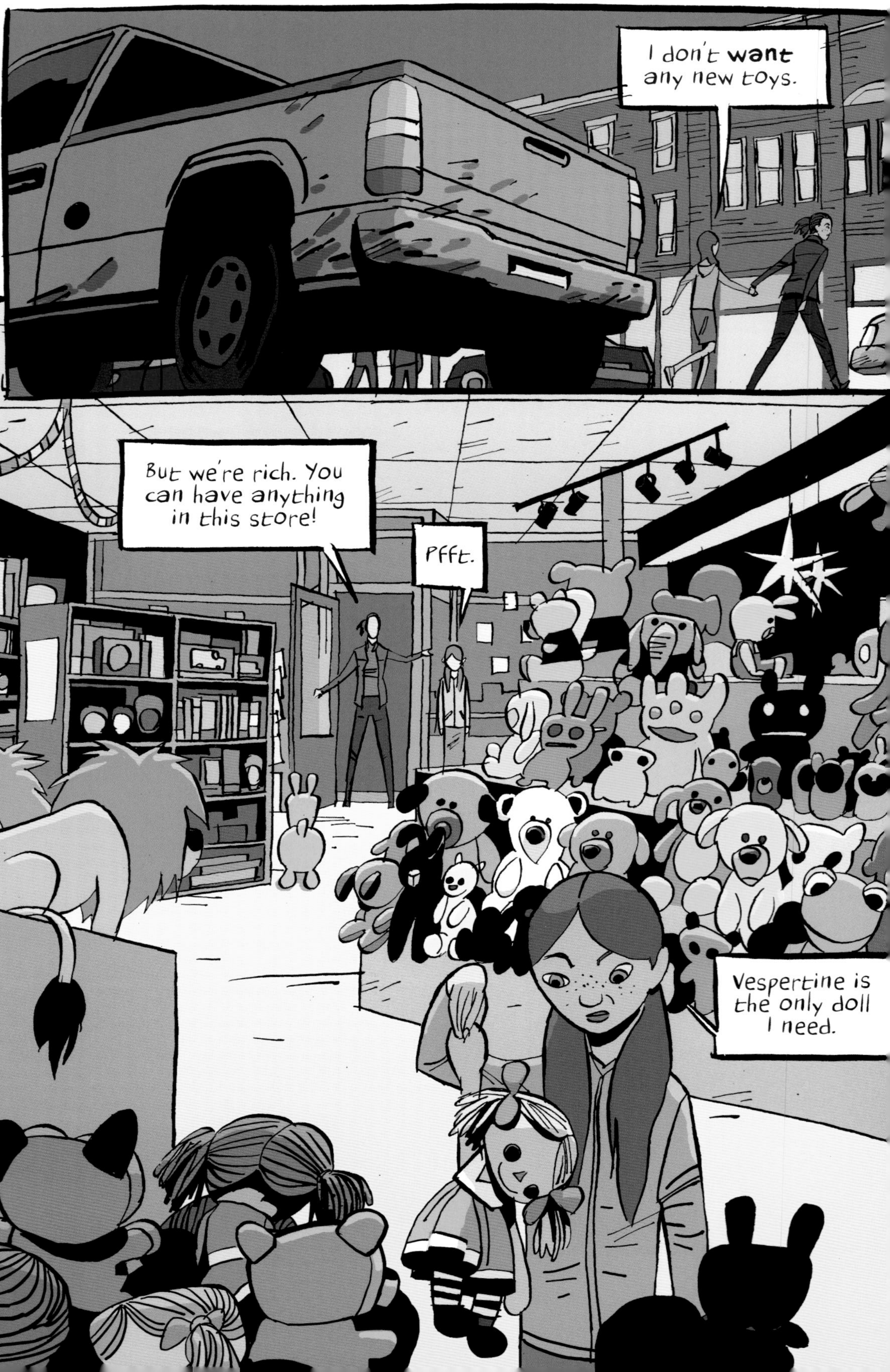
I don't **want** any new toys.
But we're rich. You can have anything in this store!
Pfft.
Vespertine is the only doll I need.

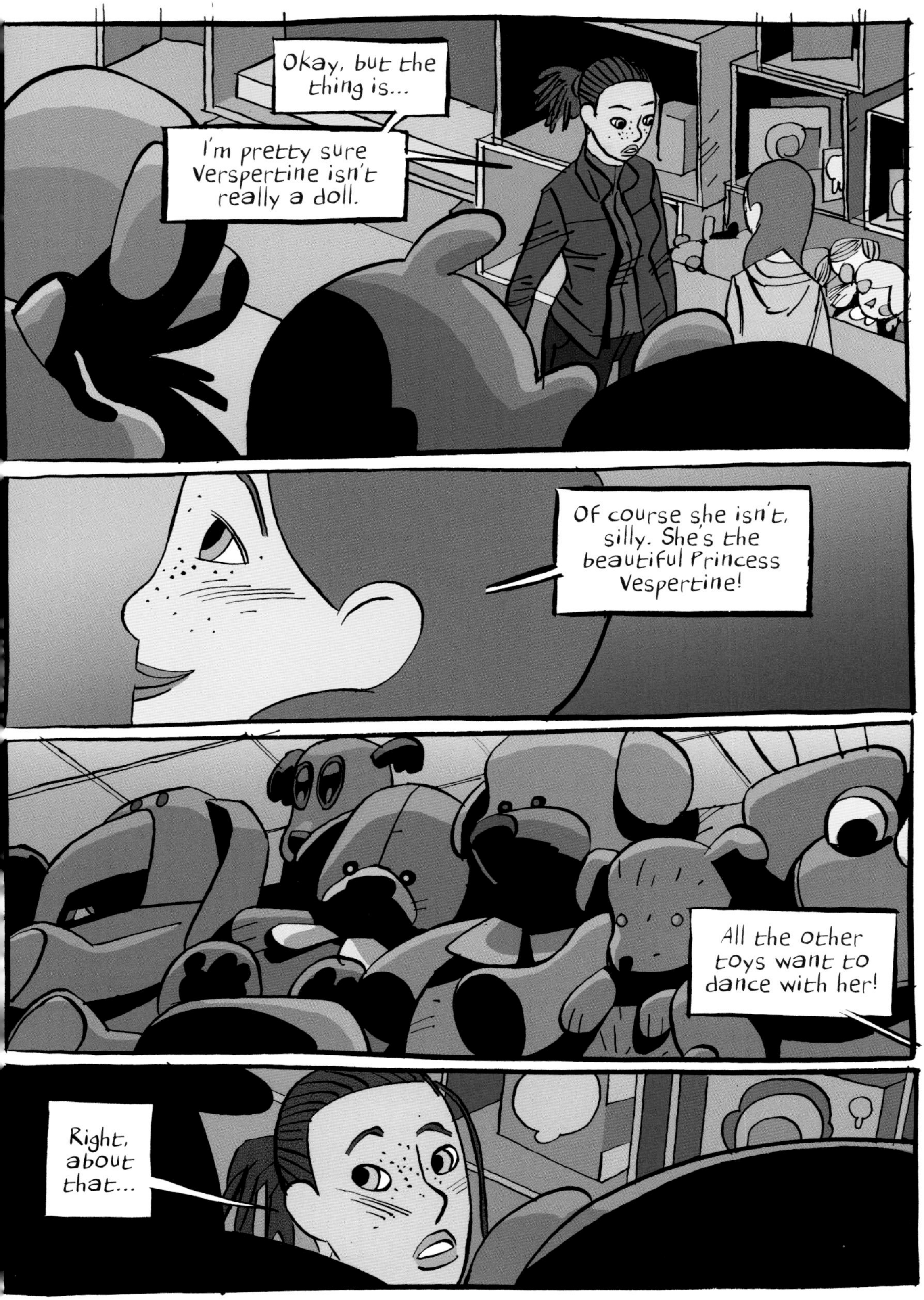

Okay, but the thing is...
I'm pretty sure Verspertine isn't really a doll.
Of course she isn't, silly. She's the beautiful Princess Vespertine!
All the other toys want to dance with her!
Right, about that...

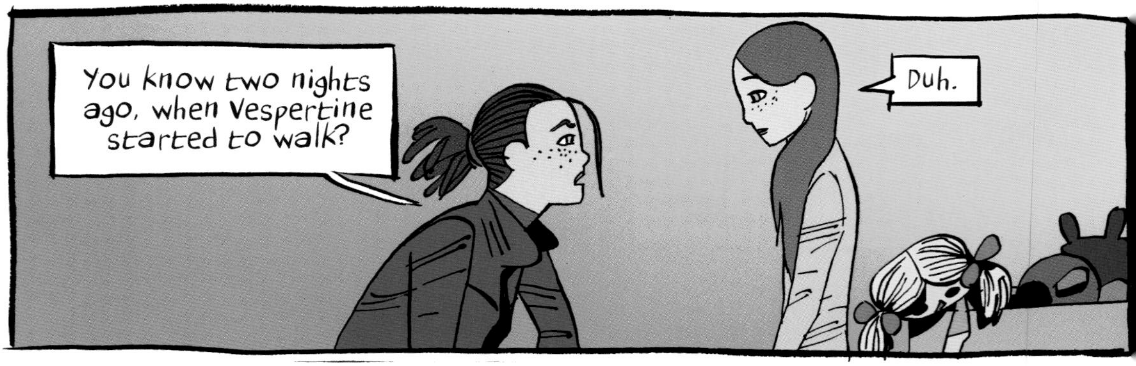
You know two nights ago, when Vespertine started to walk?
Duh.

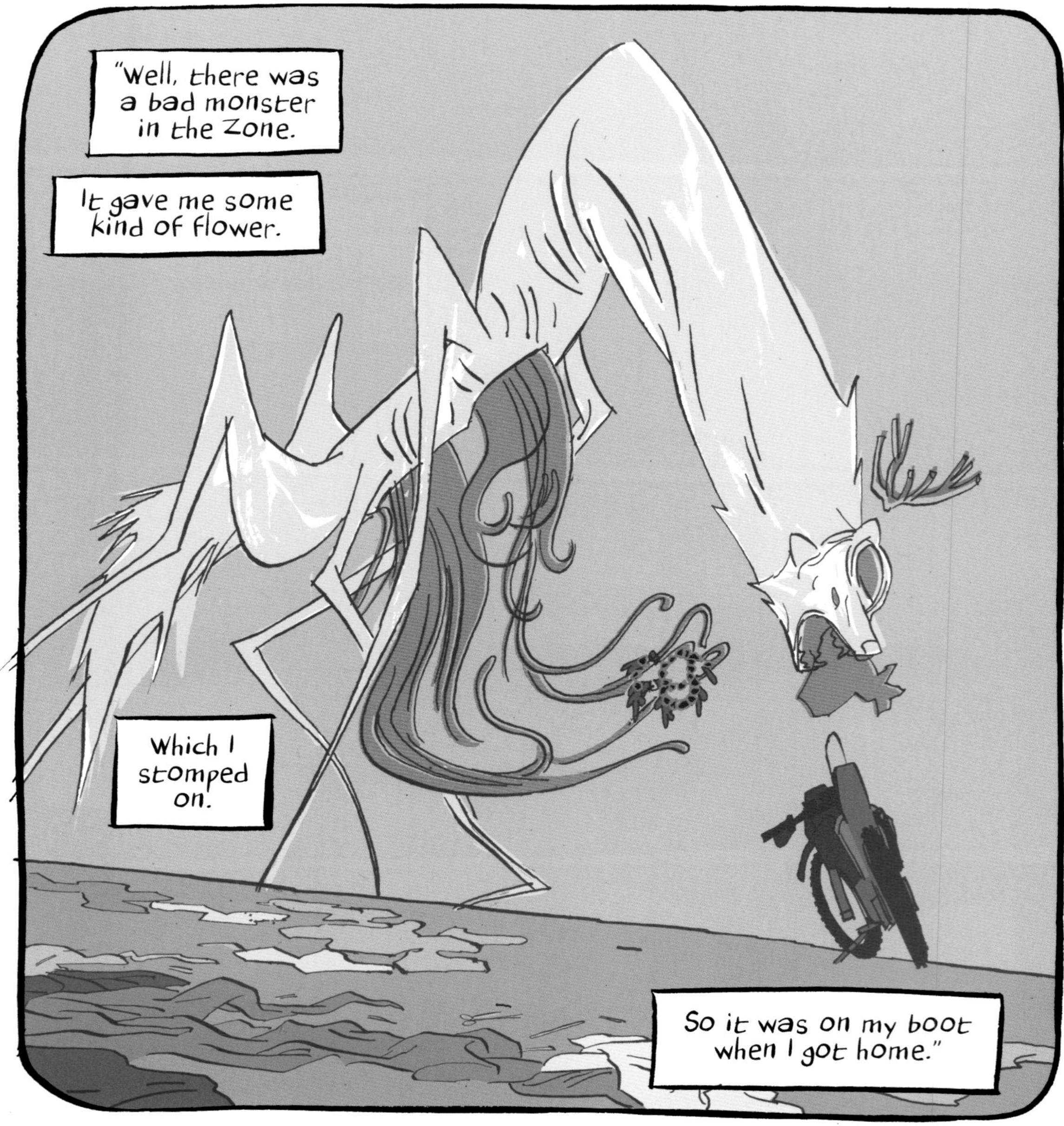
"Well, there was a bad monster in the Zone.
It gave me some kind of flower.
Which I stomped on.
So it was on my boot when I got home."

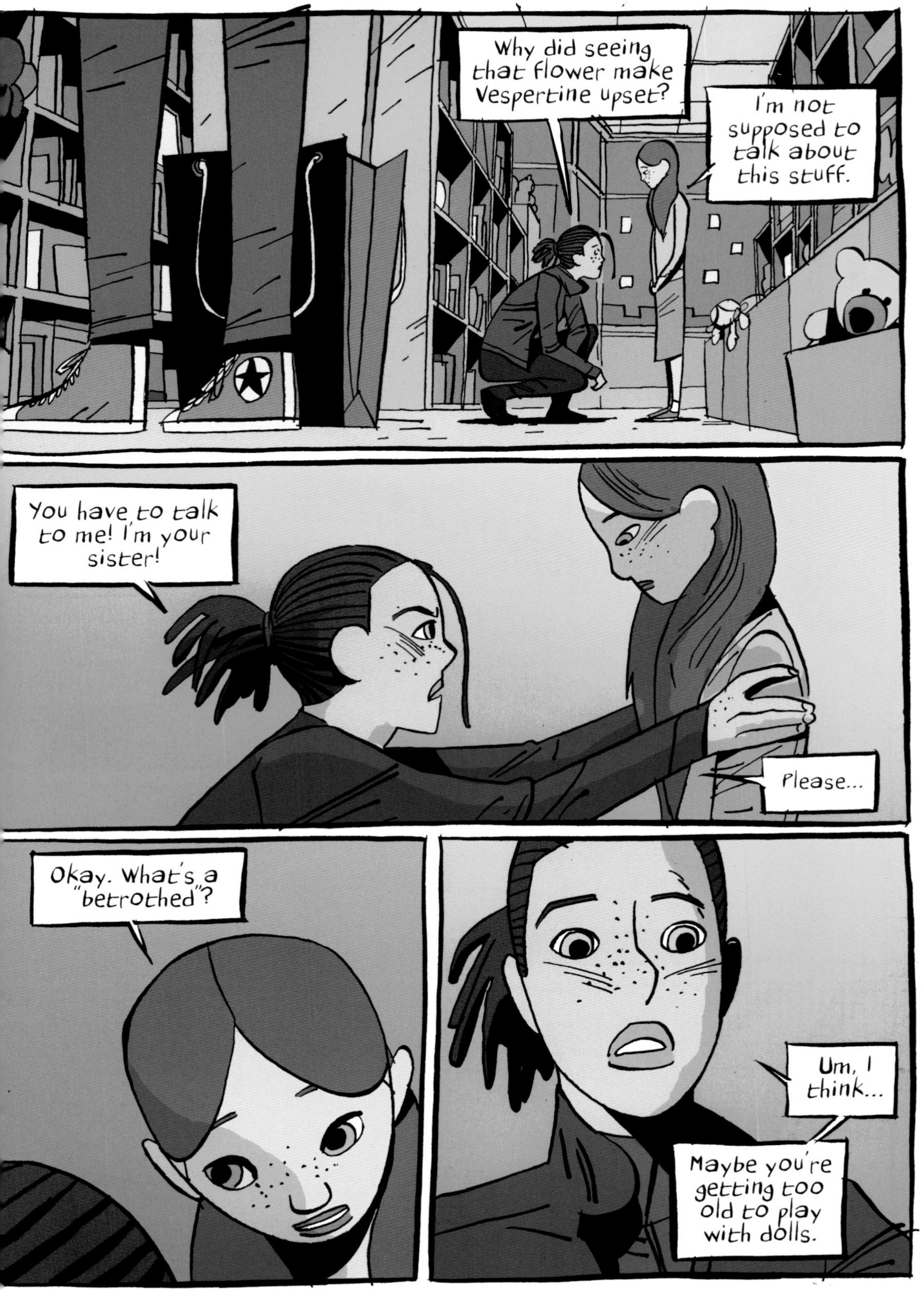
Why did seeing that flower make Vespertine upset?
I'm not supposed to talk about this stuff.
You have to talk to me! I'm your sister!
Please...
Okay. What's a "betrothed"?
Um, I think...
Maybe you're getting too old to play with dolls.

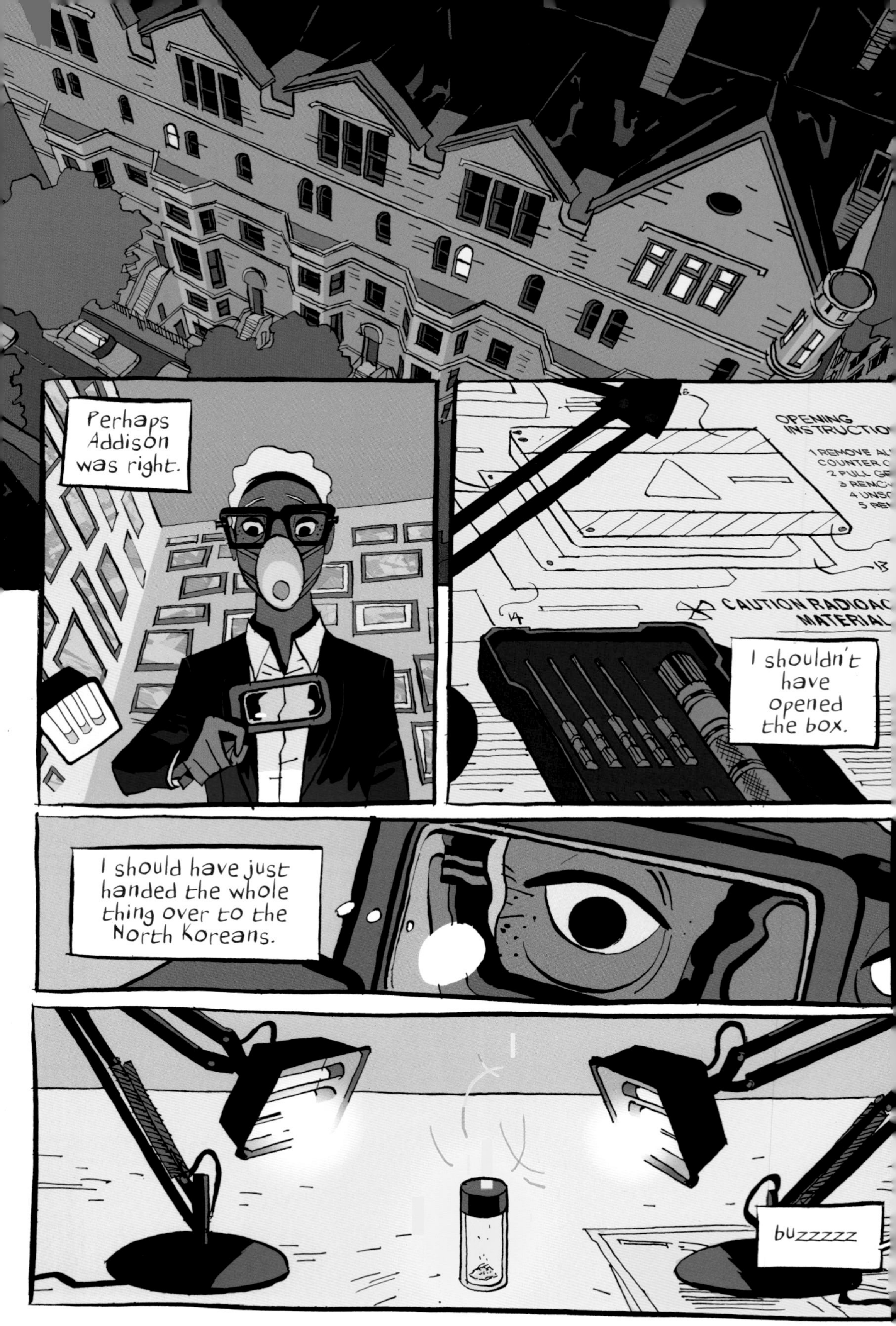

Perhaps Addison was right.
OPENING INSTRUCTIO
CAUTION RADIOAC MATERIAL
I shouldn't have opened the box.
I should have just handed the whole thing over to the North Koreans.
buzzzzz

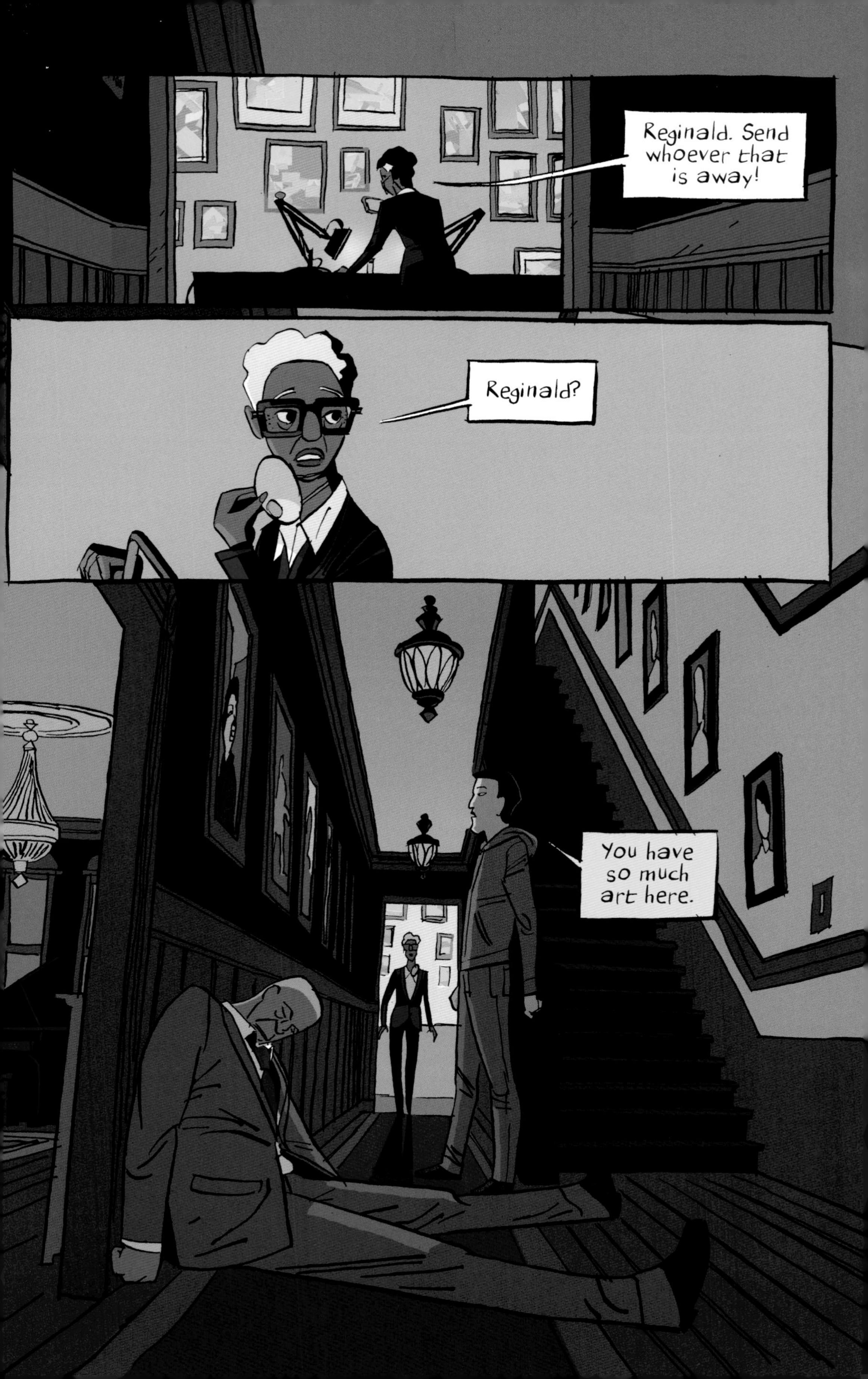
Reginald. Send whoever that is away!
Reginald?
You have so much art here.

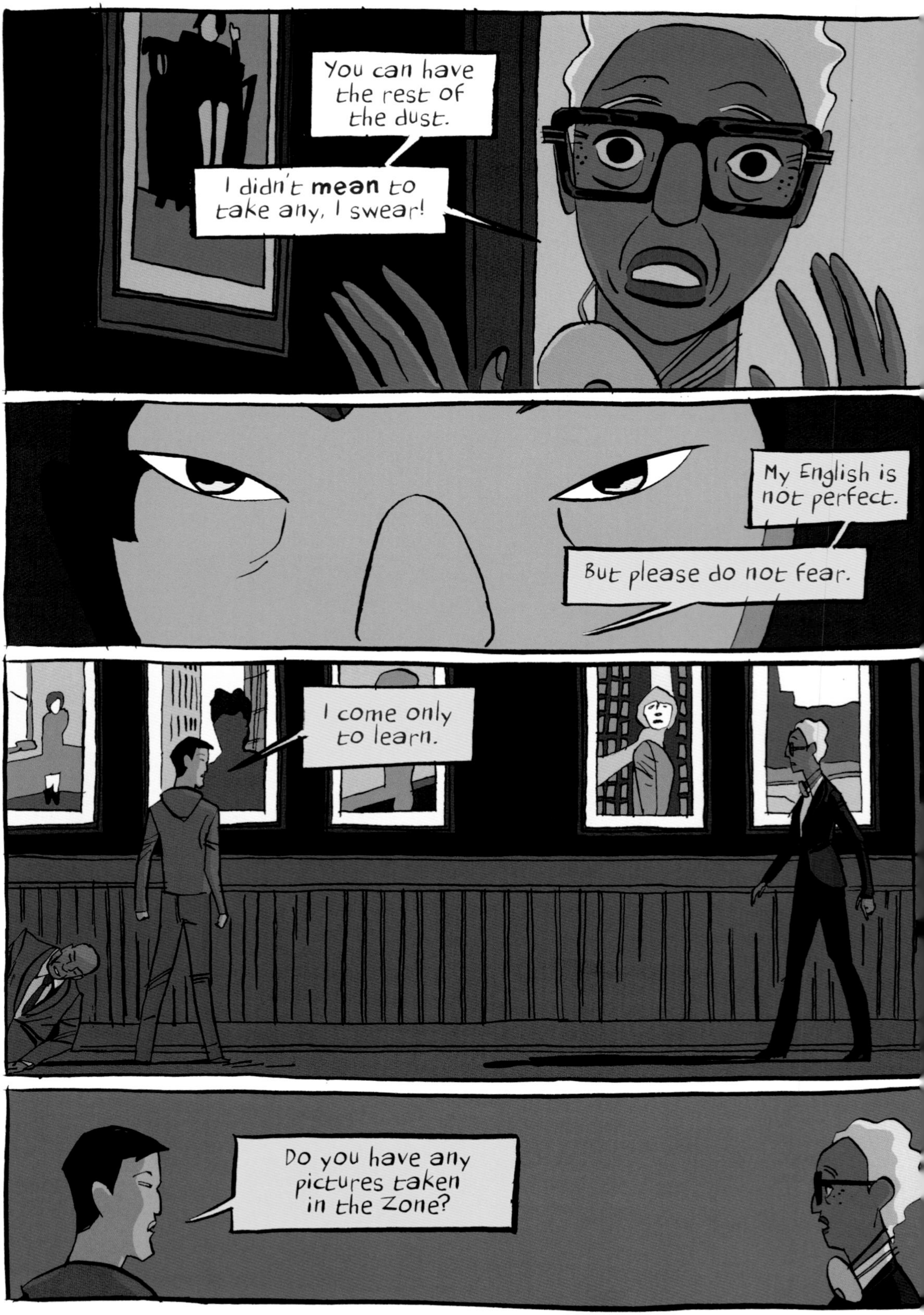
You can have the rest of the dust.
I didn't **mean** to take any, I swear!
My English is not perfect.
But please do not fear.
I come only to learn.
Do you have any pictures taken in the Zone?

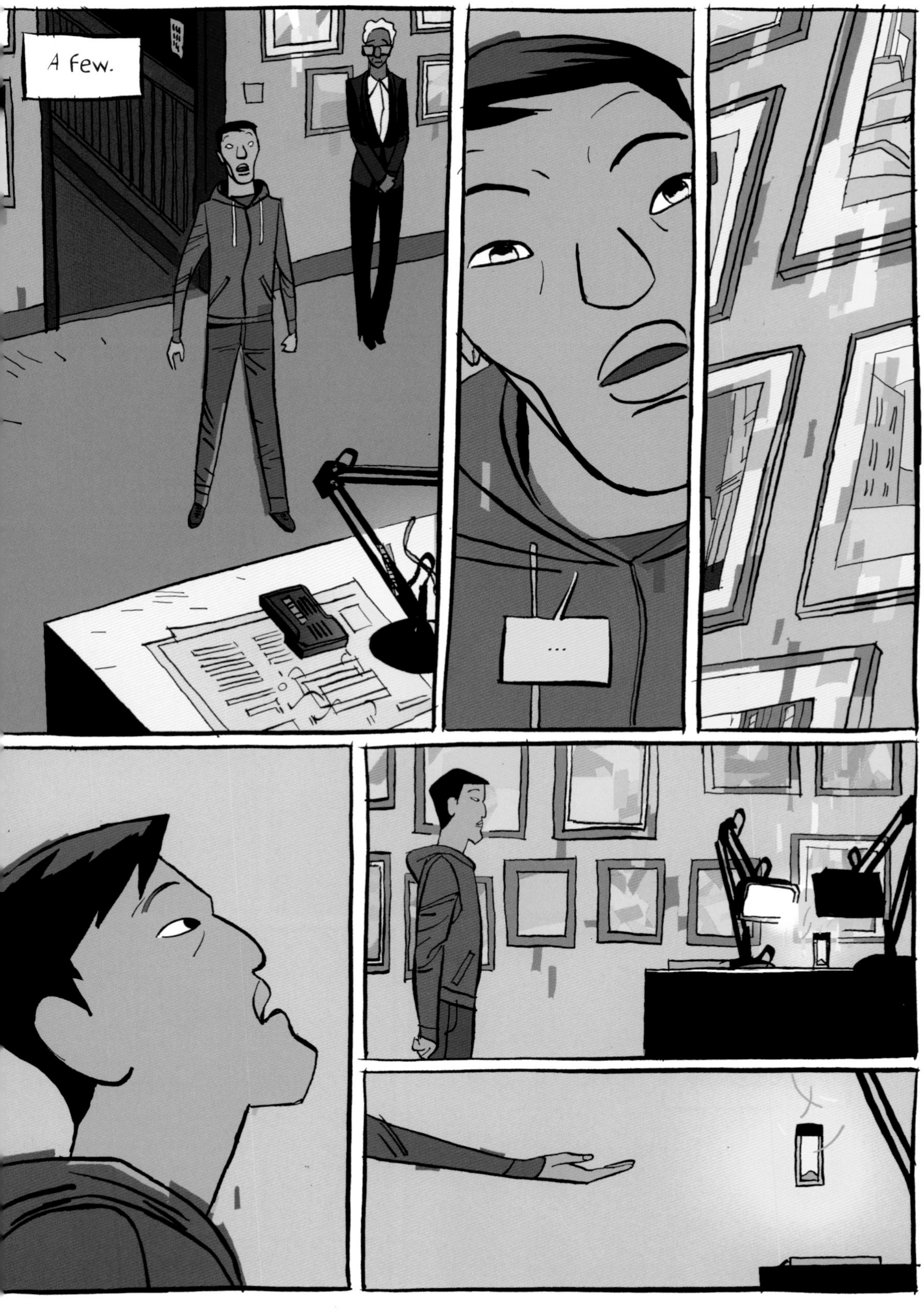
A few.
...

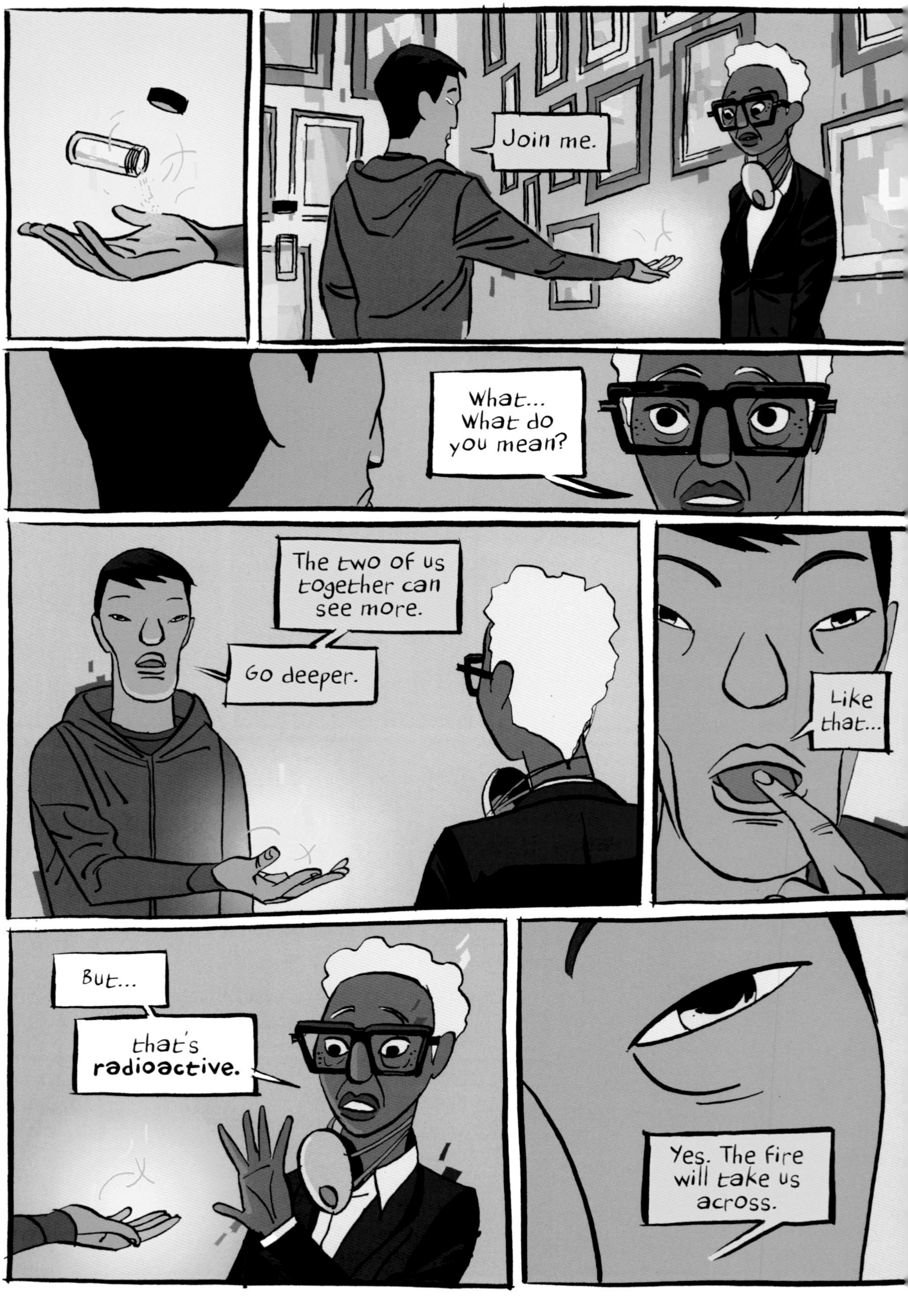
Join me.
What... What do you mean?
The two of us together can see more.
Go deeper.
Like that...
But...
that's **radioactive.**
Yes. The fire will take us across.

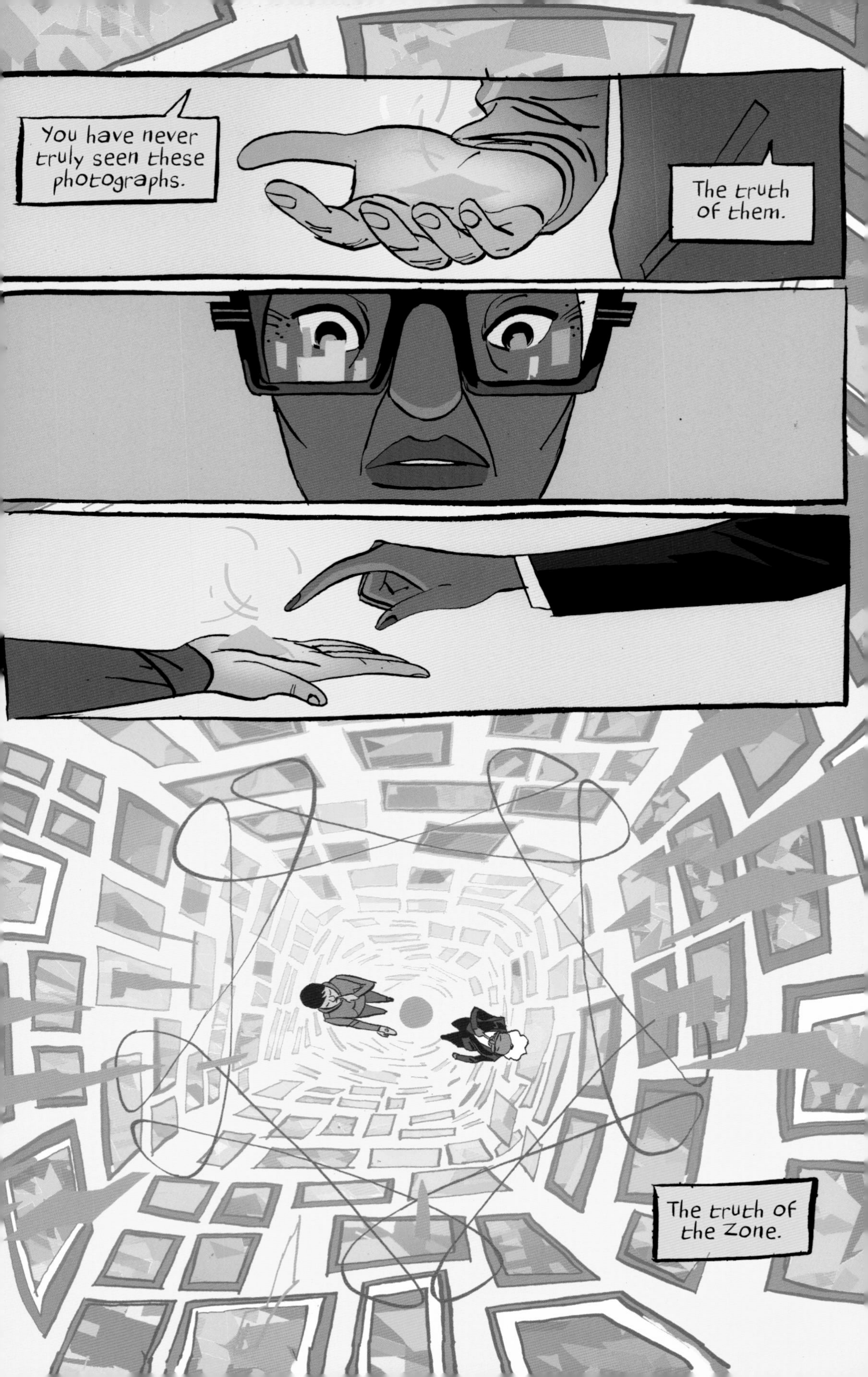
You have never truly seen these photographs.
The truth of them.
The truth of the Zone.

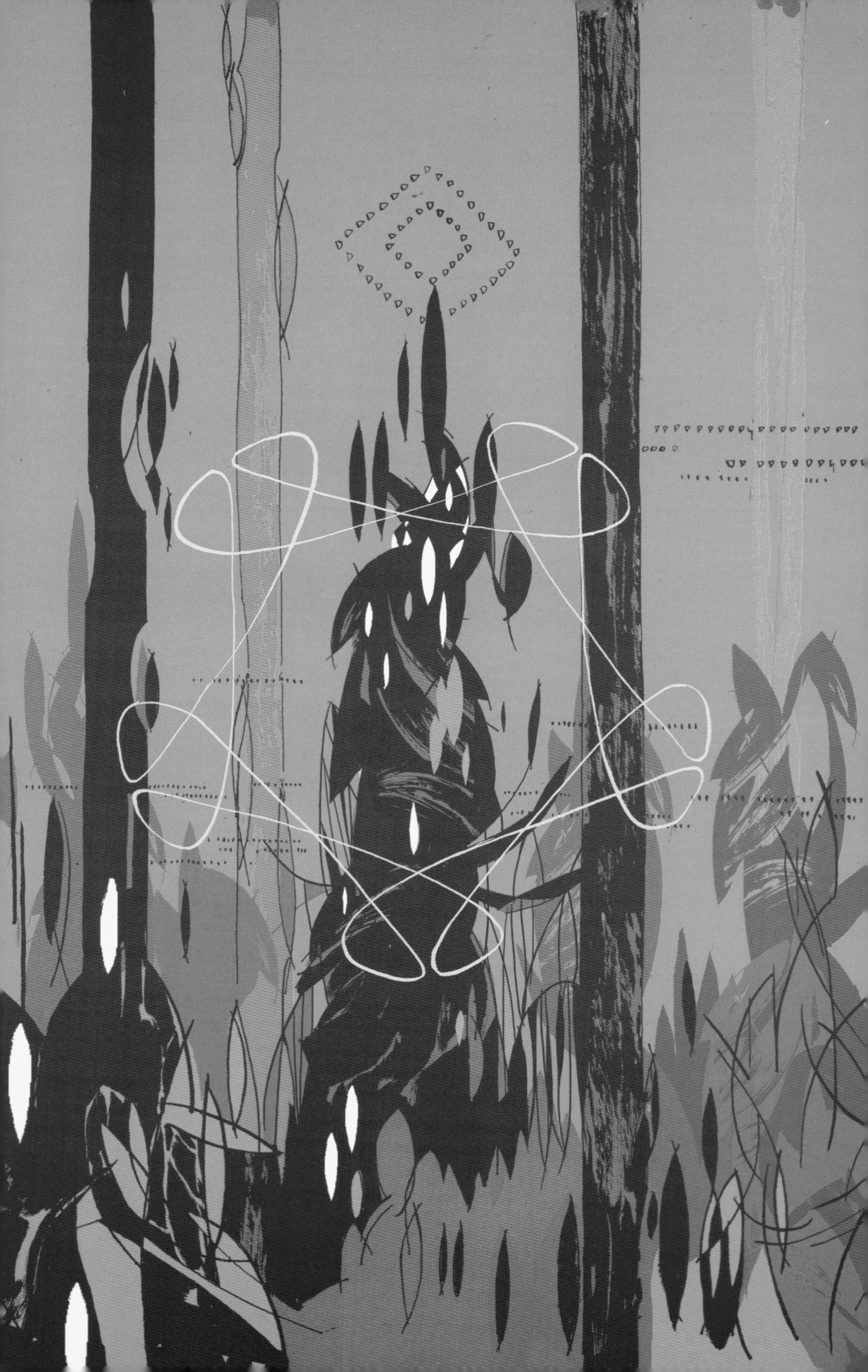

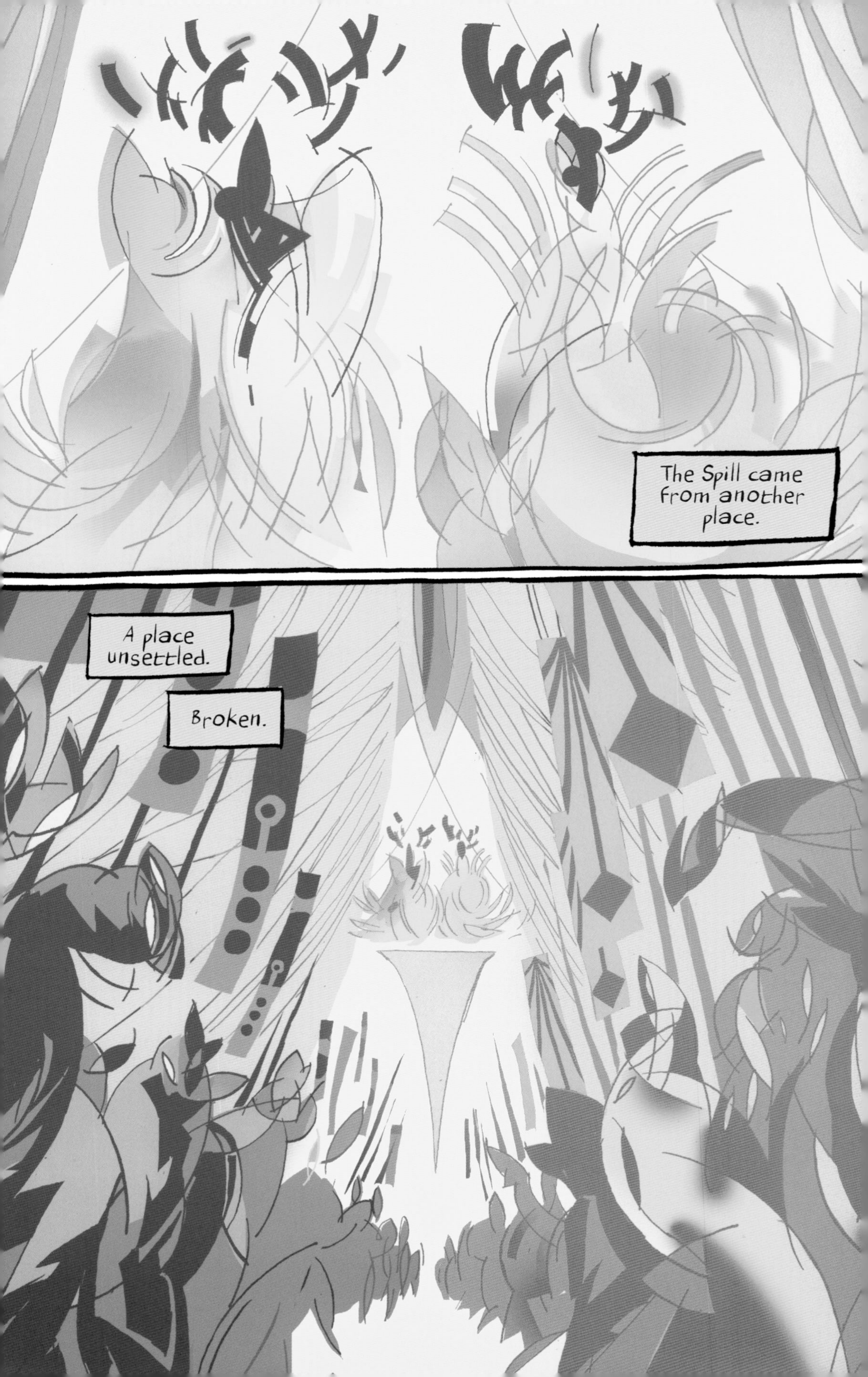
The Spill came from another place.
A place unsettled.
Broken.

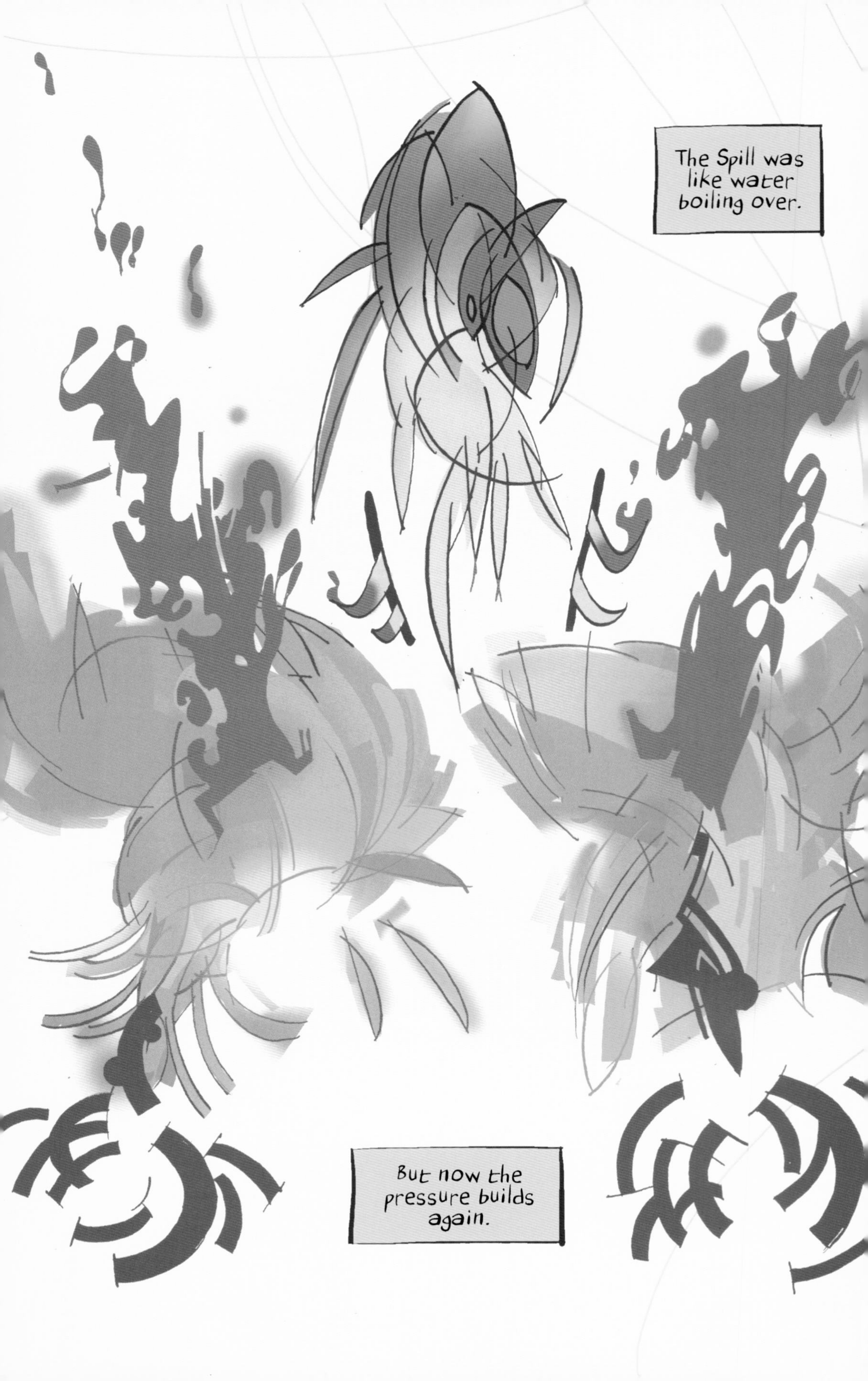
The Spill was like water boiling over.
But now the pressure builds again.

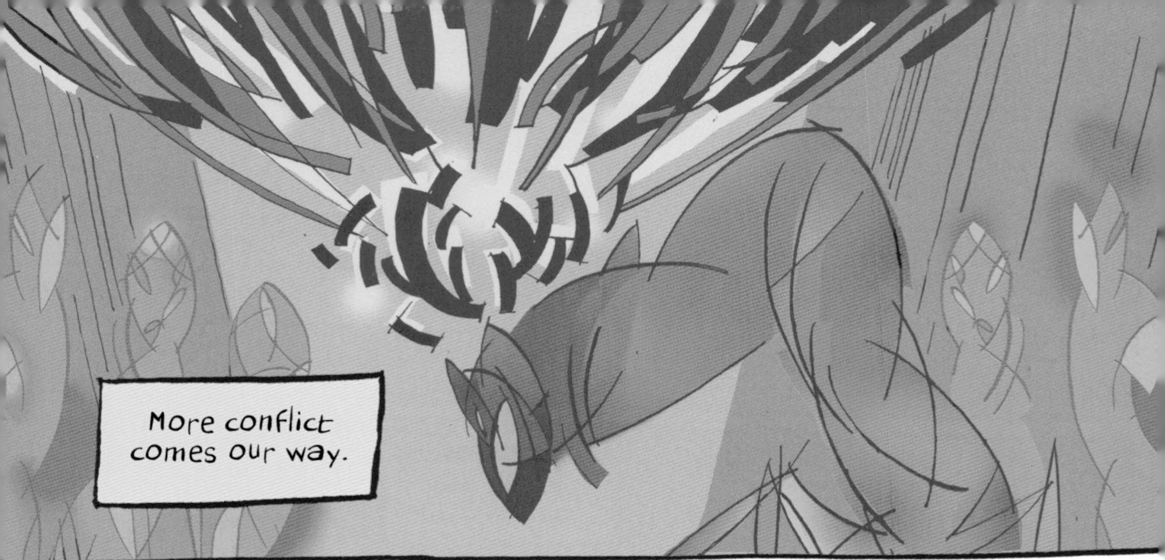
More conflict comes our way.

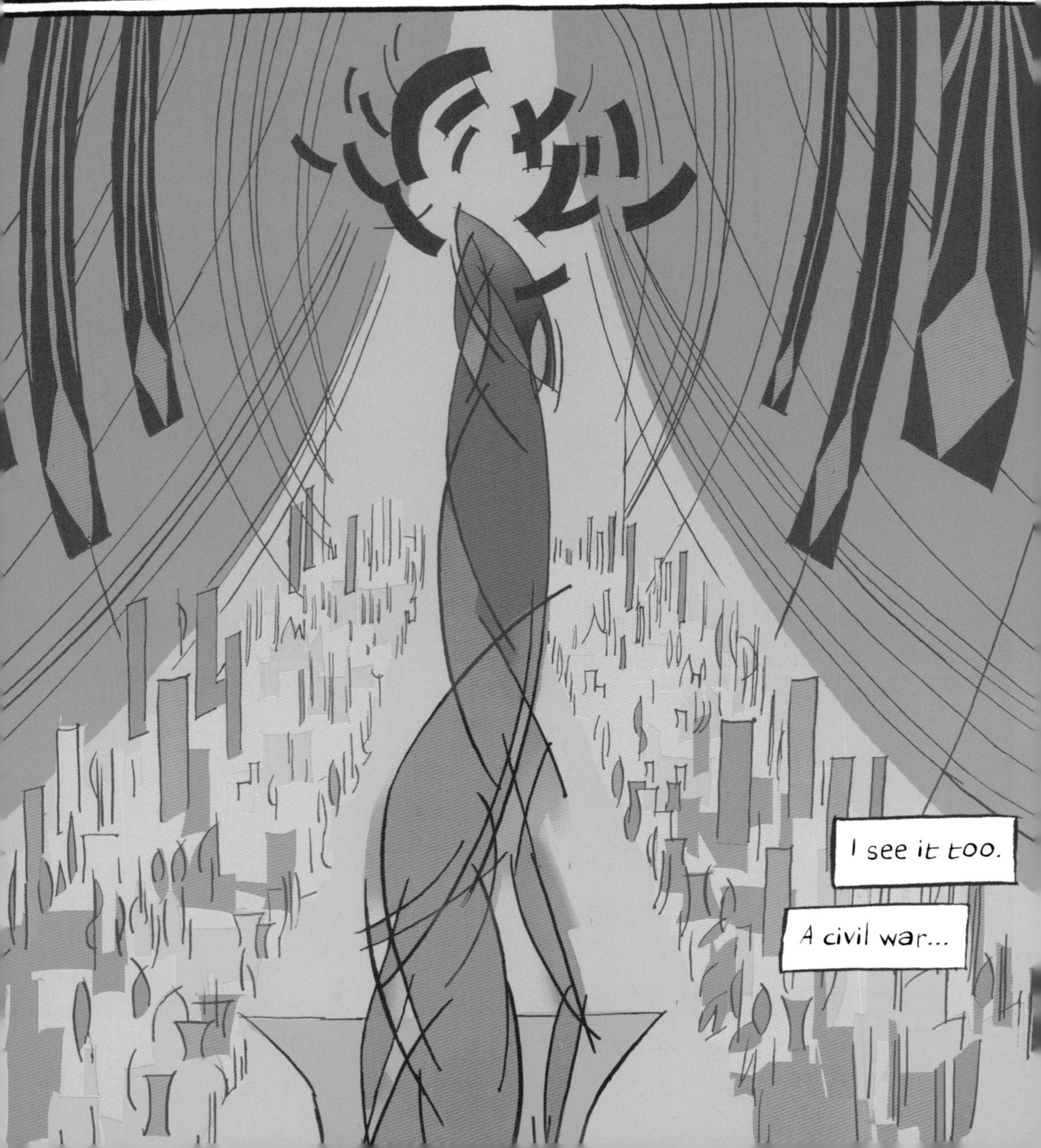
I see it too.
A civil war...

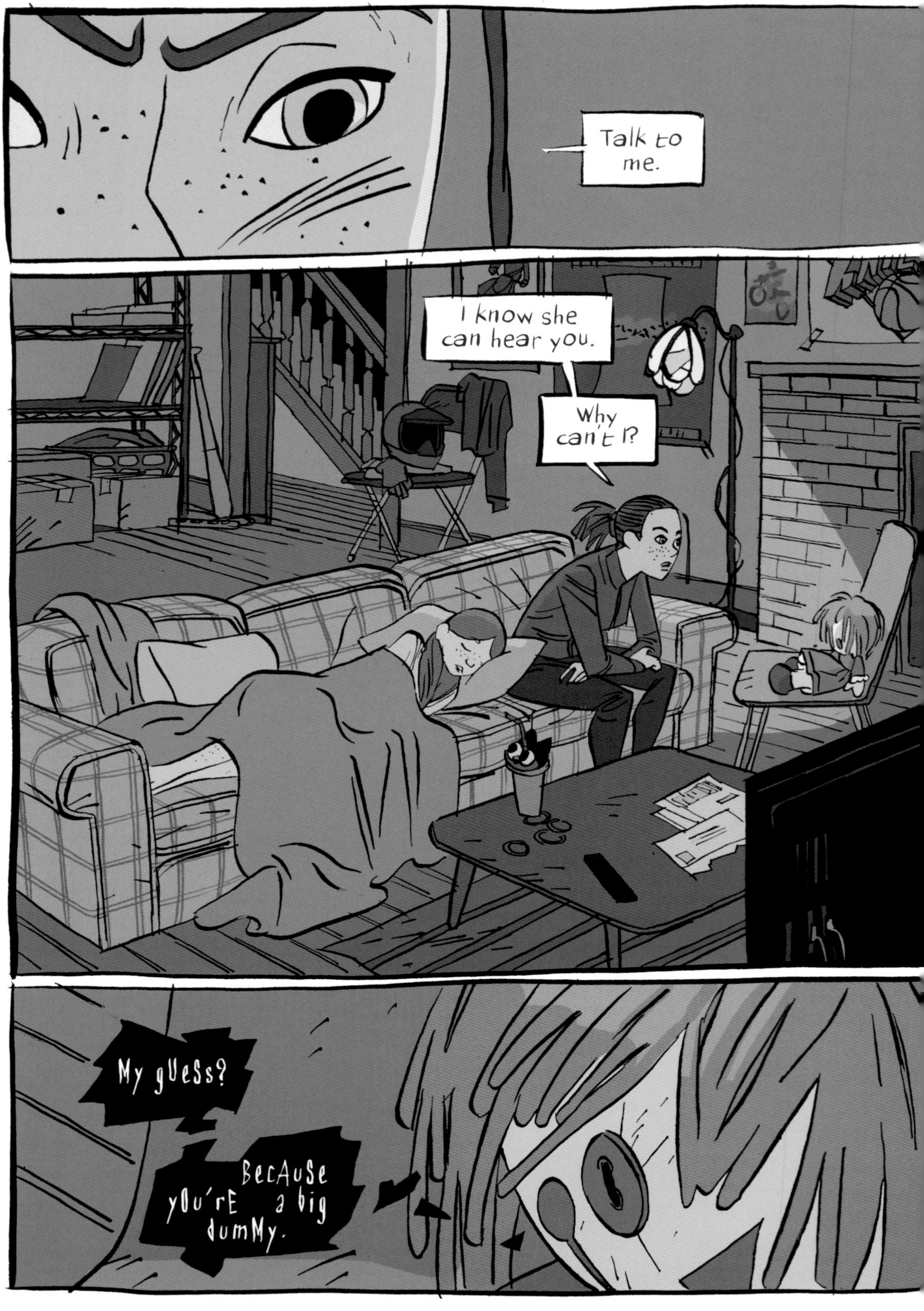
Talk to me.
I know she can hear you.
Why can't I?
My guess?
Because you're a big dummy.

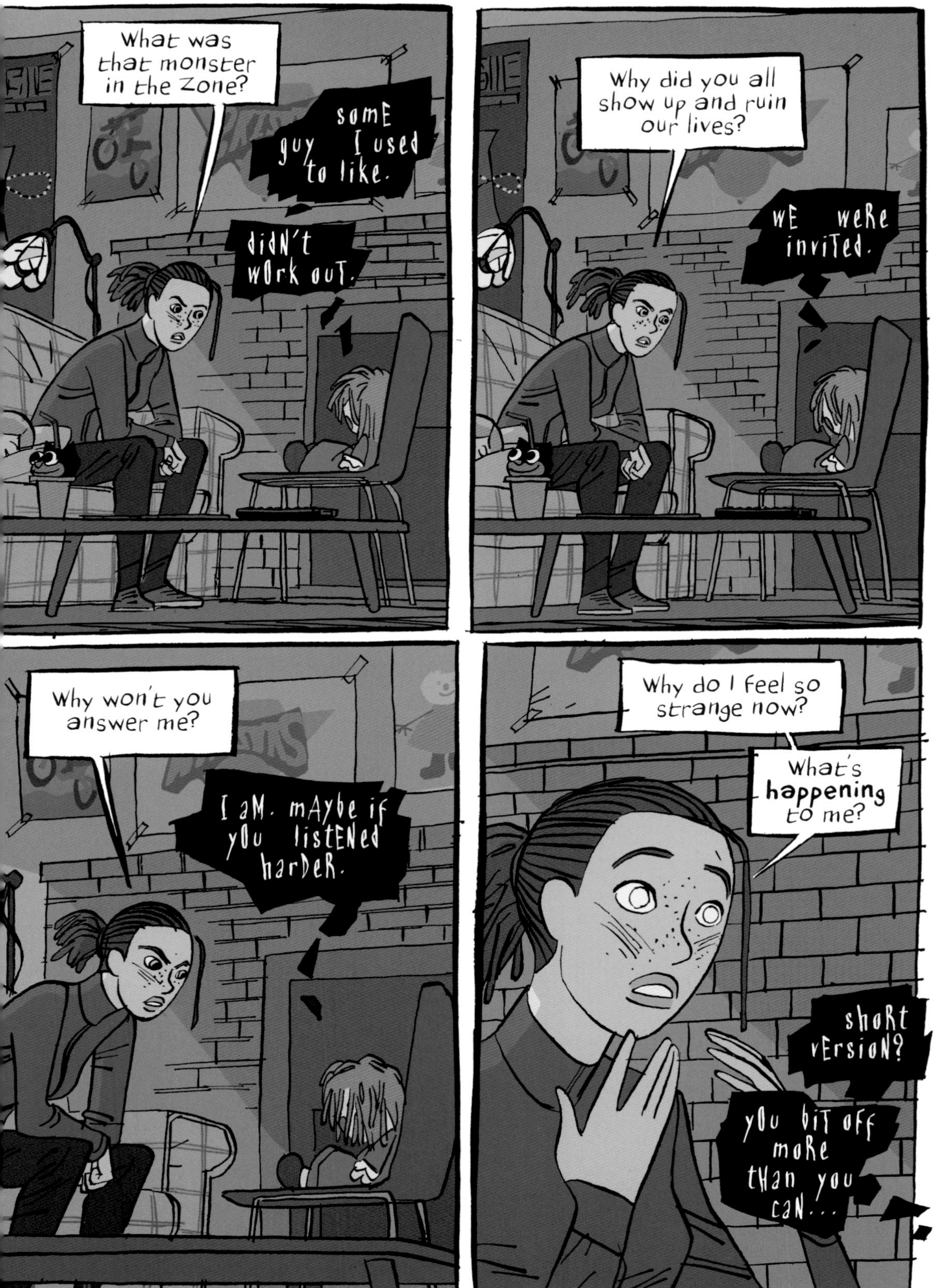
What was that monster in the Zone?
SOME guy I used to like.
didn't work out.
Why did you all show up and ruin our lives?
WE WERE invited.
Why won't you answer me?
I aM. maybe if you listENed harder.
Why do I feel so strange now?
What's **happening** to me?
short version?
you bit off more than you can...

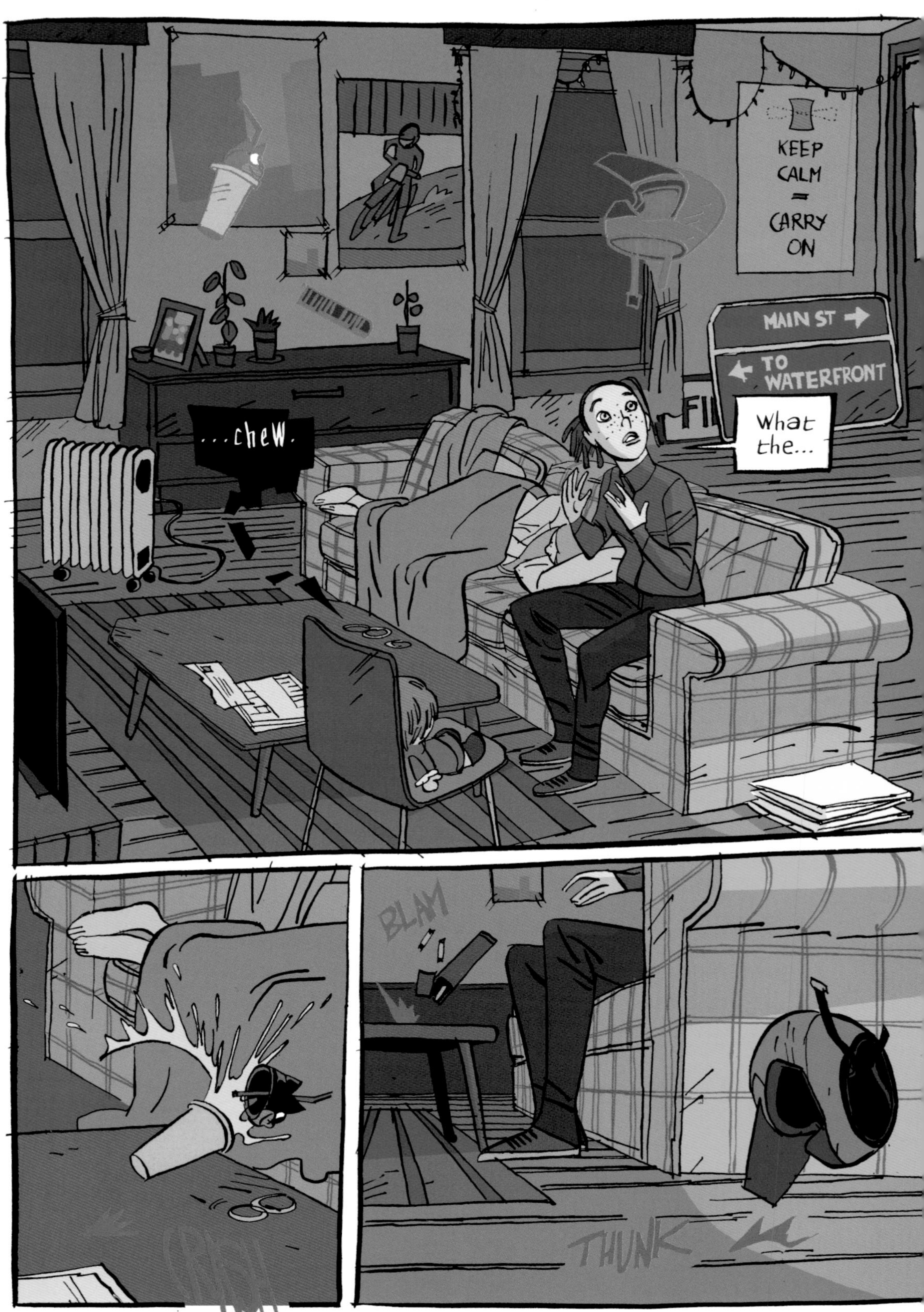
KEEP CALM = CARRY ON
MAIN ST
TO WATERFRONT
...chew.
What the...
CRASH
BLAM
THUNK

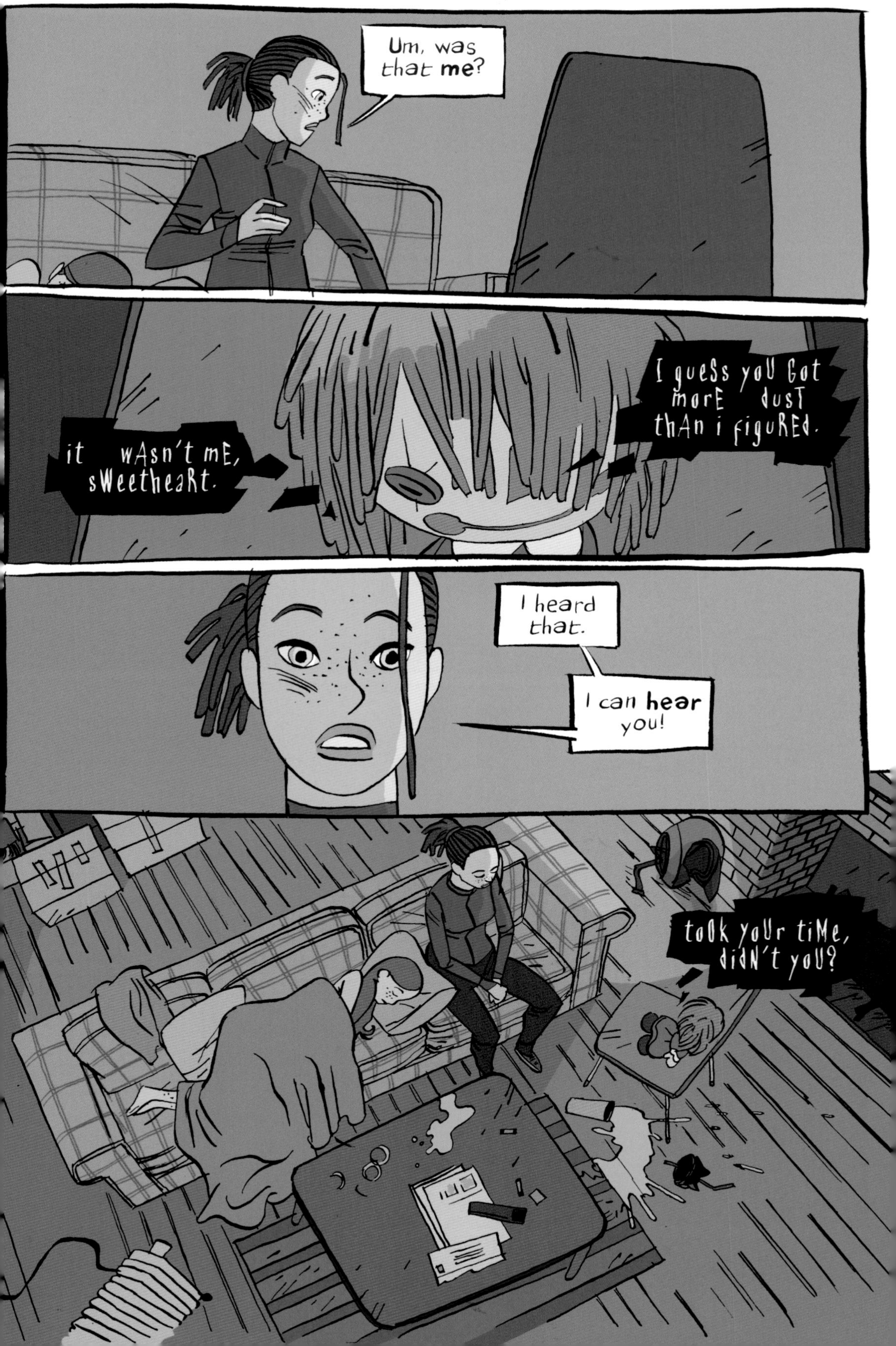
Um, was that **me**?
it wasn't me, sweetheart.
I guess you got more dust than i figured.
I heard that.
I can **hear** you!
took your time, didn't you?

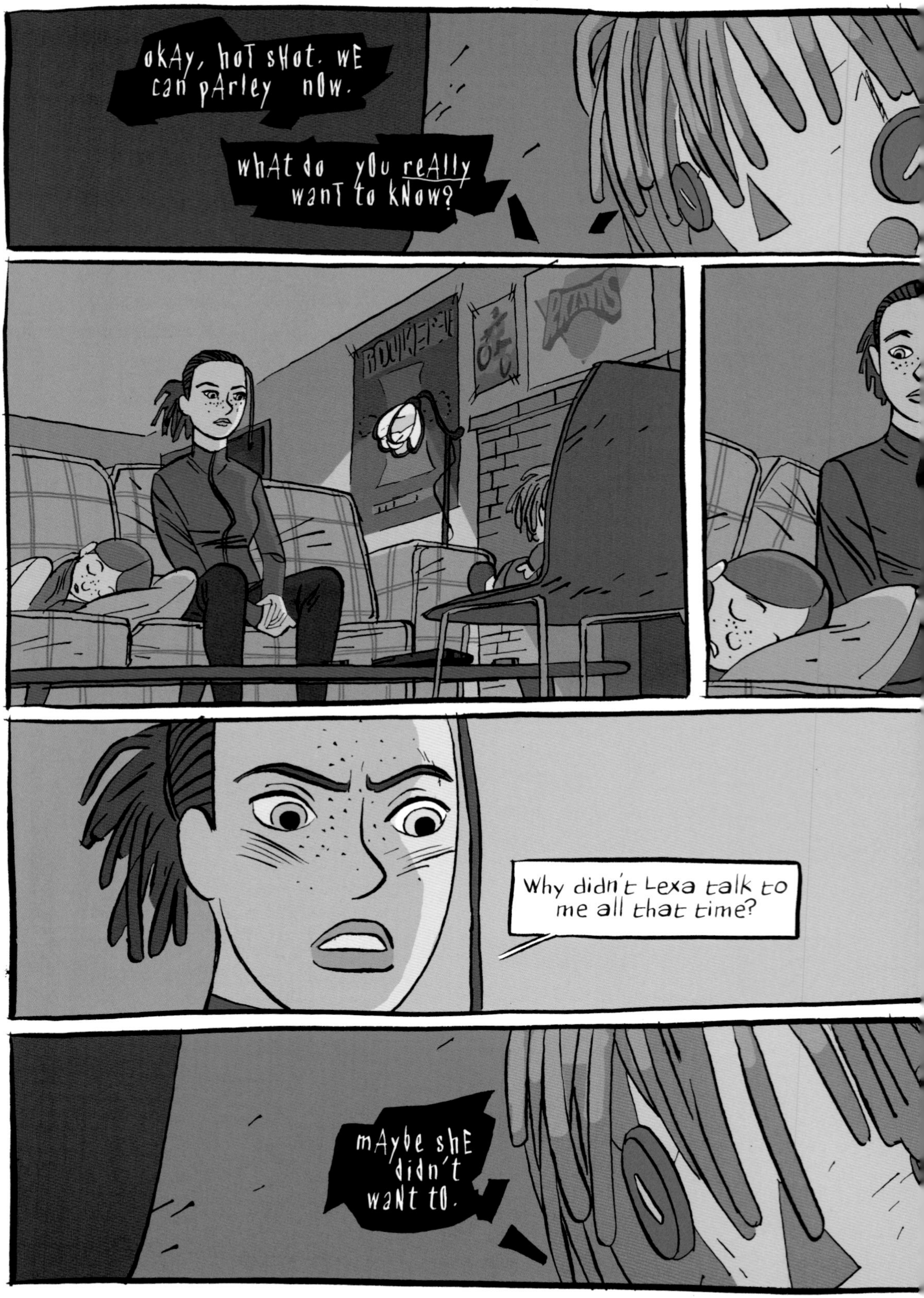
okAy, hoT shot. wE can pArley now.
whAt do you reAlly want to kNow?
Why didn't Lexa talk to me all that time?
mAybe shE didn't wAnt to.

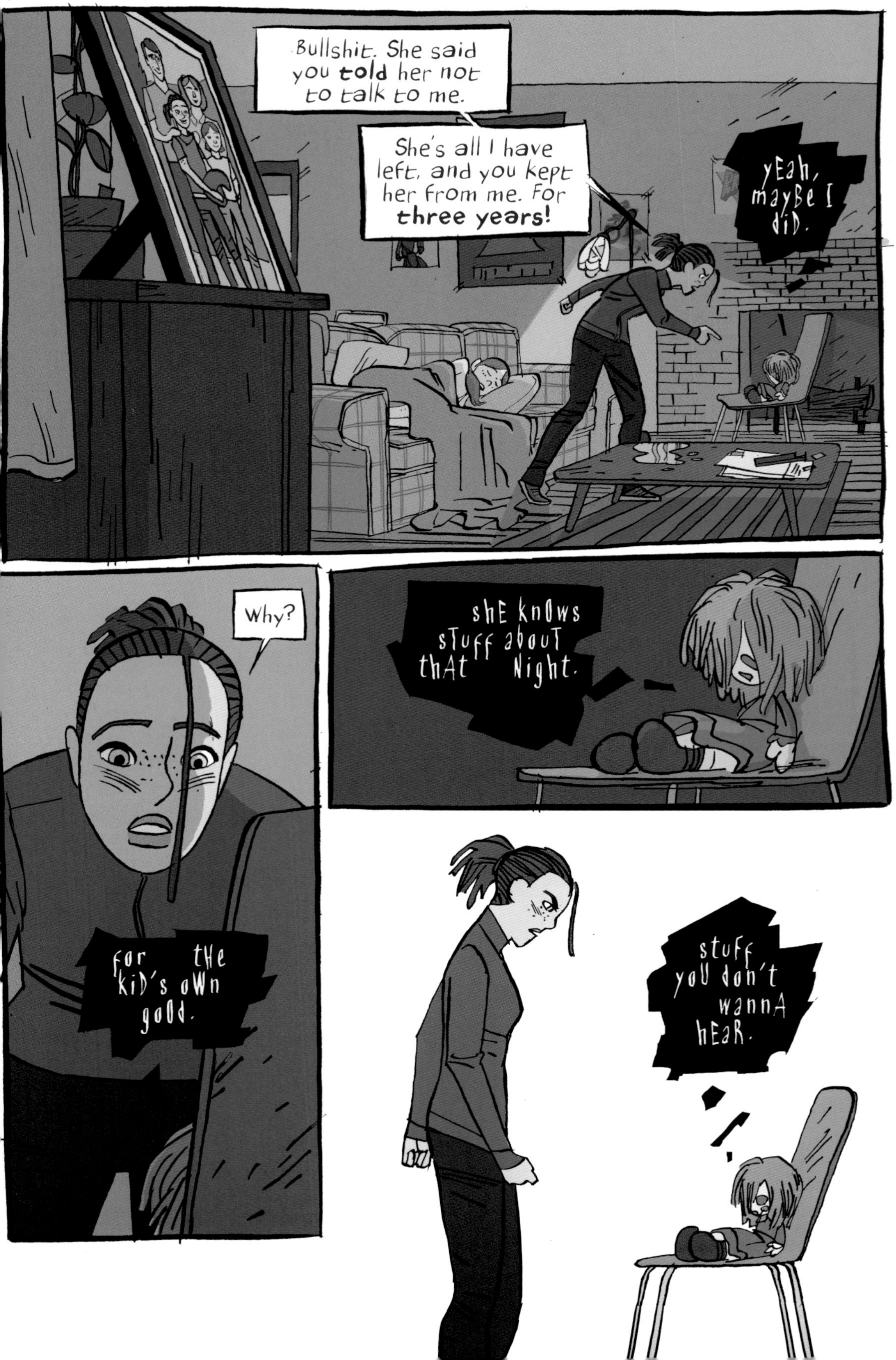

Bullshit. She said you **told** her not to talk to me.
She's all I have left, and you kept her from me. For **three years!**
yEah, maybe I diD.
Why?
for the kiD's oWn good.
shE knows stuff about thAt Night.
stuff you don't wannA hEaR.

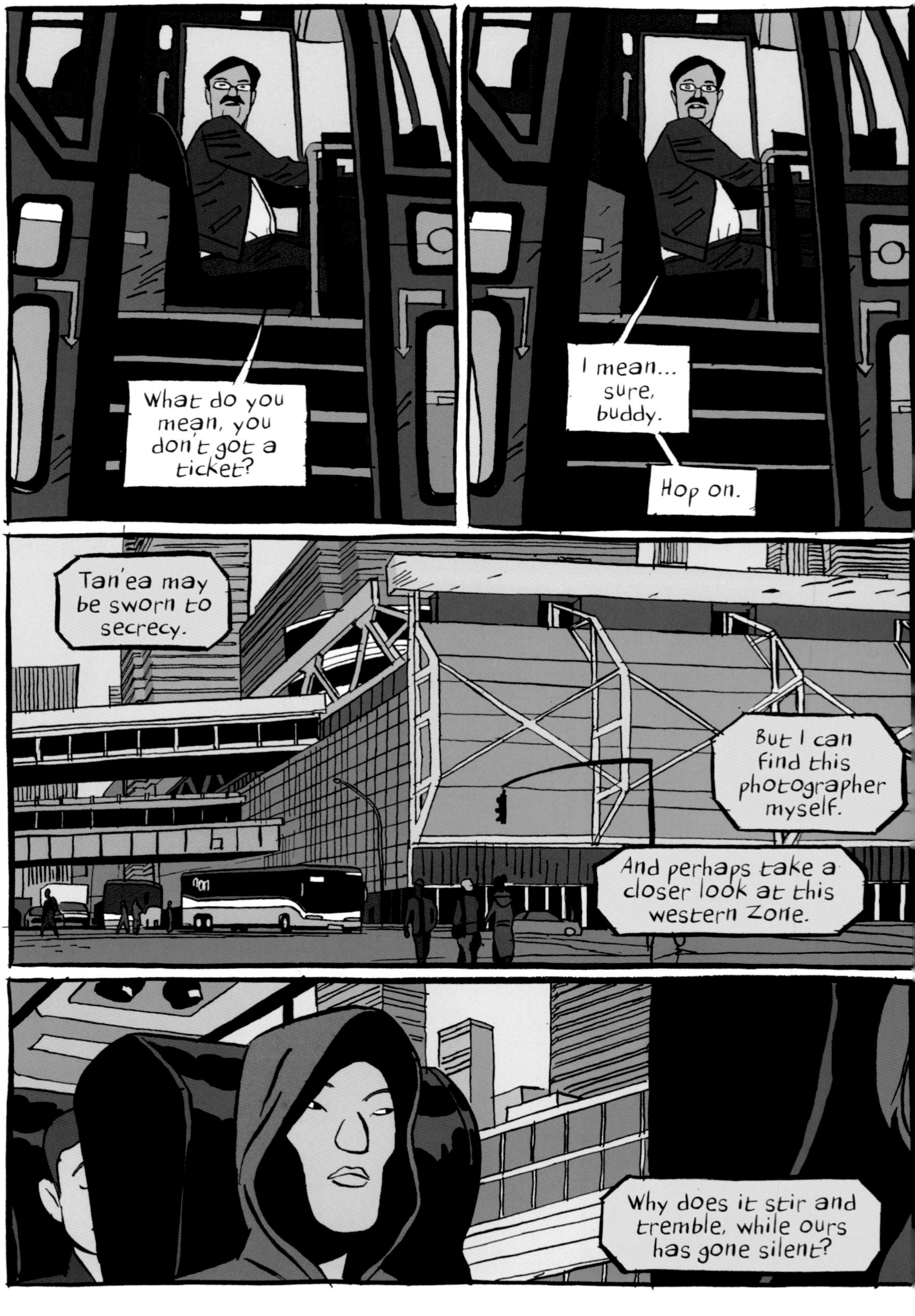
What do you mean, you don't got a ticket?
I mean... sure, buddy.
Hop on.
Tan'ea may be sworn to secrecy.
But I can find this photographer myself.
And perhaps take a closer look at this western Zone.
Why does it stir and tremble, while ours has gone silent?

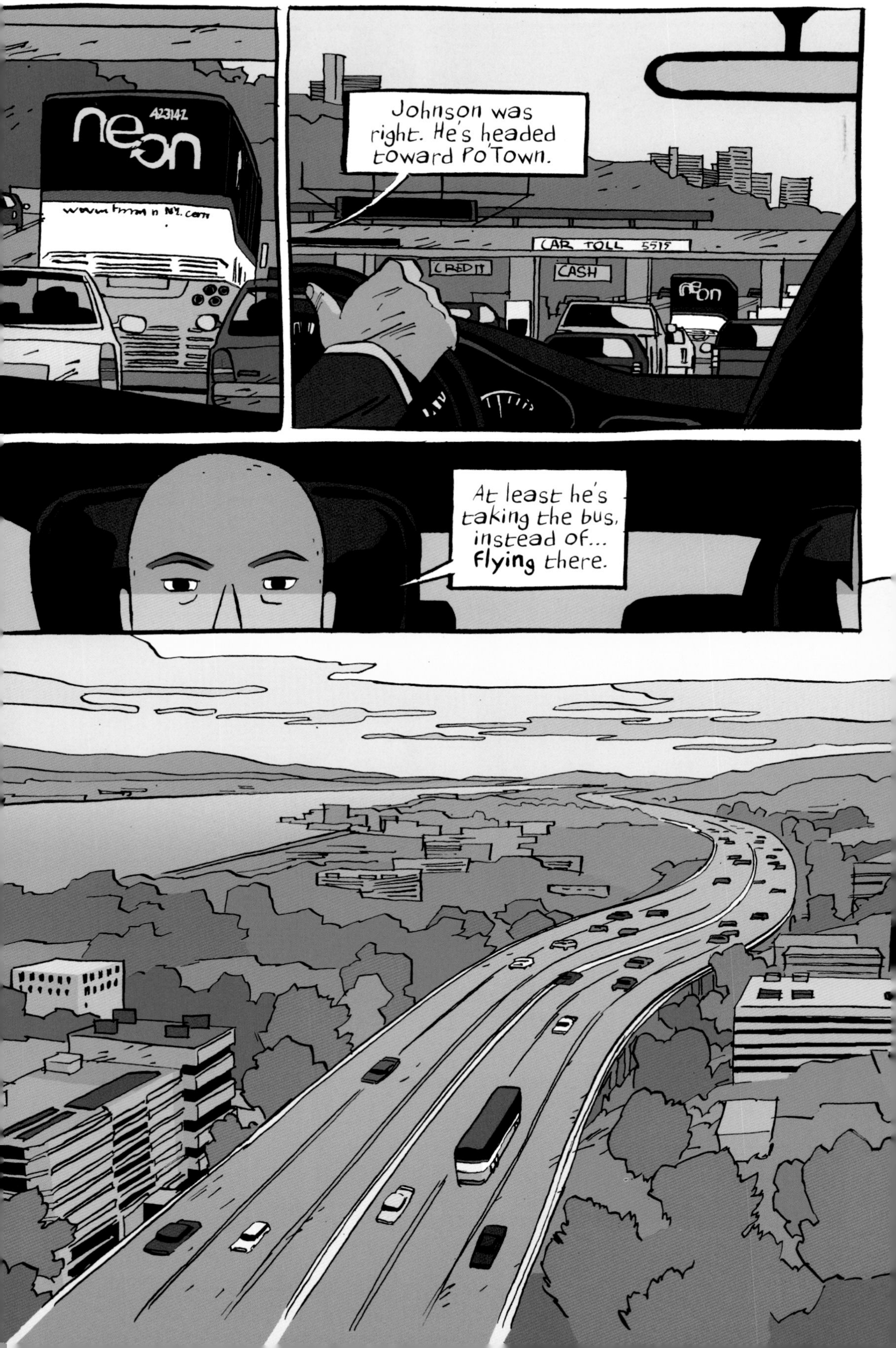
neon
423142
CAR TOLL 5515
CREDIT
CASH
Johnson was right. He's headed toward Po'Town.
At least he's taking the bus, instead of... **flying** there.

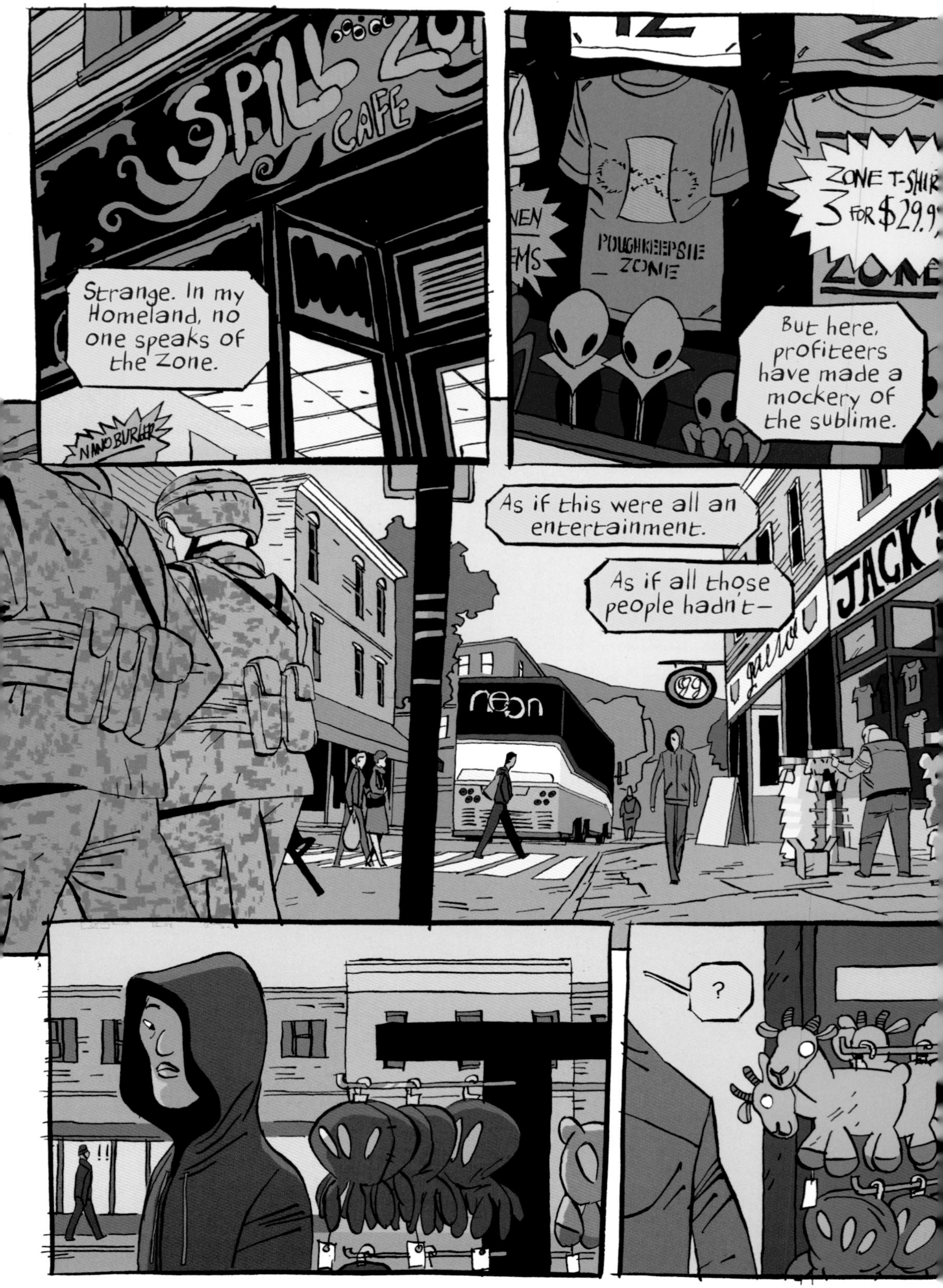

SPILL
ZO
CAFE
Strange. In my Homeland, no one speaks of the Zone.
NANO BURGER
POUGHKEEPSIE ZONE
ZONE T-SHIR
3 FOR $29.9
ZONE
But here, profiteers have made a mockery of the sublime.
As if this were all an entertainment.
As if all those people hadn't—
JACK'S
neon
99
?

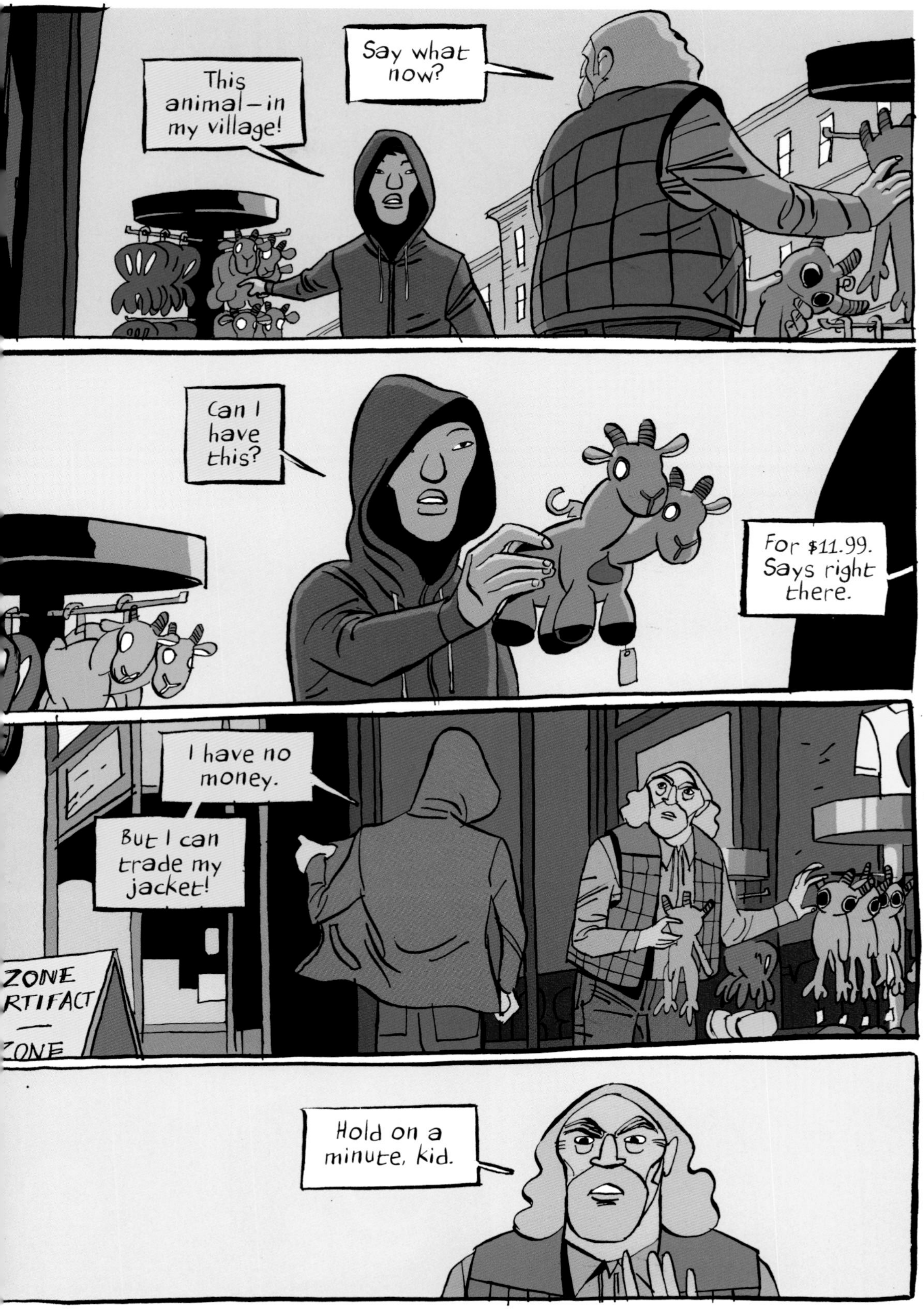
This animal—in my village!
Say what now?
Can I have this?
For $11.99. Says right there.
I have no money.
But I can trade my jacket!
ZONE
RTIFACT
ZONE
Hold on a minute, kid.

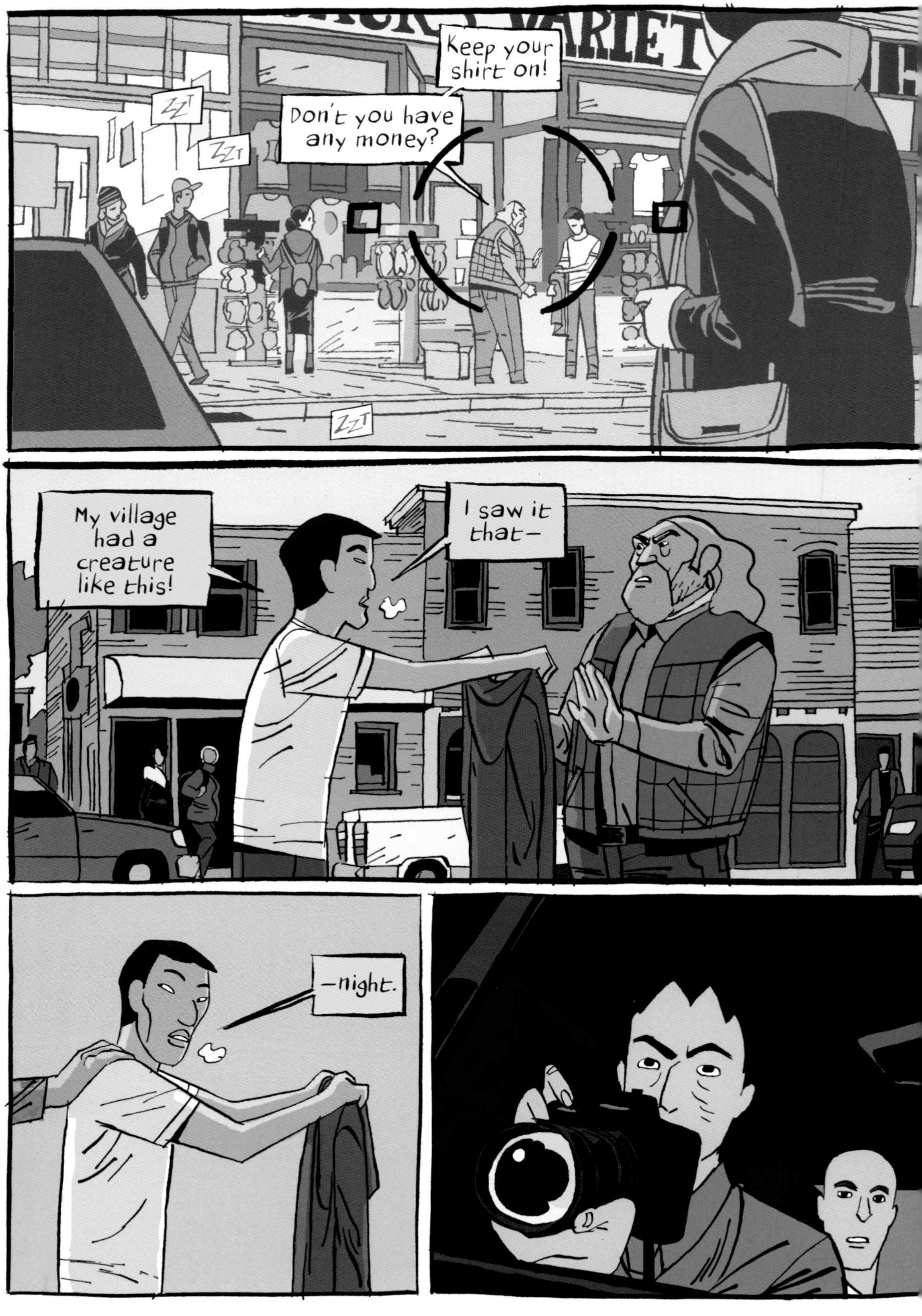
ZZT
ZZT
Don't you have any money?
Keep your shirt on!
ZZT
My village had a creature like this!
I saw it that—
—night.

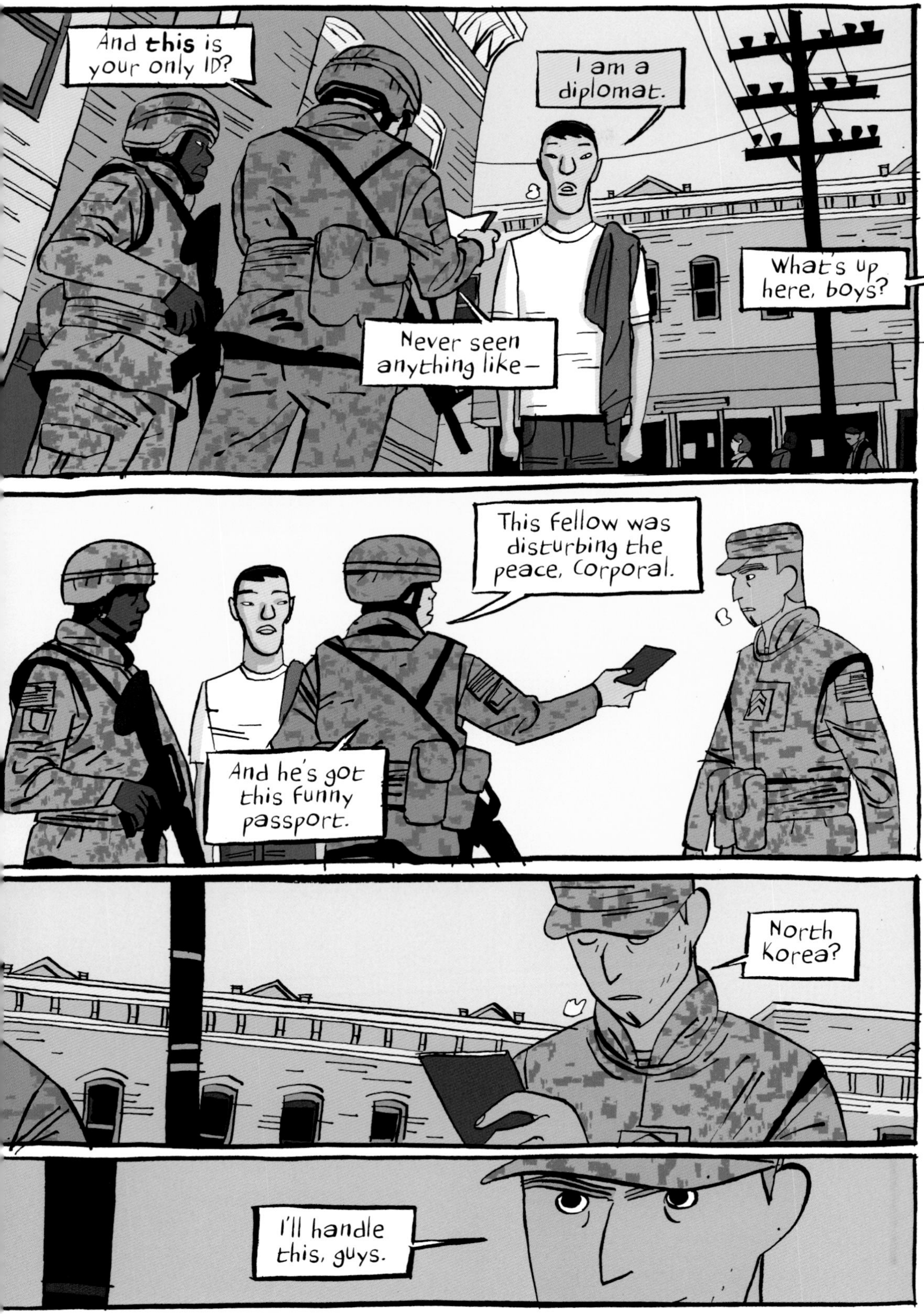

And this is your only ID?
I am a diplomat.
What's up here, boys?
Never seen anything like—
This fellow was disturbing the peace, Corporal.
And he's got this funny passport.
North Korea?
I'll handle this, guys.

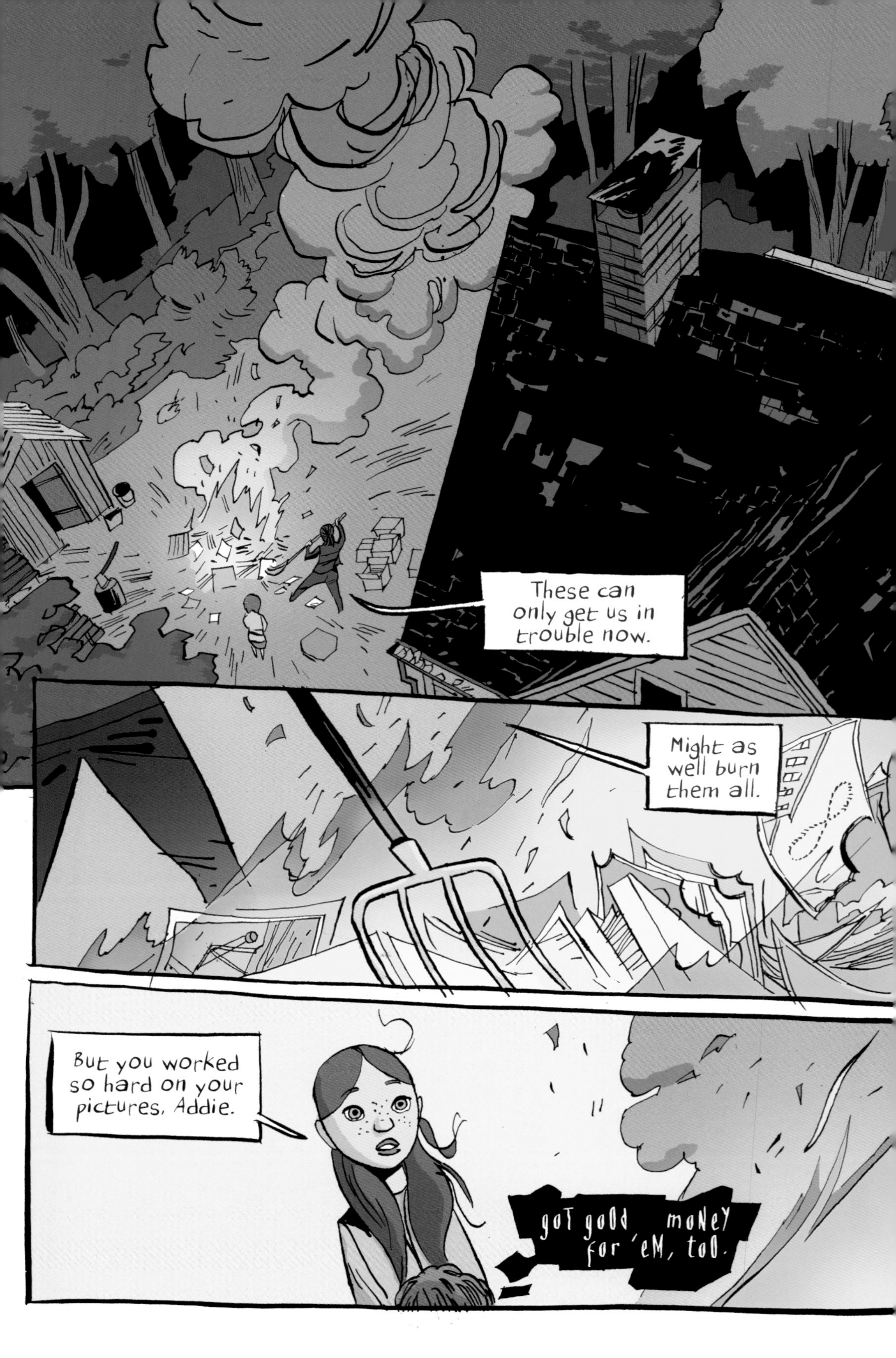
These can only get us in trouble now.
Might as well burn them all.
But you worked so hard on your pictures, Addie.
Got good money for 'em, too.

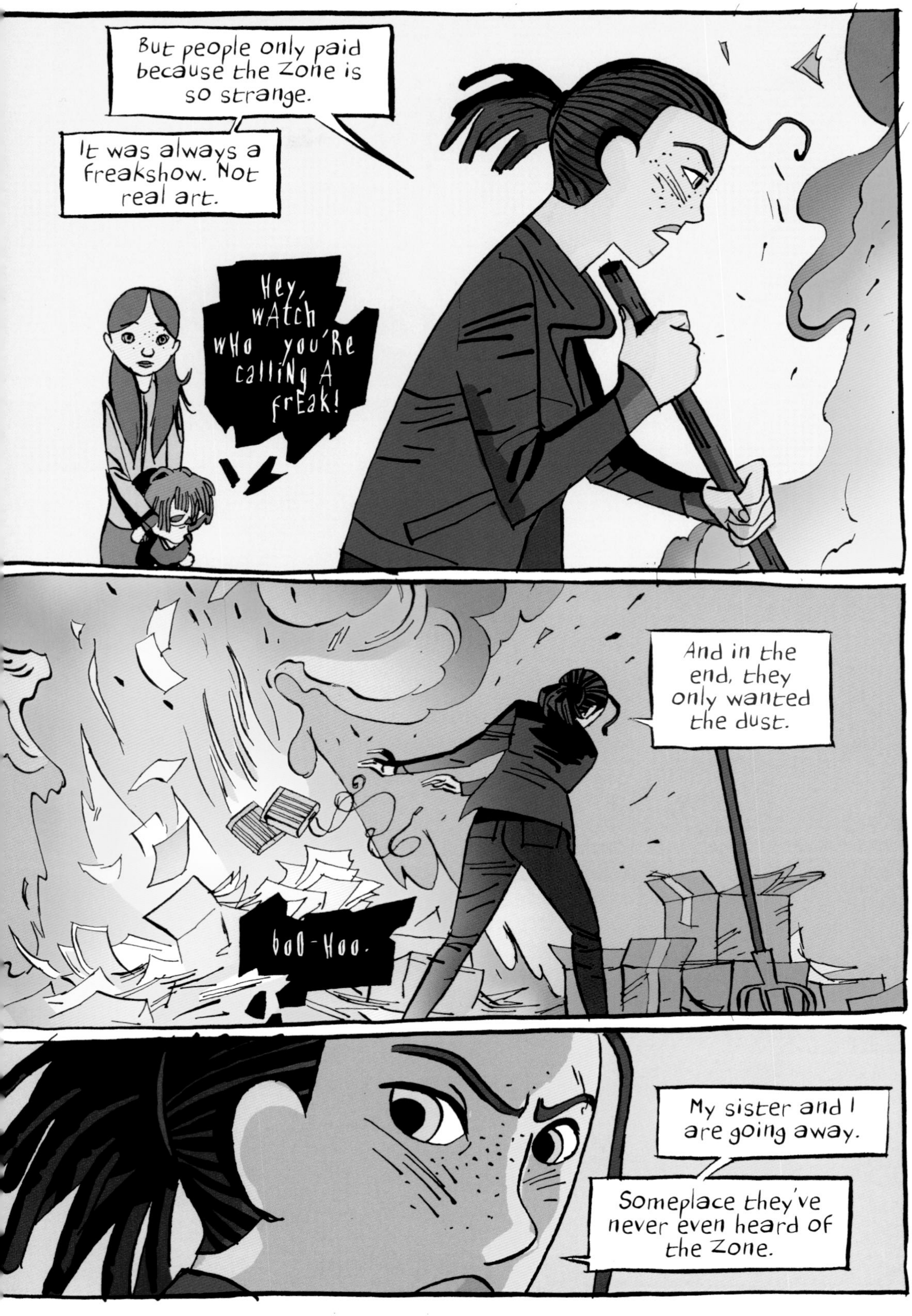
But people only paid because the Zone is so strange.
It was always a freakshow. Not real art.
Hey, watch who you're calling a freak!
And in the end, they only wanted the dust.
boo-hoo.
My sister and I are going away.
Someplace they've never even heard of the Zone.

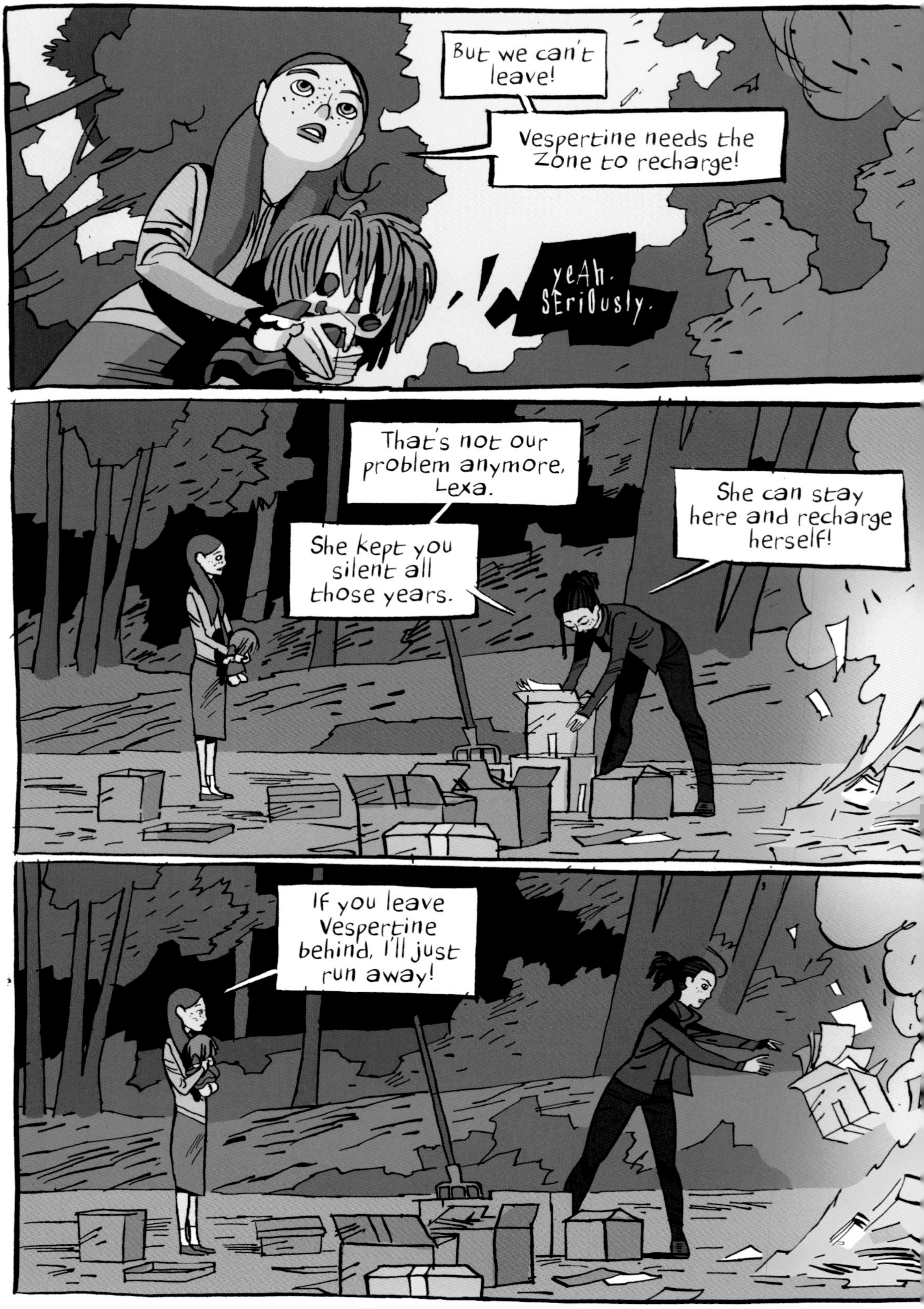
But we can't leave!
Vespertine needs the Zone to recharge!
yeAh. SEriOusly.
That's not our problem anymore, Lexa.
She kept you silent all those years.
She can stay here and recharge herself!
If you leave Vespertine behind, I'll just run away!

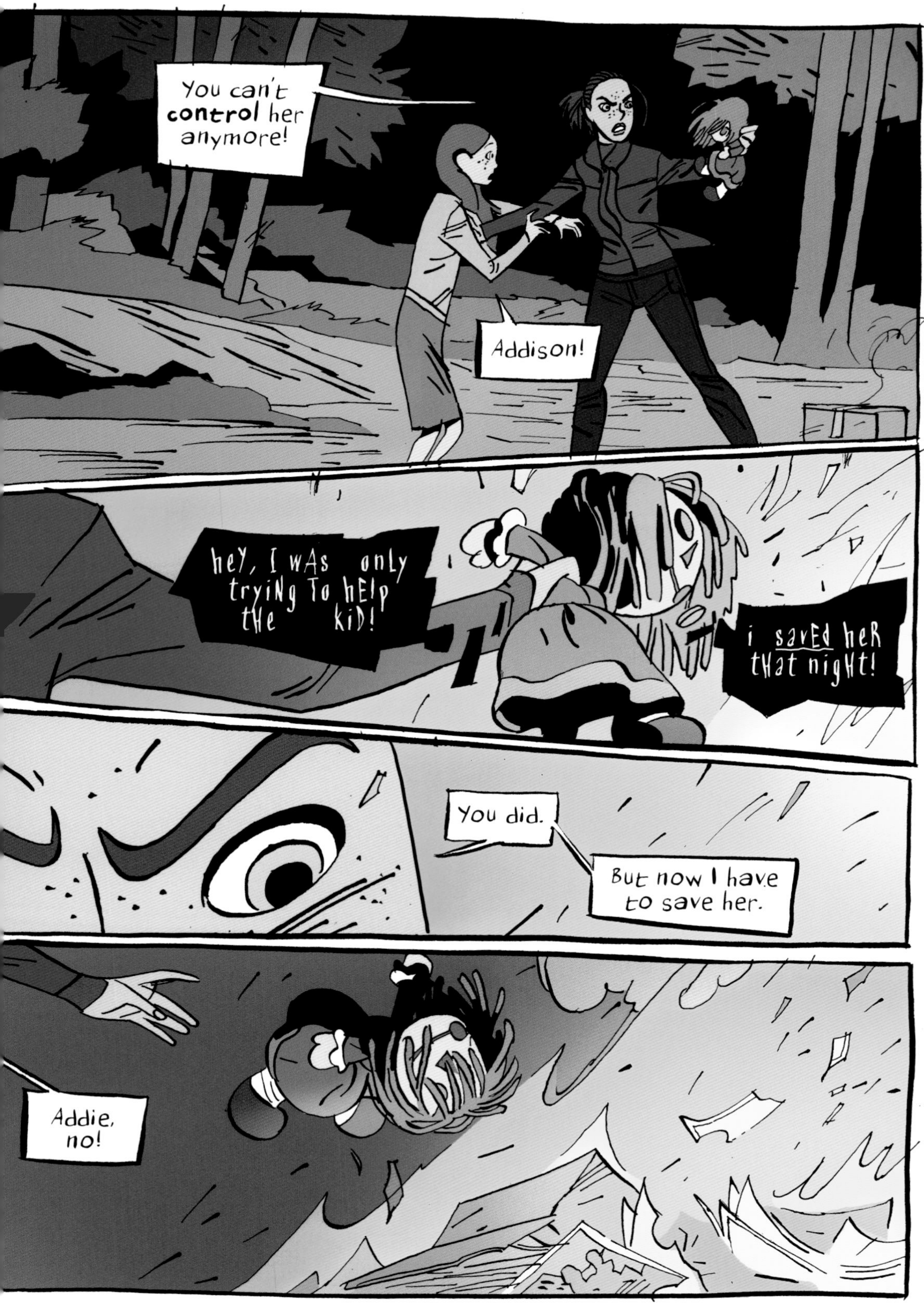
You can't **control** her anymore!
Addison!
hey, I wAs only trying to hElp the kiD!
i savEd heR that night!
You did.
But now I have to save her.
Addie, no!

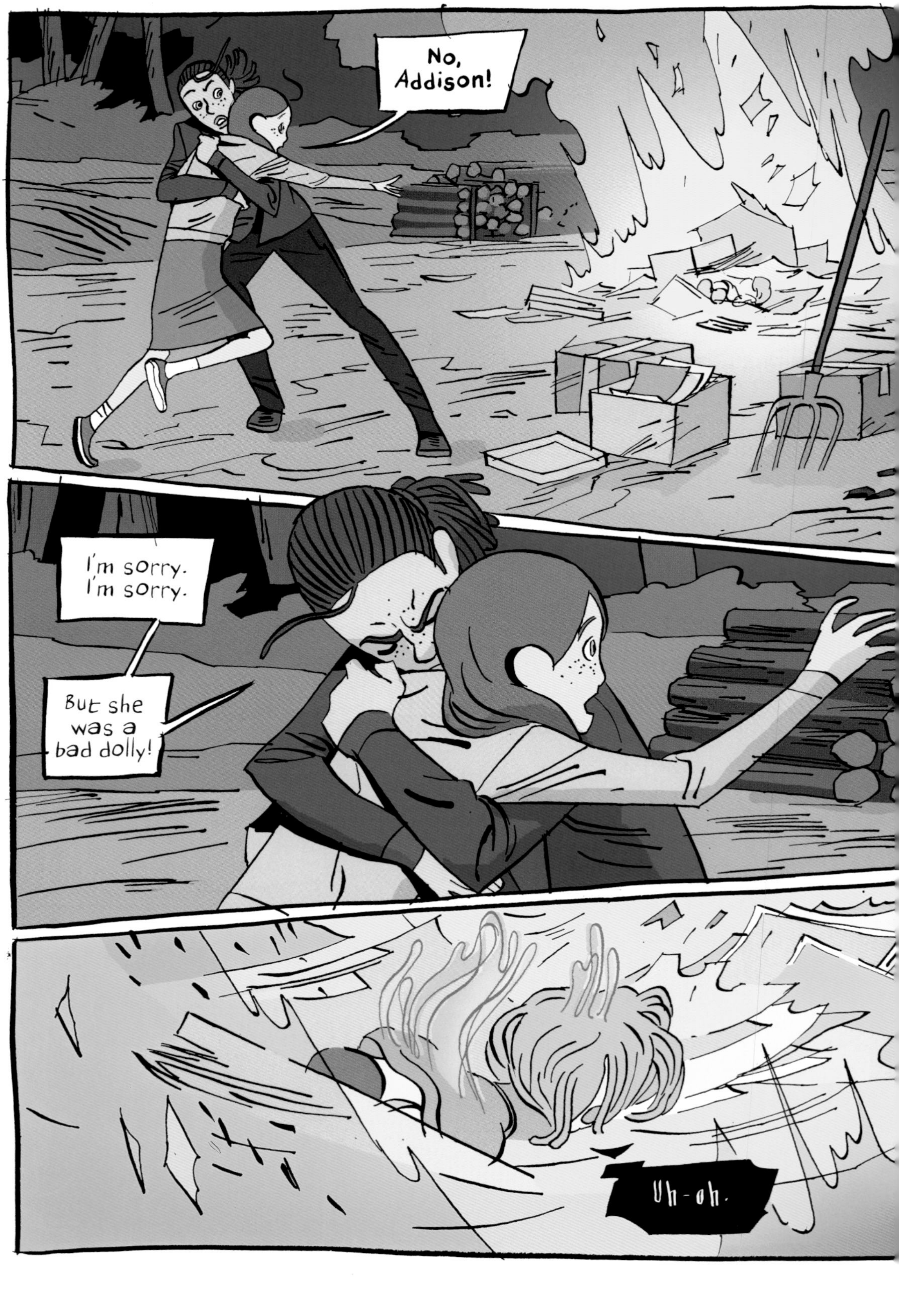
No, Addison!
I'm sorry. I'm sorry.
But she was a bad dolly!
Uh-oh.

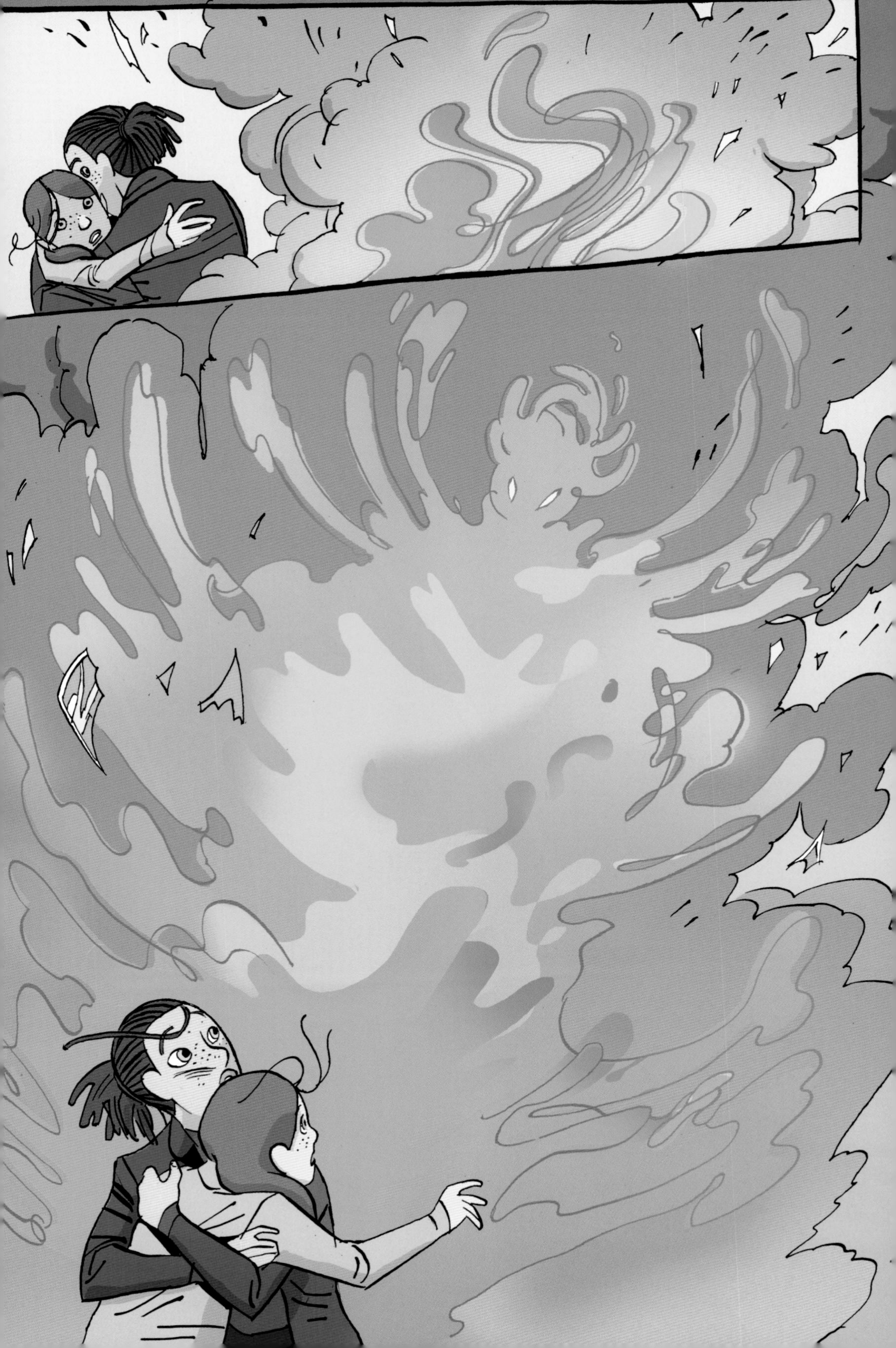

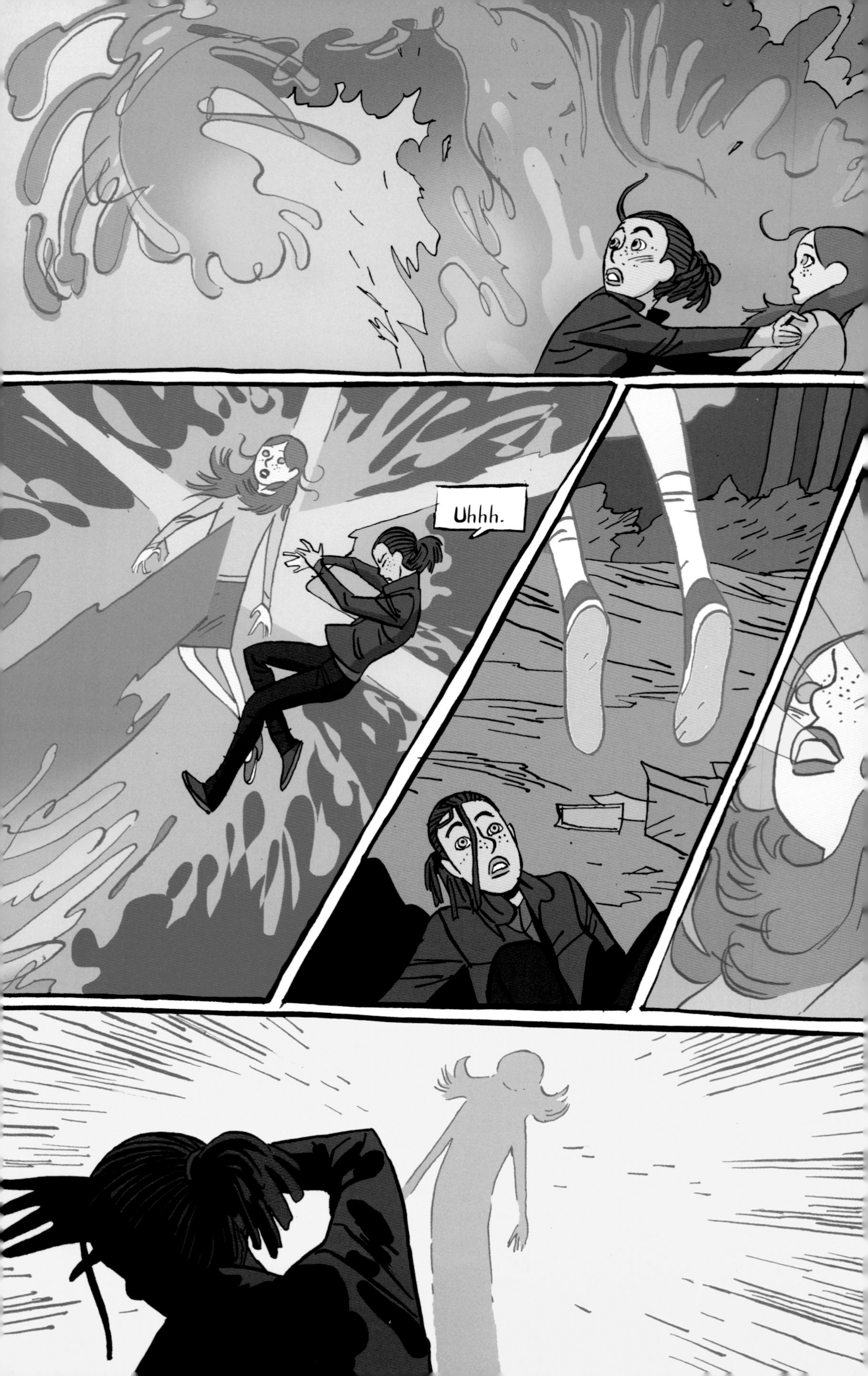
Uhhh.

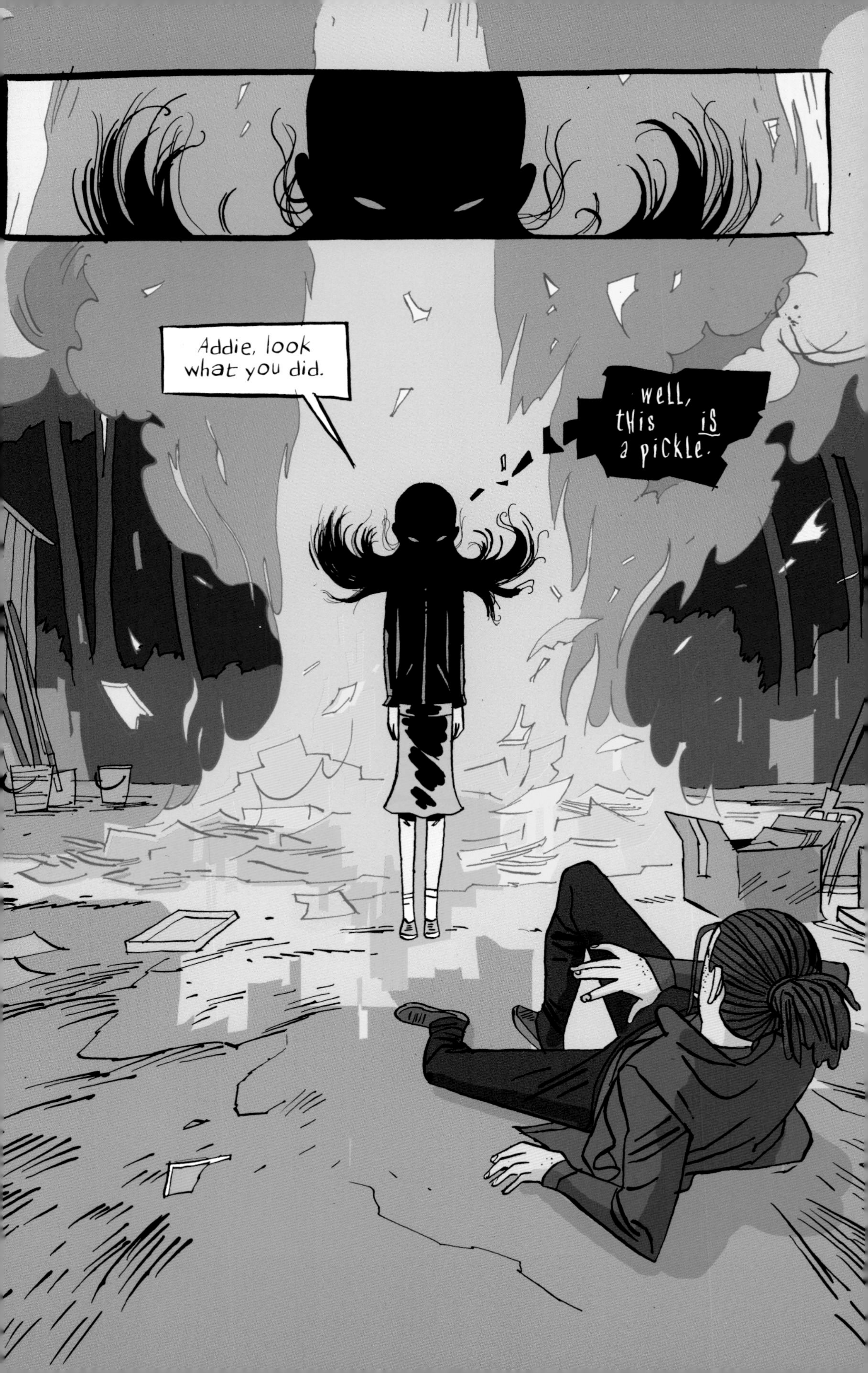
Addie, look what you did.
well, this is a pickle.

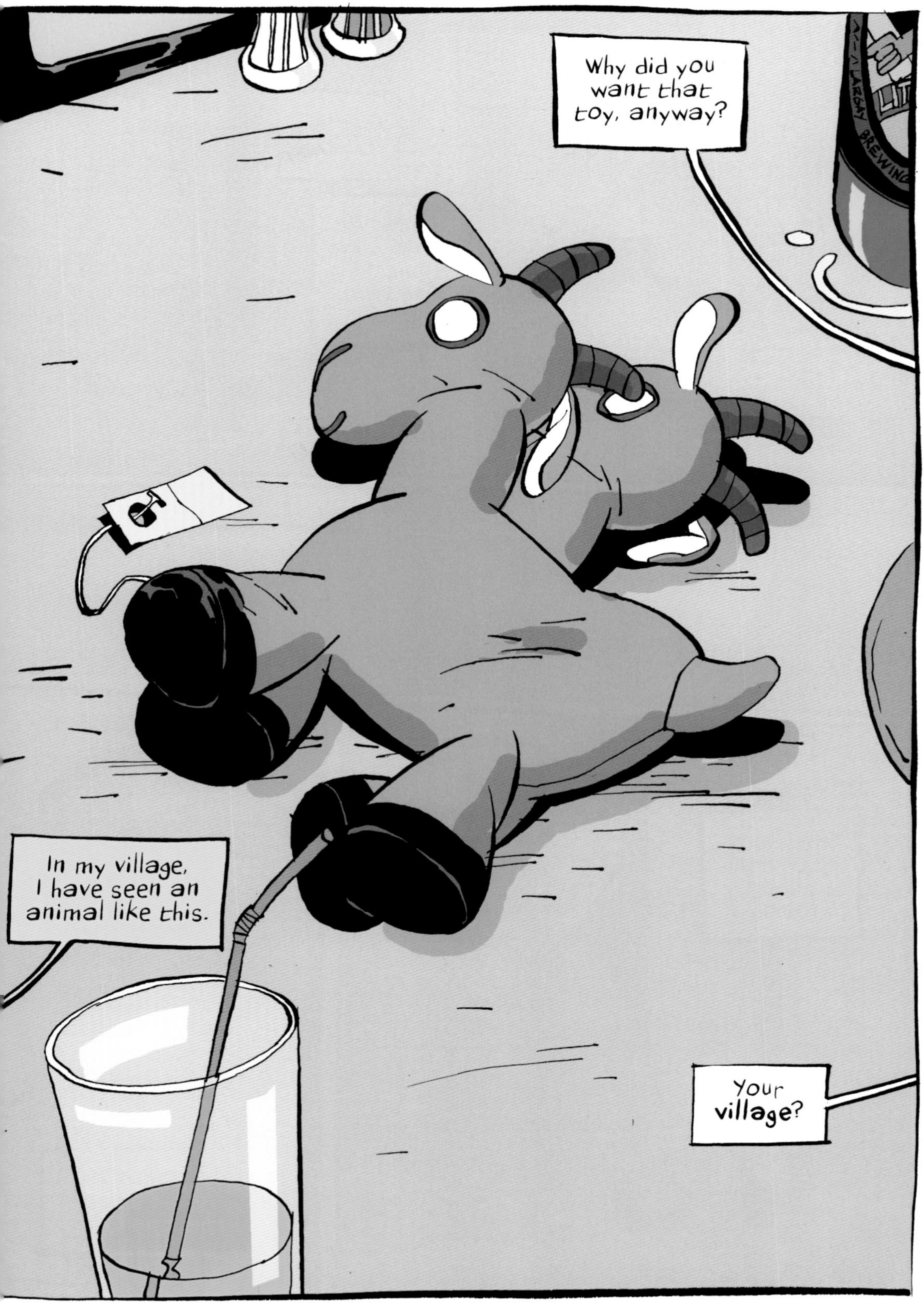
Why did you want that toy, anyway?
In my village, I have seen an animal like this.
Your village?

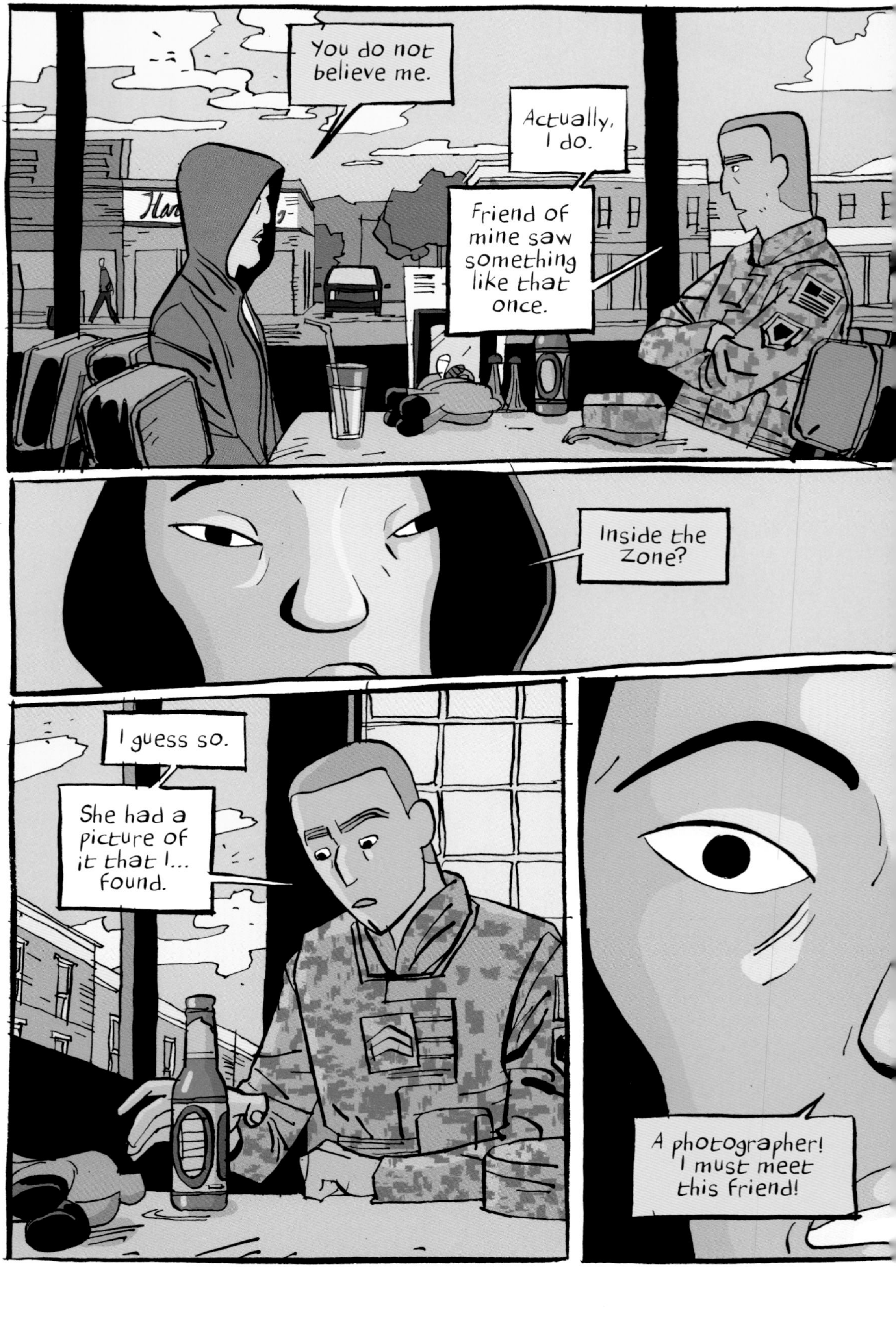
You do not believe me.
Actually, I do.
Friend of mine saw something like that once.
Inside the Zone?
I guess so.
She had a picture of it that I... found.
A photographer! I must meet this friend!

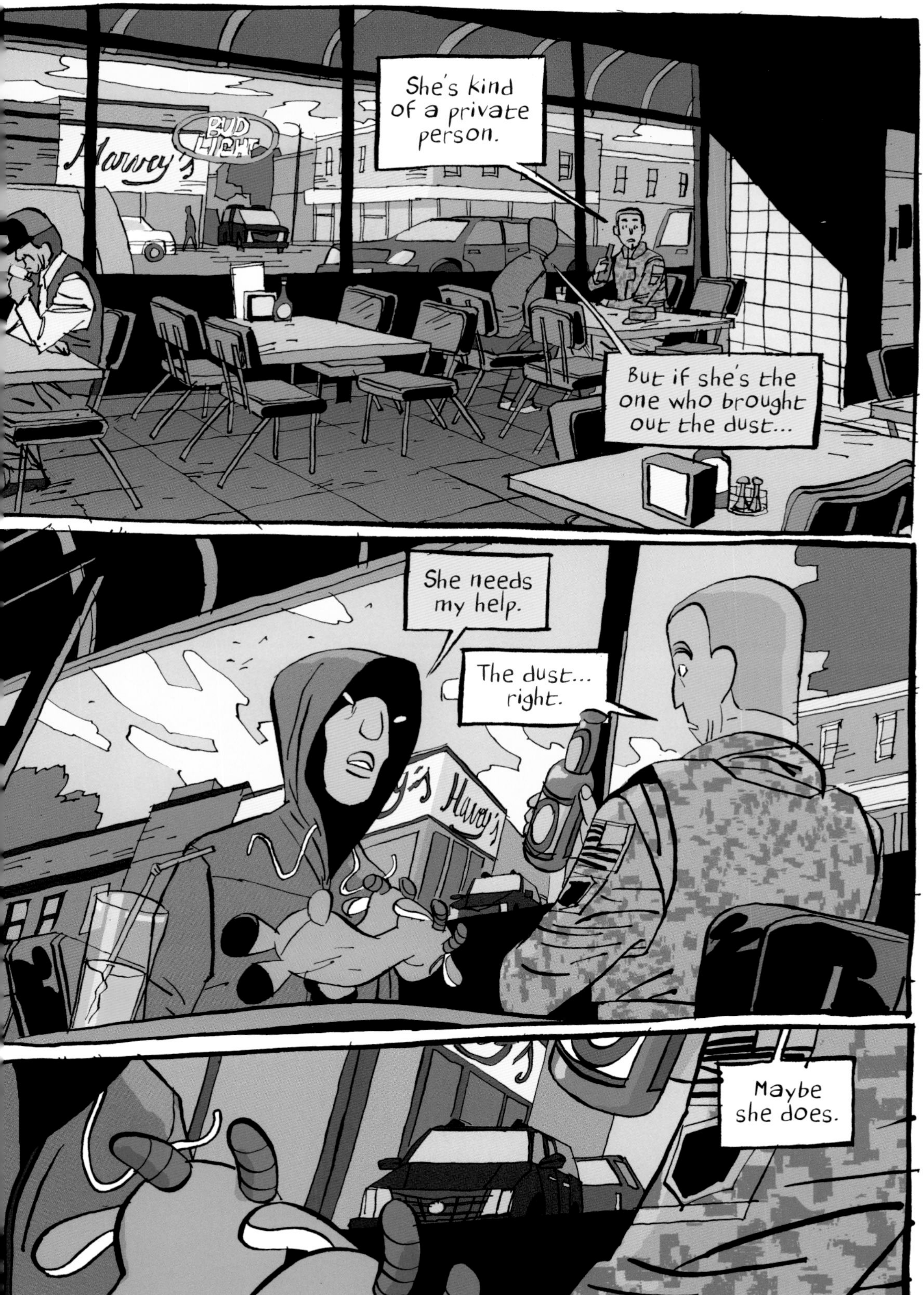
She's kind of a private person.
But if she's the one who brought out the dust...
BUD LIGHT
Harvey's
She needs my help.
The dust... right.
Maybe she does.

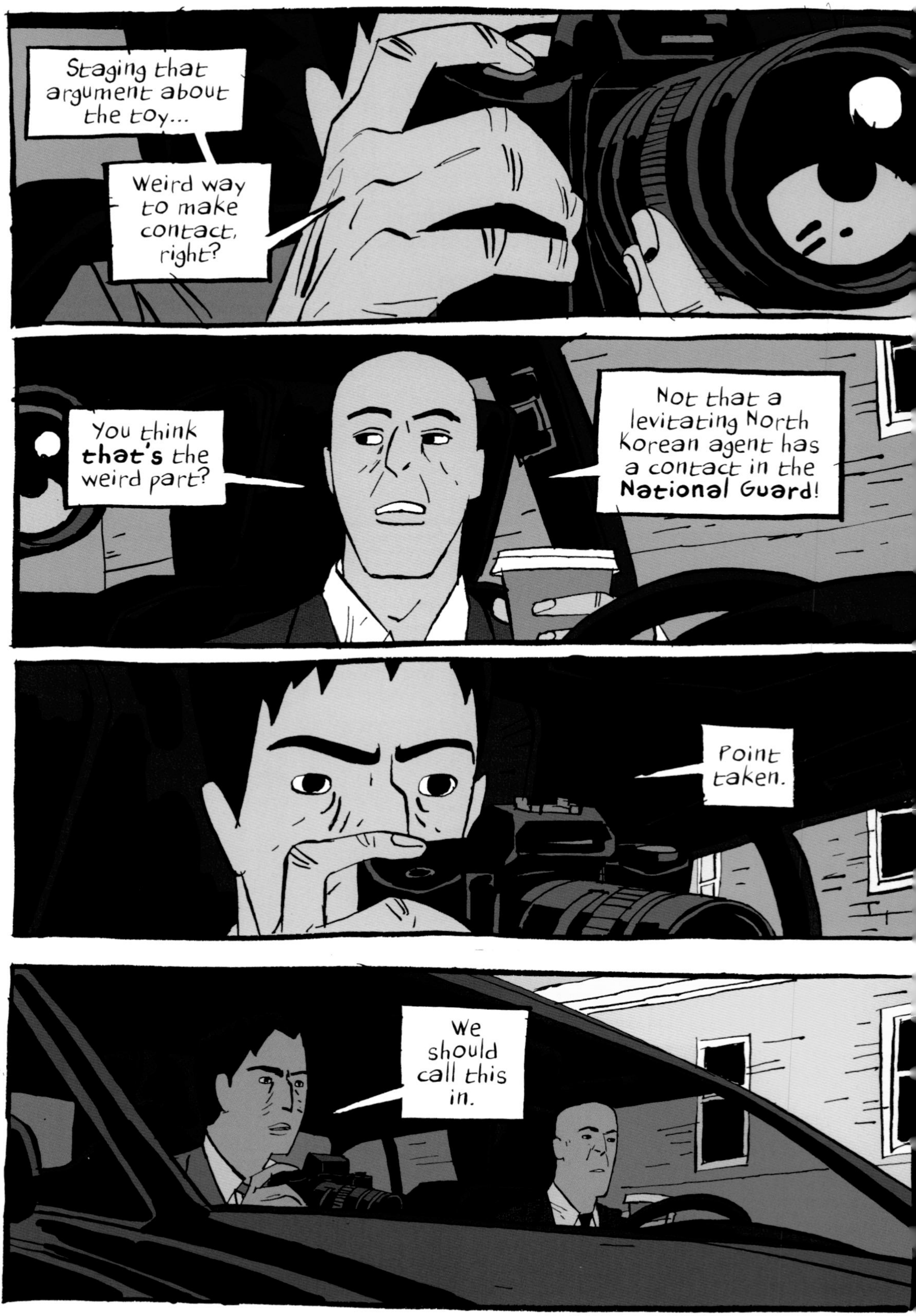
Staging that argument about the toy...
Weird way to make contact, right?
You think **that's** the weird part?
Not that a levitating North Korean agent has a contact in the **National Guard**!
Point taken.
We should call this in.

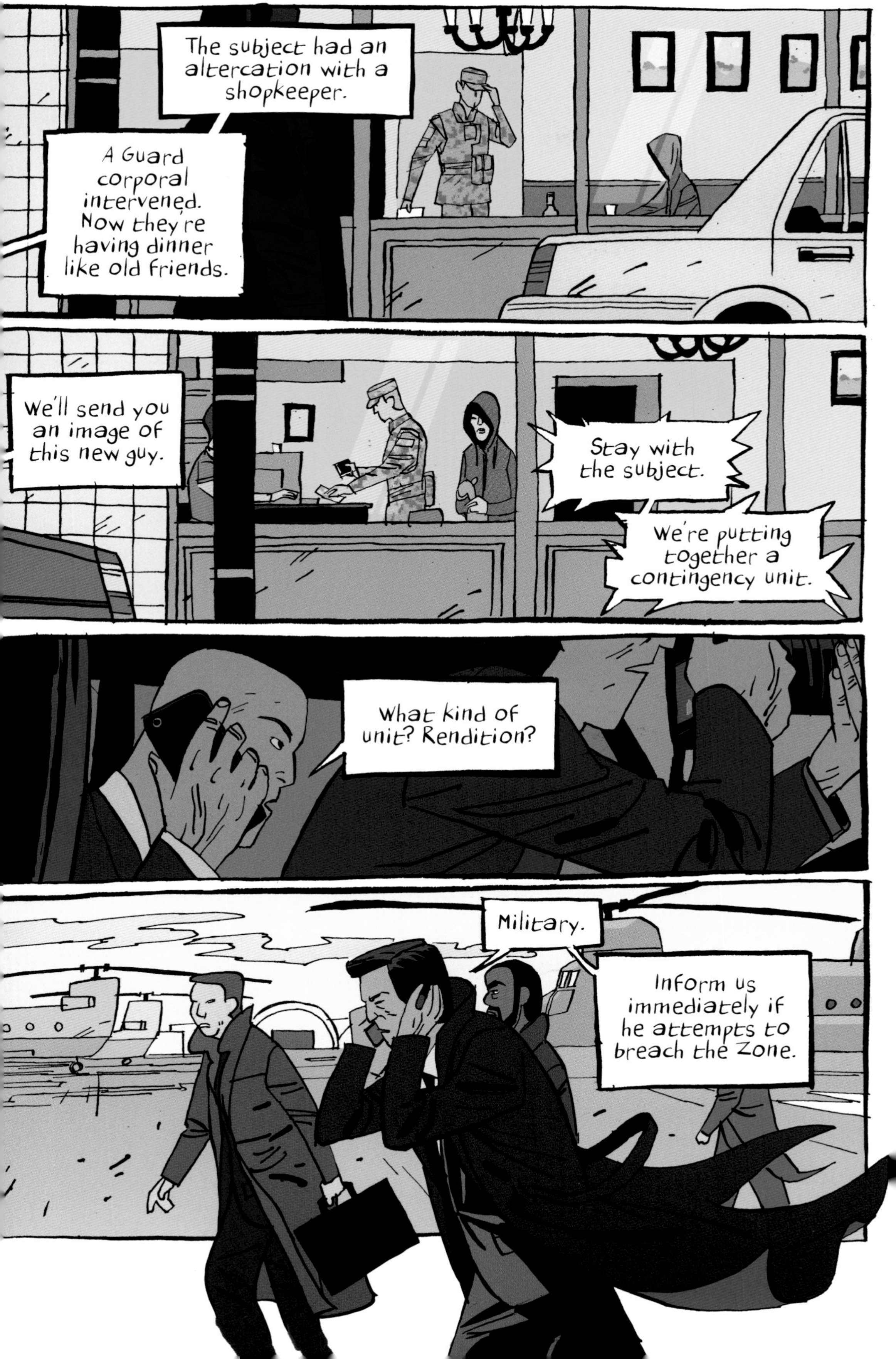
The subject had an altercation with a shopkeeper.
A Guard corporal intervened. Now they're having dinner like old friends.
We'll send you an image of this new guy.
Stay with the subject.
We're putting together a contingency unit.
What kind of unit? Rendition?
Military.
Inform us immediately if he attempts to breach the Zone.

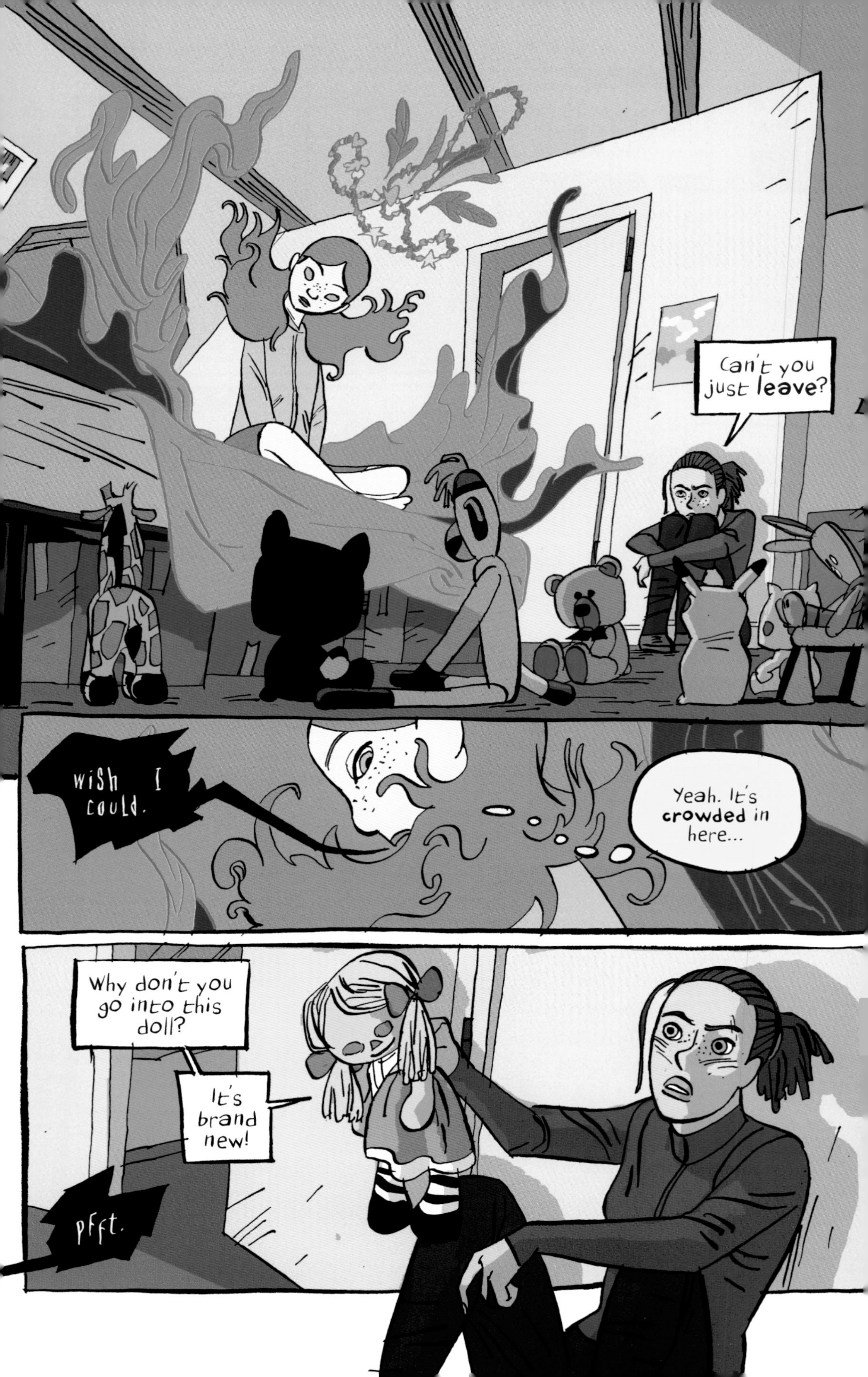
Can't you just leave?
wish I could.
Yeah. It's crowded in here...
Why don't you go into this doll?
It's brand new!
pfft.

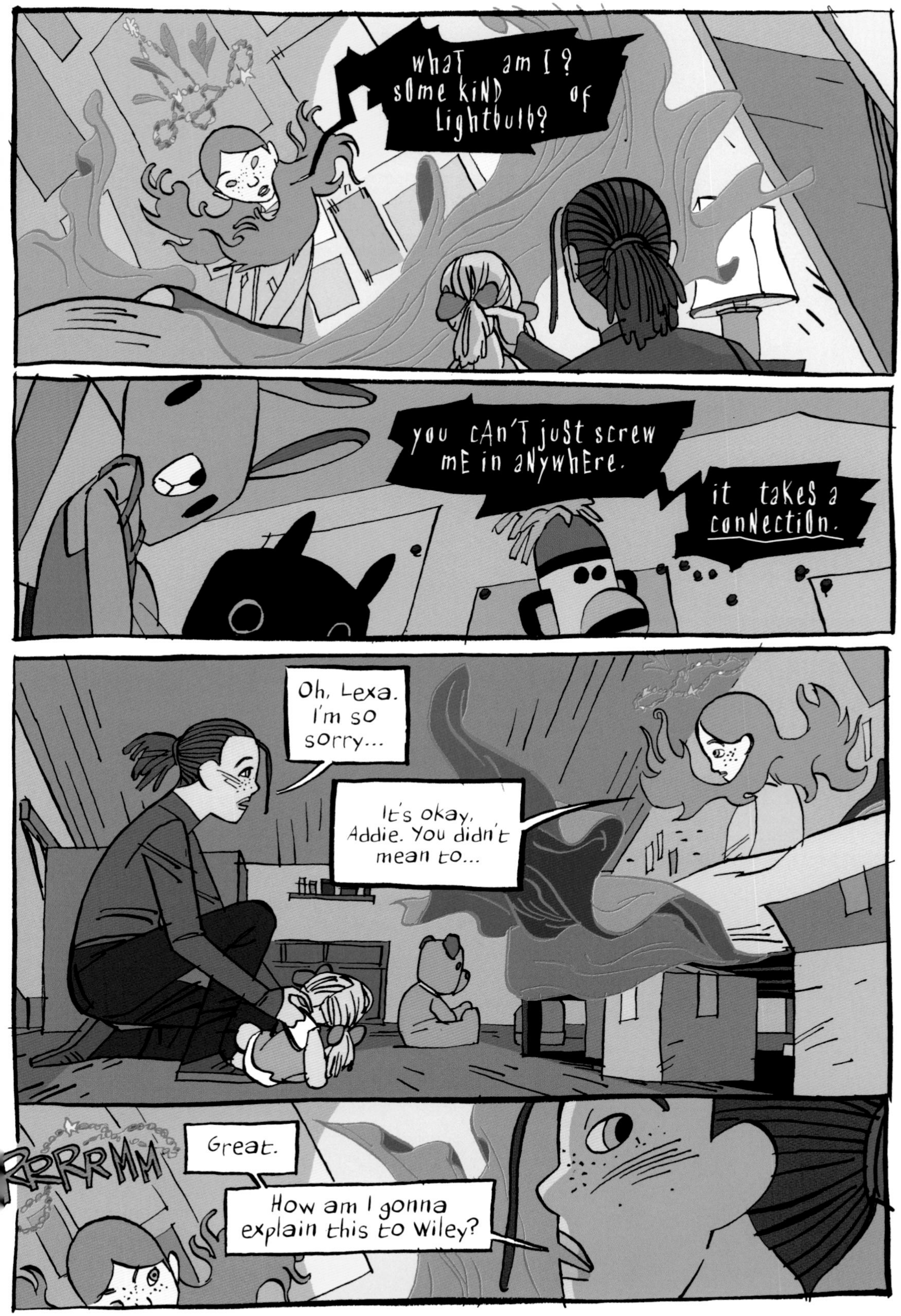
what am I? some kind of lightbulb?
you can't just screw me in anywhere.
it takes a connection.
Oh, Lexa. I'm so sorry...
It's okay, Addie. You didn't mean to...
RRRRRMM
Great.
How am I gonna explain this to Wiley?

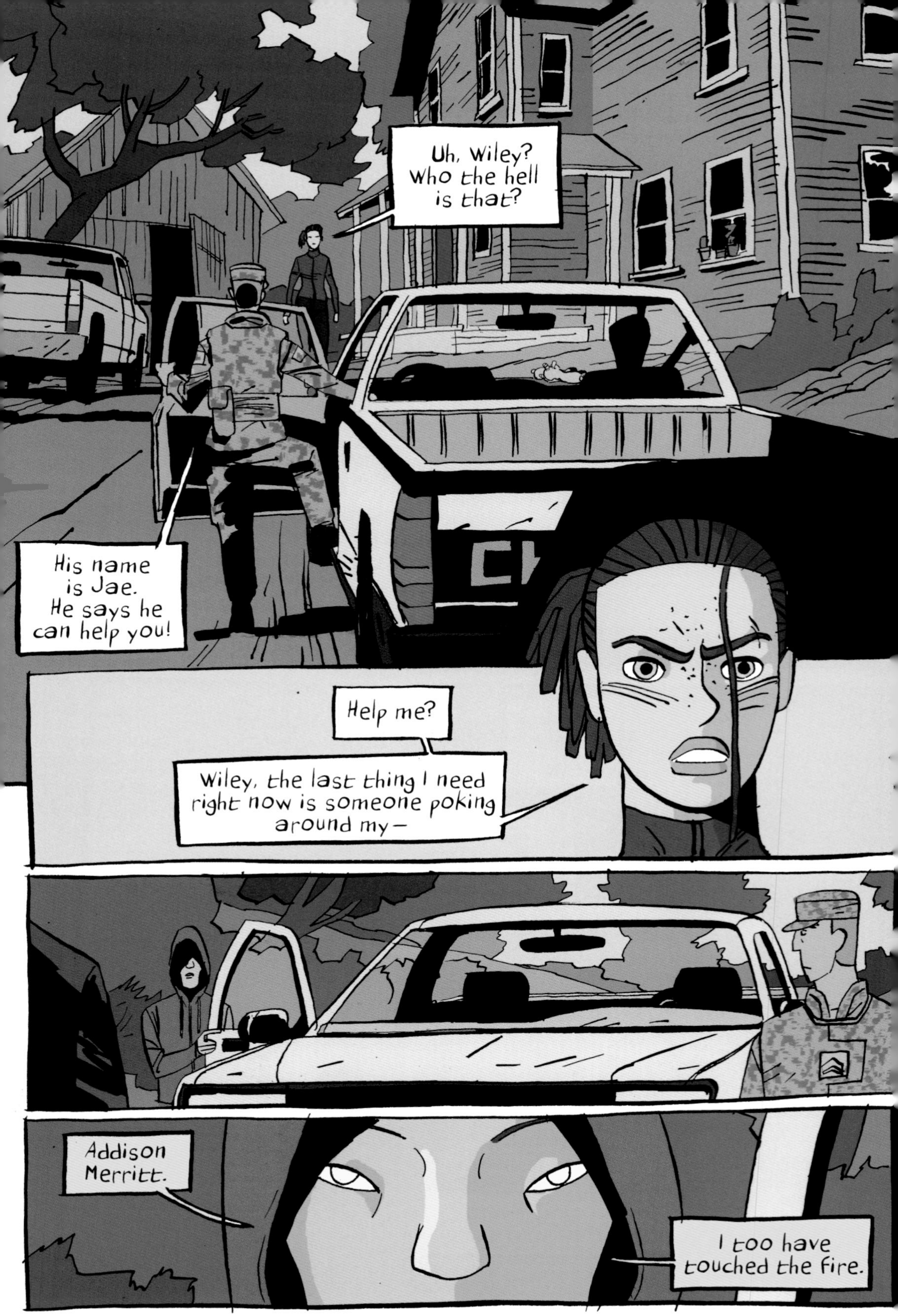
Uh, Wiley? Who the hell is that?
His name is Jae. He says he can help you!
Help me?
Wiley, the last thing I need right now is someone poking around my—
Addison Merritt.
I too have touched the fire.

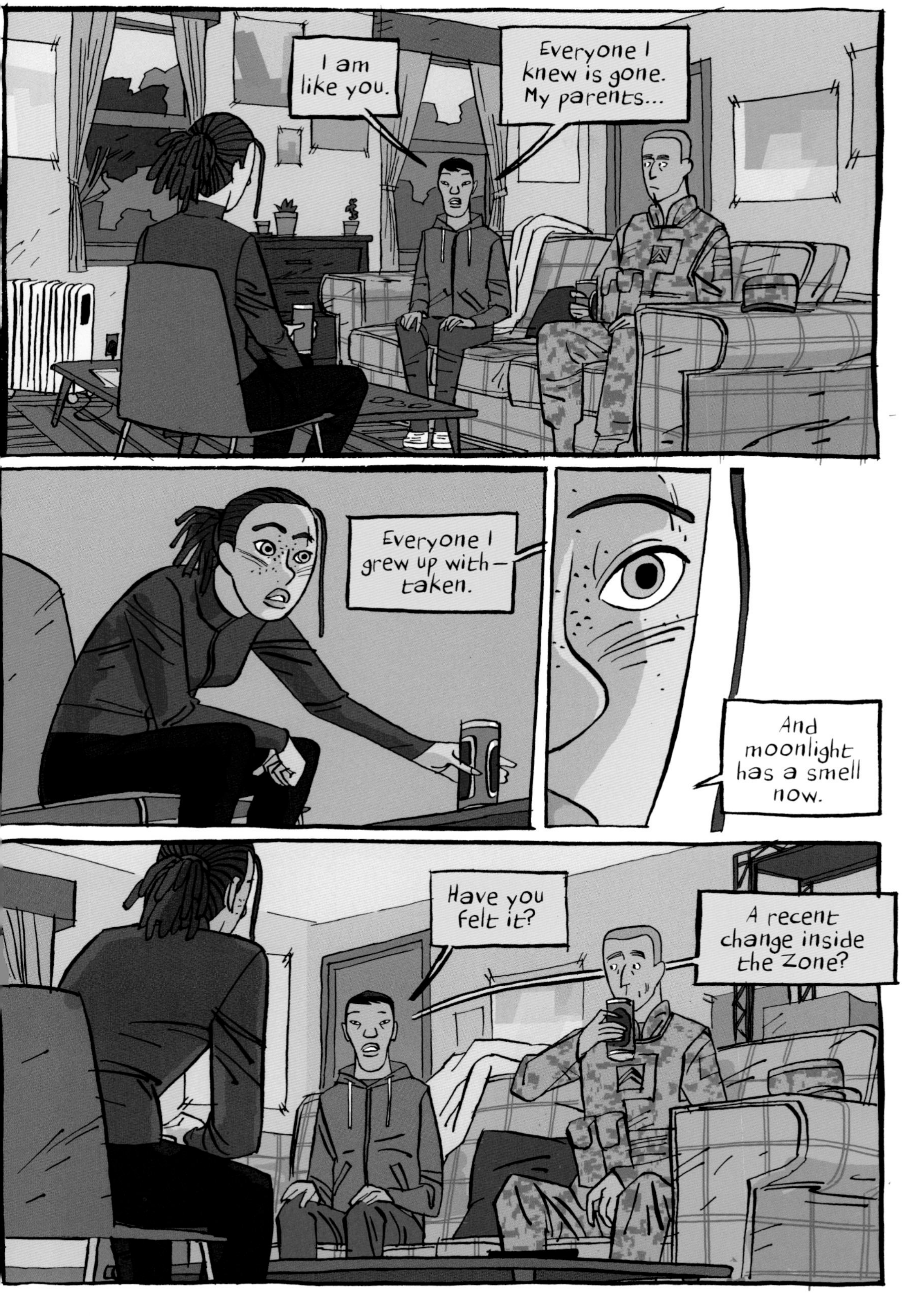
I am like you.
Everyone I knew is gone. My parents...
Everyone I grew up with—taken.
And moonlight has a smell now.
Have you felt it?
A recent change inside the Zone?

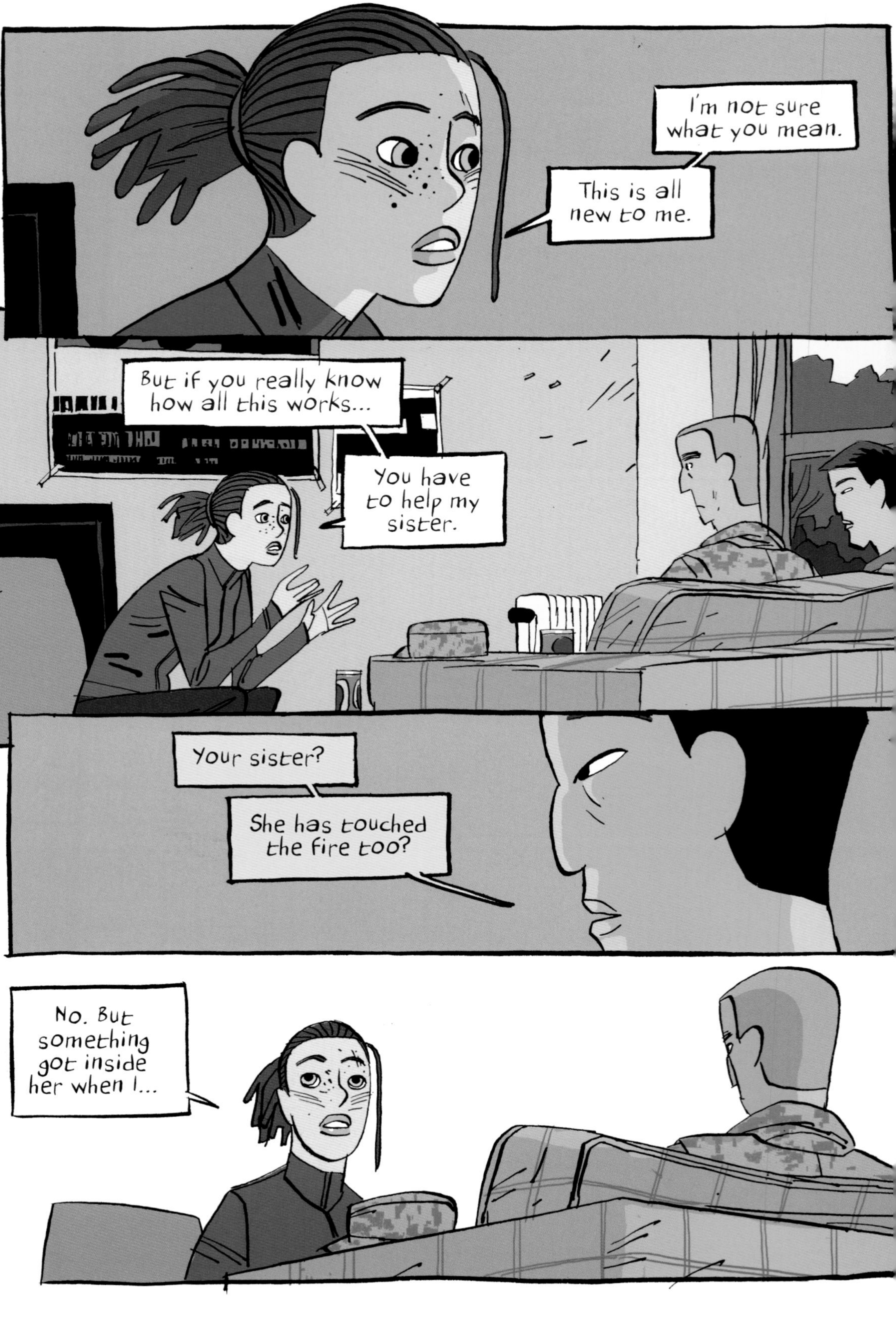
I'm not sure what you mean.
This is all new to me.
But if you really know how all this works...
You have to help my sister.
Your sister?
She has touched the fire too?
No. But something got inside her when I...

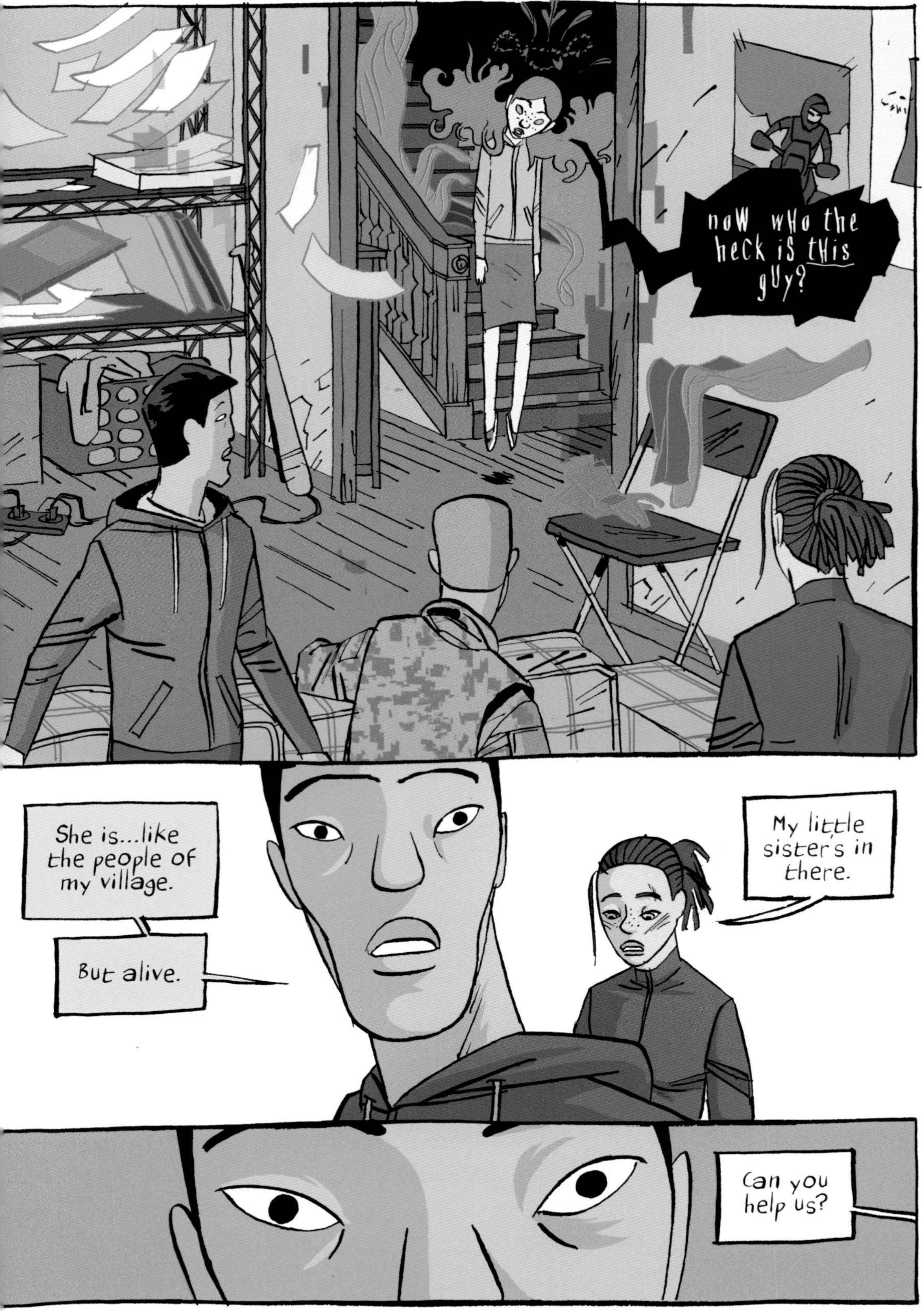
now who the heck is this guy?
She is...like the people of my village.
But alive.
My little sister's in there.
Can you help us?

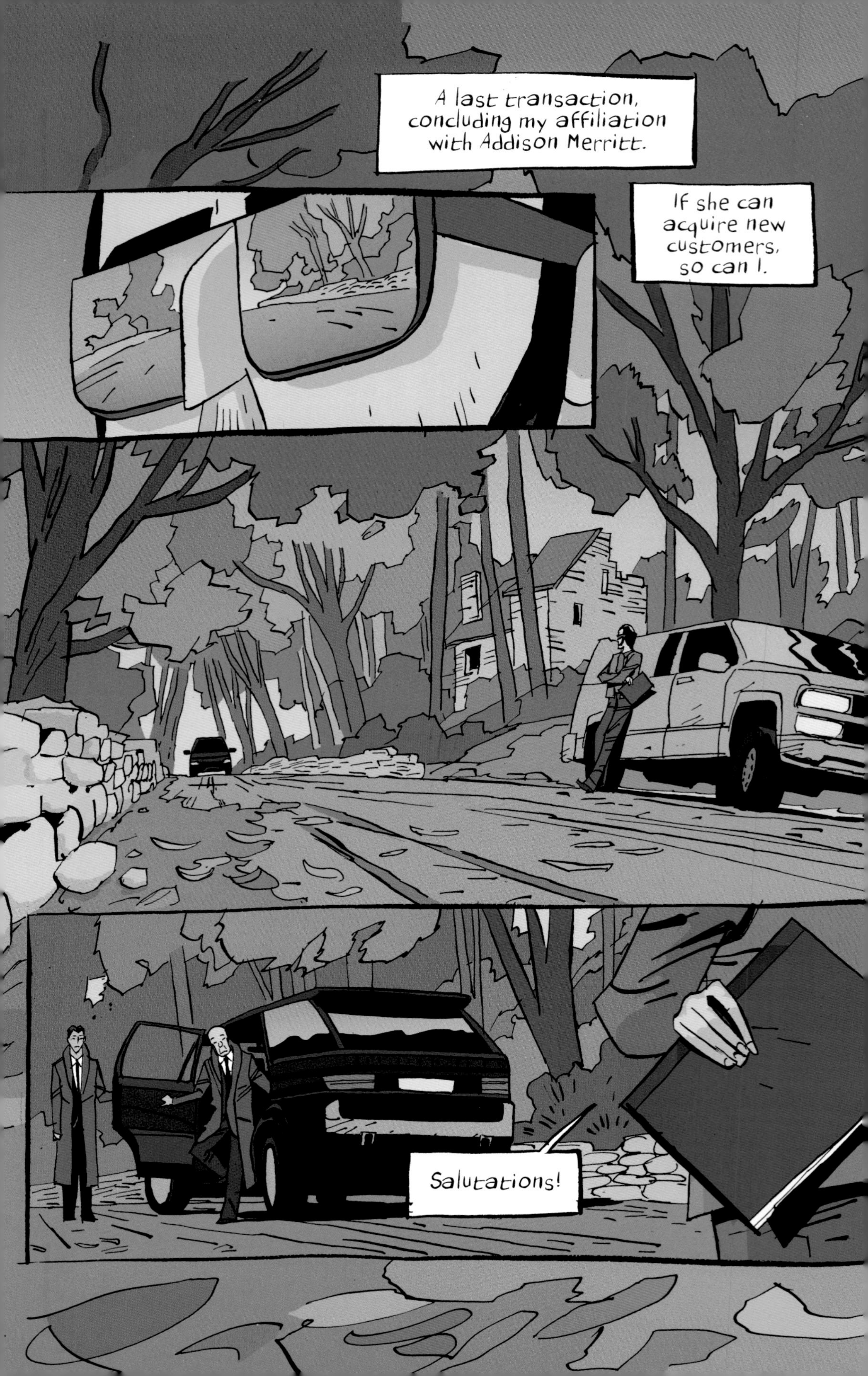
A last transaction, concluding my affiliation with Addison Merritt.
If she can acquire new customers, so can I.
Salutations!

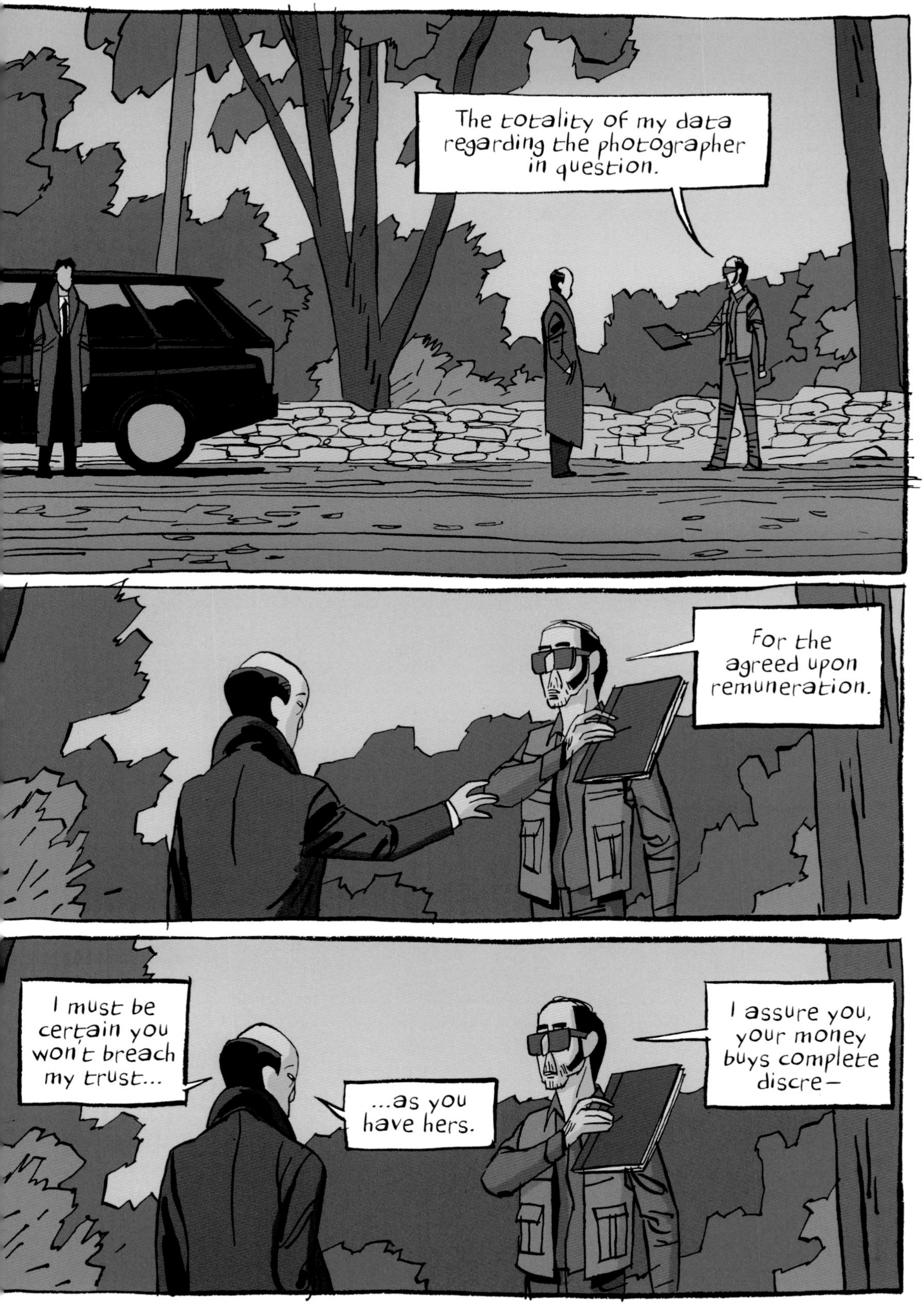
The totality of my data regarding the photographer in question.
For the agreed upon remuneration.
I must be certain you won't breach my trust...
...as you have hers.
I assure you, your money buys complete discre—

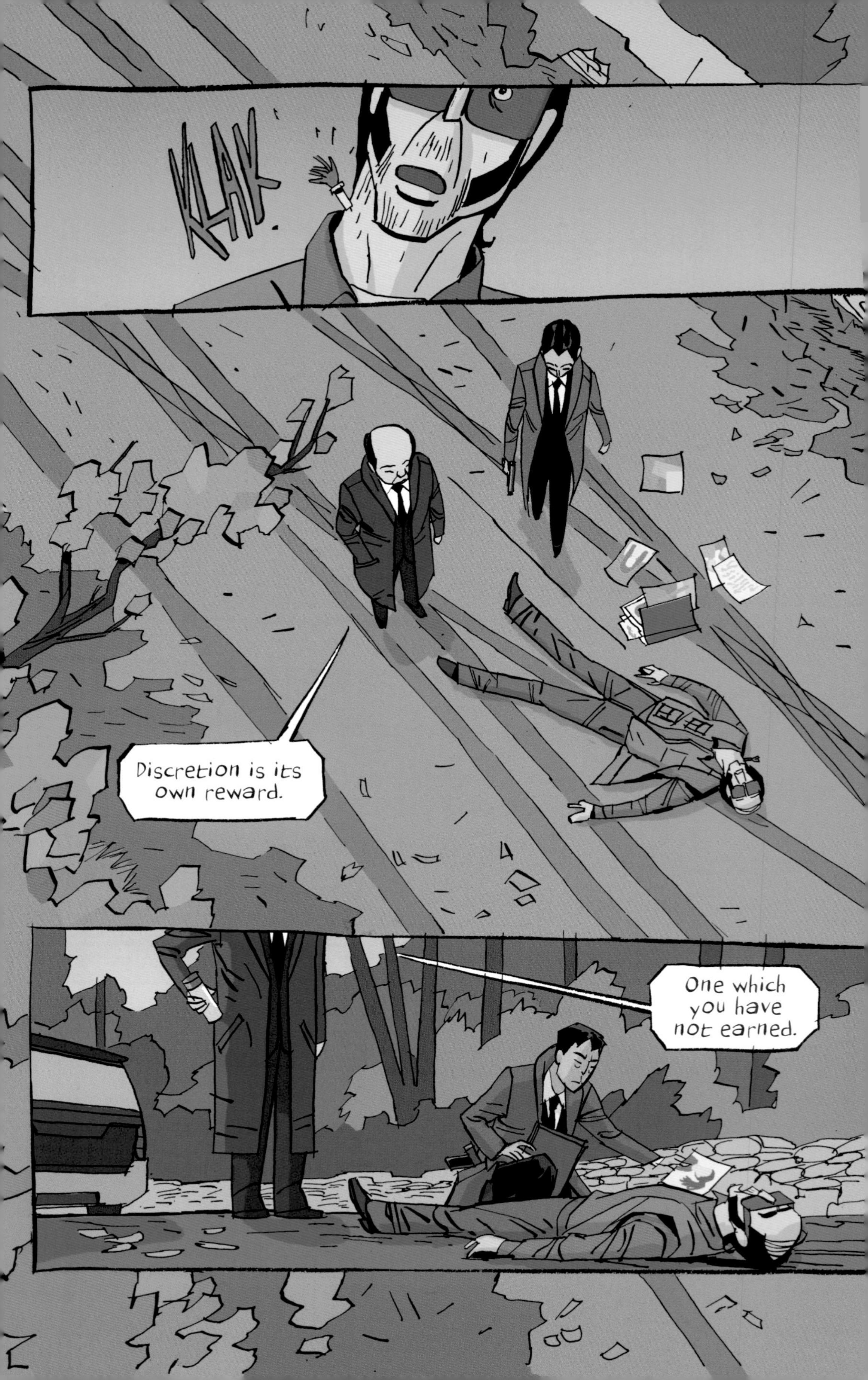
KLAK
Discretion is its own reward.
One which you have not earned.

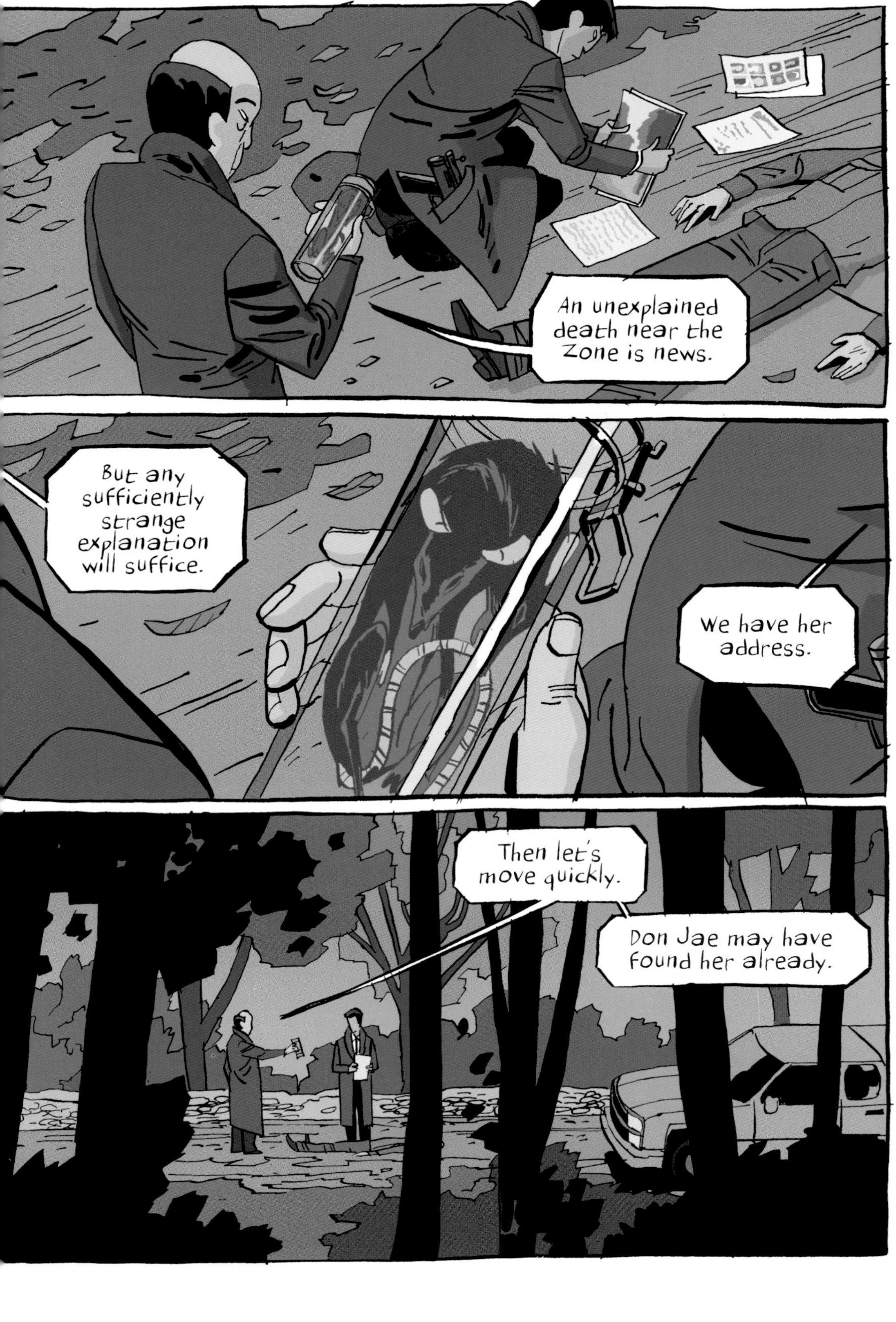
An unexplained death near the Zone is news.
But any sufficiently strange explanation will suffice.
We have her address.
Then let's move quickly.
Don Jae may have found her already.

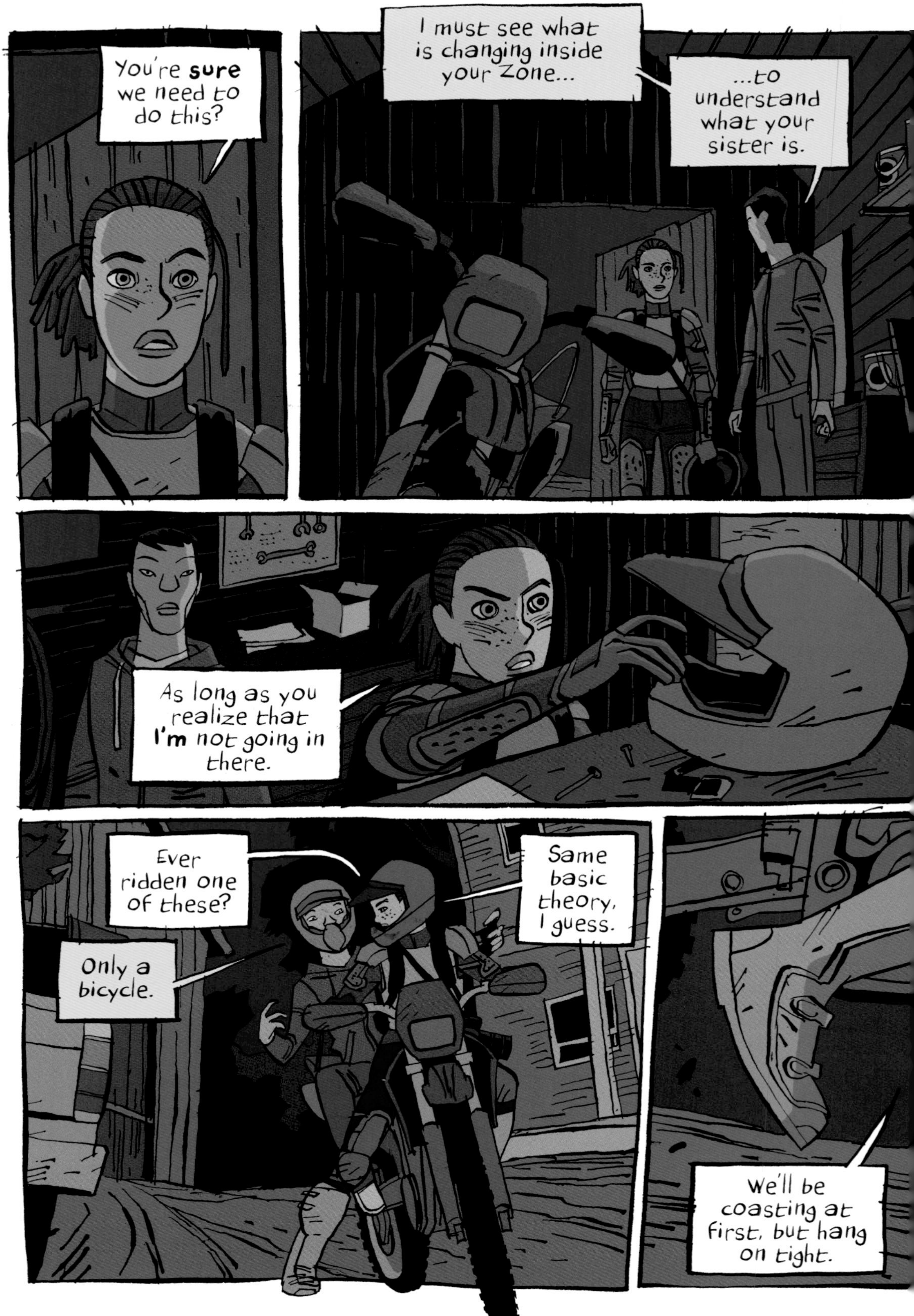
You're **sure** we need to do this?
I must see what is changing inside your Zone...
...to understand what your sister is.
As long as you realize that **I'm** not going in there.
Ever ridden one of these?
Only a bicycle.
Same basic theory, I guess.
We'll be coasting at first, but hang on tight.

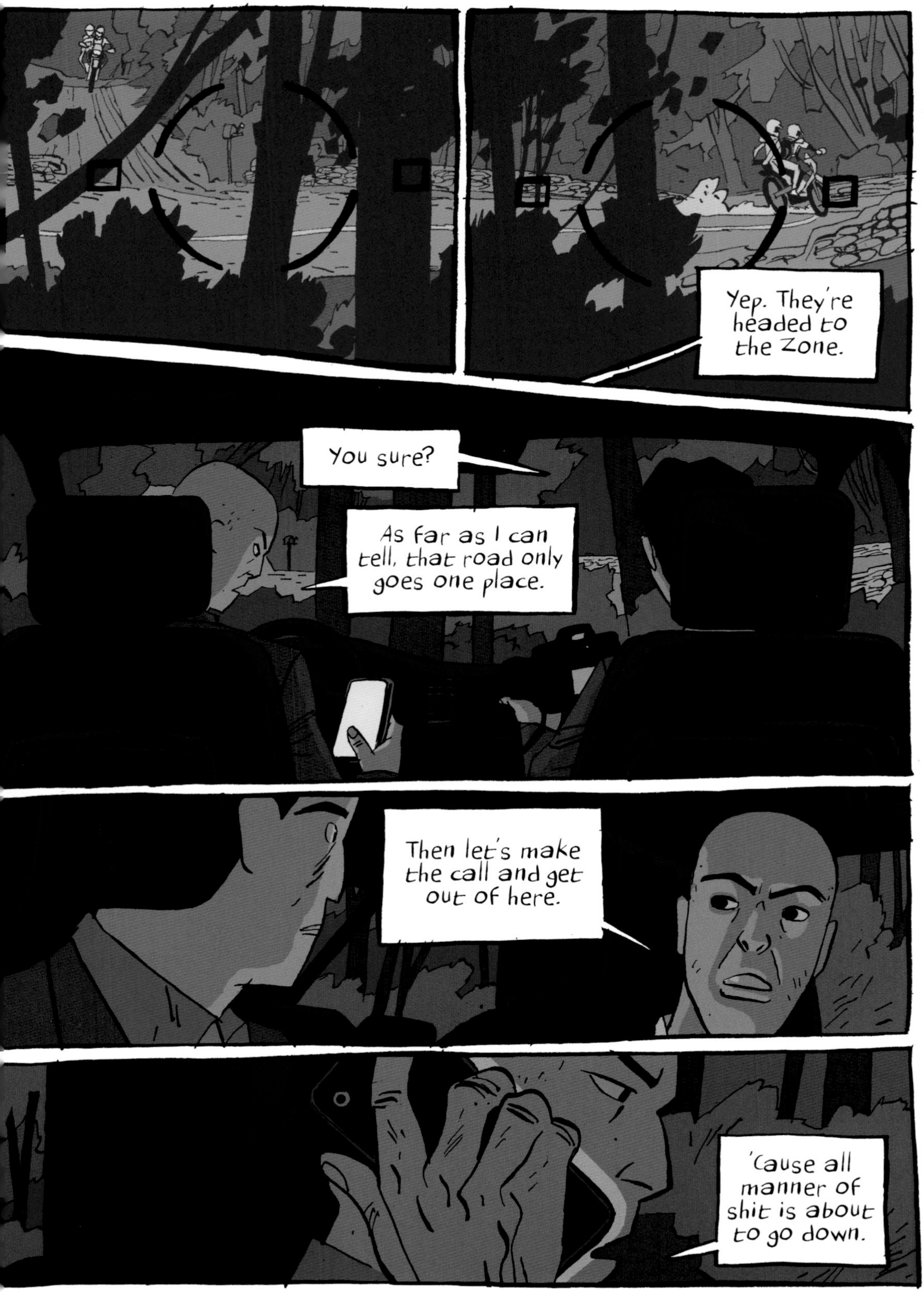
Yep. They're headed to the Zone.
You sure?
As far as I can tell, that road only goes one place.
Then let's make the call and get out of here.
'Cause all manner of shit is about to go down.

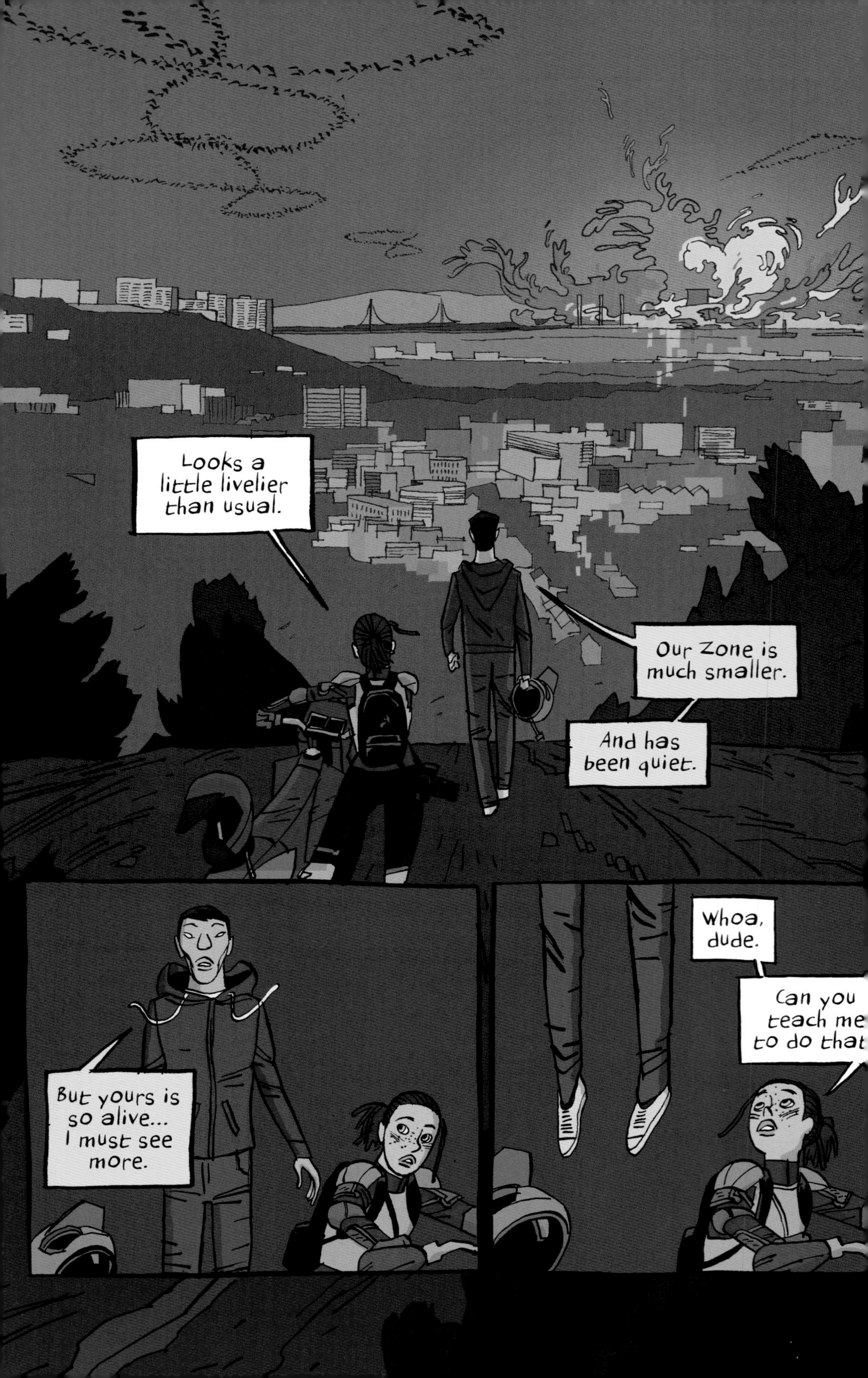
Looks a little livelier than usual.
Our Zone is much smaller.
And has been quiet.
But yours is so alive... I must see more.
Whoa, dude.
Can you teach me to do that

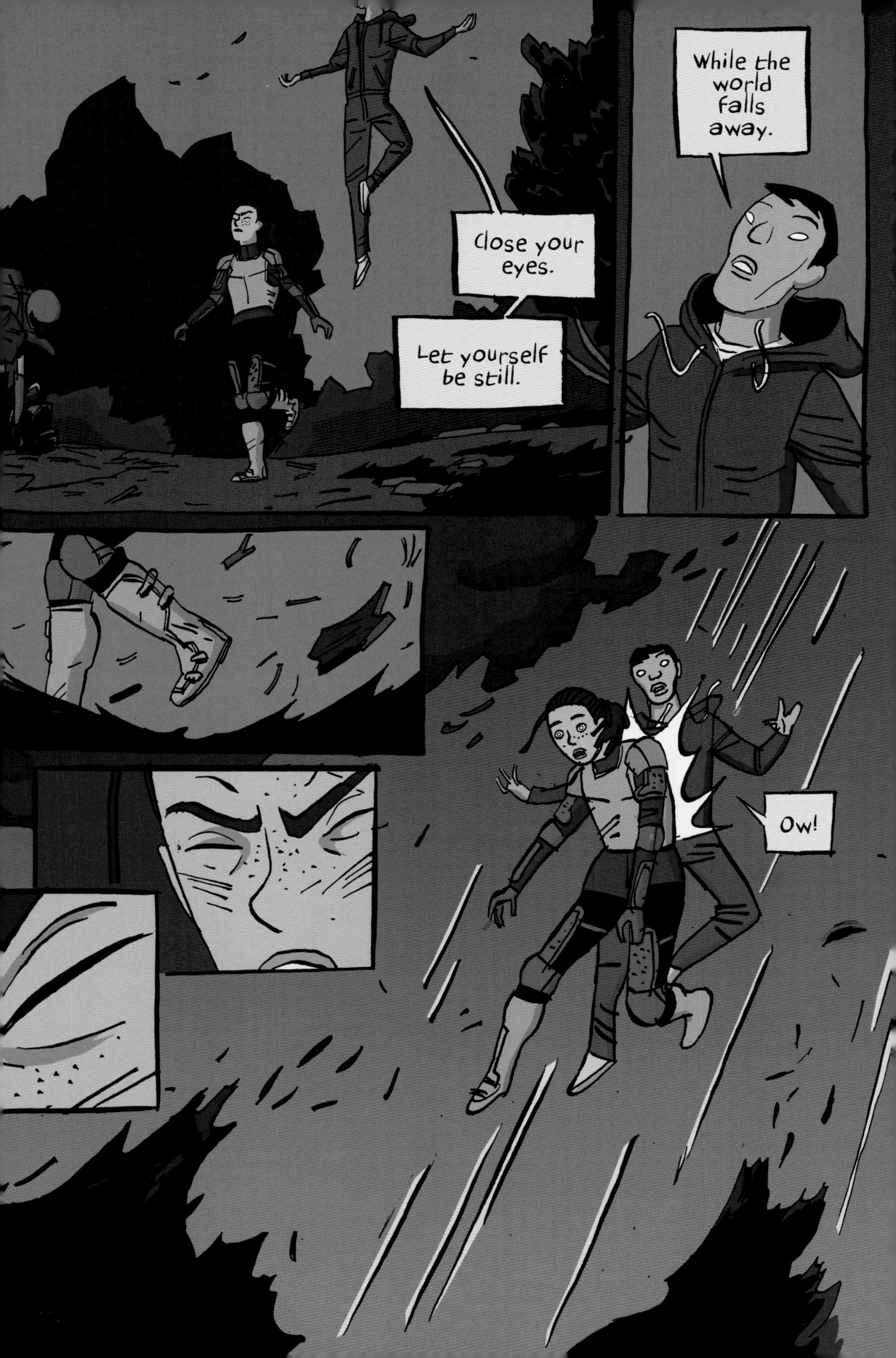
Close your eyes.
Let yourself be still.
While the world falls away.
Ow!

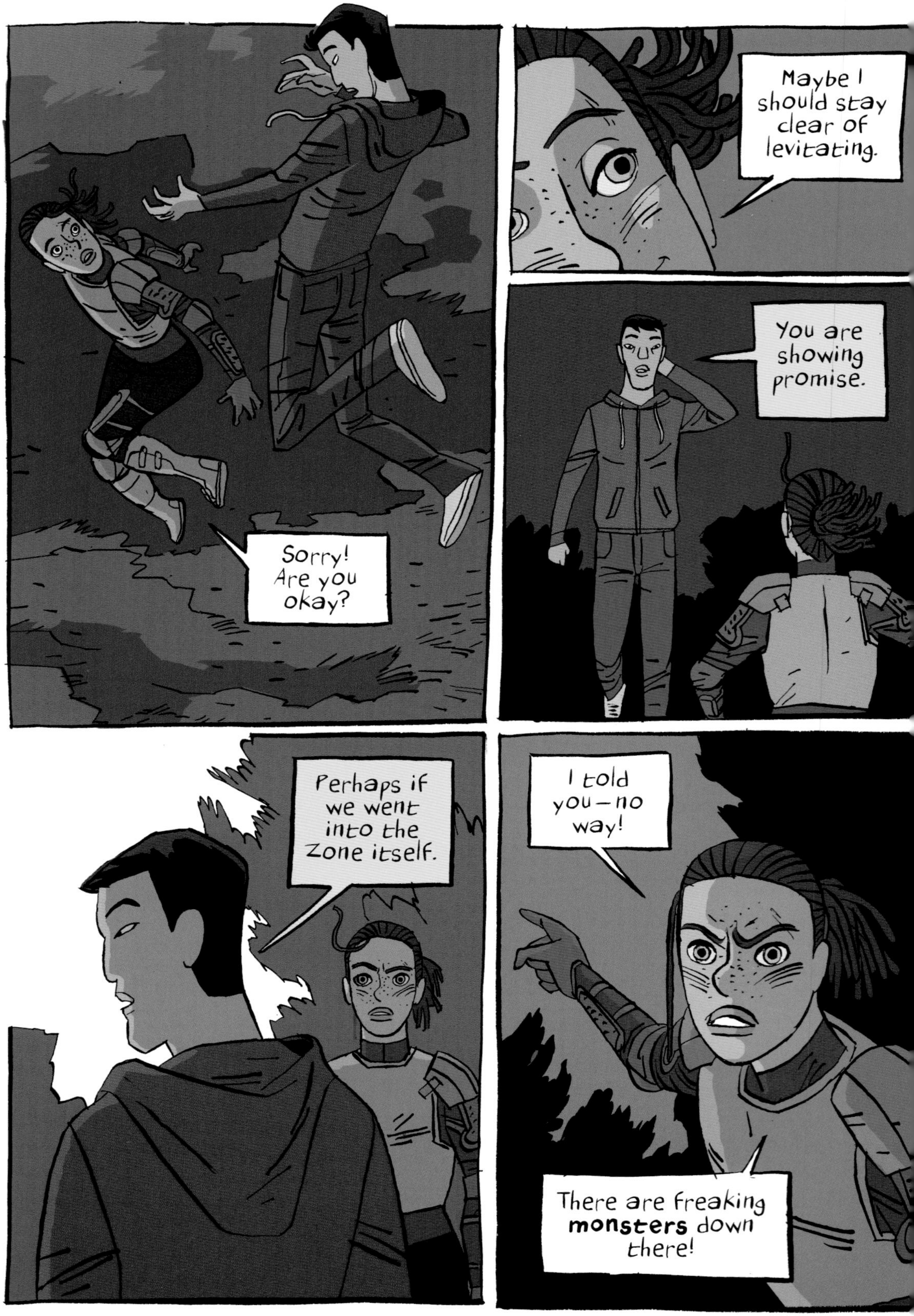
Sorry! Are you okay?
Maybe I should stay clear of levitating.
You are showing promise.
Perhaps if we went into the Zone itself.
I told you—no way!
There are freaking **monsters** down there!

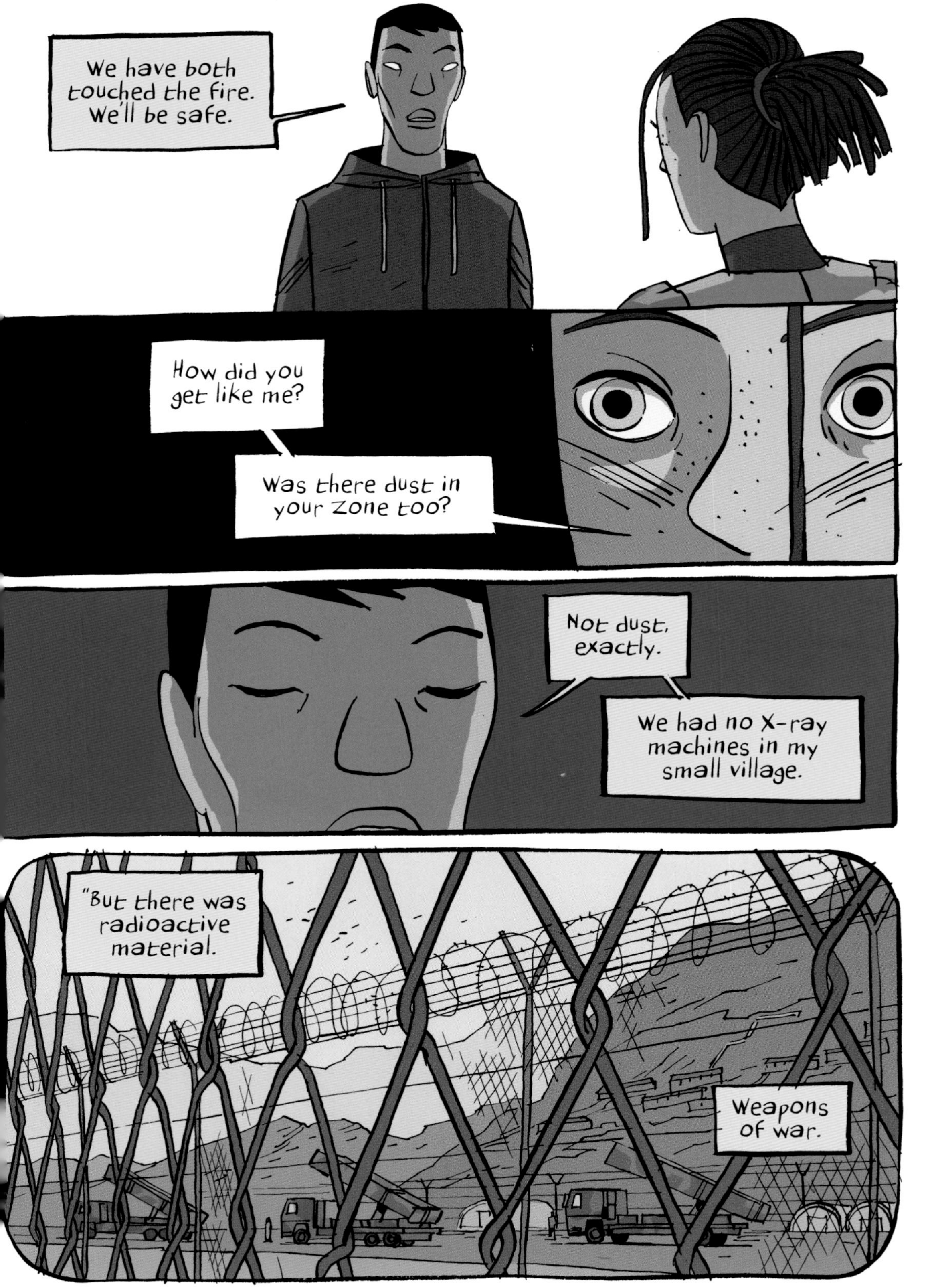
We have both touched the fire. We'll be safe.
How did you get like me?
Was there dust in your zone too?
Not dust, exactly.
We had no X-ray machines in my small village.
"But there was radioactive material.
Weapons of war.

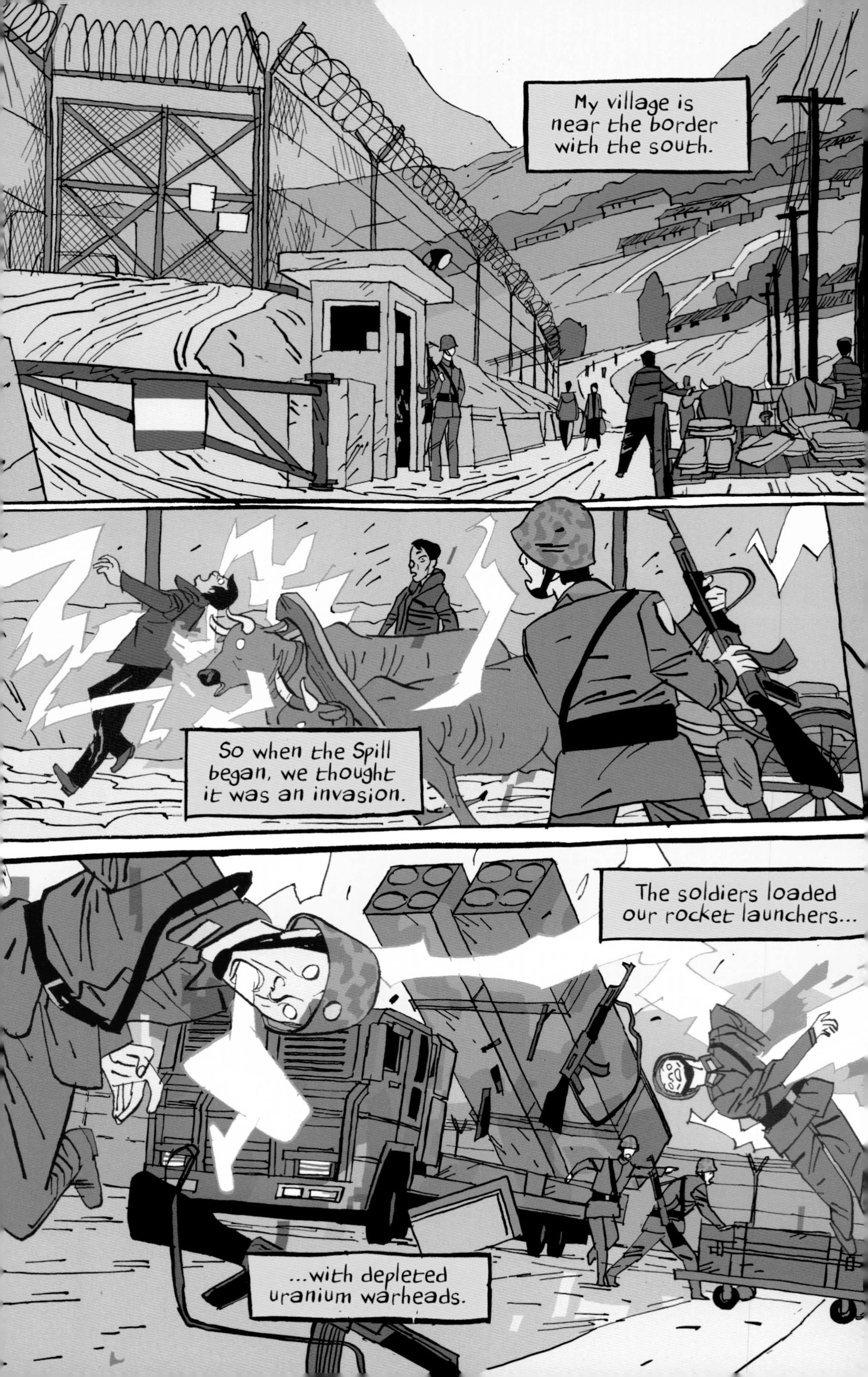
My village is near the border with the south.
So when the Spill began, we thought it was an invasion.
The soldiers loaded our rocket launchers...
...with depleted uranium warheads.

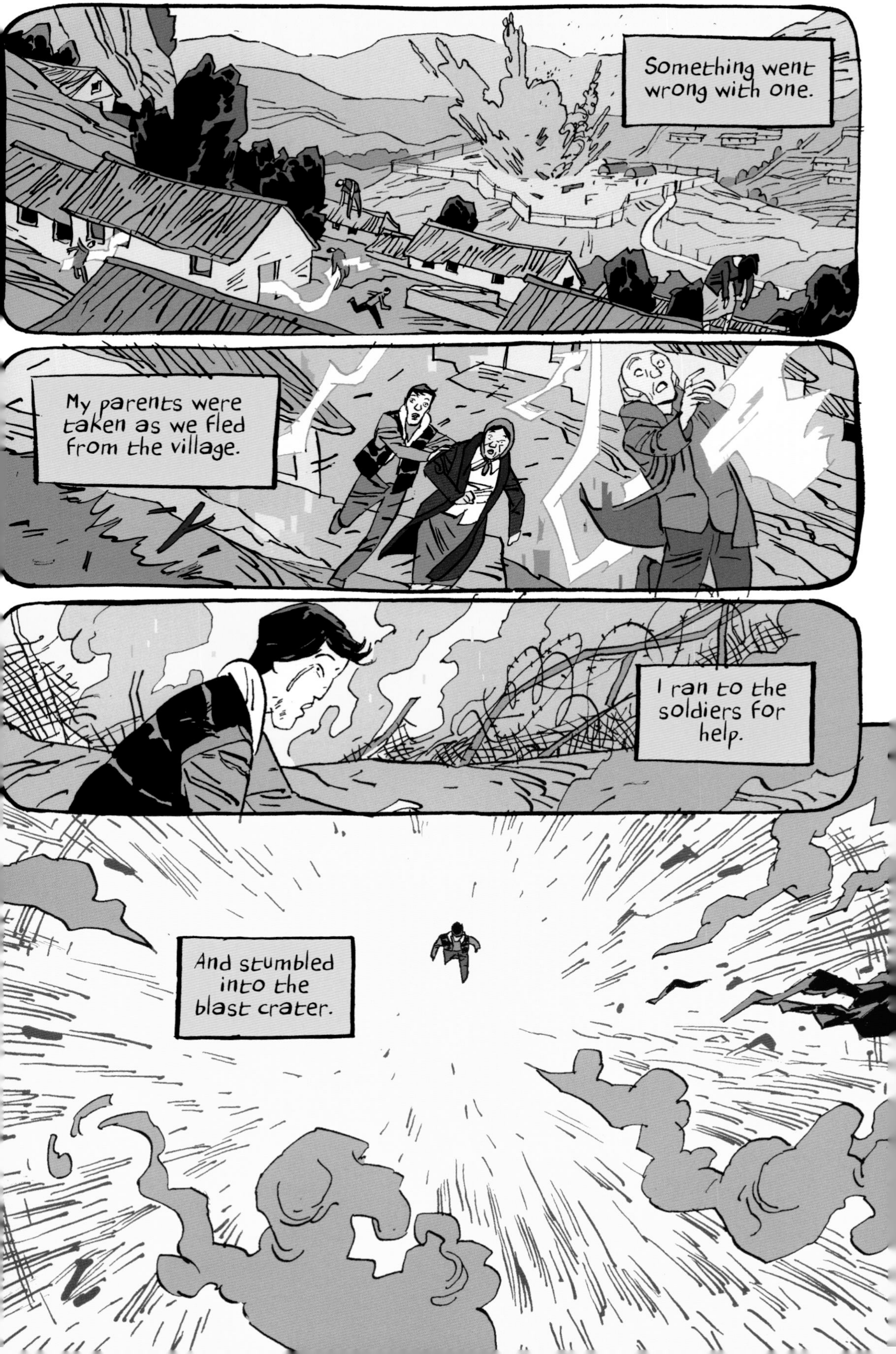
Something went wrong with one.
My parents were taken as we fled from the village.
I ran to the soldiers for help.
And stumbled into the blast crater.

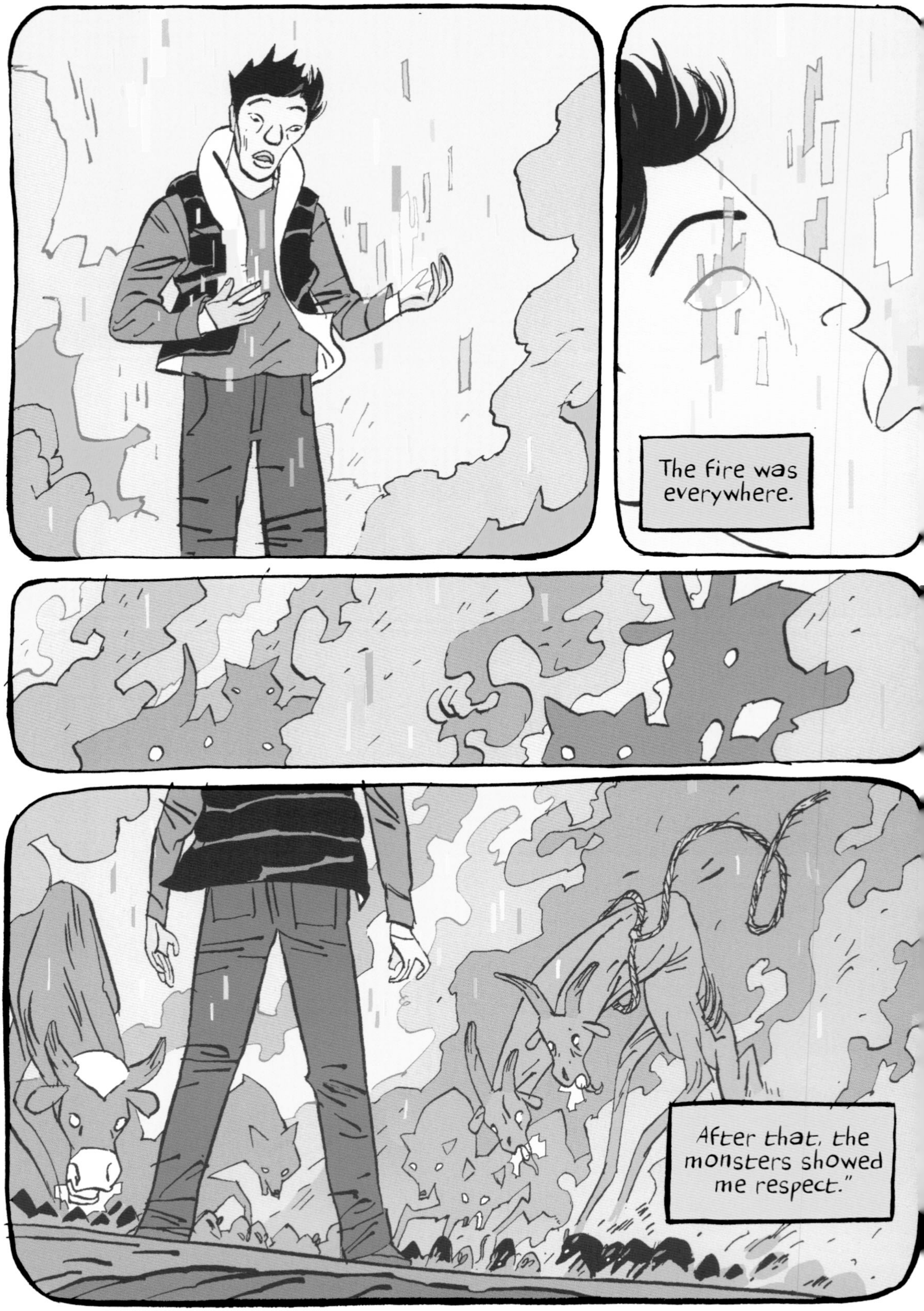

The fire was everywhere.
After that, the monsters showed me respect."

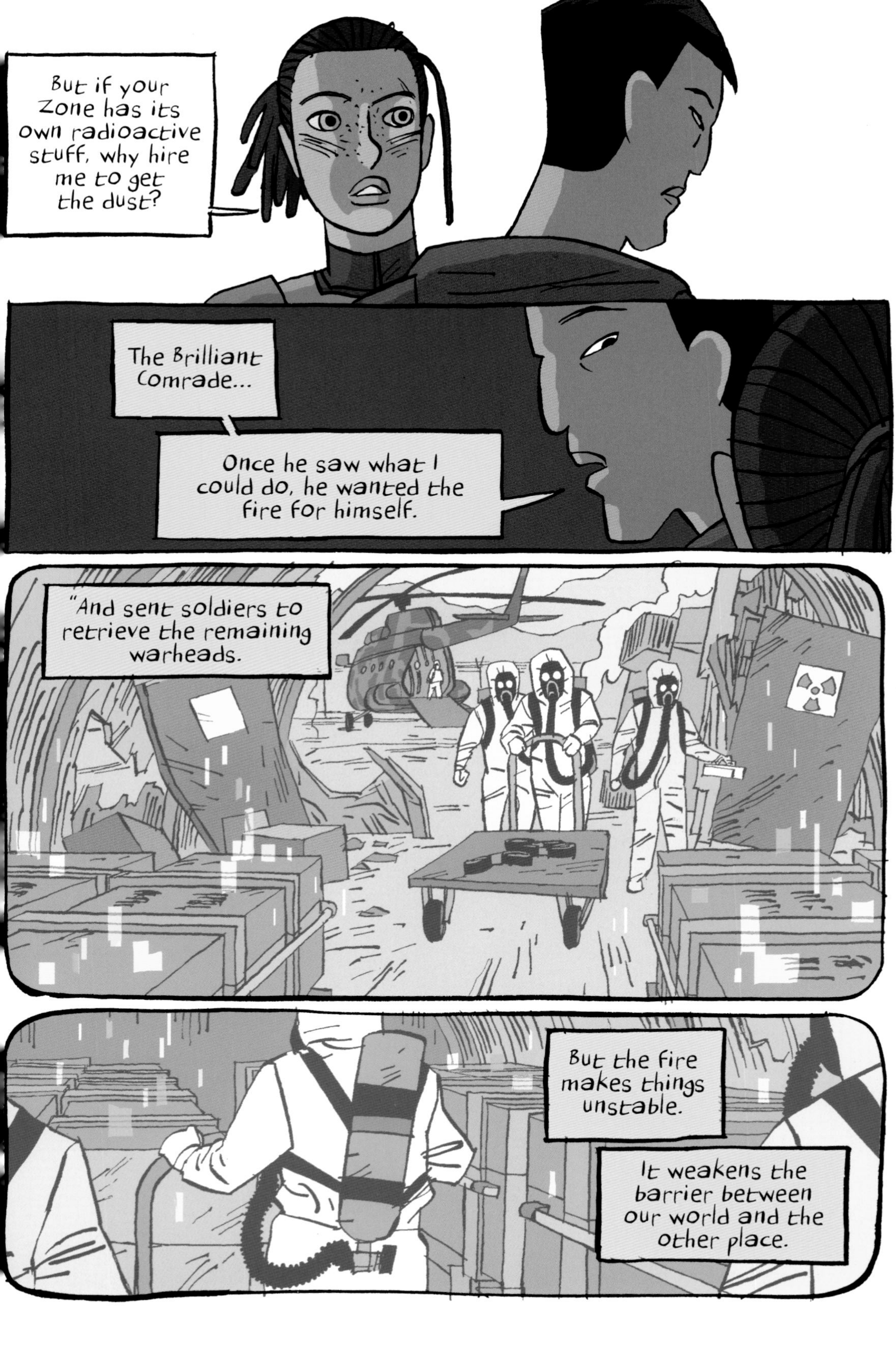
But if your Zone has its own radioactive stuff, why hire me to get the dust?
The Brilliant Comrade...
Once he saw what I could do, he wanted the fire for himself.
"And sent soldiers to retrieve the remaining warheads.
But the fire makes things unstable.
It weakens the barrier between our world and the other place.

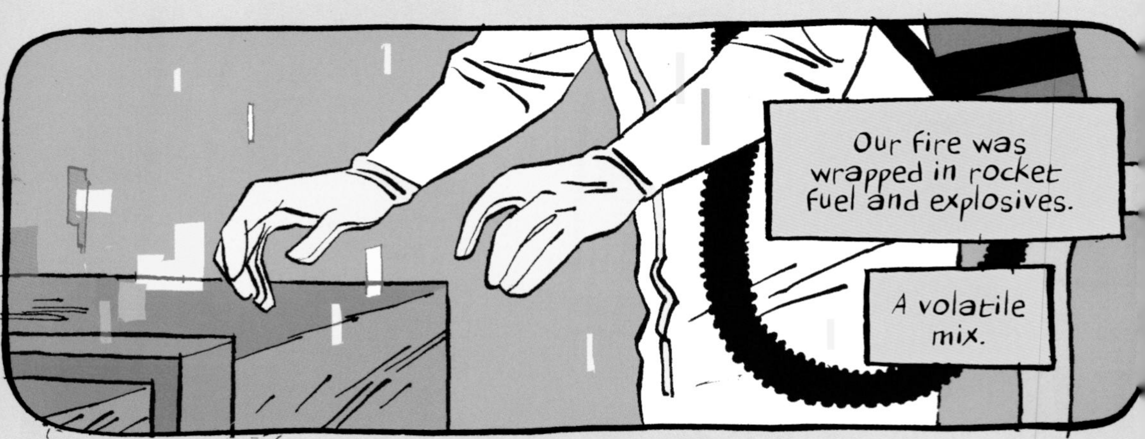
Our fire was wrapped in rocket fuel and explosives.
A volatile mix.

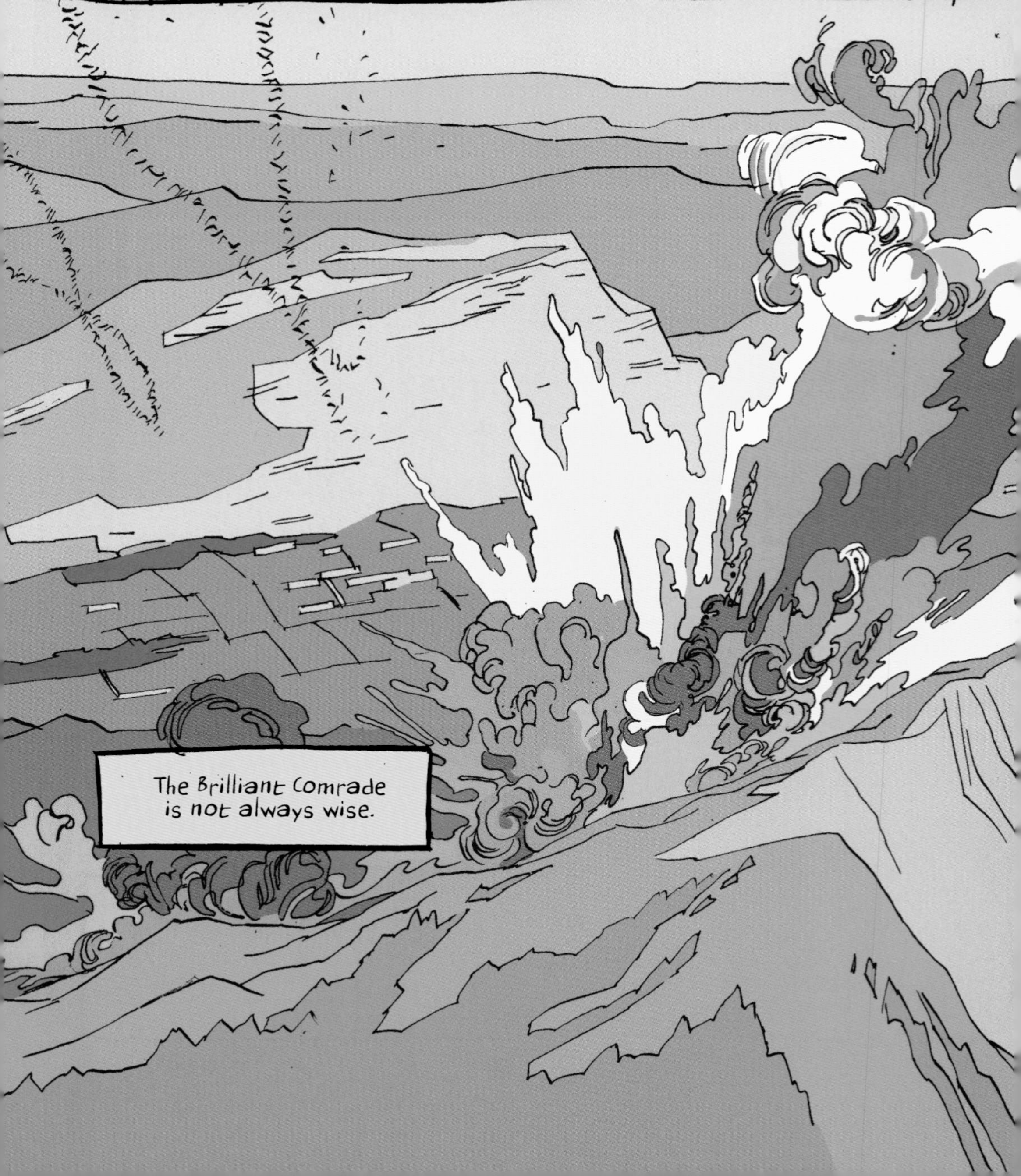
The Brilliant Comrade is not always wise.

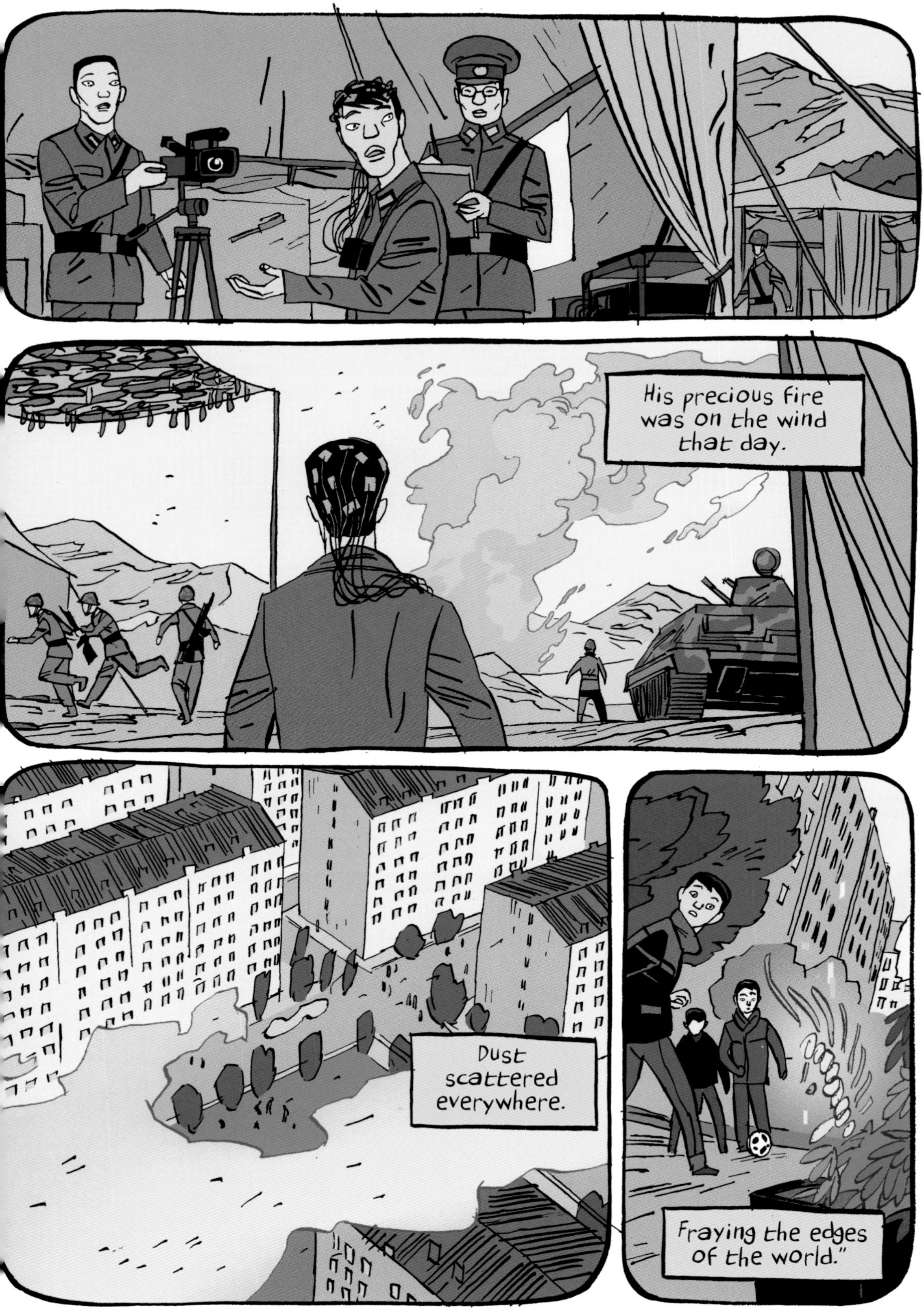
His precious fire was on the wind that day.
Dust scattered everywhere.
Fraying the edges of the world."

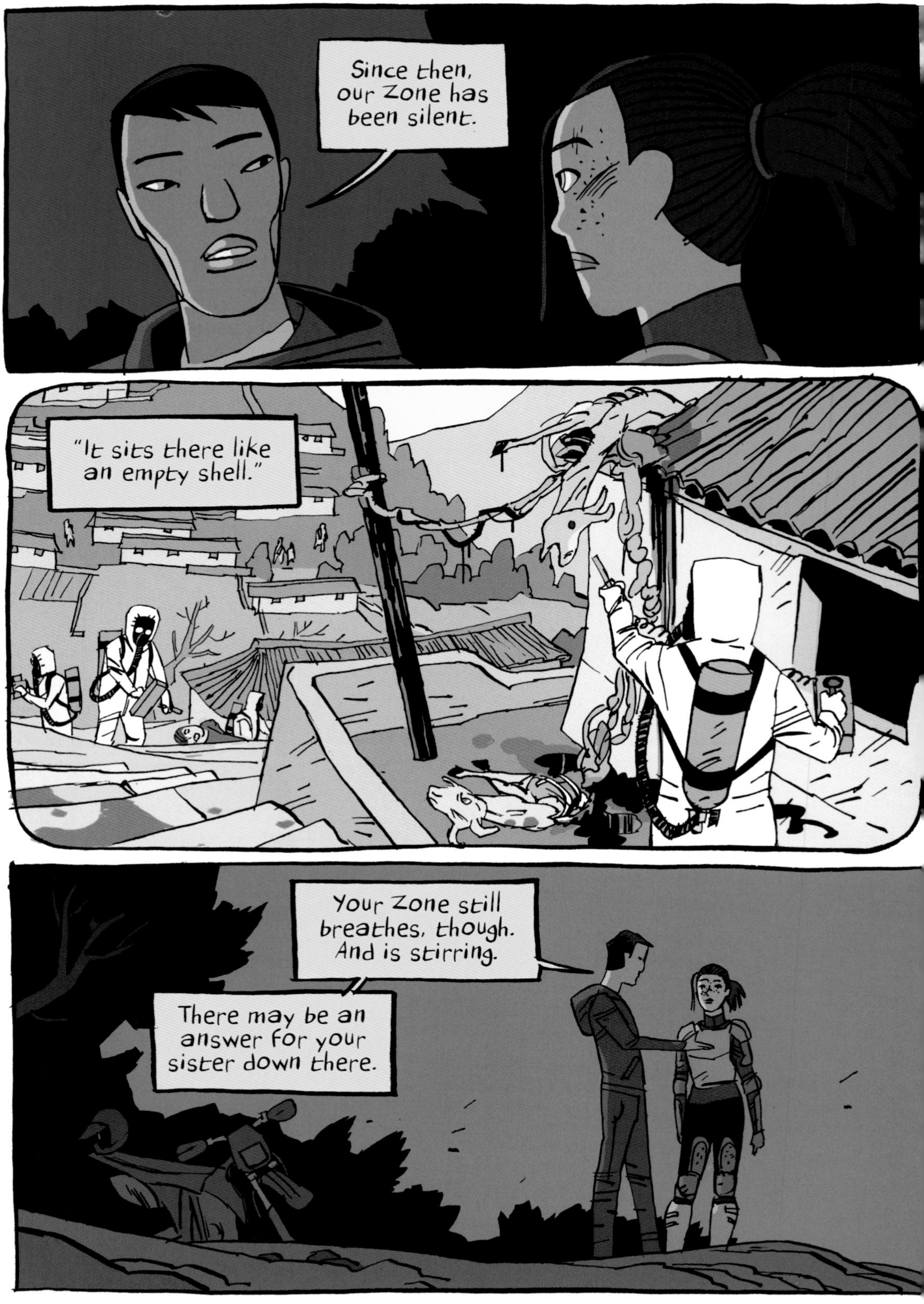
Since then, our Zone has been silent.
"It sits there like an empty shell."
Your Zone still breathes, though. And is stirring.
There may be an answer for your sister down there.

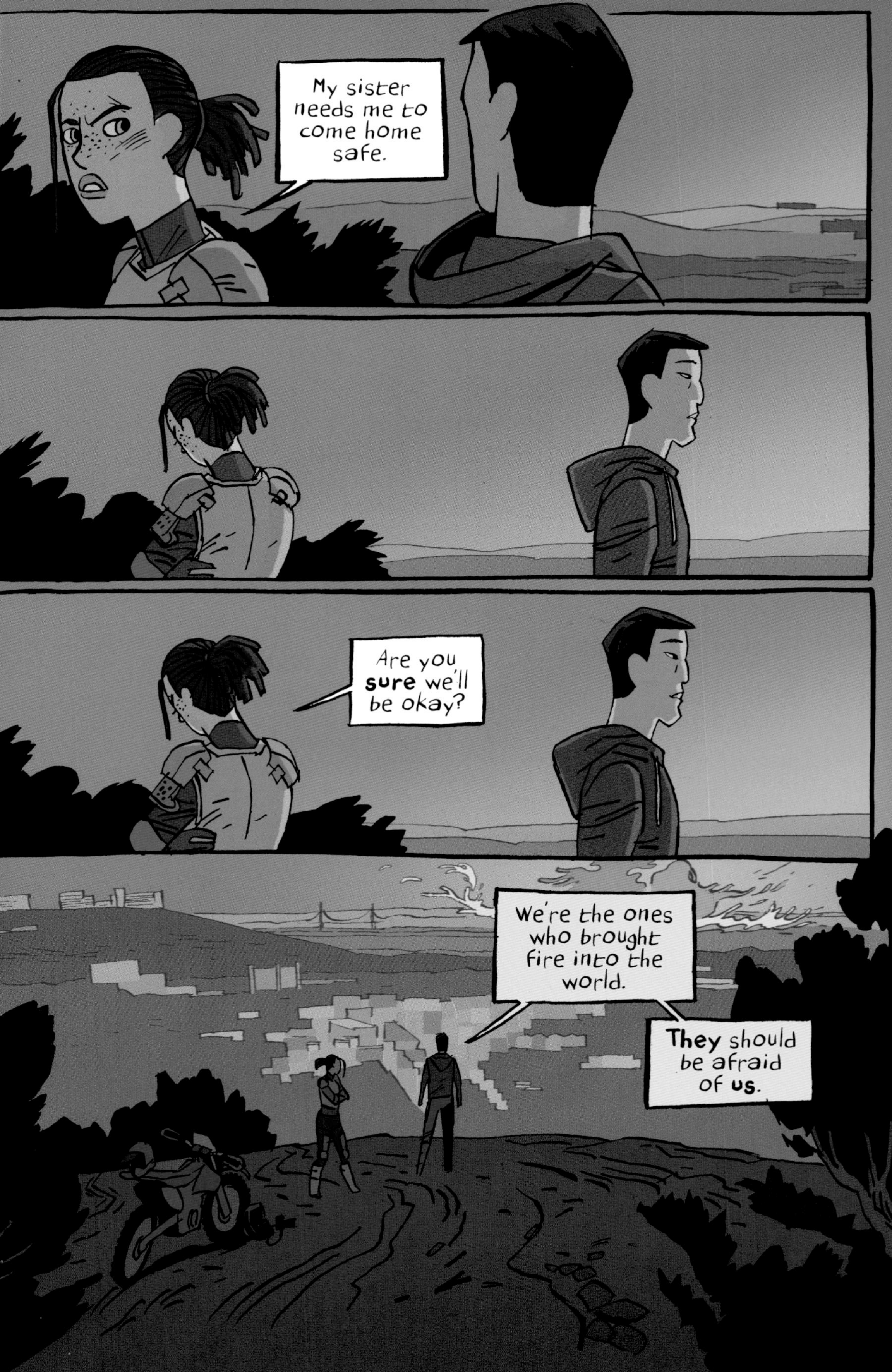
My sister needs me to come home safe.
Are you **sure** we'll be okay?
We're the ones who brought fire into the world.
They should be afraid of **us**.

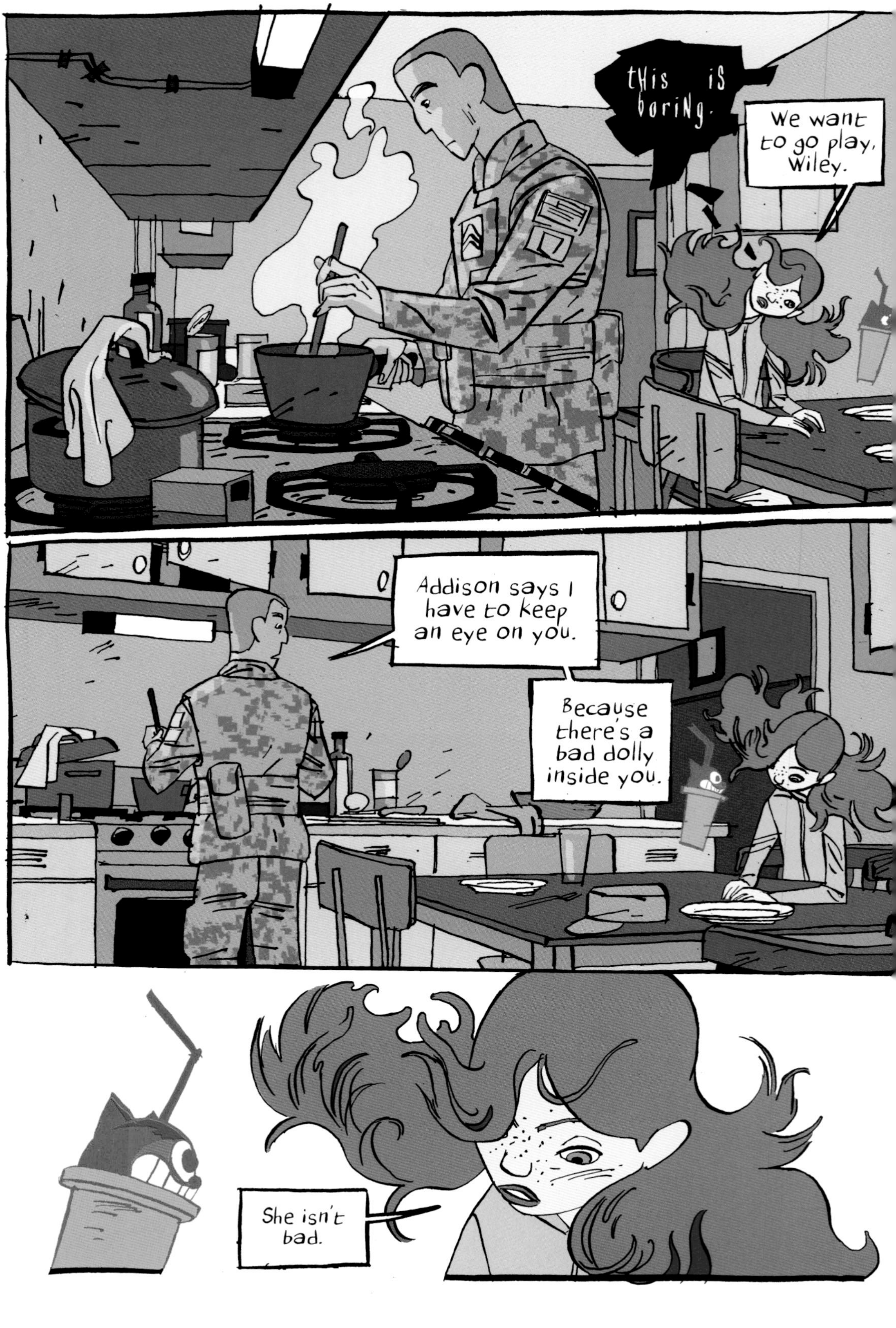
this is boring.
We want to go play, Wiley.
Addison says I have to keep an eye on you.
Because there's a bad dolly inside you.
She isn't bad.

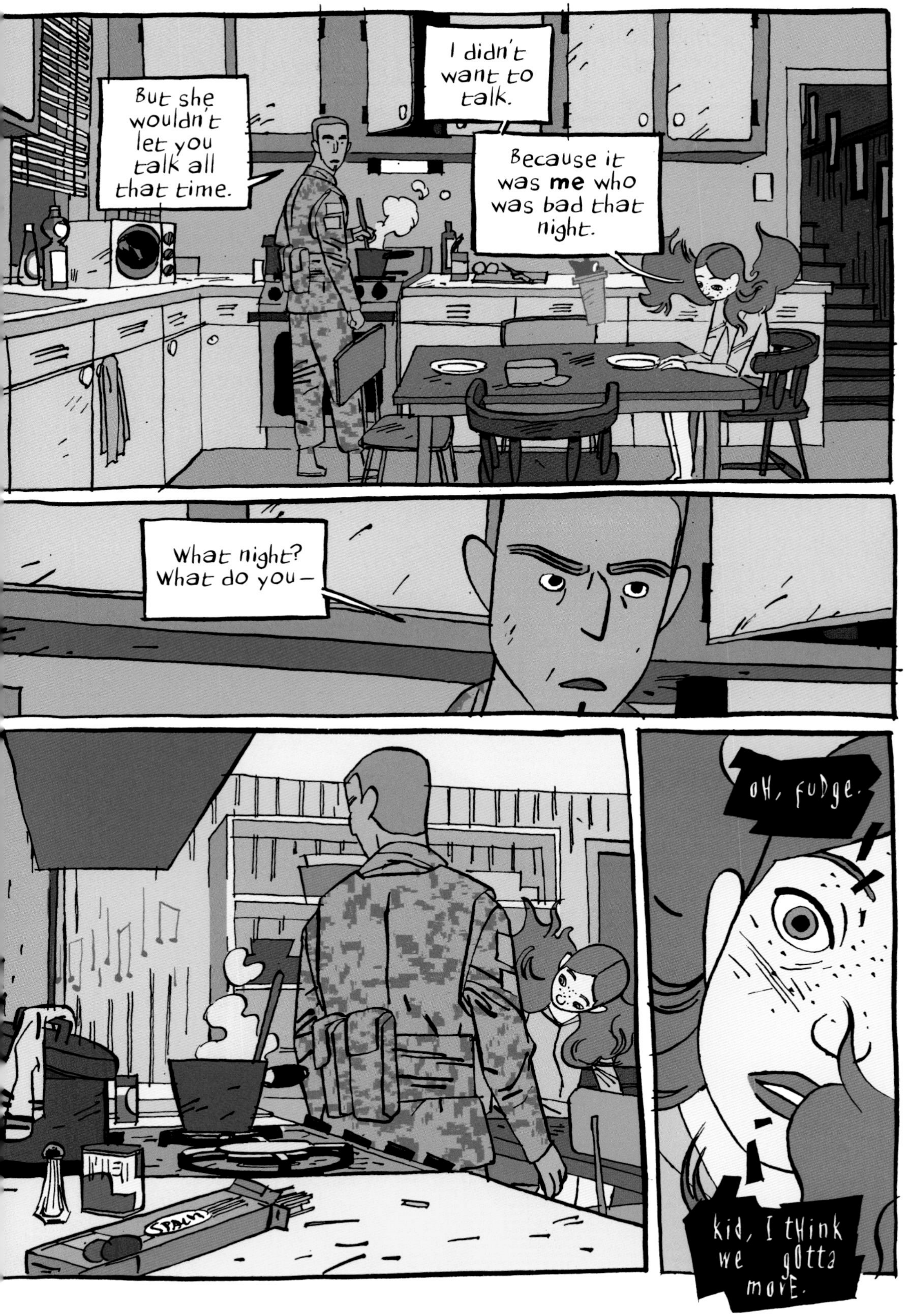
But she wouldn't let you talk all that time.
I didn't want to talk.
Because it was **me** who was bad that night.
What night? What do you—
SPAM
OH, FUDGE.
KID, I THINK WE GOTTA MOVE.

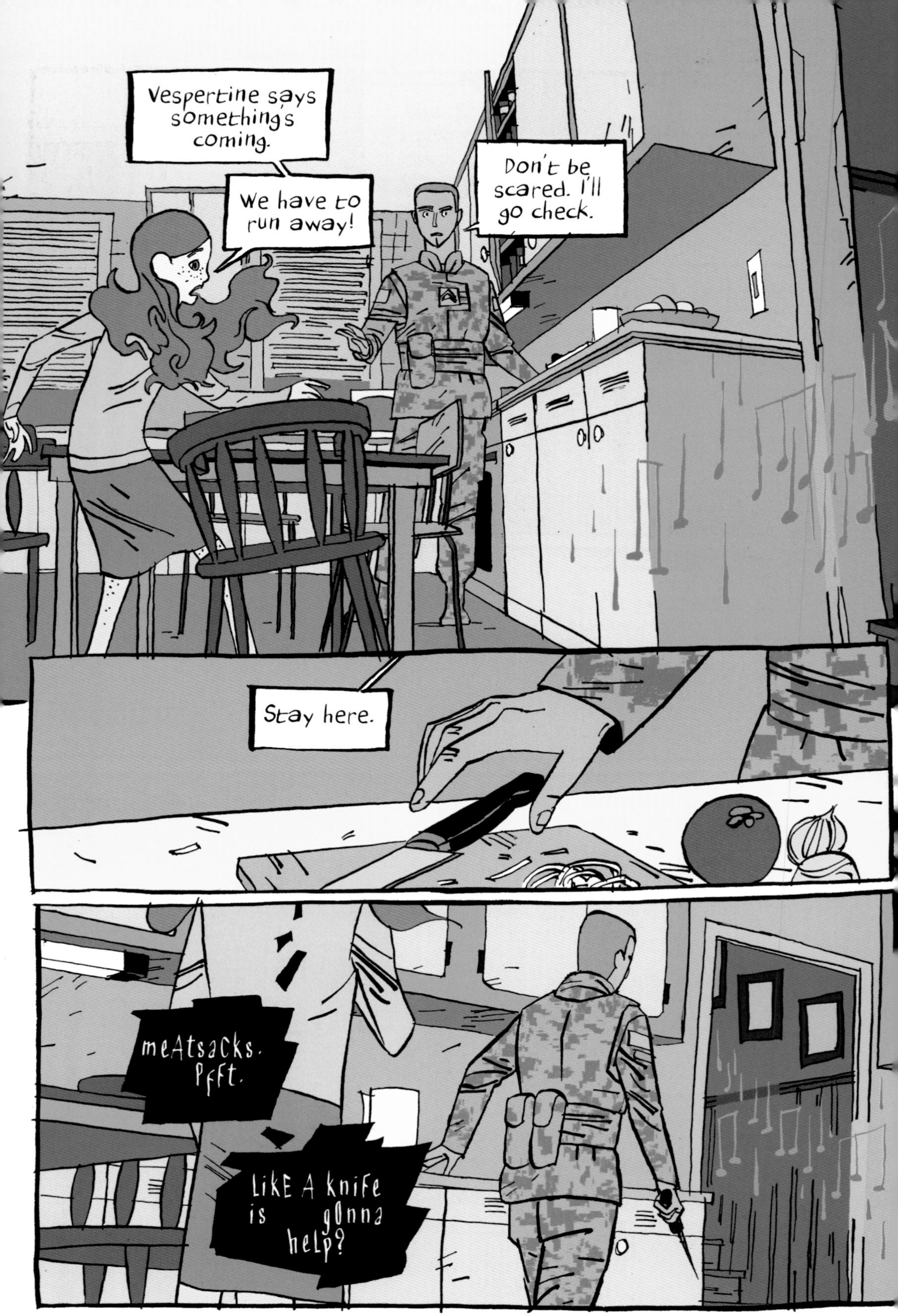
Vespertine says something's coming.
We have to run away!
Don't be scared. I'll go check.
Stay here.
meAtsacks. PfFt.
LiKE A knifE is g0nna helP?

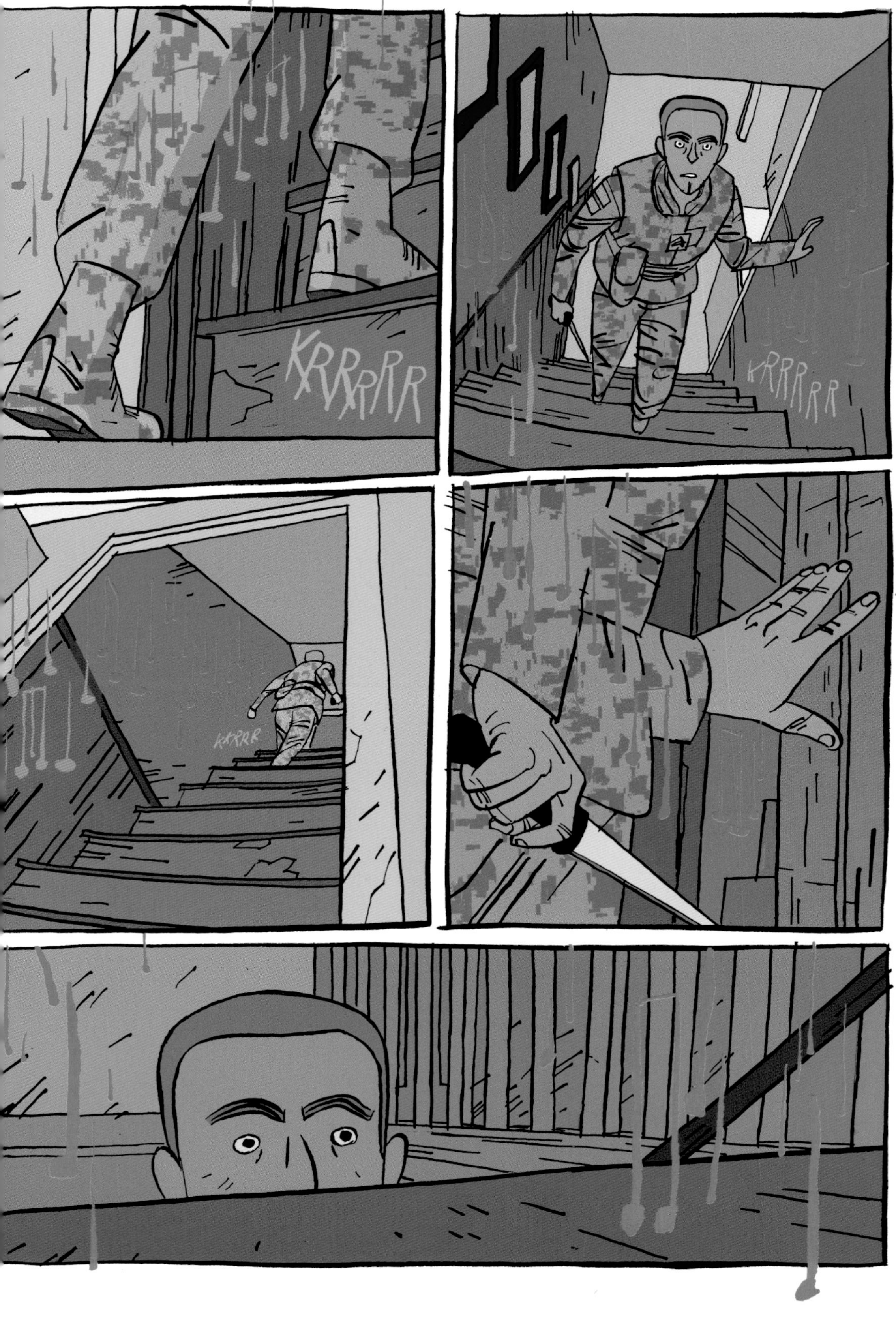
KRRRRRR
KRRRRRR
KRRRR

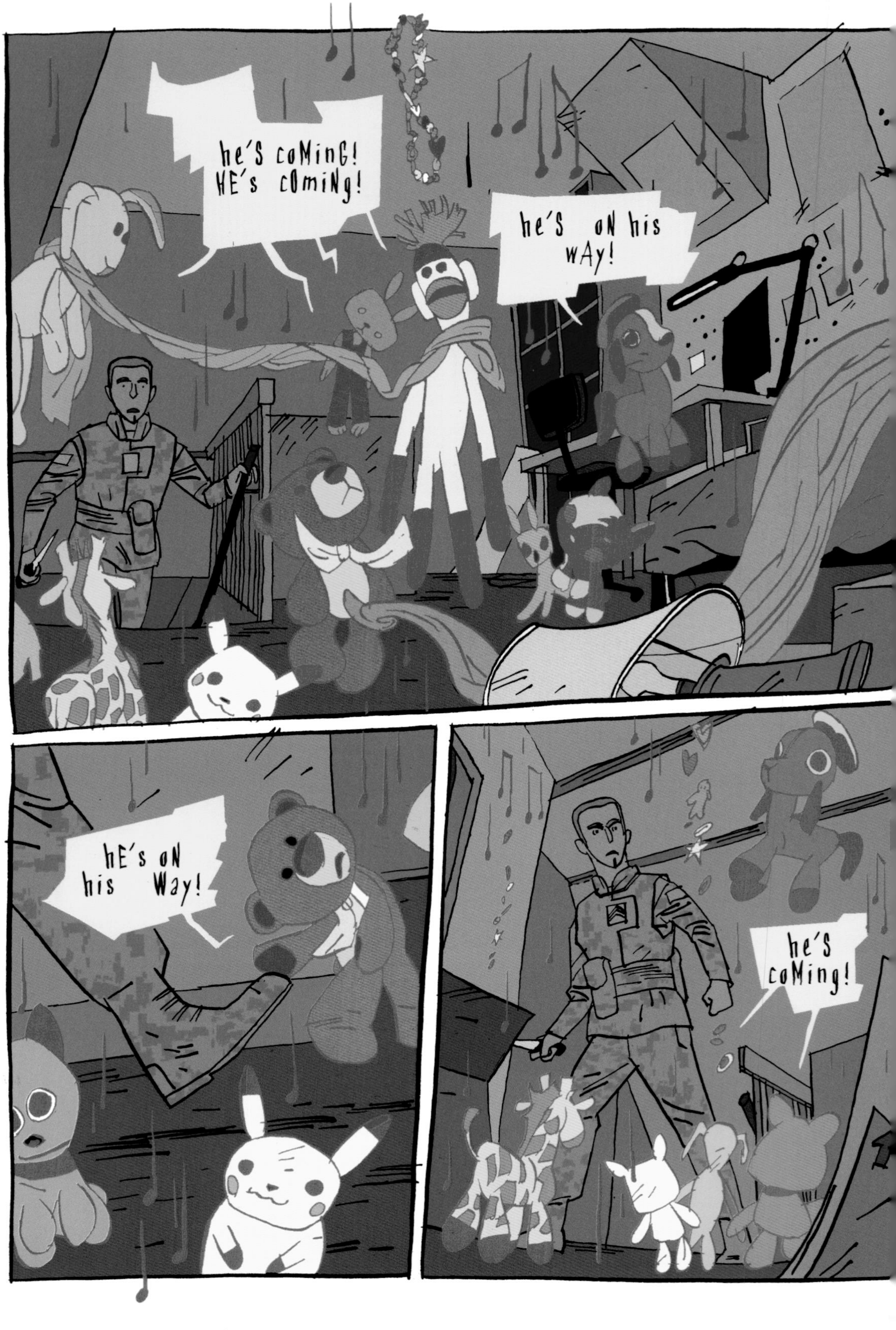
he's coMinG!
HE's cOmiNg!
he's oN his wAy!
hE's oN his Way!
he's coMing!

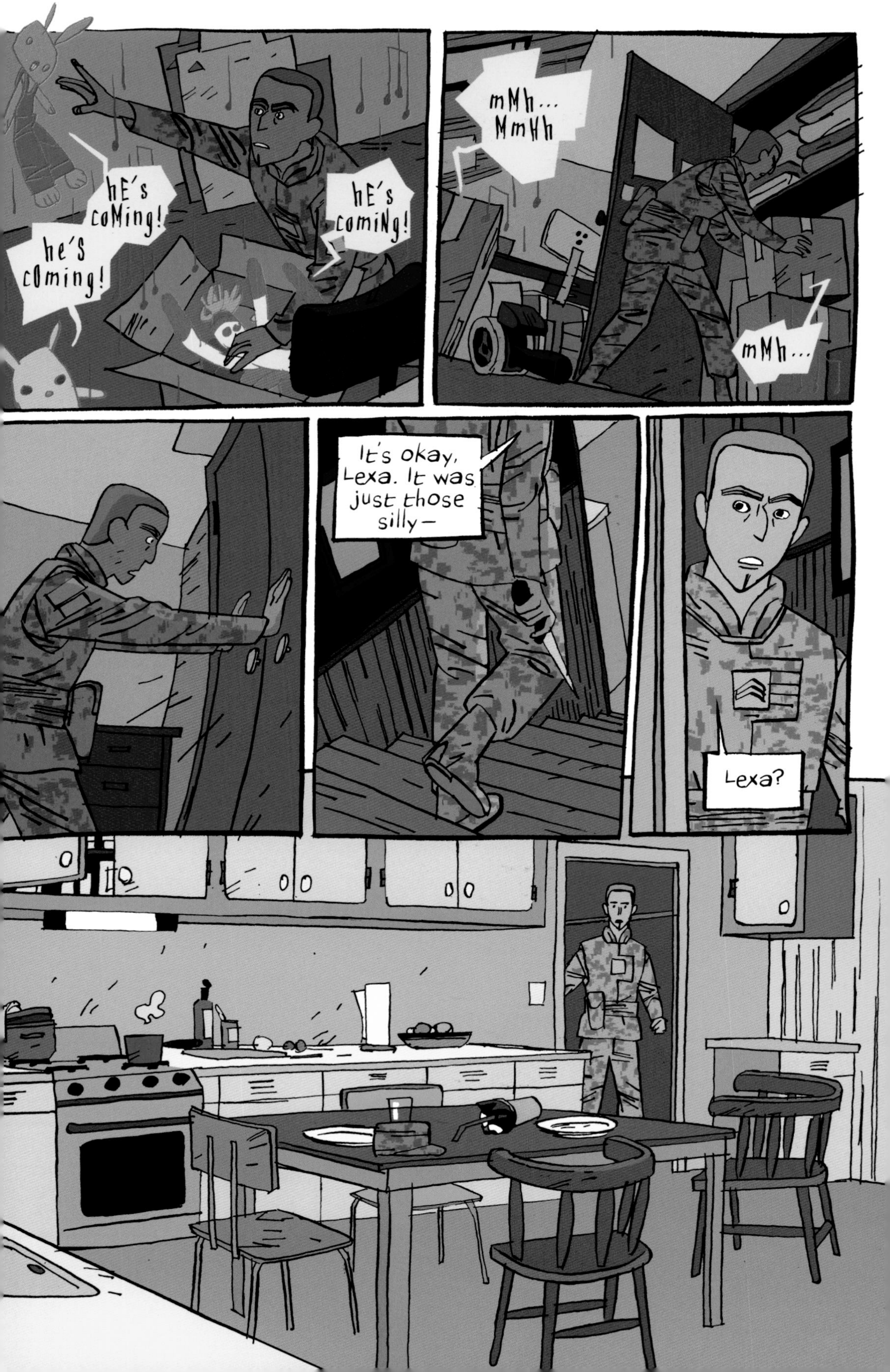
hE's coMing!
he's coming!
hE's coMiNg!
mMh... MmHh
mMh...
It's okay, Lexa. It was just those silly—
Lexa?

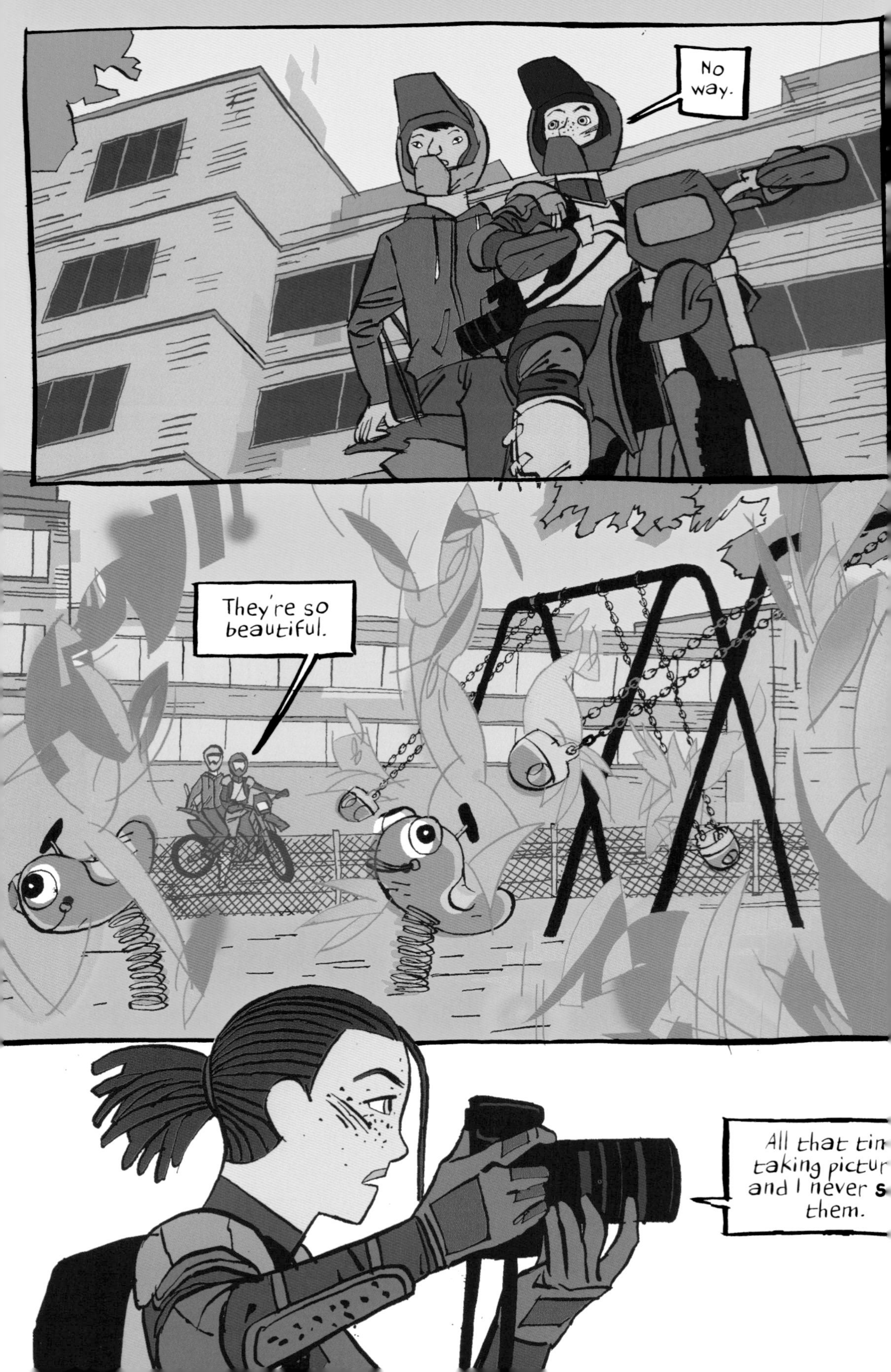
No way.
They're so beautiful.
All that tin taking pictur and I never s them.

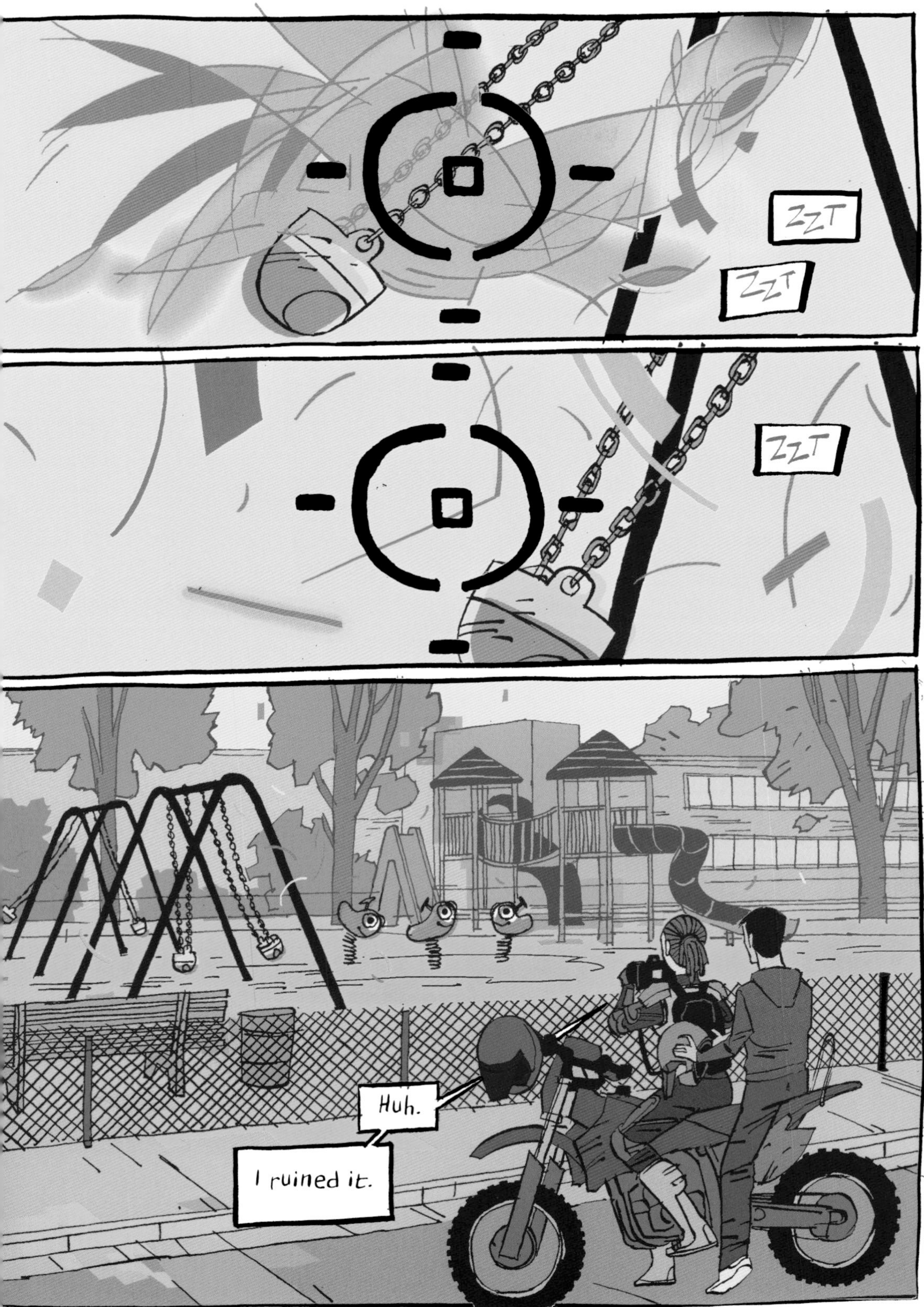
ZZT
ZZT
ZZT
Huh.
I ruined it.

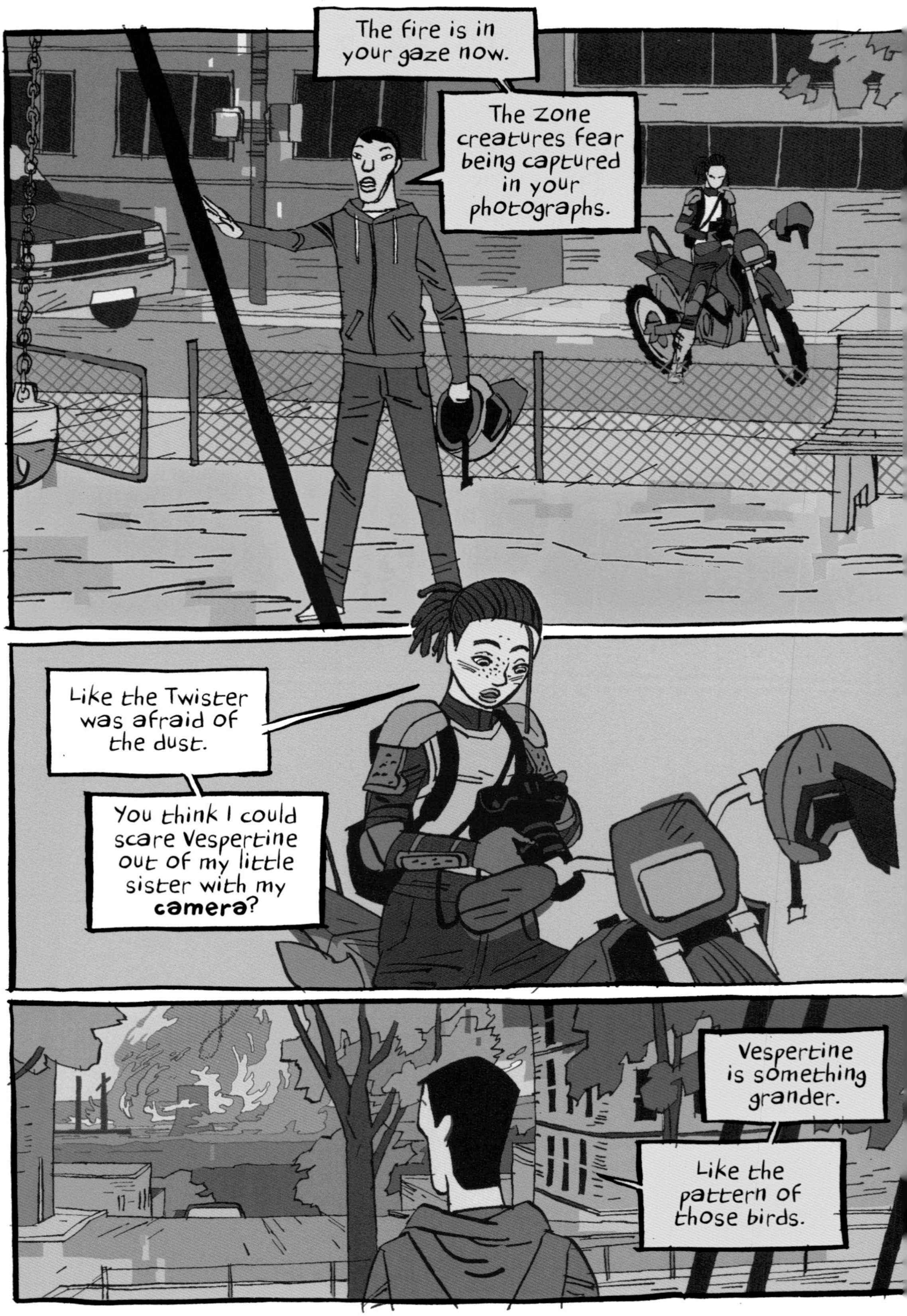
The fire is in your gaze now.
The zone creatures fear being captured in your photographs.
Like the Twister was afraid of the dust.
You think I could scare Vespertine out of my little sister with my **camera**?
Vespertine is something grander.
Like the pattern of those birds.

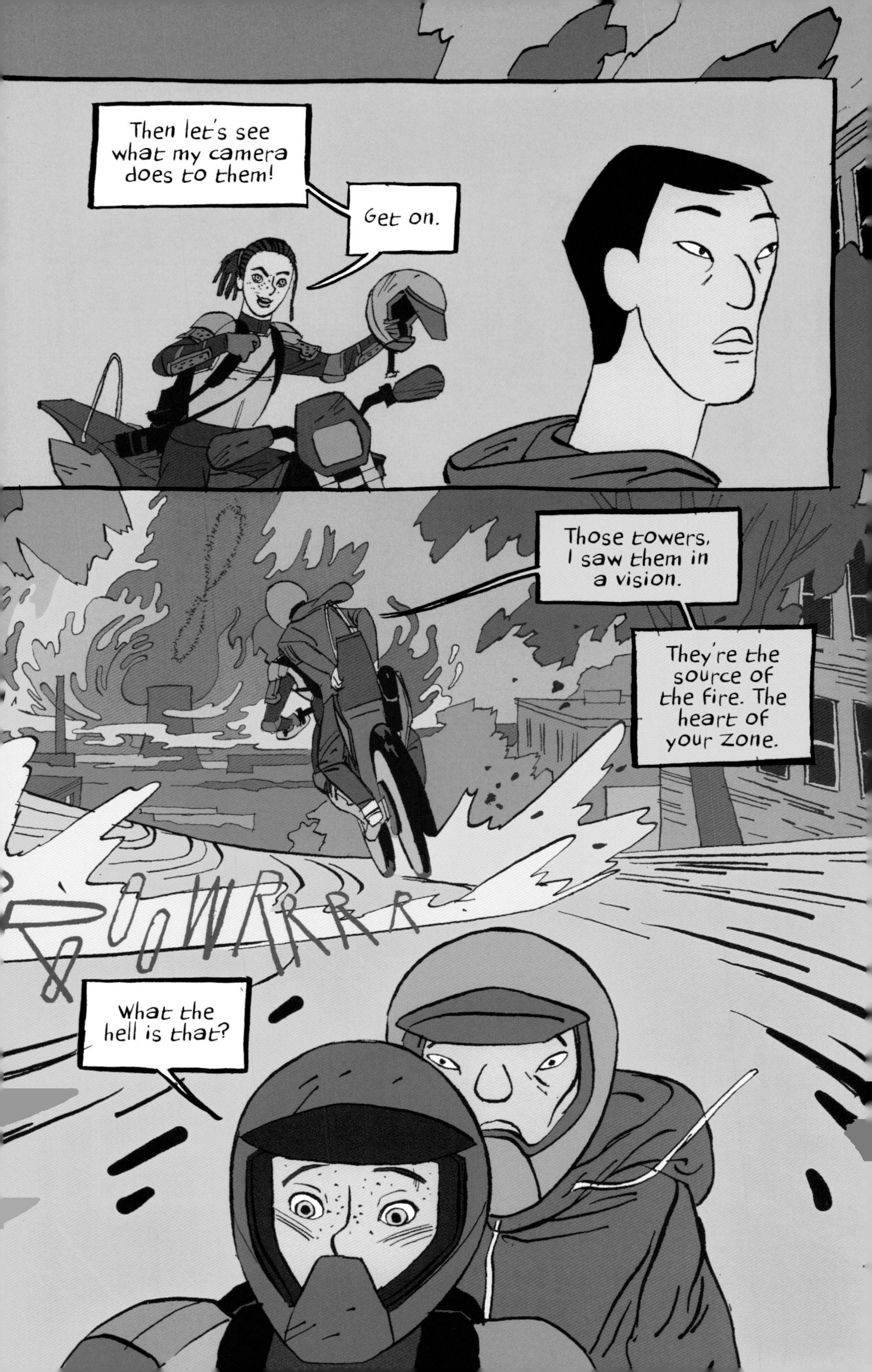
Then let's see what my camera does to them!
Get on.
Those towers, I saw them in a vision.
They're the source of the fire. The heart of your zone.
VOOWRRRRR
What the hell is that?

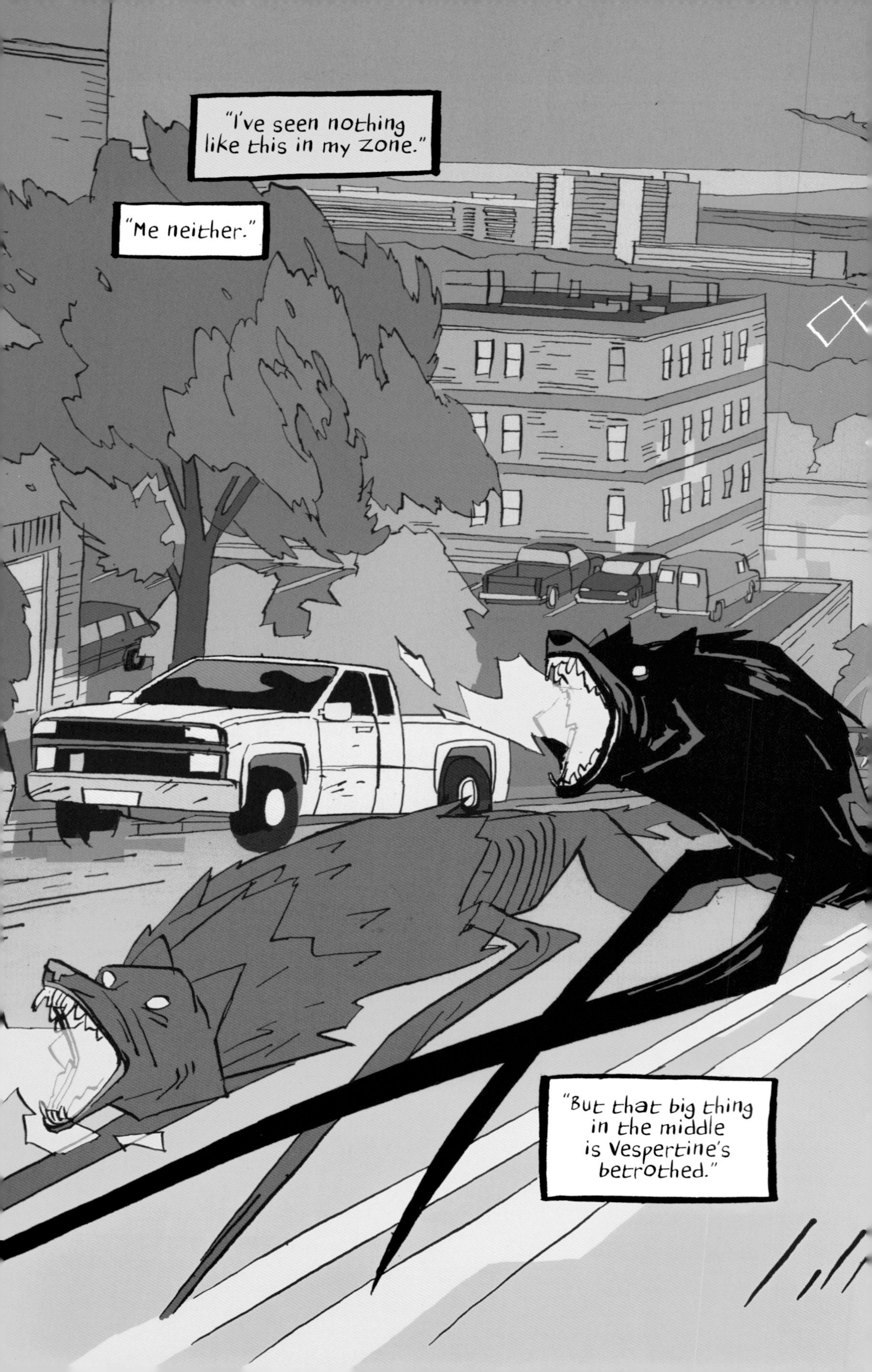
"I've seen nothing like this in my zone."
"Me neither."
"But that big thing in the middle is Vespertine's betrothed."

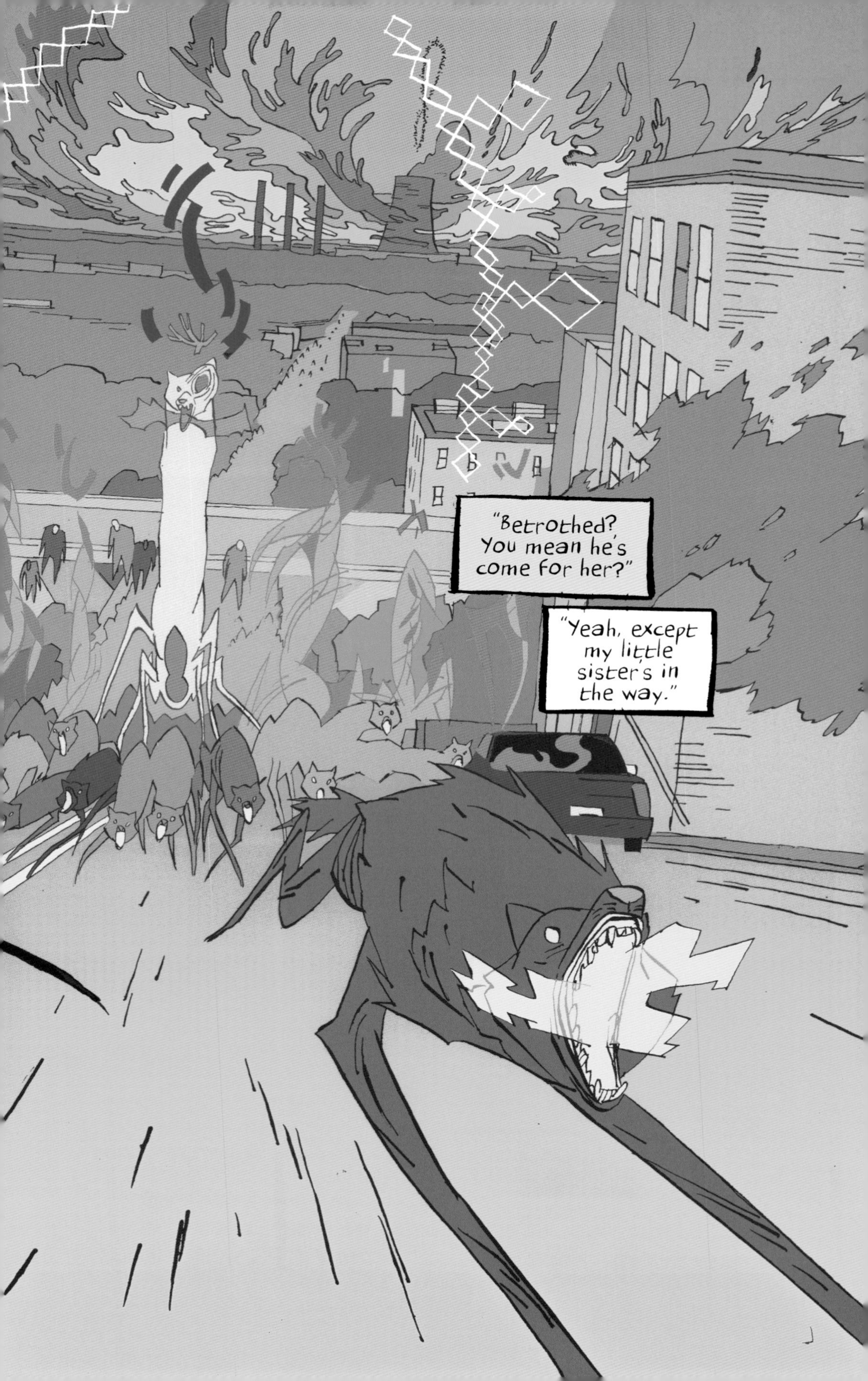
"Betrothed? You mean he's come for her?"
"Yeah, except my little sister's in the way."

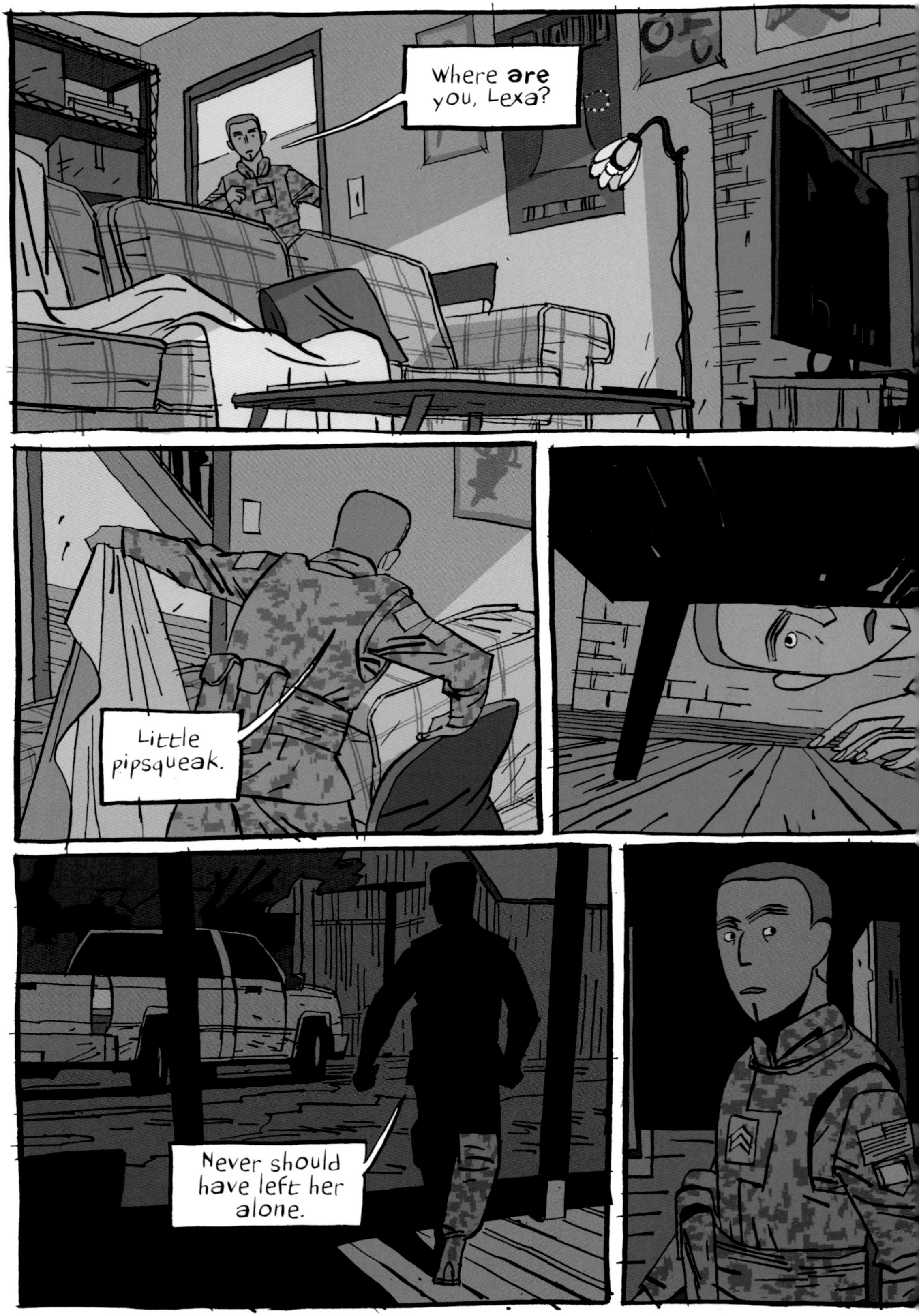
Where are you, Lexa?
Little pipsqueak.
Never should have left her alone.

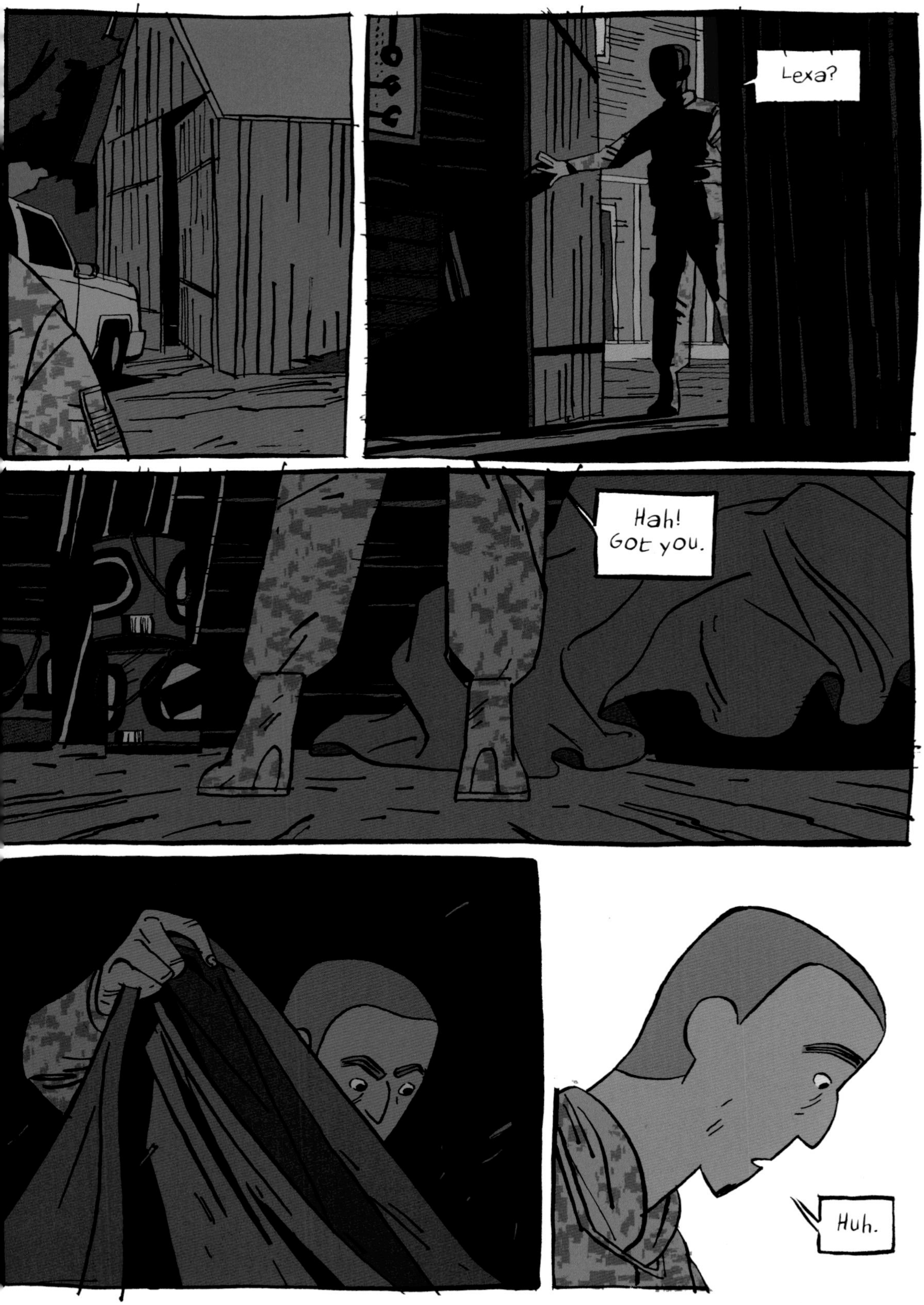
Lexa?
Hah! Got you.
Huh.

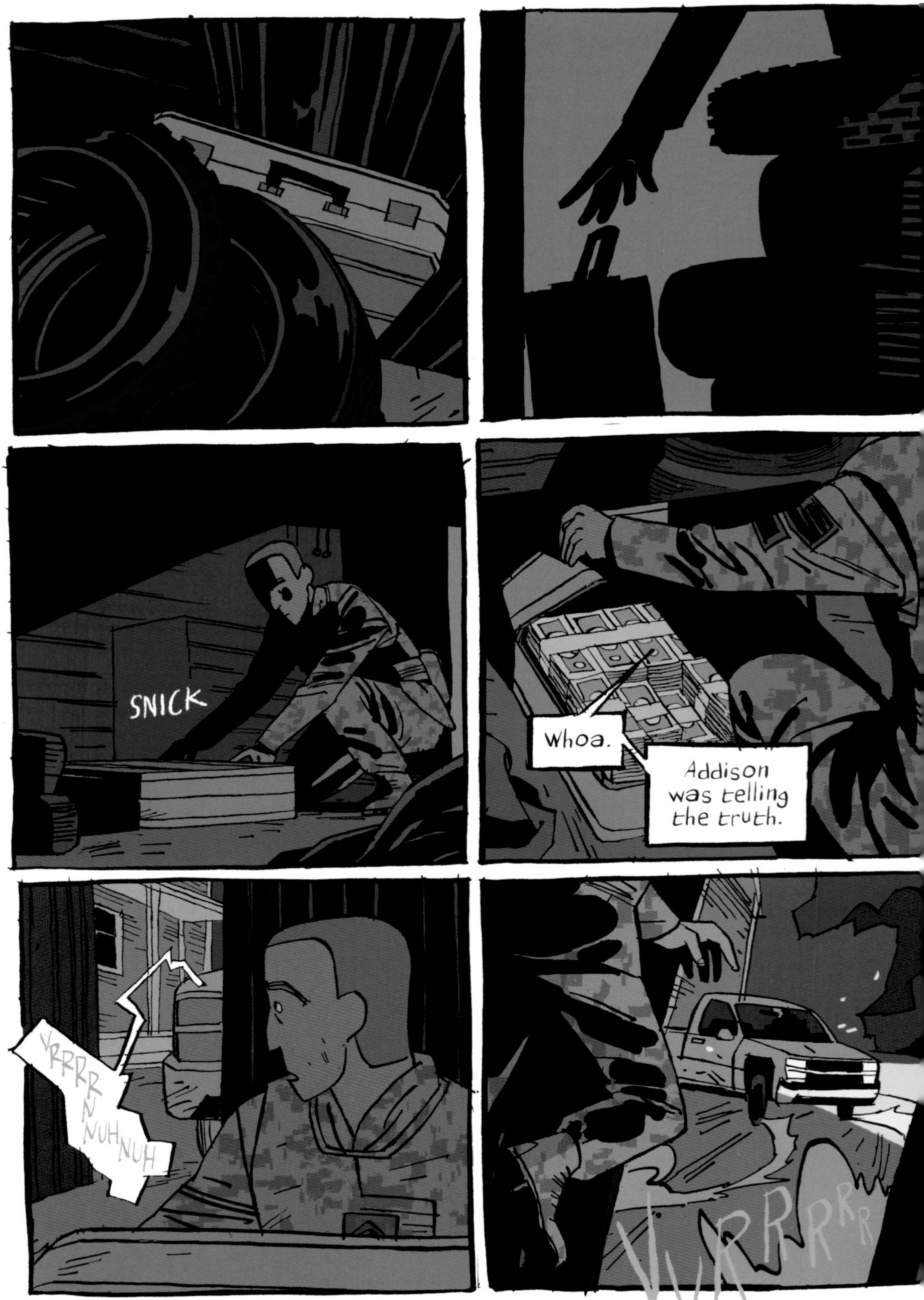
SNICK
Whoa.
Addison was telling the truth.
VRRRR N NUH NUH
VVRRRRR

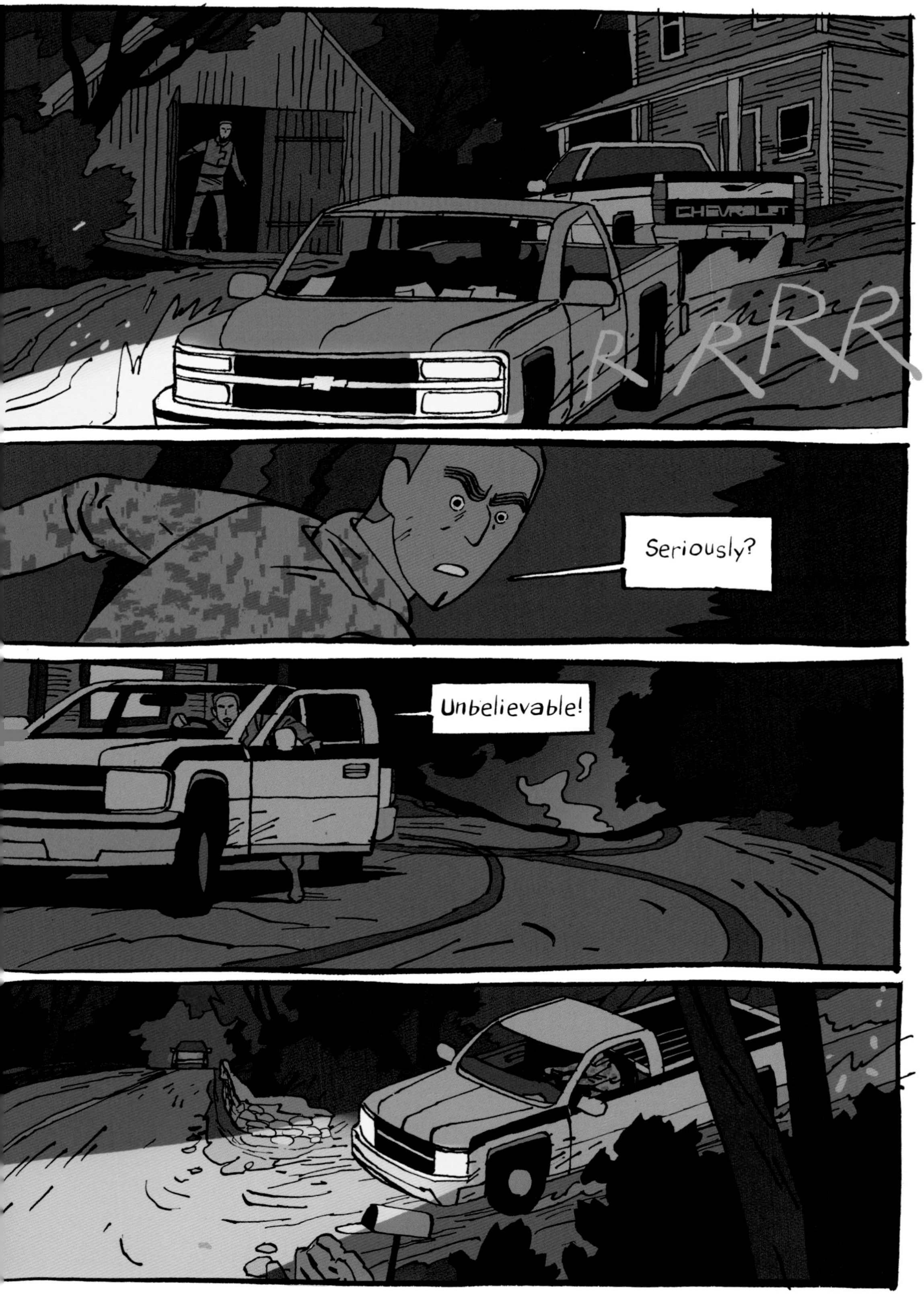
CHEVROLET
RRRR
Seriously?
Unbelievable!

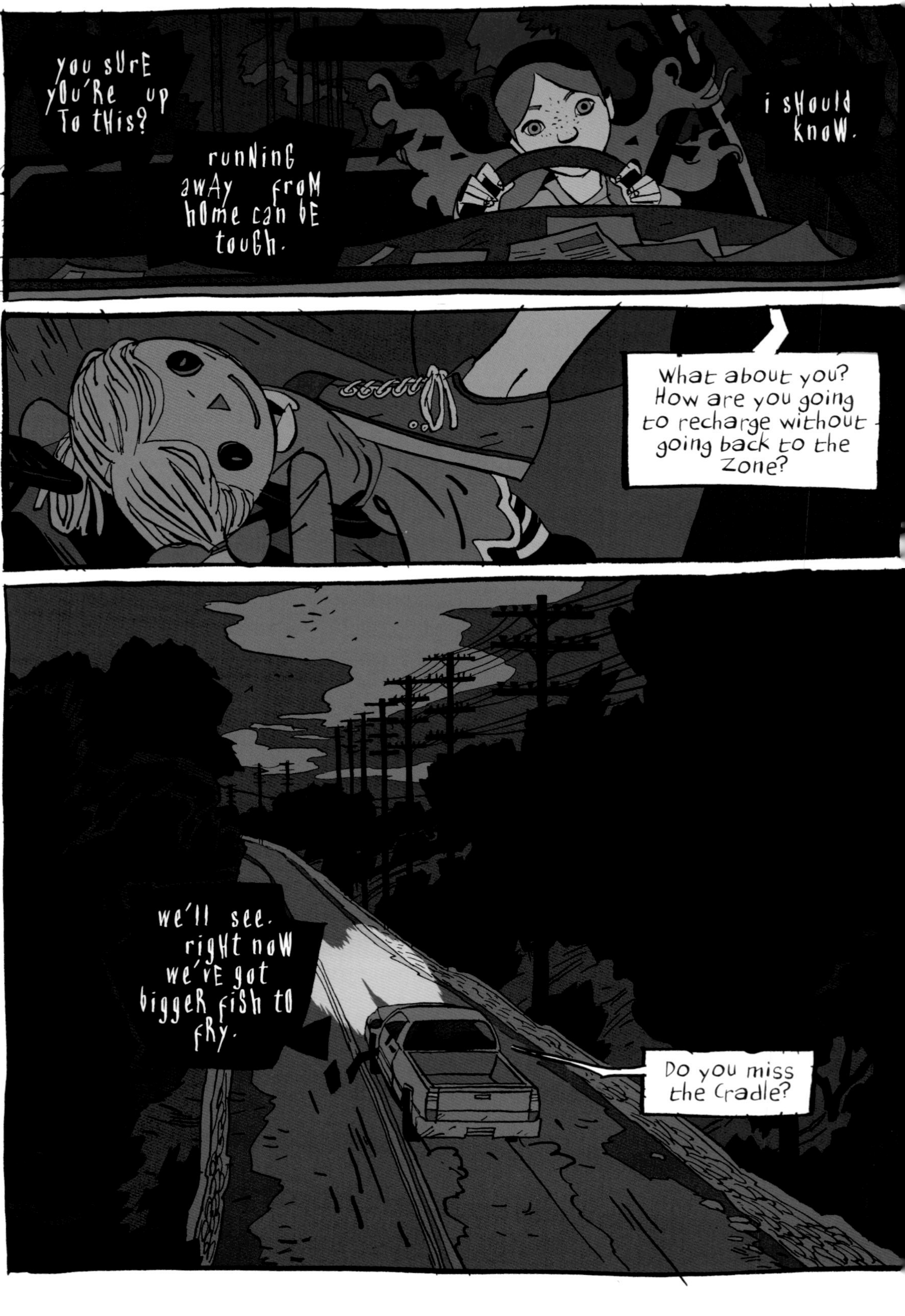
you sure you're up to this?
running away from home can be tough.
i should know.
What about you? How are you going to recharge without going back to the Zone?
we'll see. right now we've got bigger fish to fry.
Do you miss the Cradle?

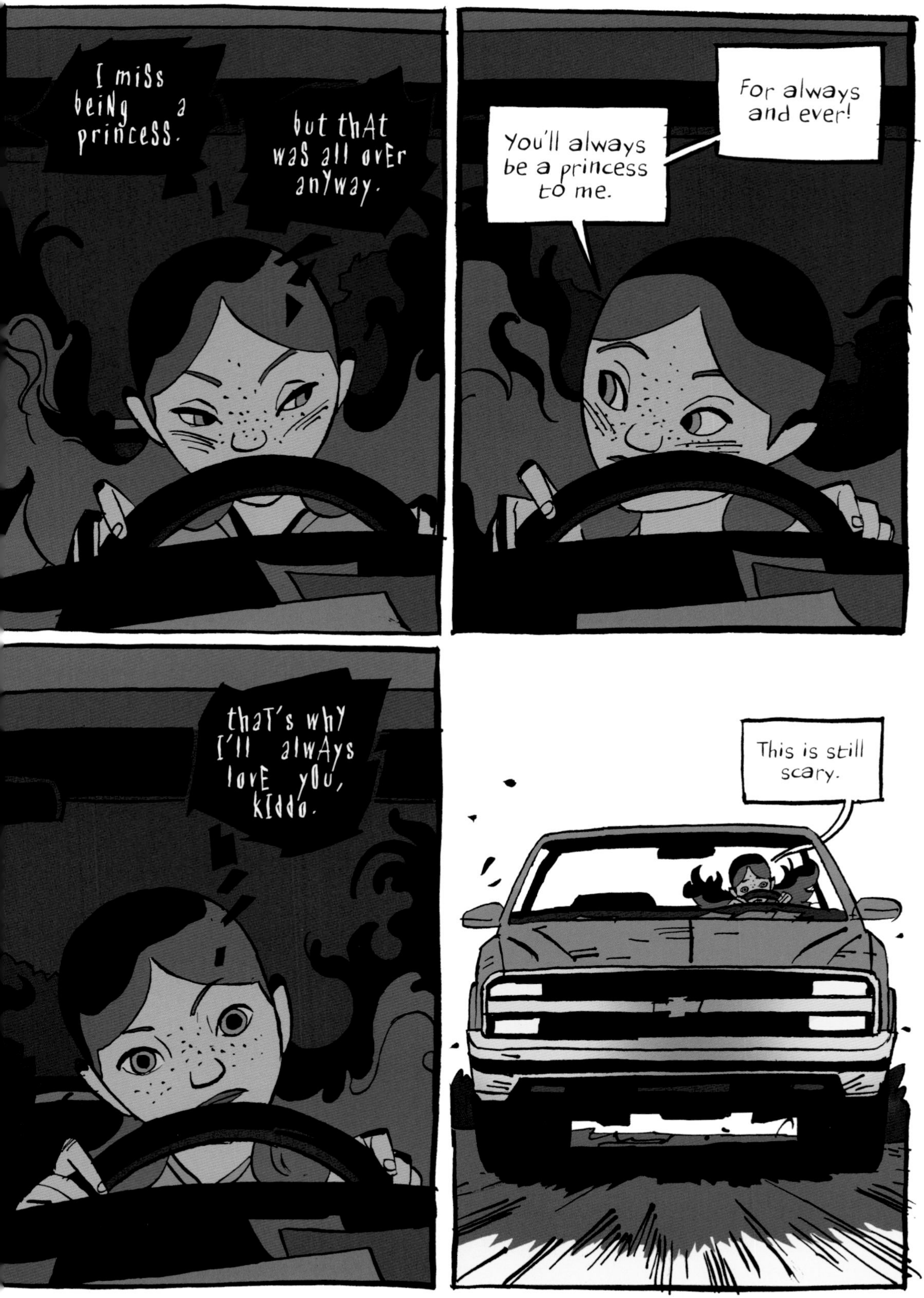
I miss being a princess.
but that was all over anyway.
You'll always be a princess to me.
For always and ever!
that's why I'll always love you, kiddo.
This is still scary.

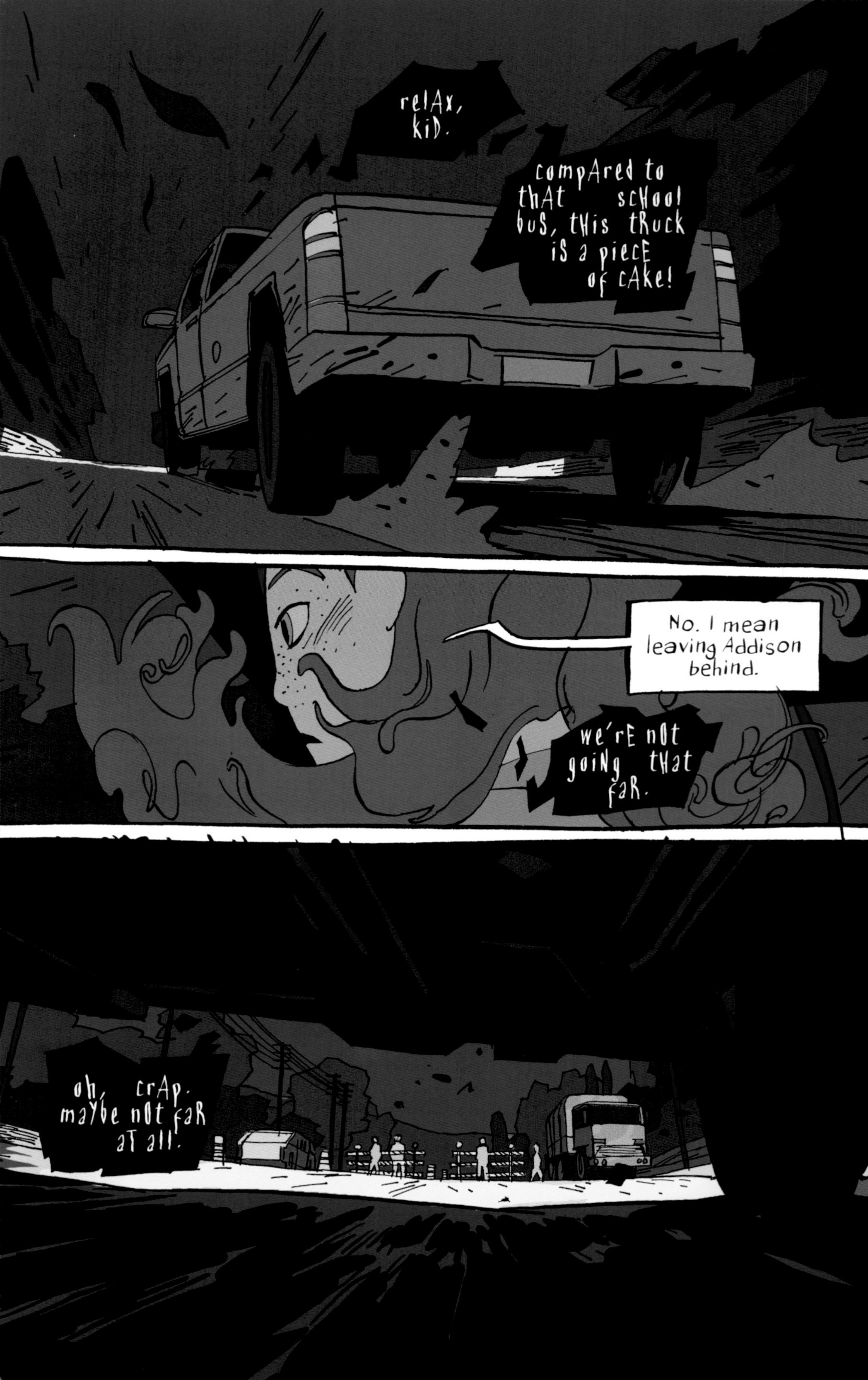
relax, kid.
compared to that school bus, this truck is a piece of cake!
No. I mean leaving Addison behind.
we're not going that far.
oh, crap. maybe not far at all.

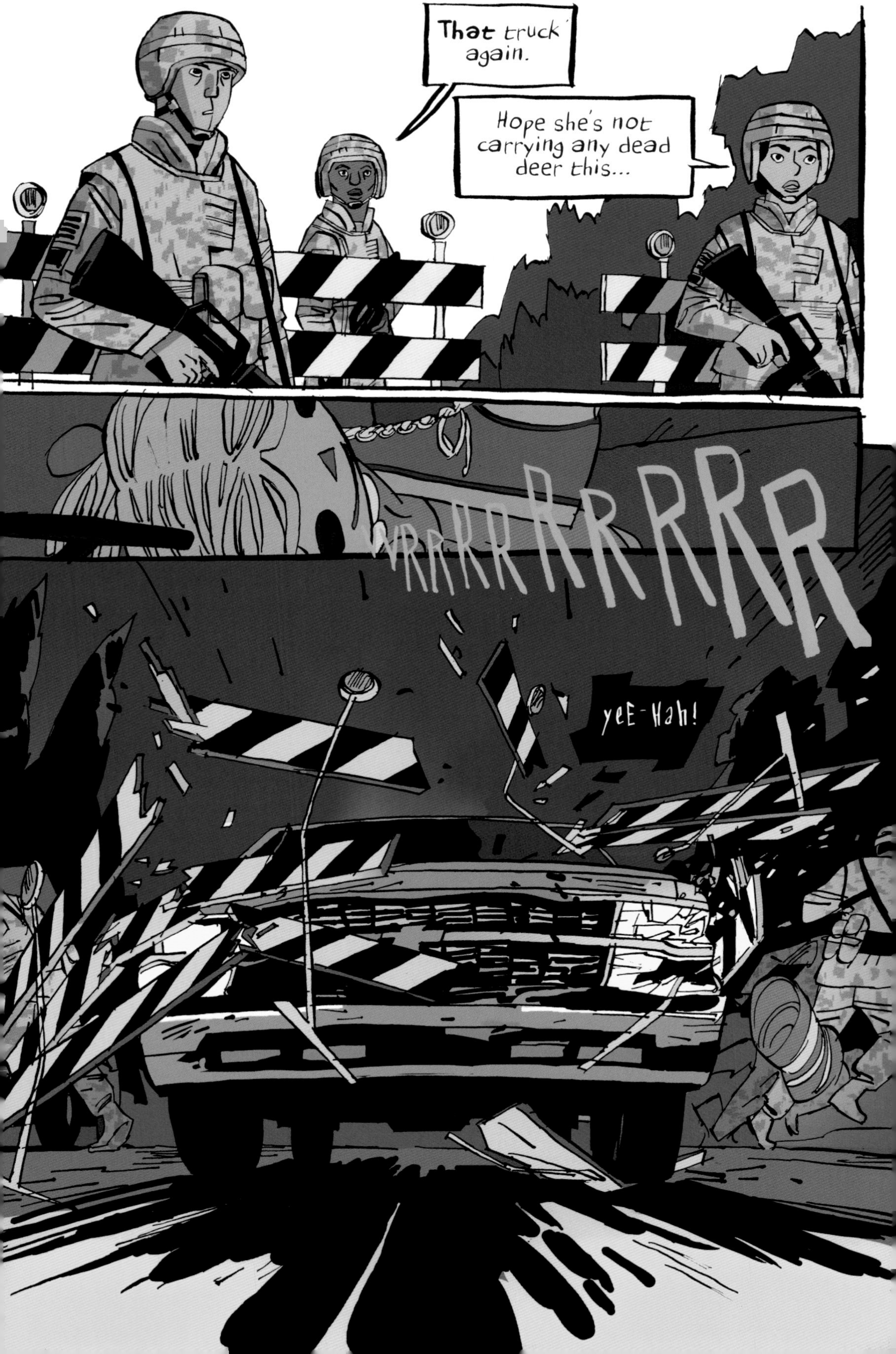

That truck again.
Hope she's not carrying any dead deer this...
VRRRRRRRRRRR
yeE-Hah!

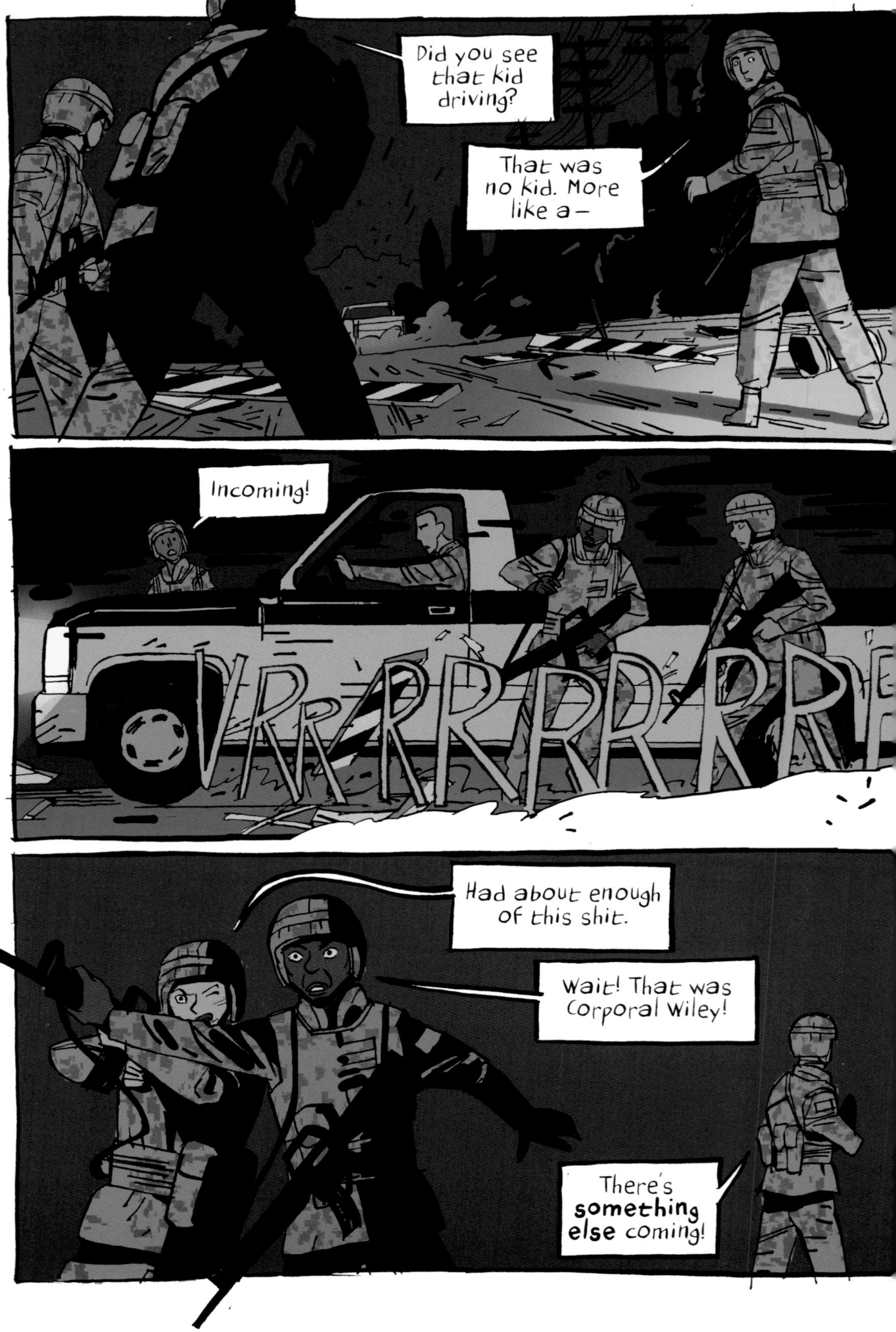
Did you see that kid driving?
That was no kid. More like a—
Incoming!
VRRRRRRRR
Had about enough of this shit.
Wait! That was Corporal Wiley!
There's **something else** coming!

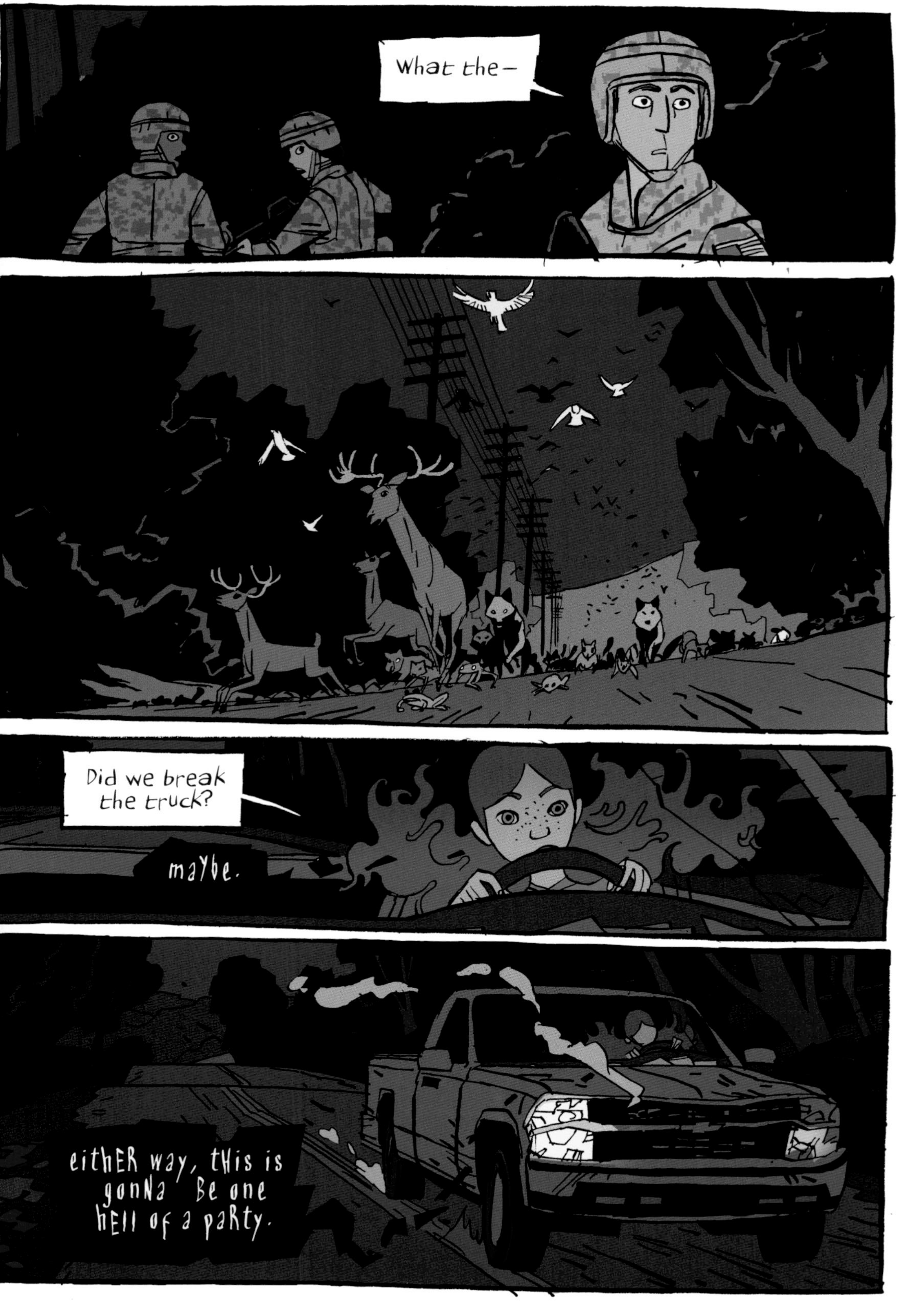
What the–
Did we break the truck?
maybe.
either way, this is gonna be one hell of a party.

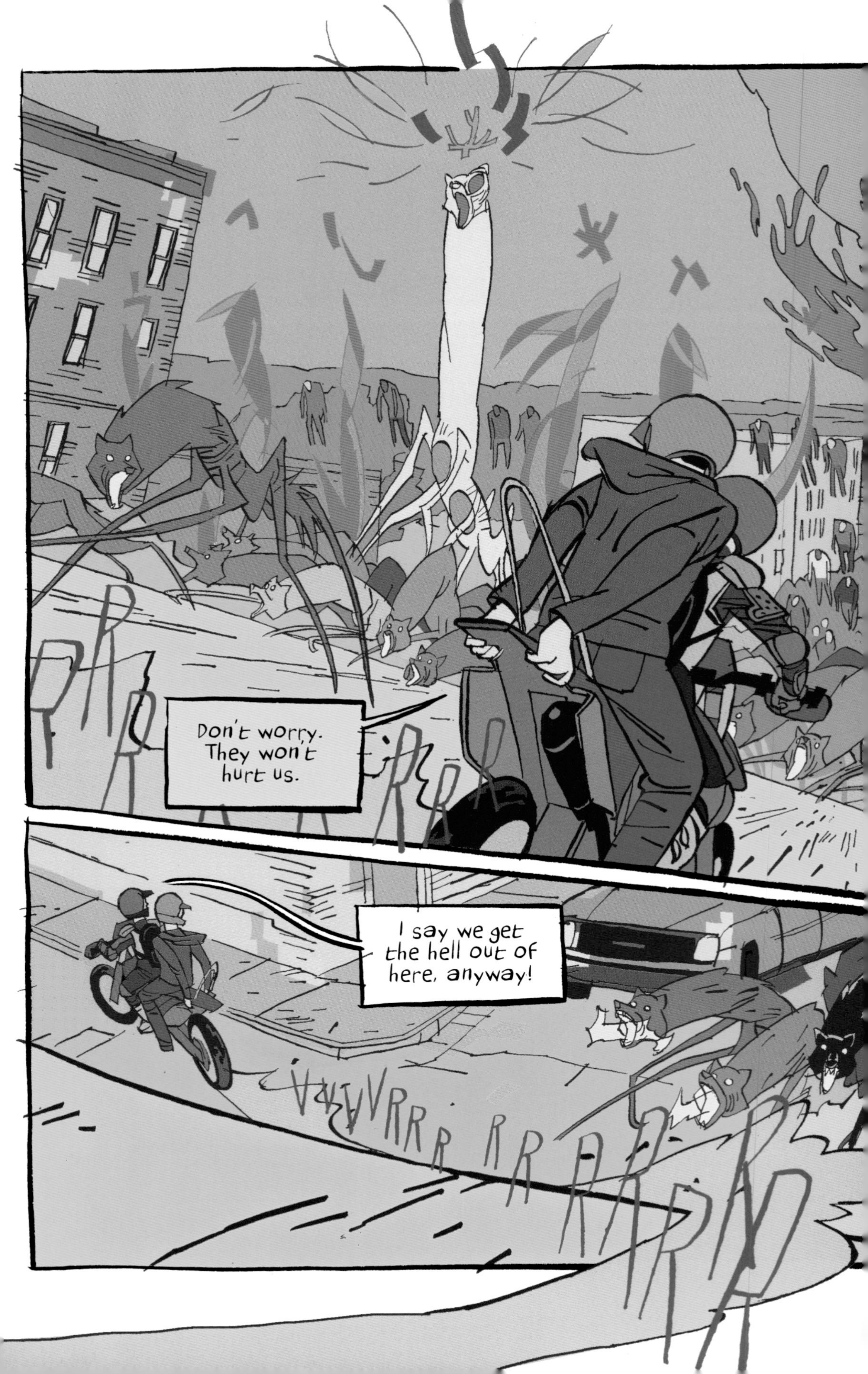
Don't worry. They won't hurt us.
I say we get the hell out of here, anyway!

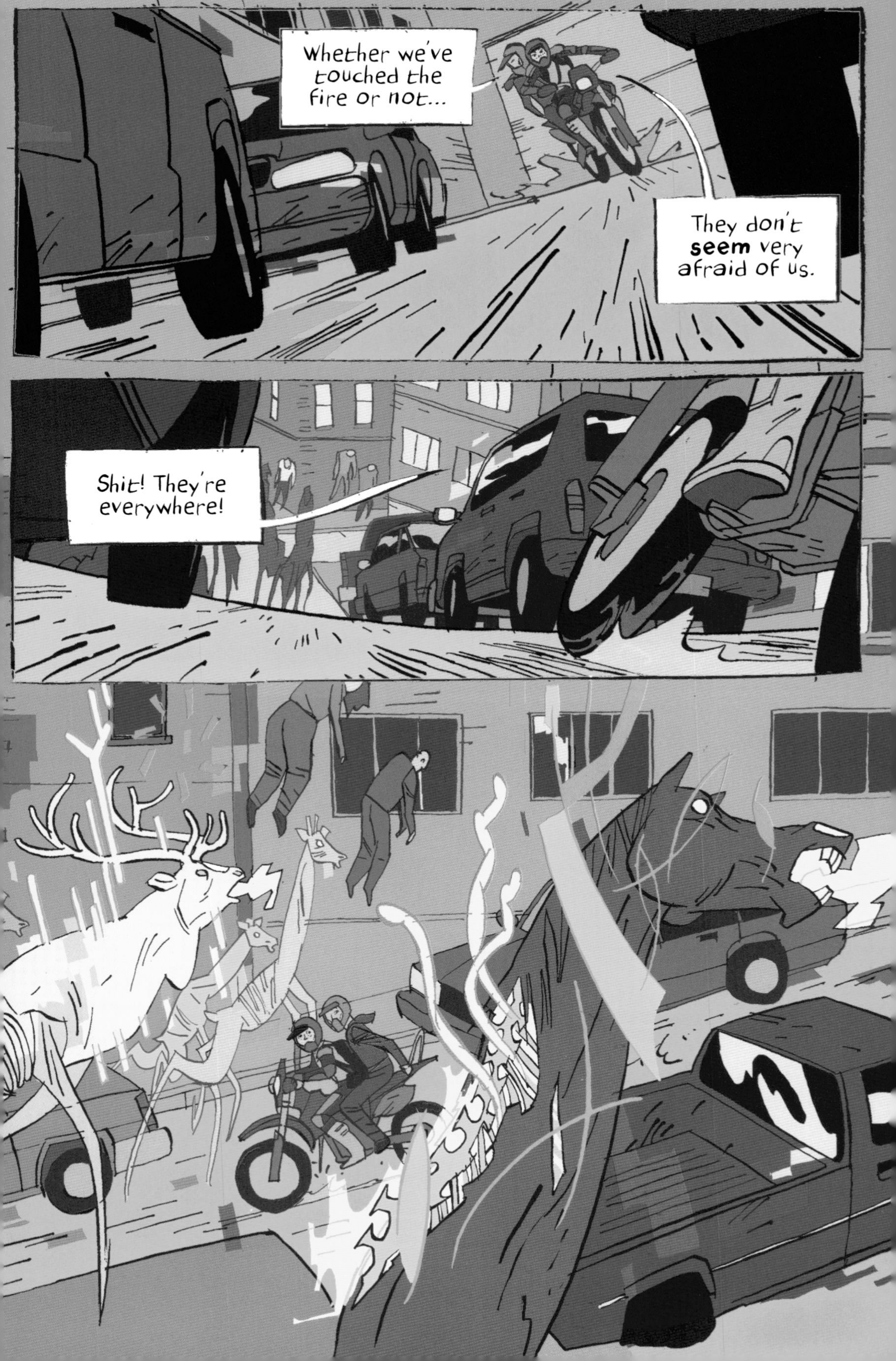
Whether we've touched the fire or not...
They don't **seem** very afraid of us.
Shit! They're everywhere!

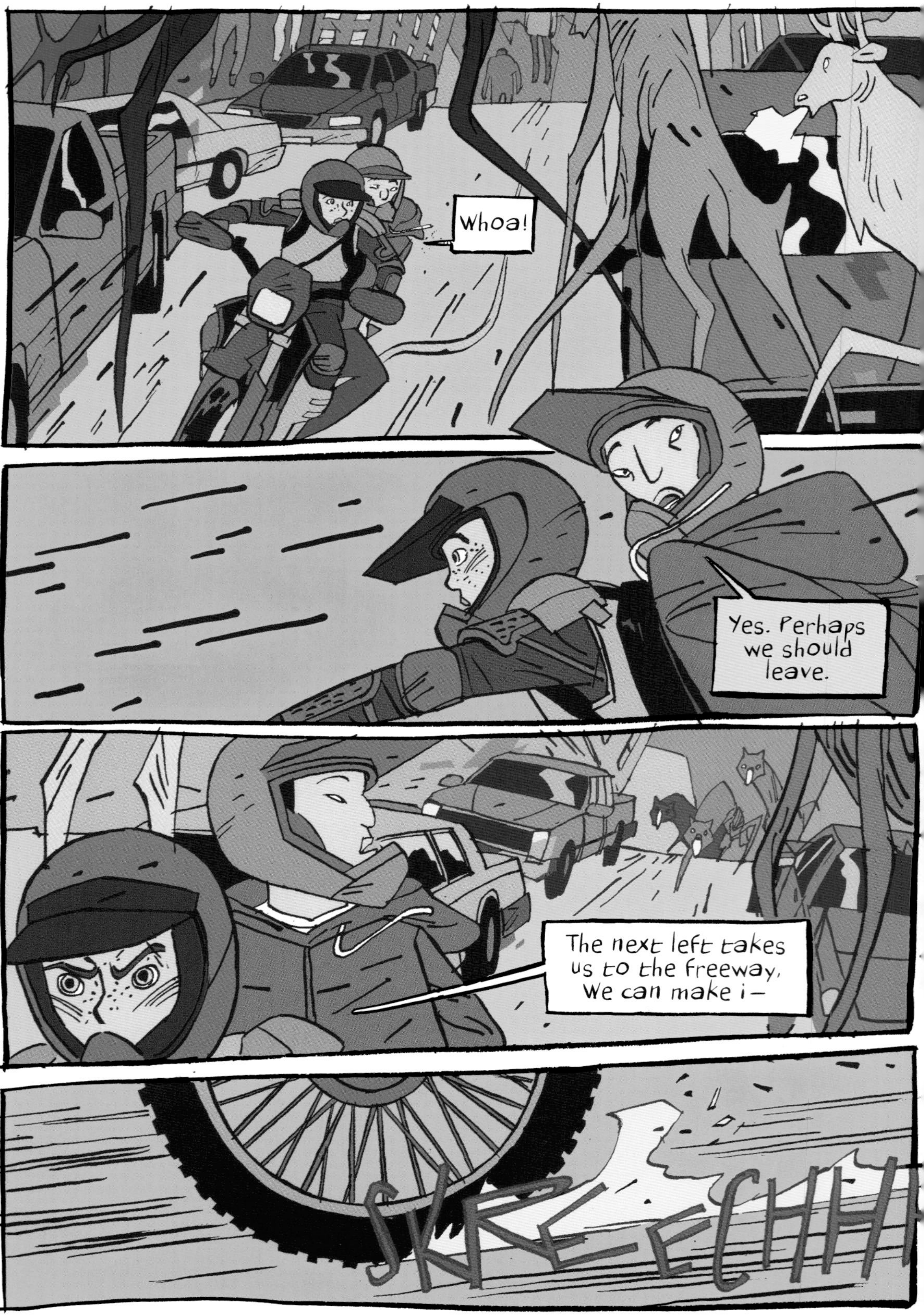
Whoa!
Yes. Perhaps we should leave.
The next left takes us to the freeway, We can make i–
SKREECHH

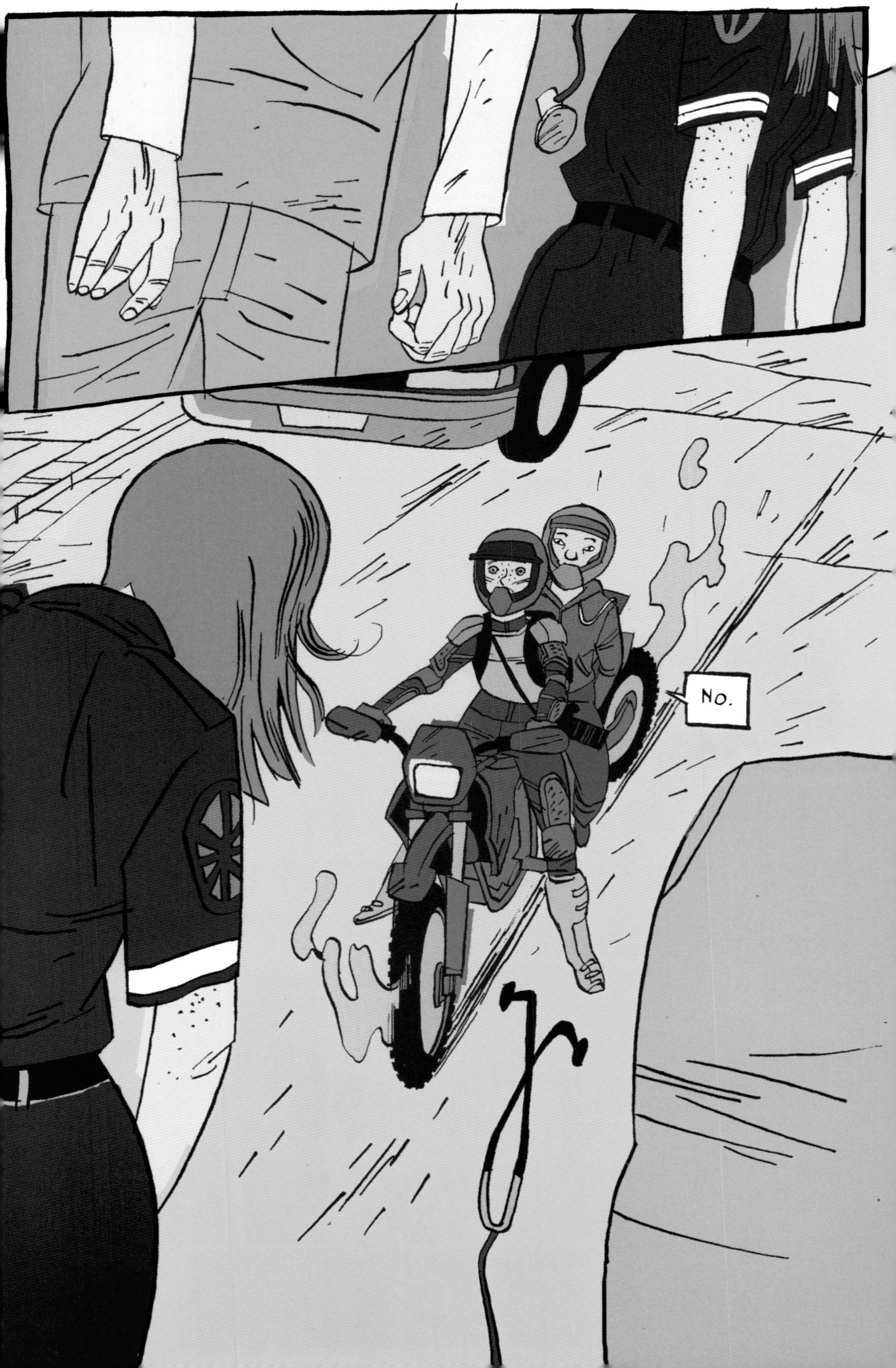
NO.

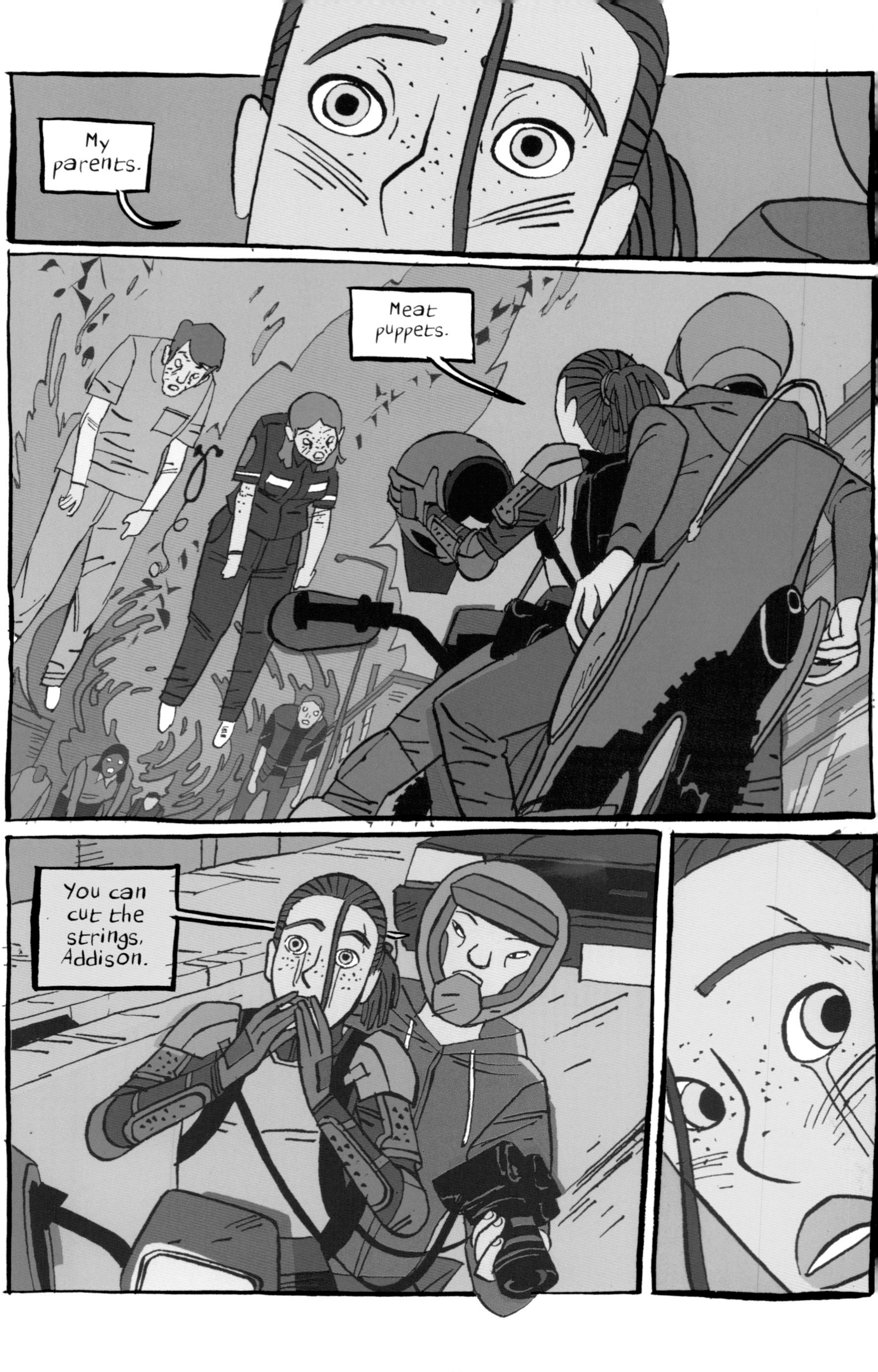
My parents.
Meat puppets.
You can cut the strings, Addison.

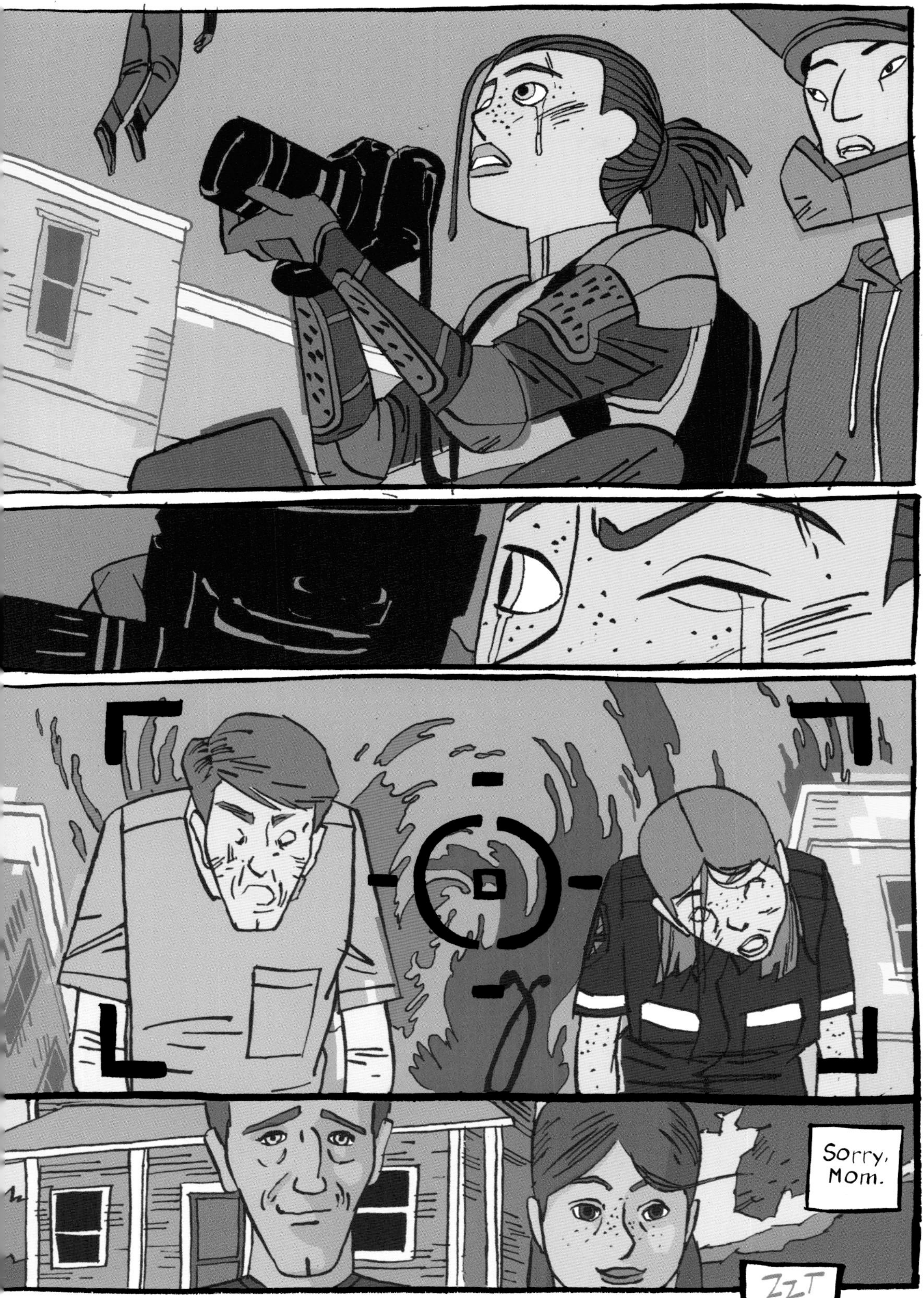
Sorry, Mom.
ZZT

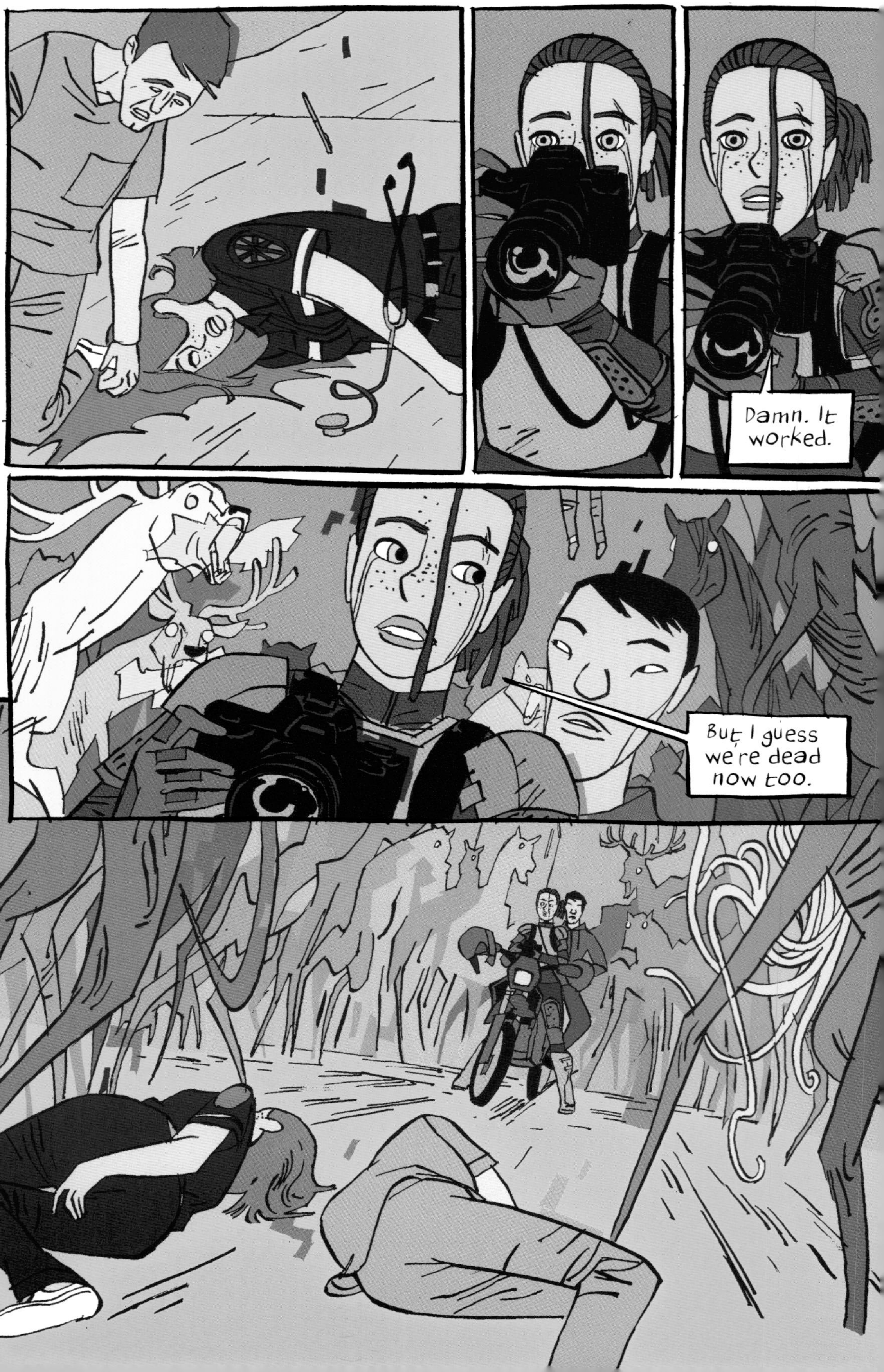
Damn. It worked.
But I guess we're dead now too.

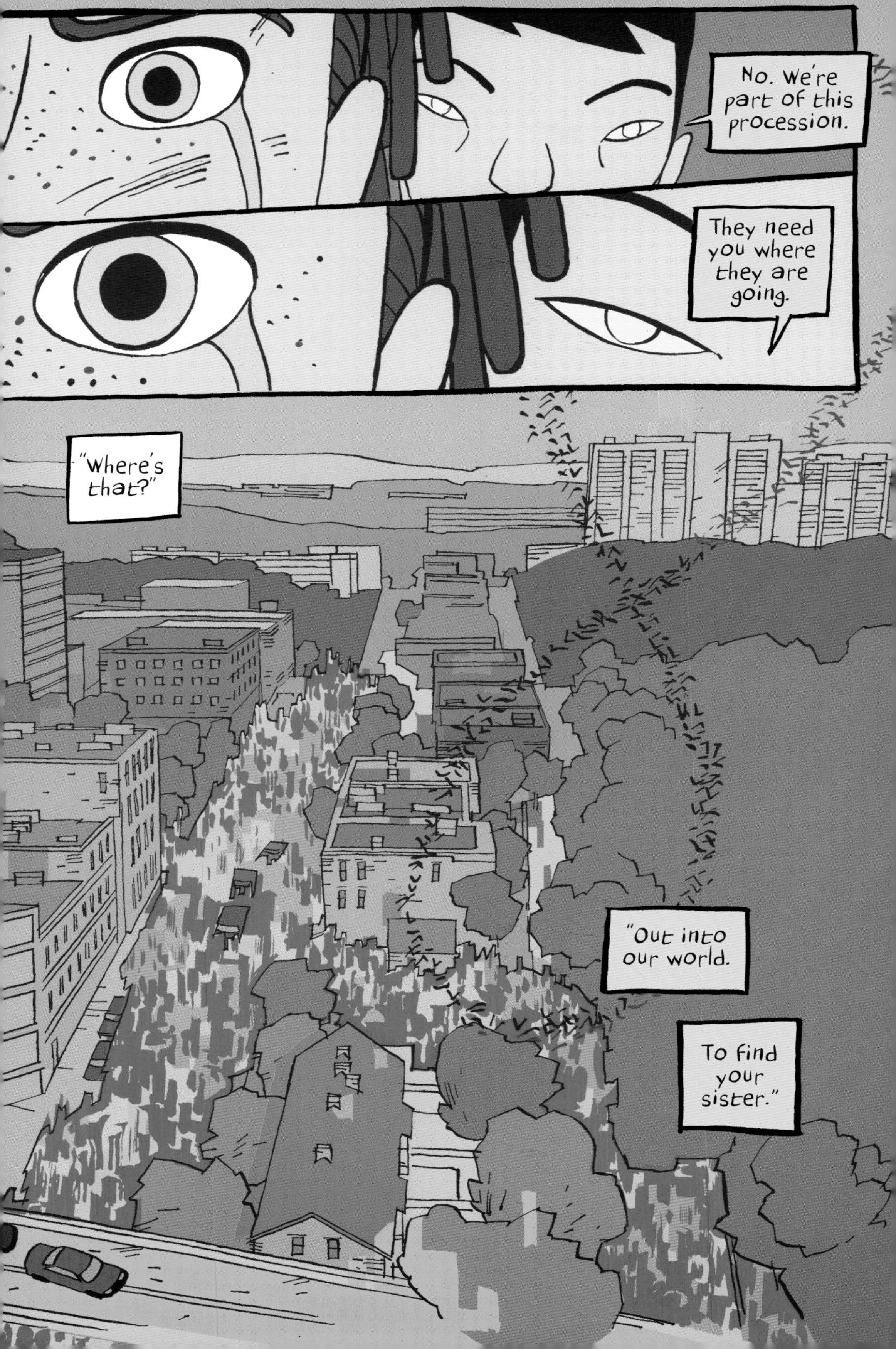
No. We're part of this procession.
They need you where they are going.
"Where's that?"
"Out into our world.
To find your sister."

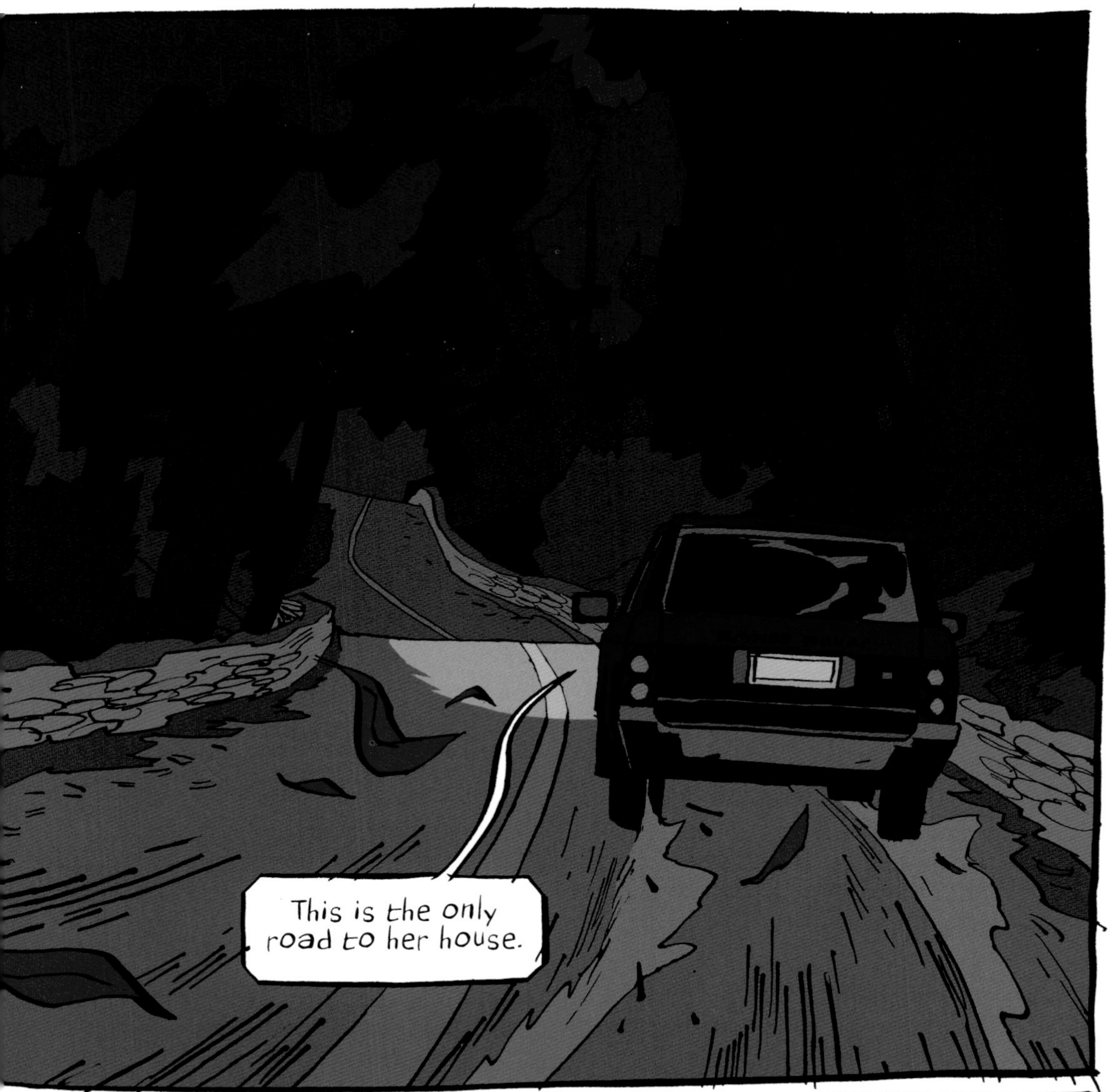
This is the only road to her house.

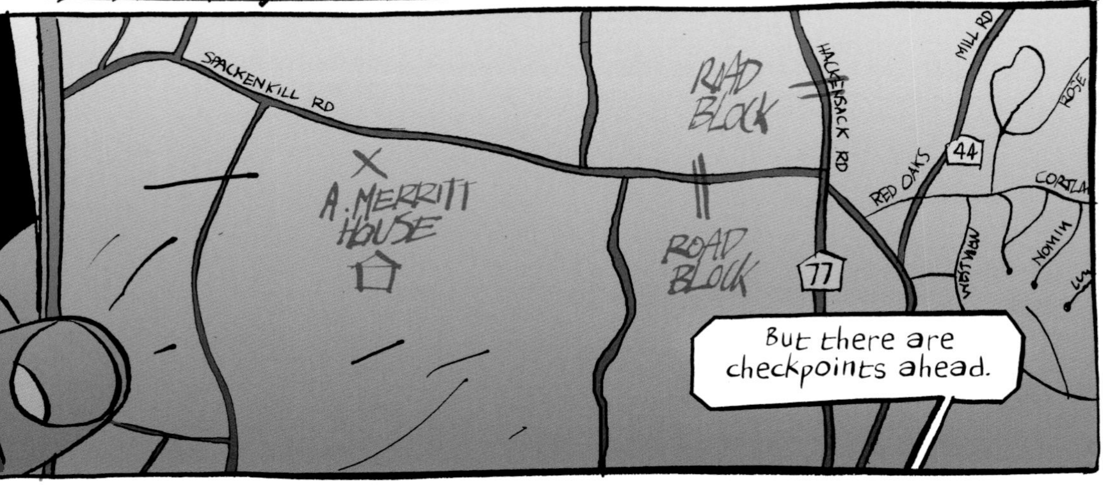
SPACKENKILL RD
ROAD BLOCK
HACKENSACK RD
MILL RD
ROSE
44
RED OAKS
A. MERRITT HOUSE
ROAD BLOCK
77
But there are checkpoints ahead.

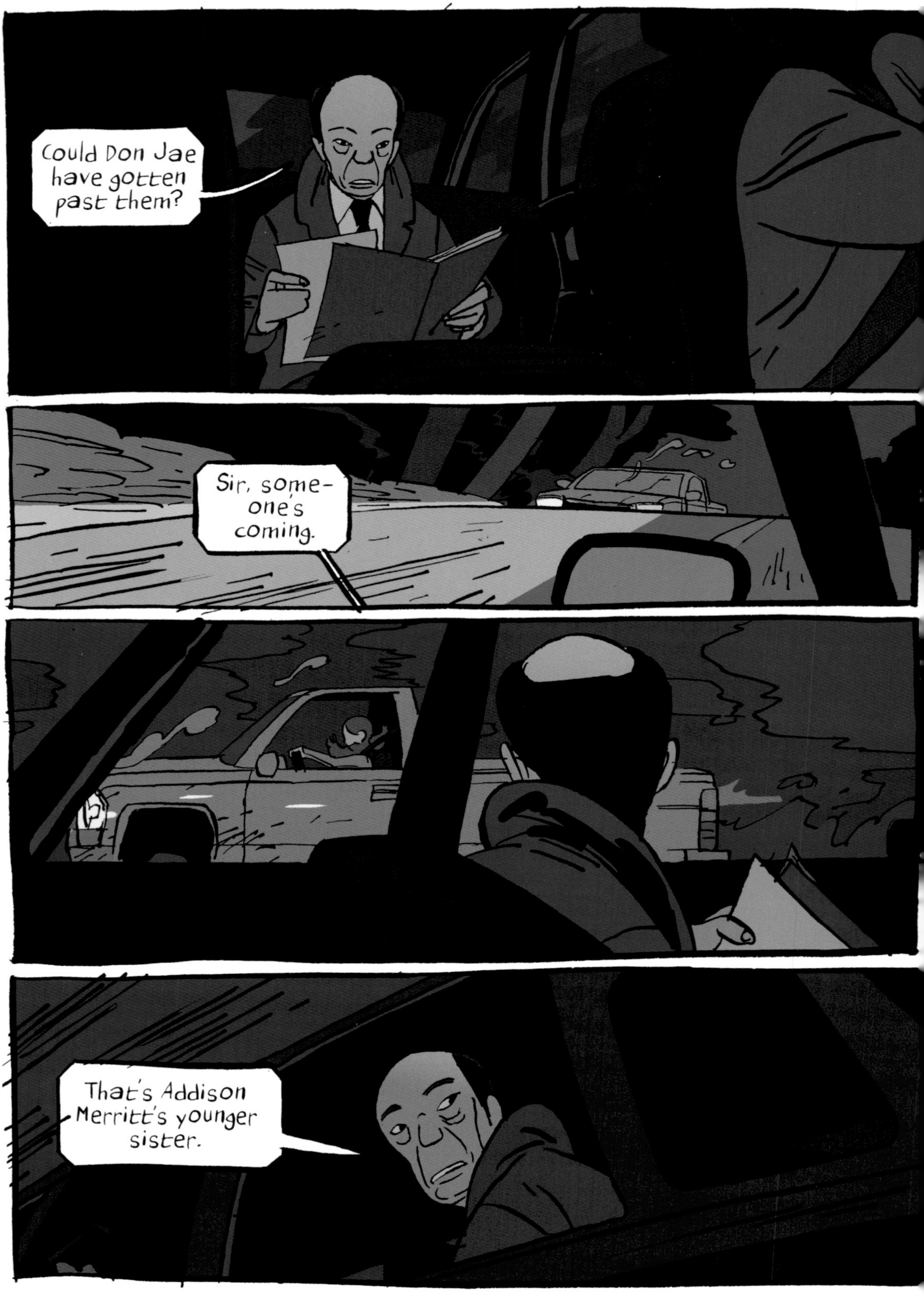
Could Don Jae have gotten past them?
Sir, someone's coming.
That's Addison Merritt's younger sister.

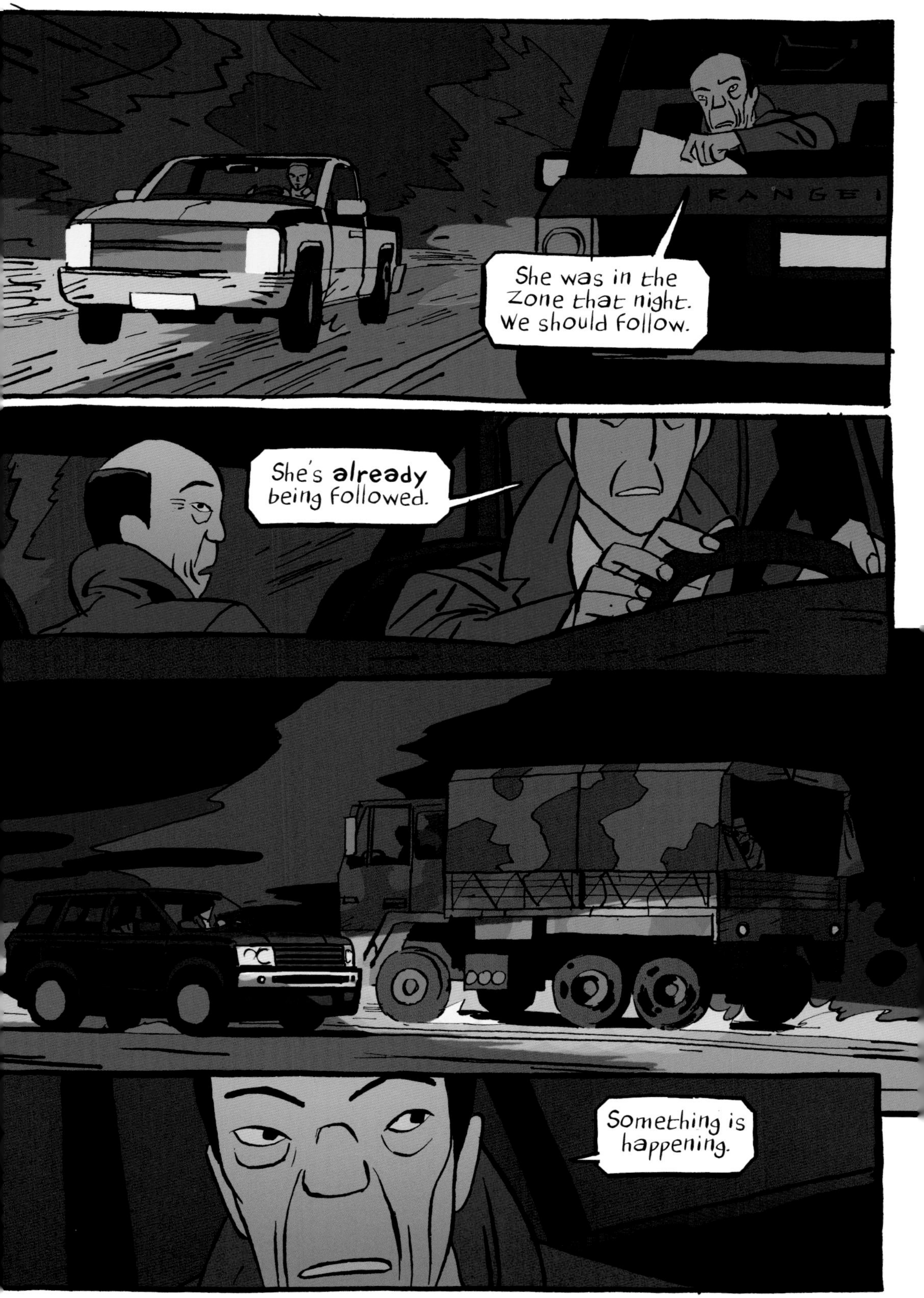
She was in the Zone that night. We should follow.
She's **already** being followed.
Something is happening.

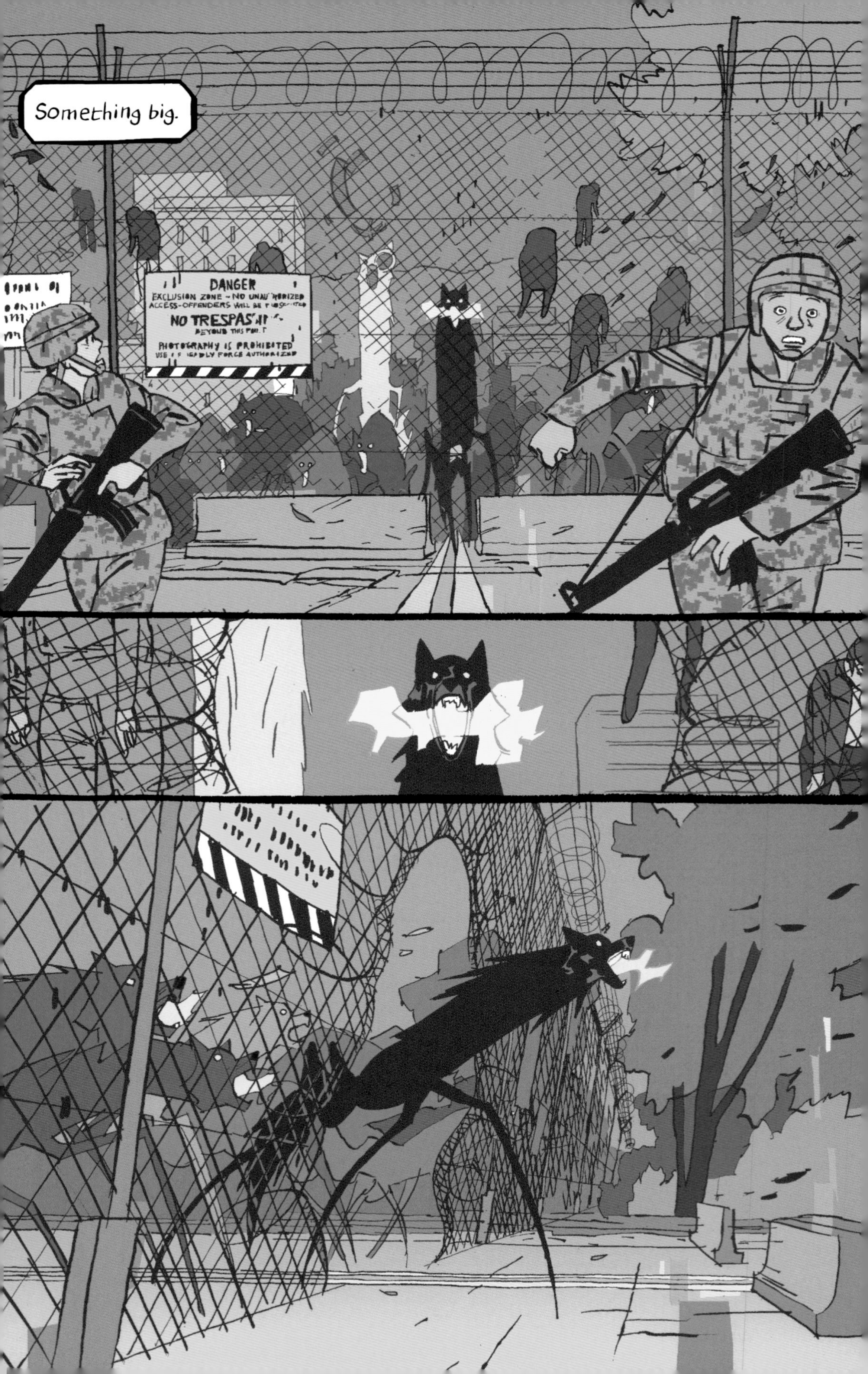
Something big.
DANGER
PHOTOGRAPHY IS PROHIBITED

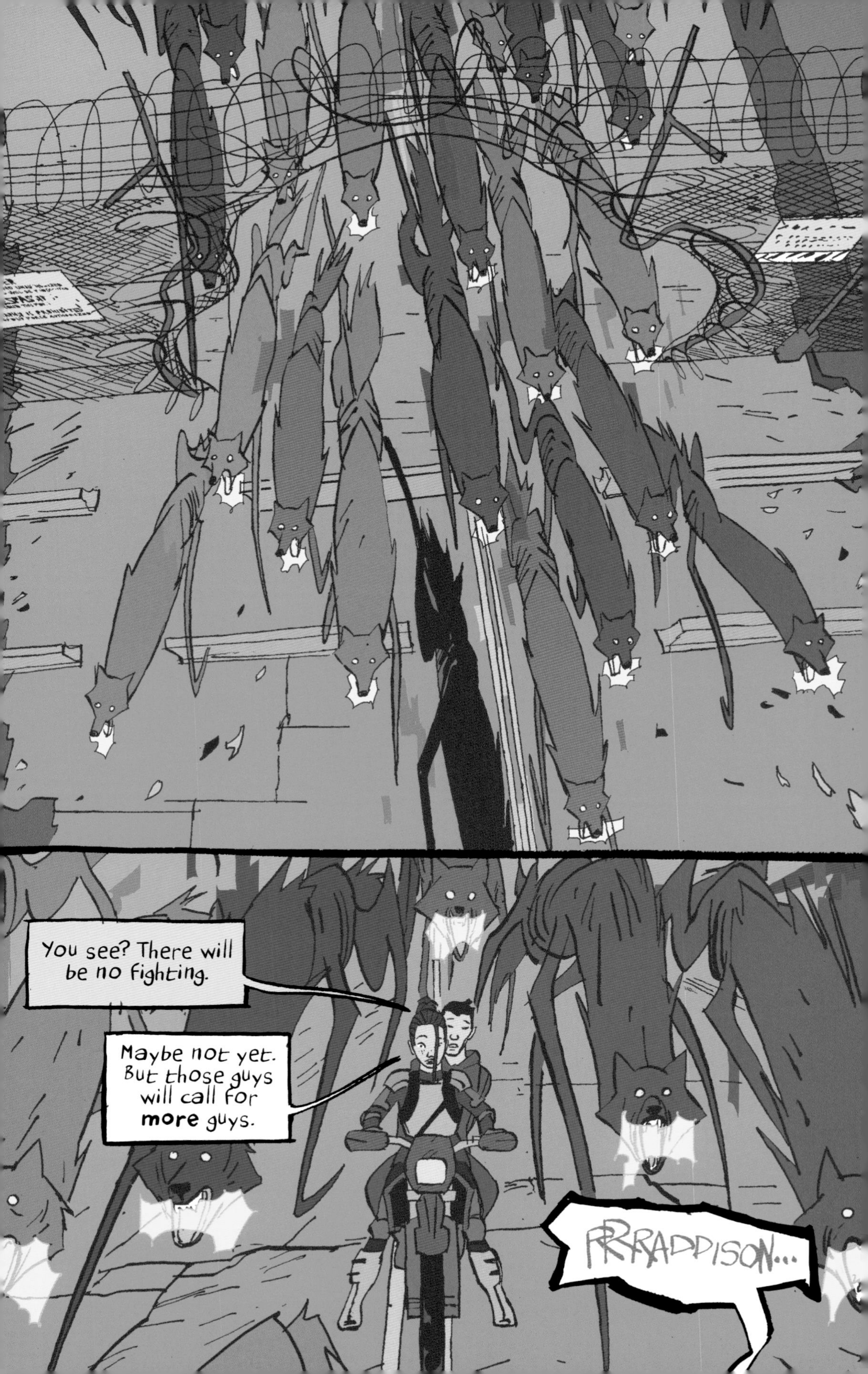
You see? There will be no fighting.
Maybe not yet. But those guys will call for **more** guys.
RRRRADDISON...

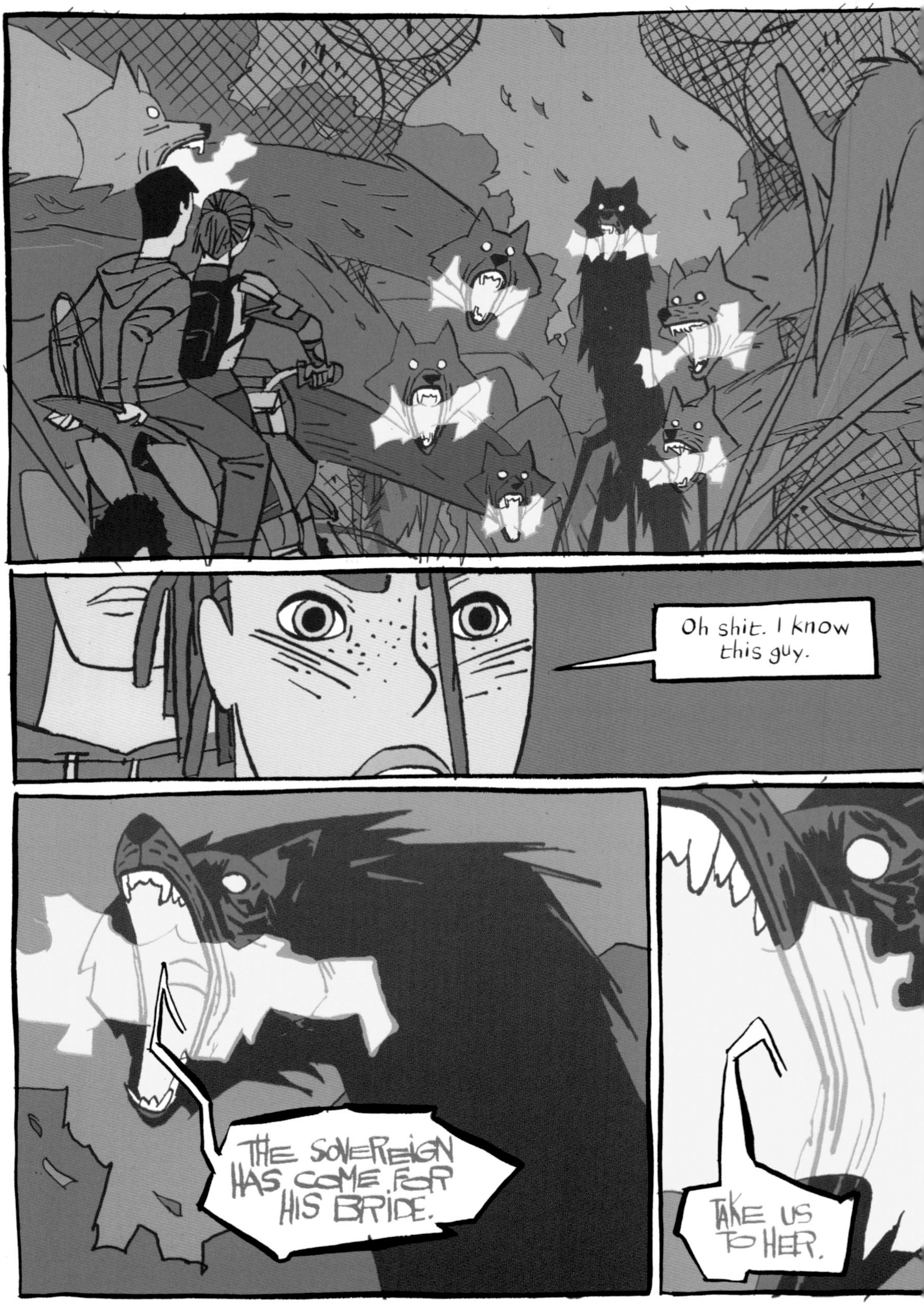
Oh shit. I know this guy.
THE SOVEREIGN HAS COME FOR HIS BRIDE.
TAKE US TO HER.

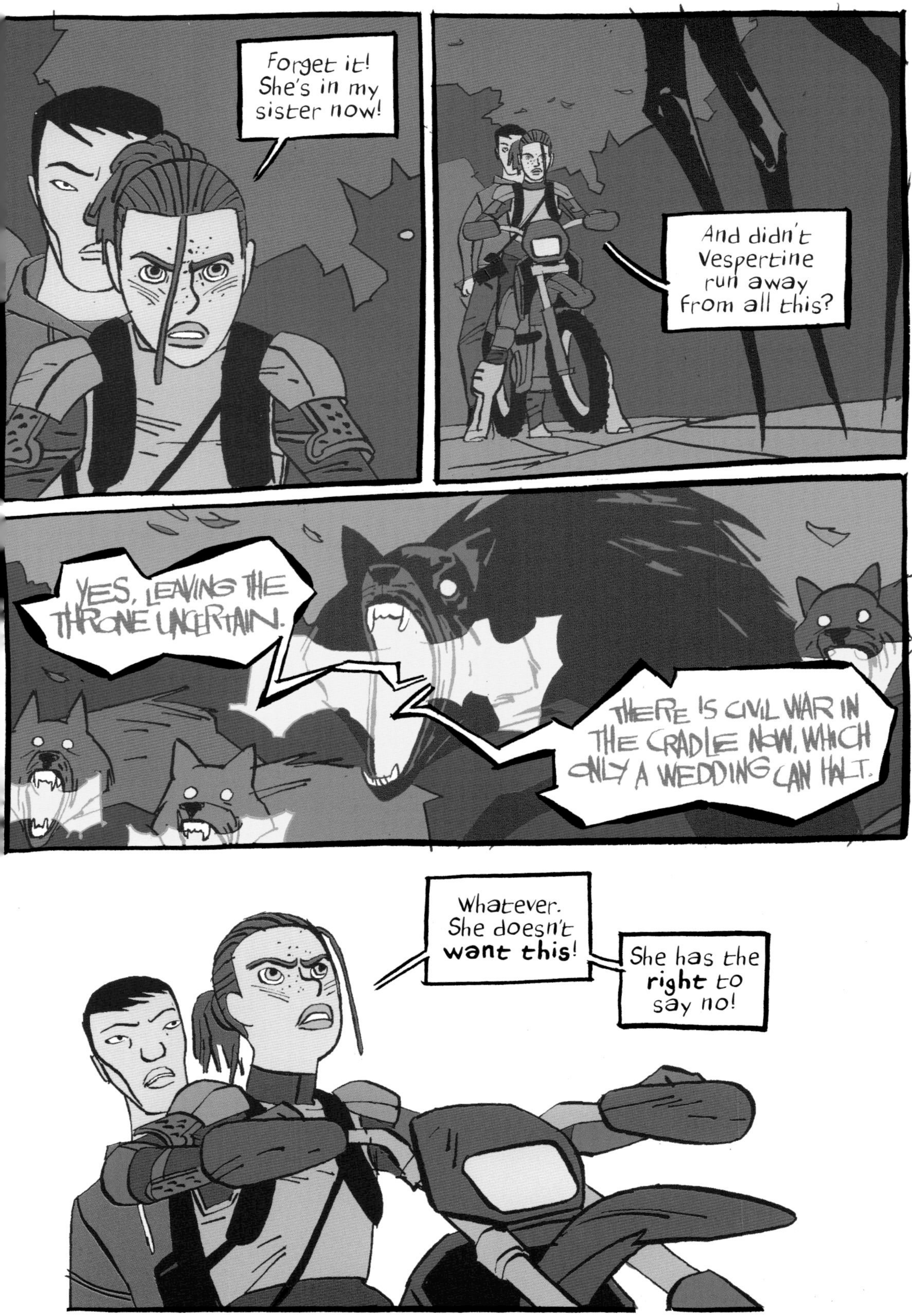
Forget it! She's in my sister now!
And didn't Vespertine run away from all this?
YES, LEAVING THE THRONE UNCERTAIN.
THERE IS CIVIL WAR IN THE CRADLE NOW, WHICH ONLY A WEDDING CAN HALT.
Whatever. She doesn't **want this**!
She has the **right** to say no!

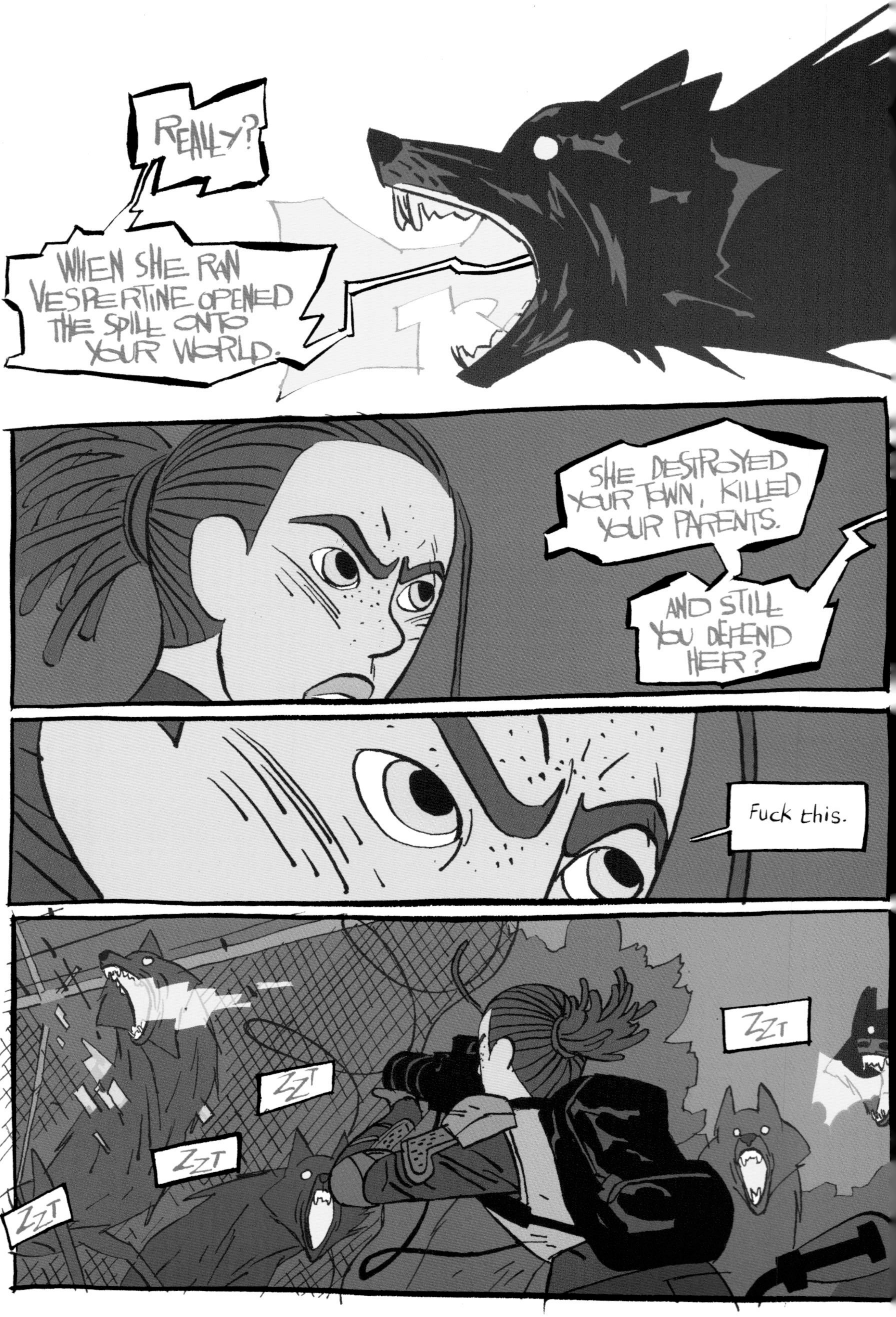
REALLY?
WHEN SHE RAN VESPERTINE OPENED THE SPILL ONTO YOUR WORLD.
SHE DESTROYED YOUR TOWN, KILLED YOUR PARENTS.
AND STILL YOU DEFEND HER?
Fuck this.
ZZT
ZZT
ZZT
ZZT

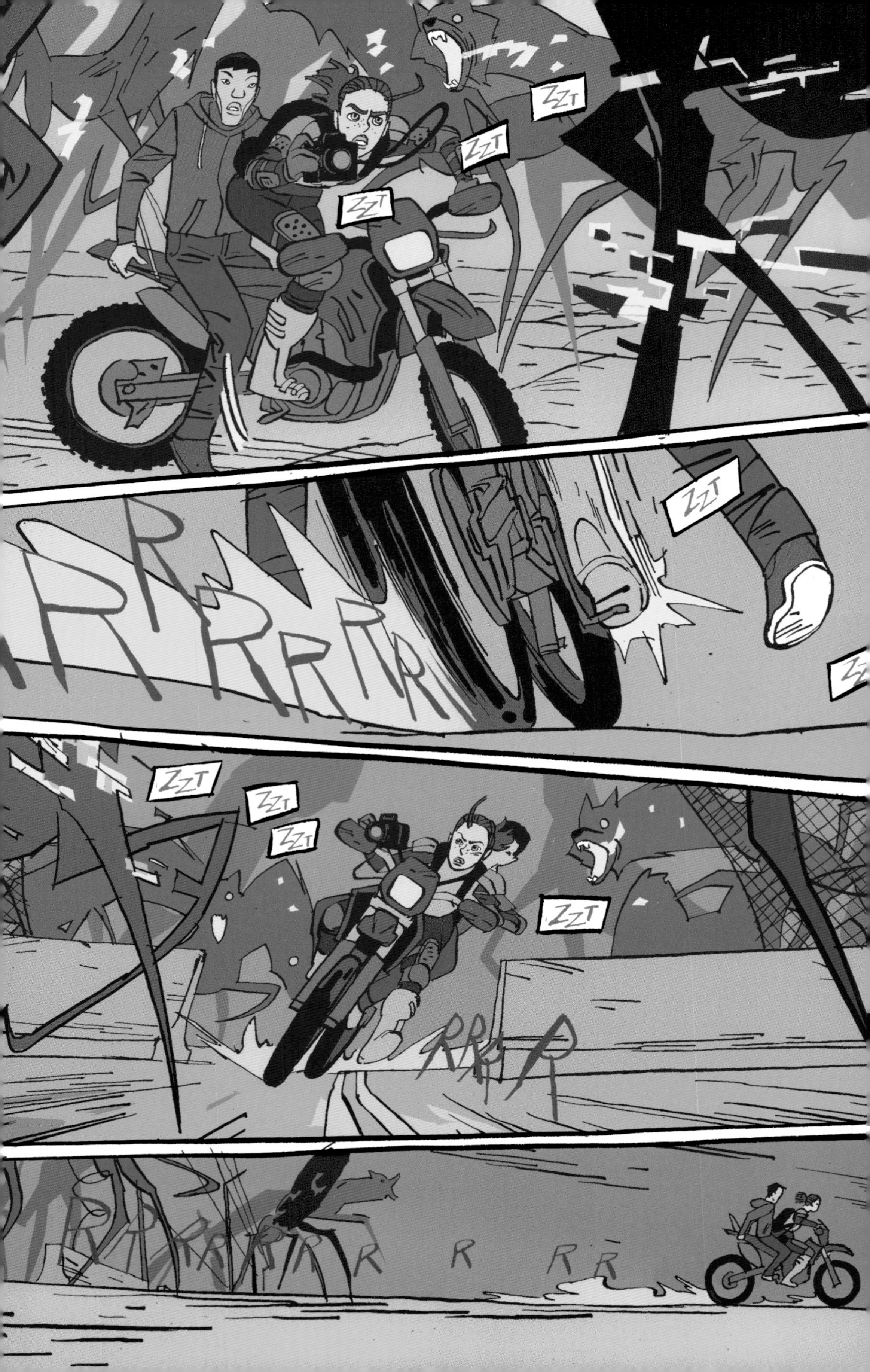
ZZT
ZZT
ZZT
ZZT
RRRRRRRR
ZZT
ZZT
ZZT
ZZT
RRRR
RRRRRRR R R RR

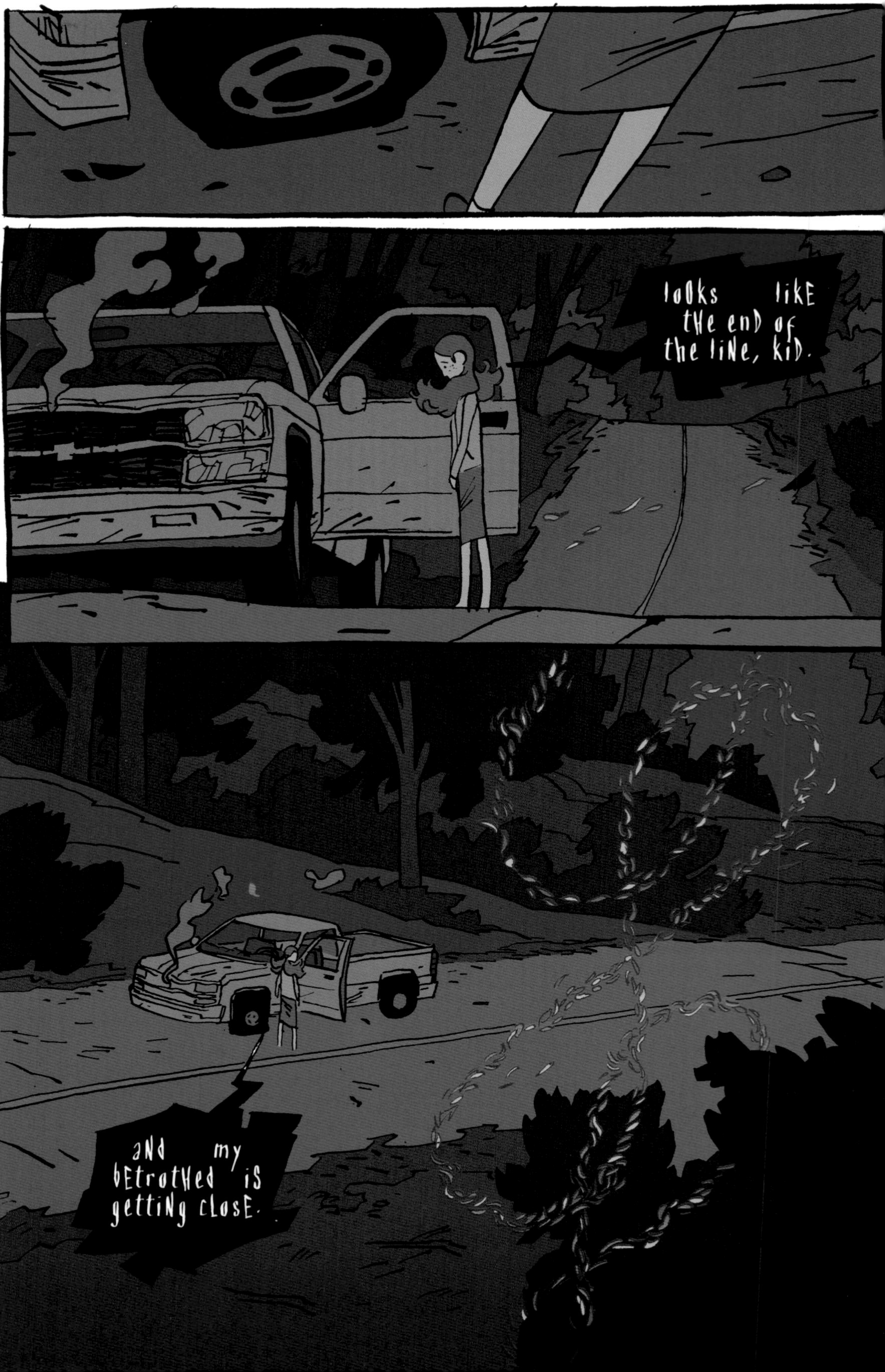
looks like the end of the line, kid.
and my betrothed is getting close.

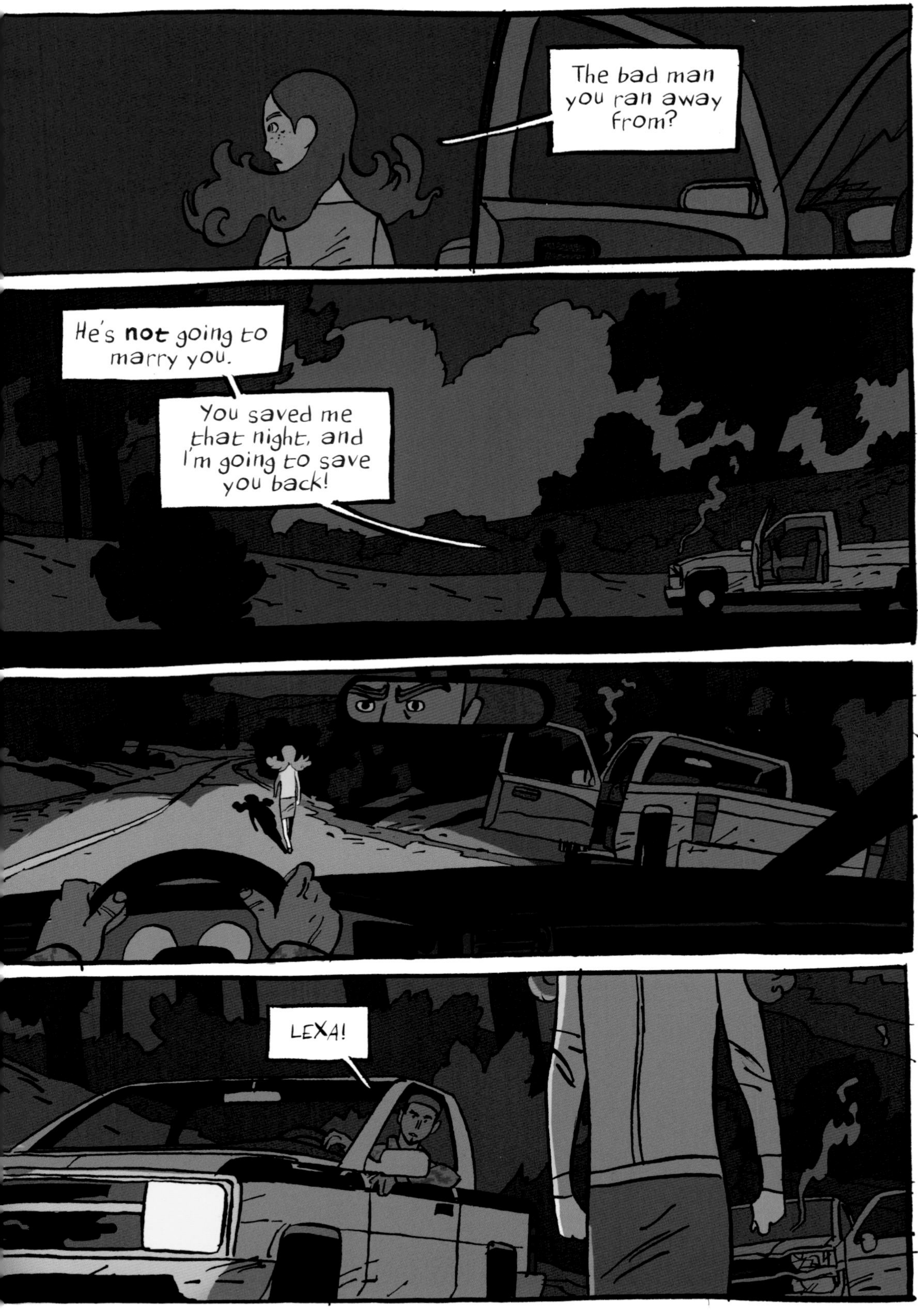
The bad man you ran away from?
He's **not** going to marry you.
You saved me that night, and I'm going to save you back!
LEXA!

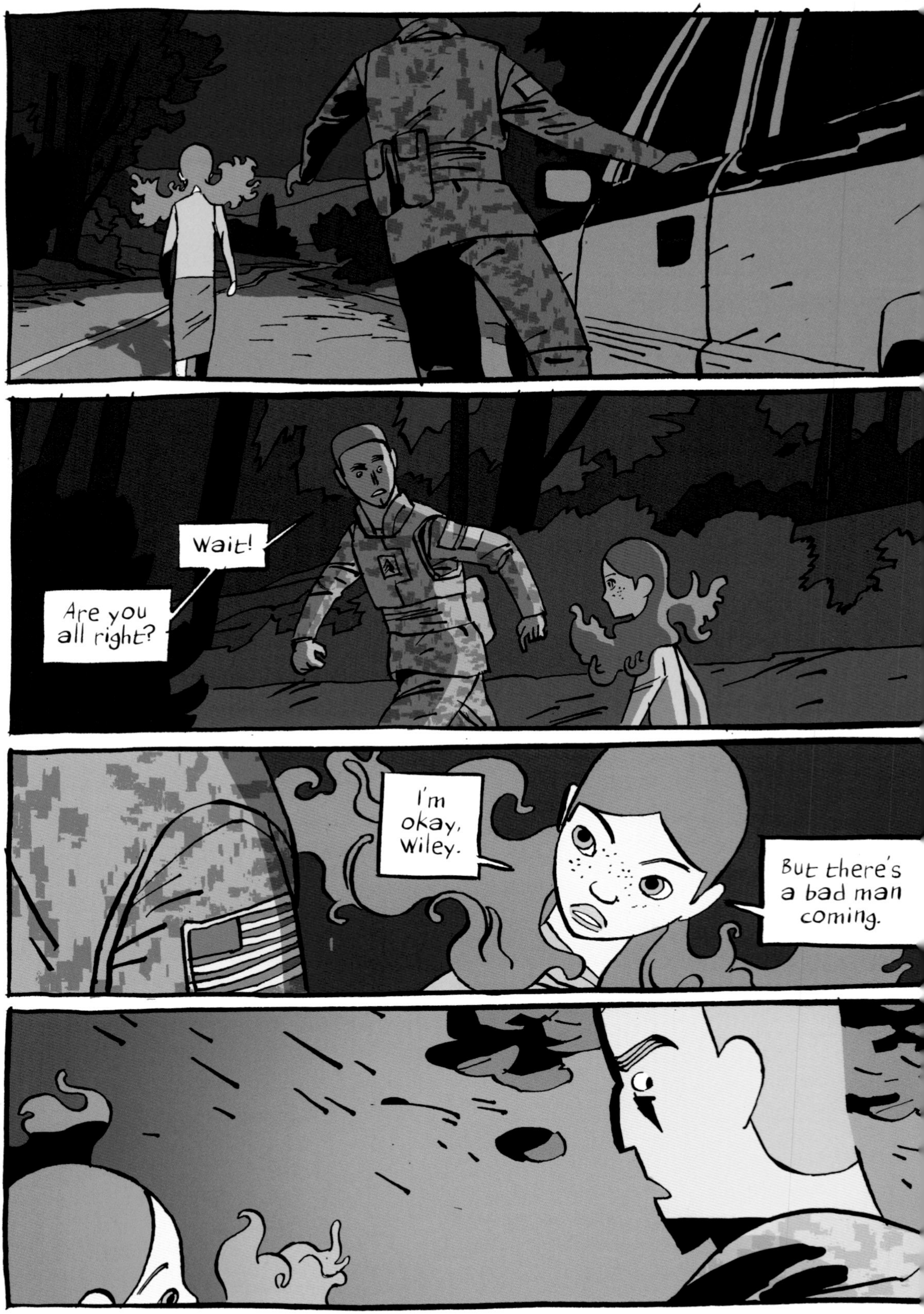
Wait!
Are you all right?
I'm okay, Wiley.
But there's a bad man coming.

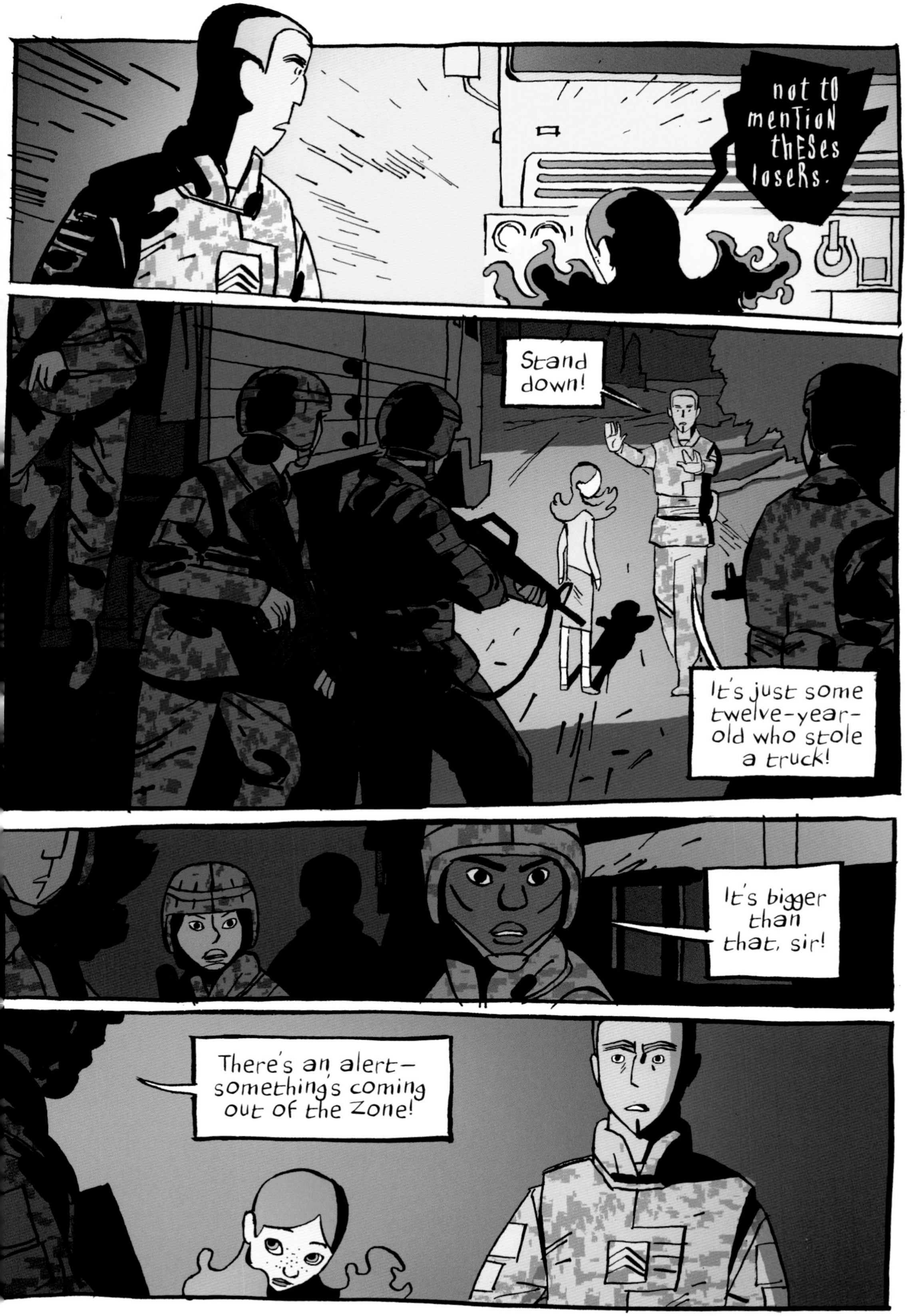
not to mention theses losers.
Stand down!
It's just some twelve-year-old who stole a truck!
It's bigger than that, sir!
There's an alert—something's coming out of the Zone!

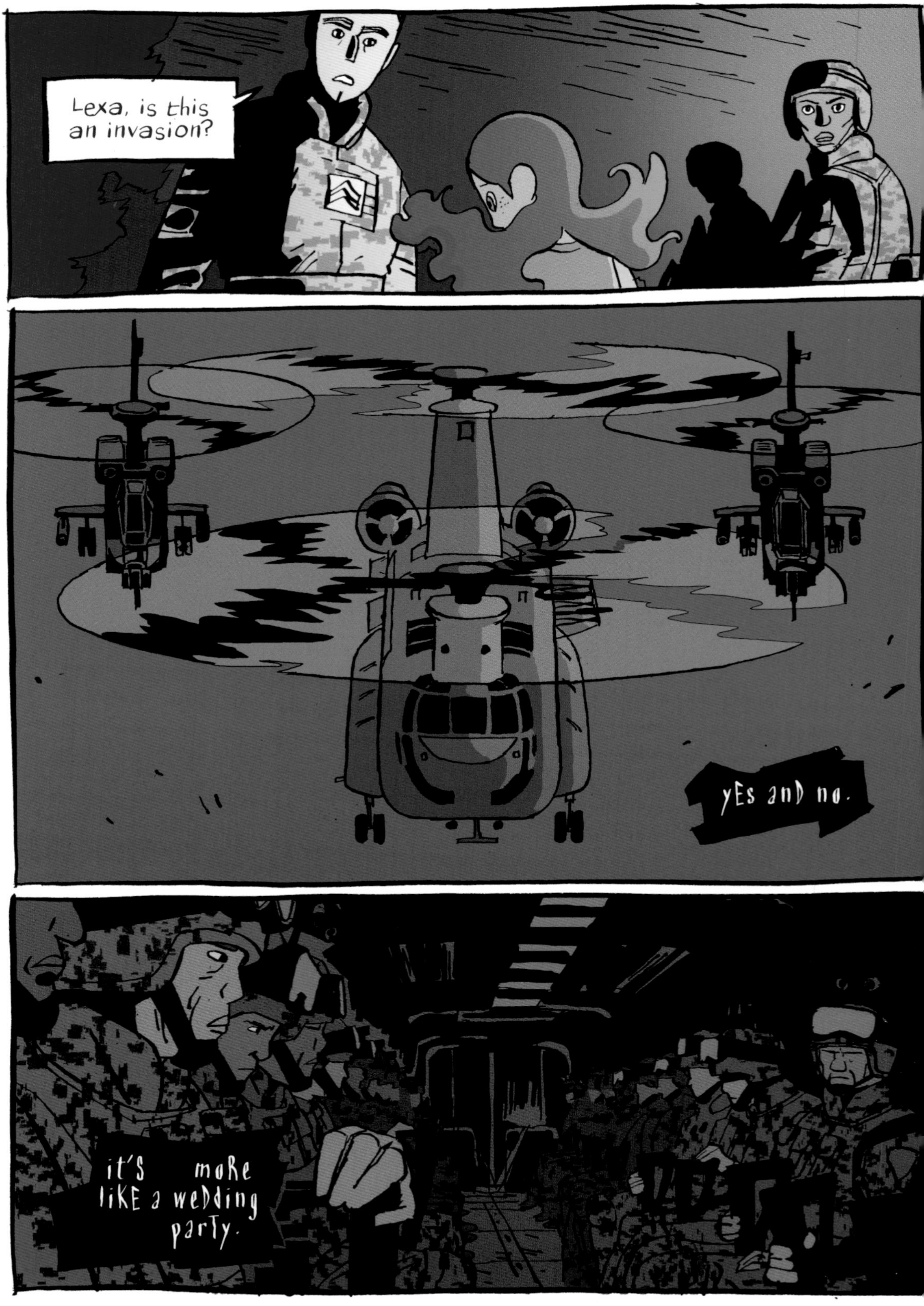
Lexa, is this an invasion?
yEs anD no.
it's more like a weDDing party.

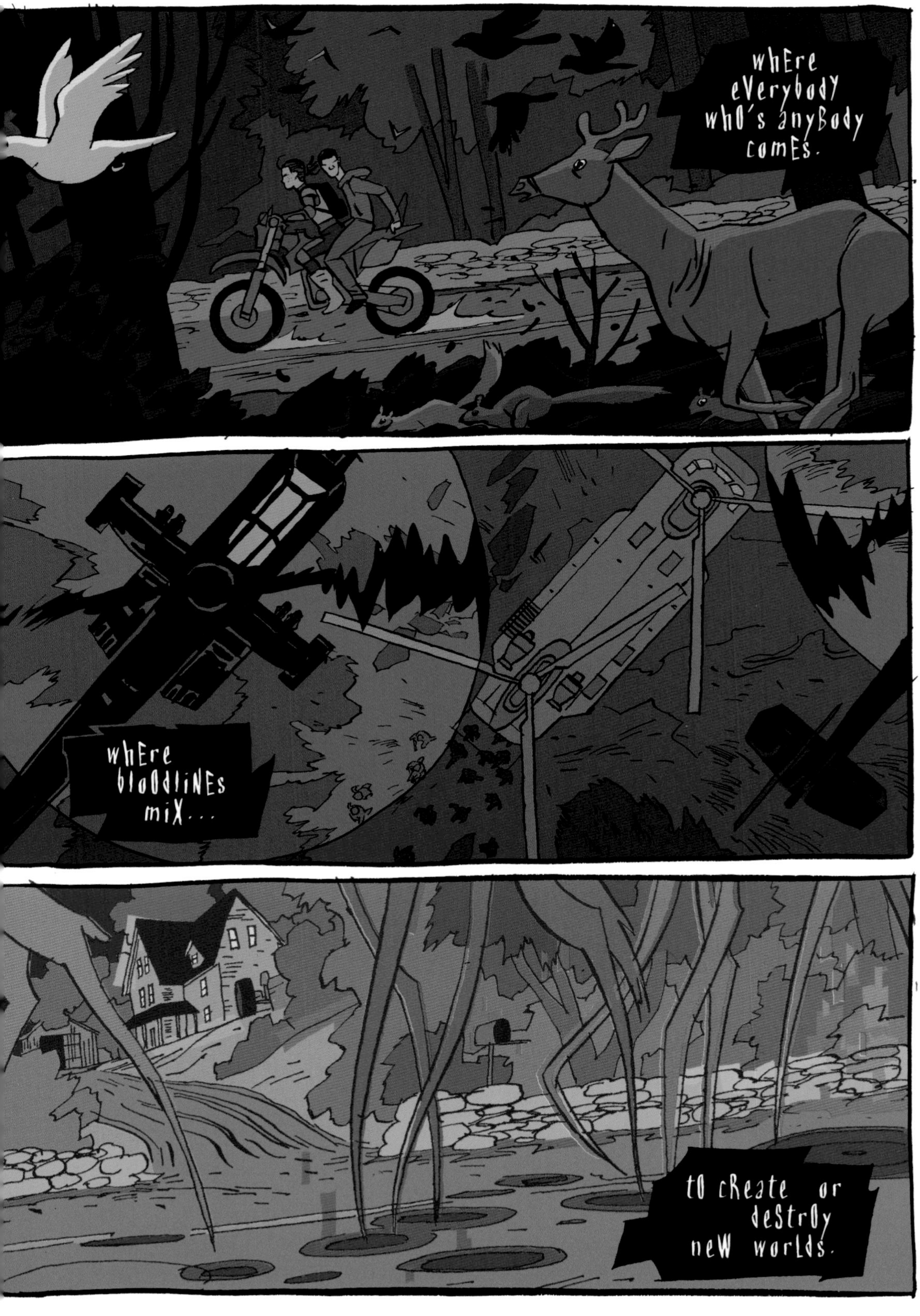
where everybody who's anybody comes.
where bloodlines mix...
to create or destroy new worlds.

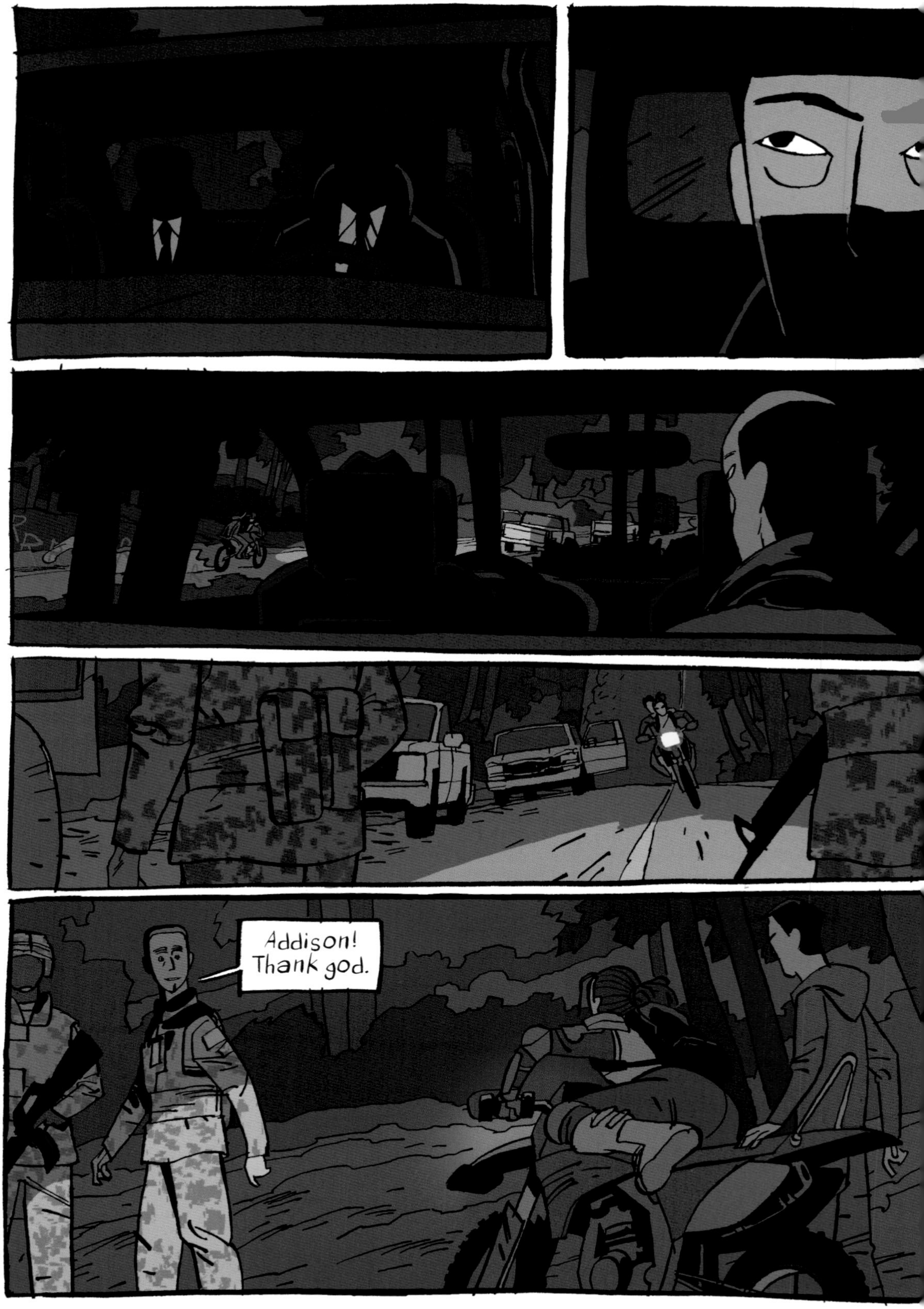
Addison! Thank god.

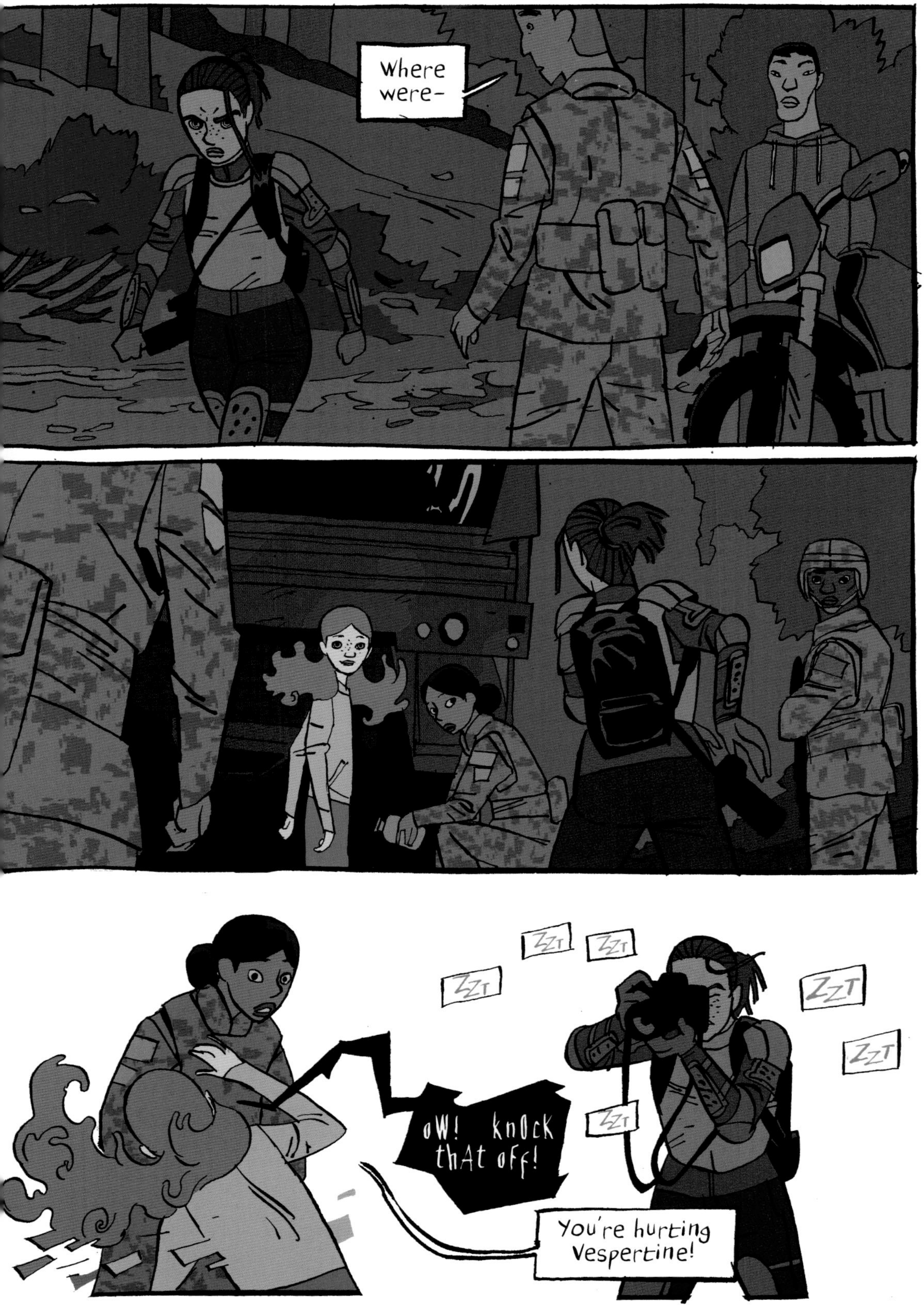
Where were-
ZZT
ZZT
ZZT
ZZT
ZZT
ZZT
OW! KNOCK THAT OFF!
You're hurting Vespertine!

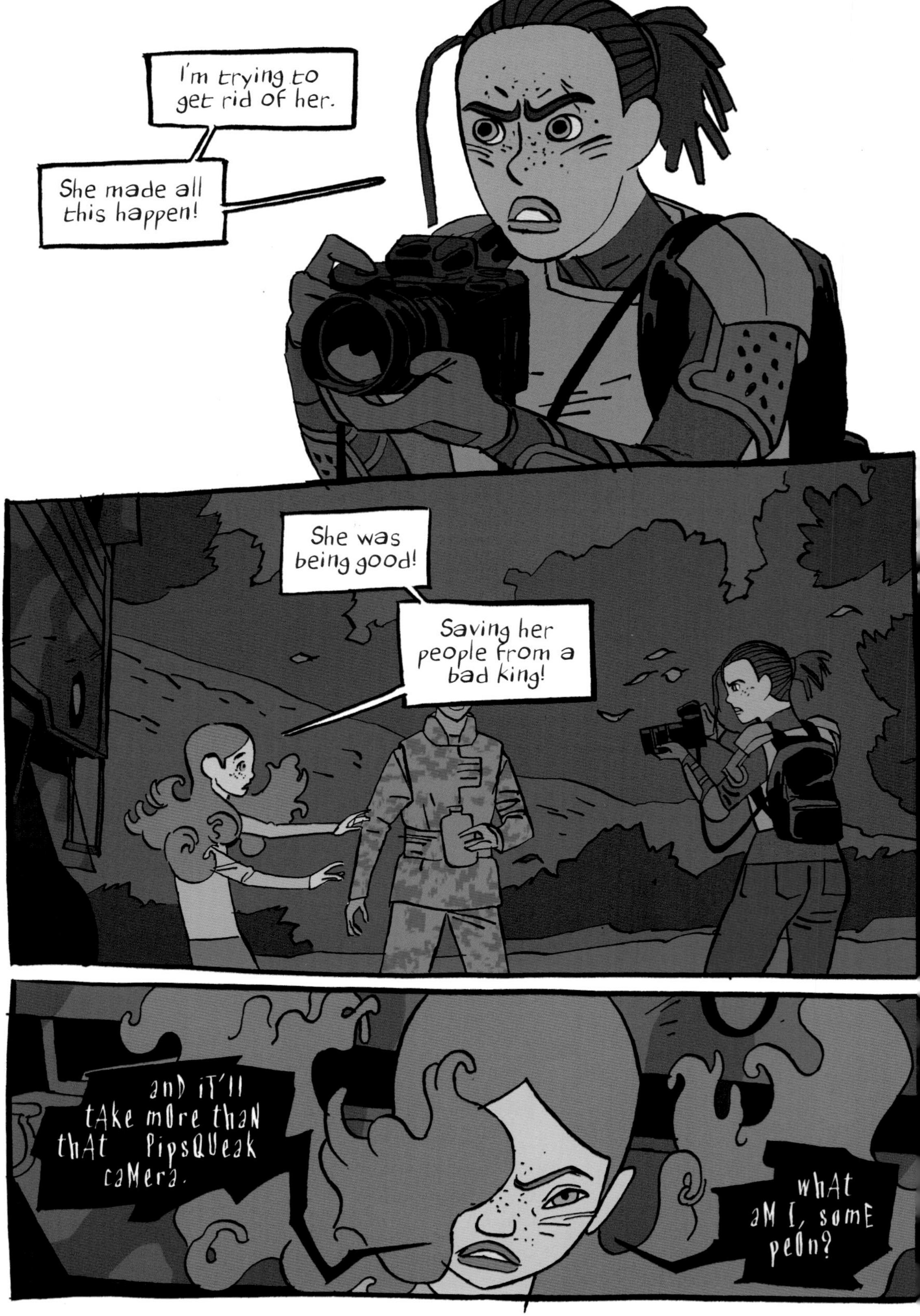
I'm trying to get rid of her.
She made all this happen!
She was being good!
Saving her people from a bad king!
and it'll take more than that pipsqueak camera.
what am I, some peon?

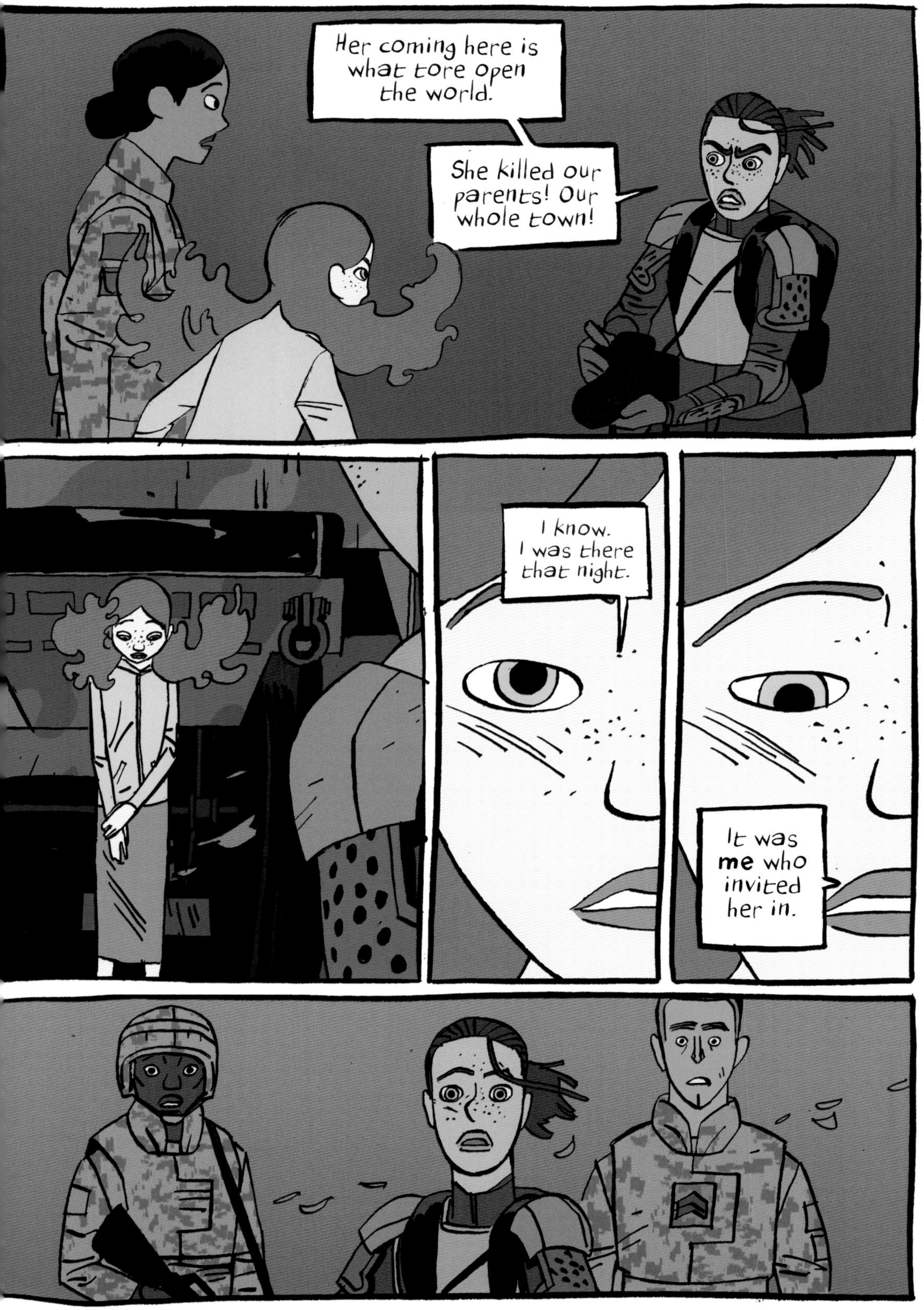
Her coming here is what tore open the world.
She killed our parents! Our whole town!
I know. I was there that night.
It was **me** who invited her in.

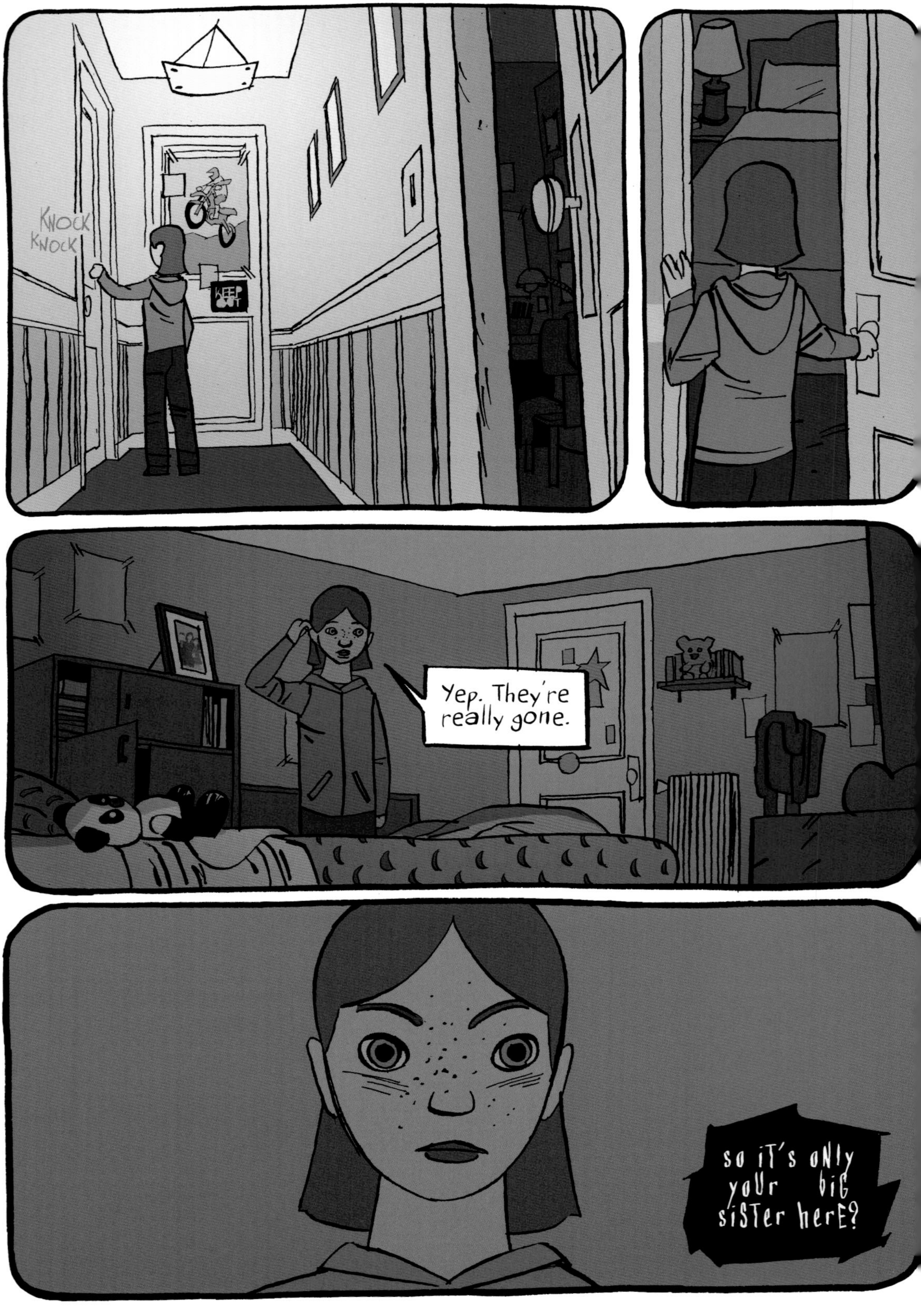
KNOCK
KNOCK
KEEP OUT
Yep. They're really gone.
so it's only your big sister here?

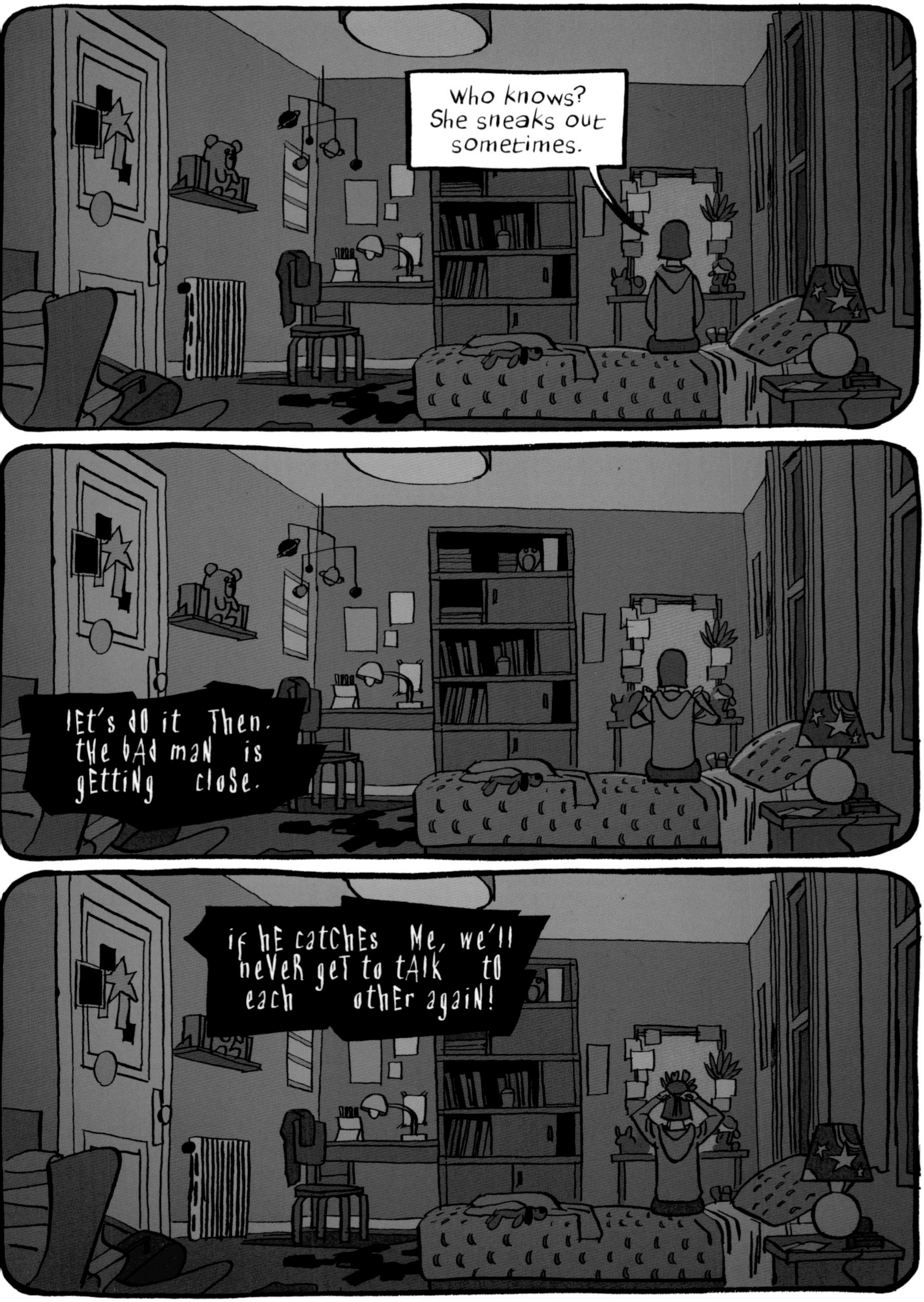
Who knows? She sneaks out sometimes.
lEt's do it Then. tHe bAd maN is gEttiNg close.
if hE catchEs Me, we'll neveR get to tAlk to each other agaiN!

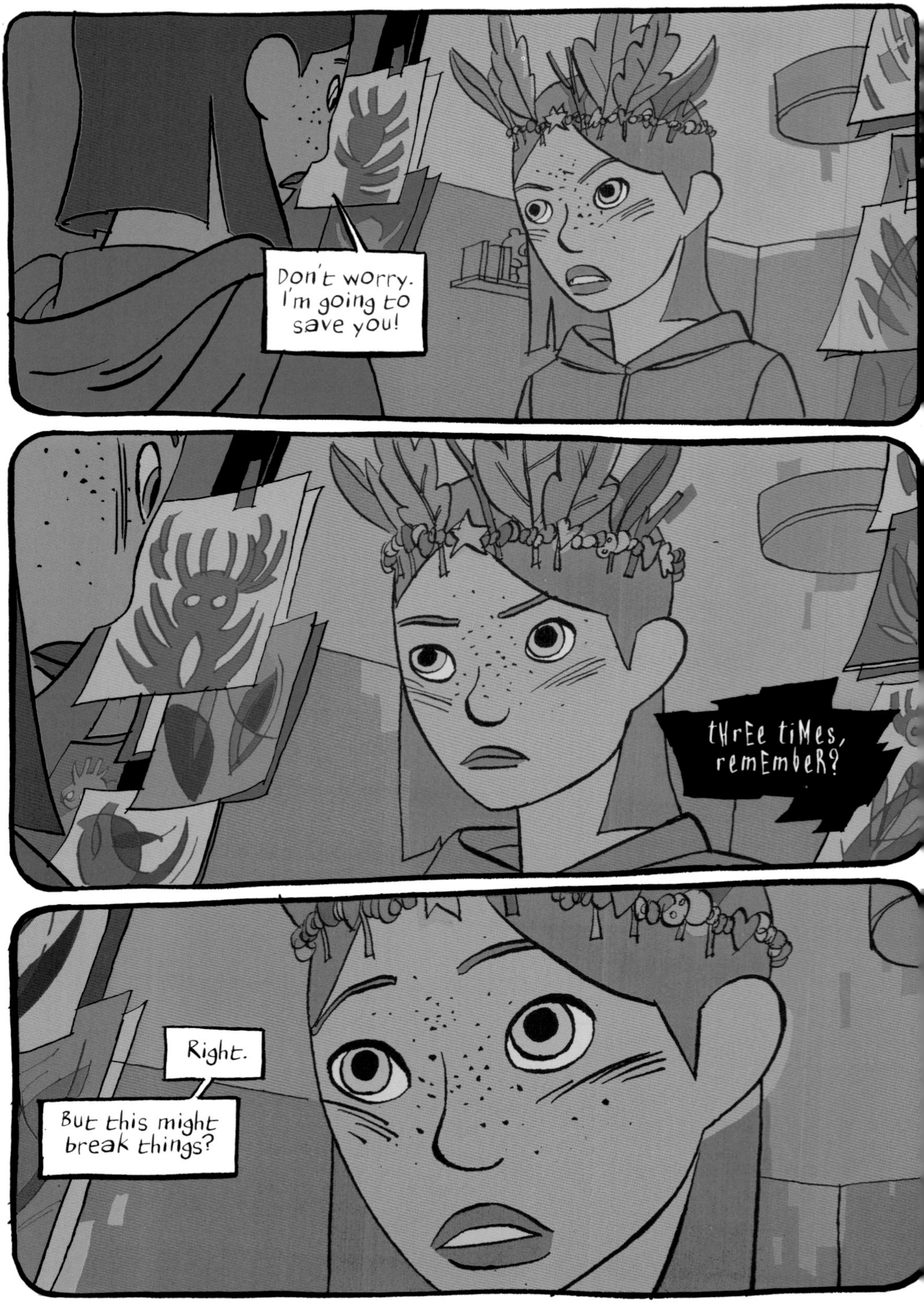
Don't worry. I'm going to save you!
three times, remember?
Right.
But this might break things?

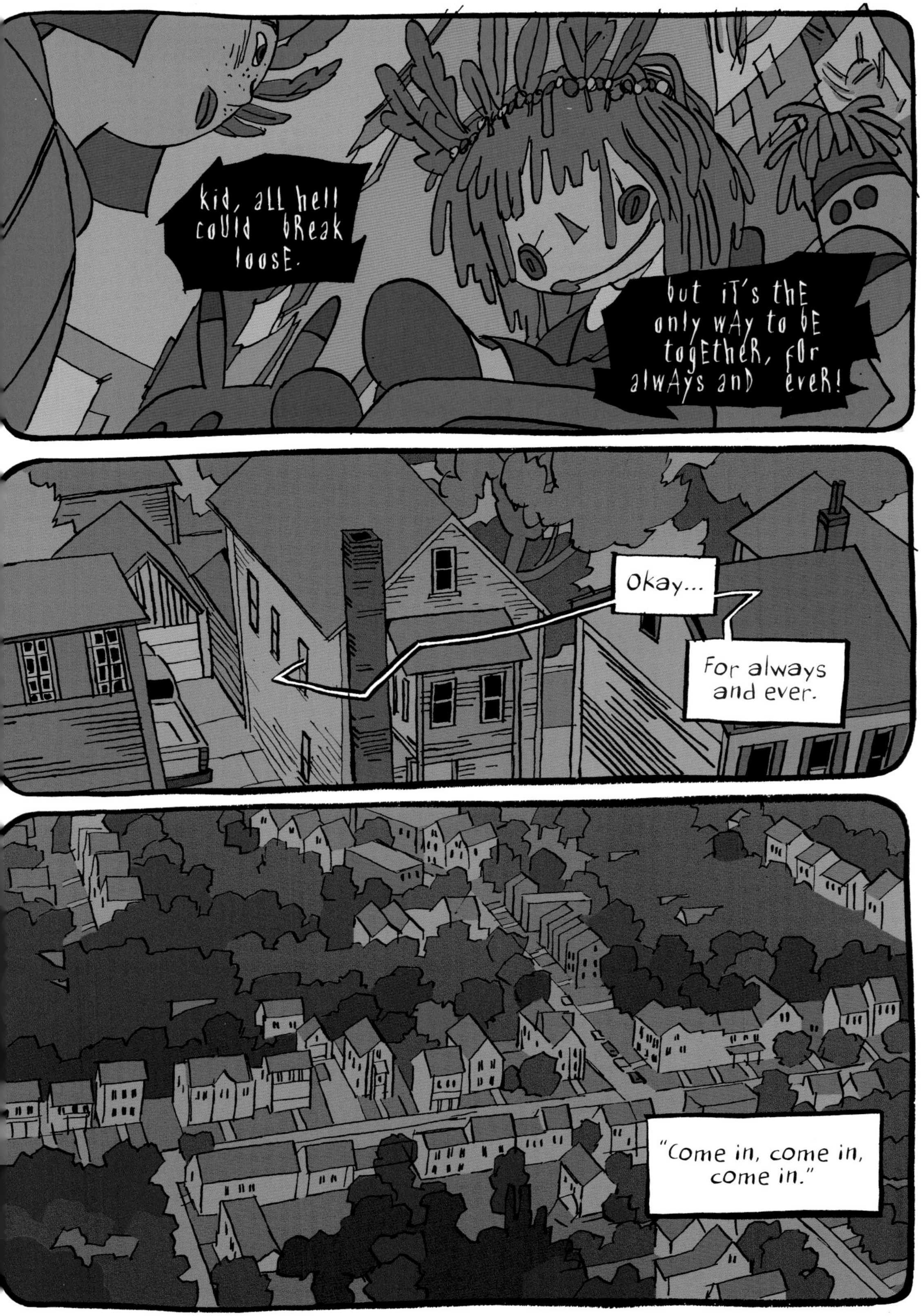
kid, all hell could break loose.
but it's the only way to be together, for always and ever!
Okay...
For always and ever.
"Come in, come in, come in."

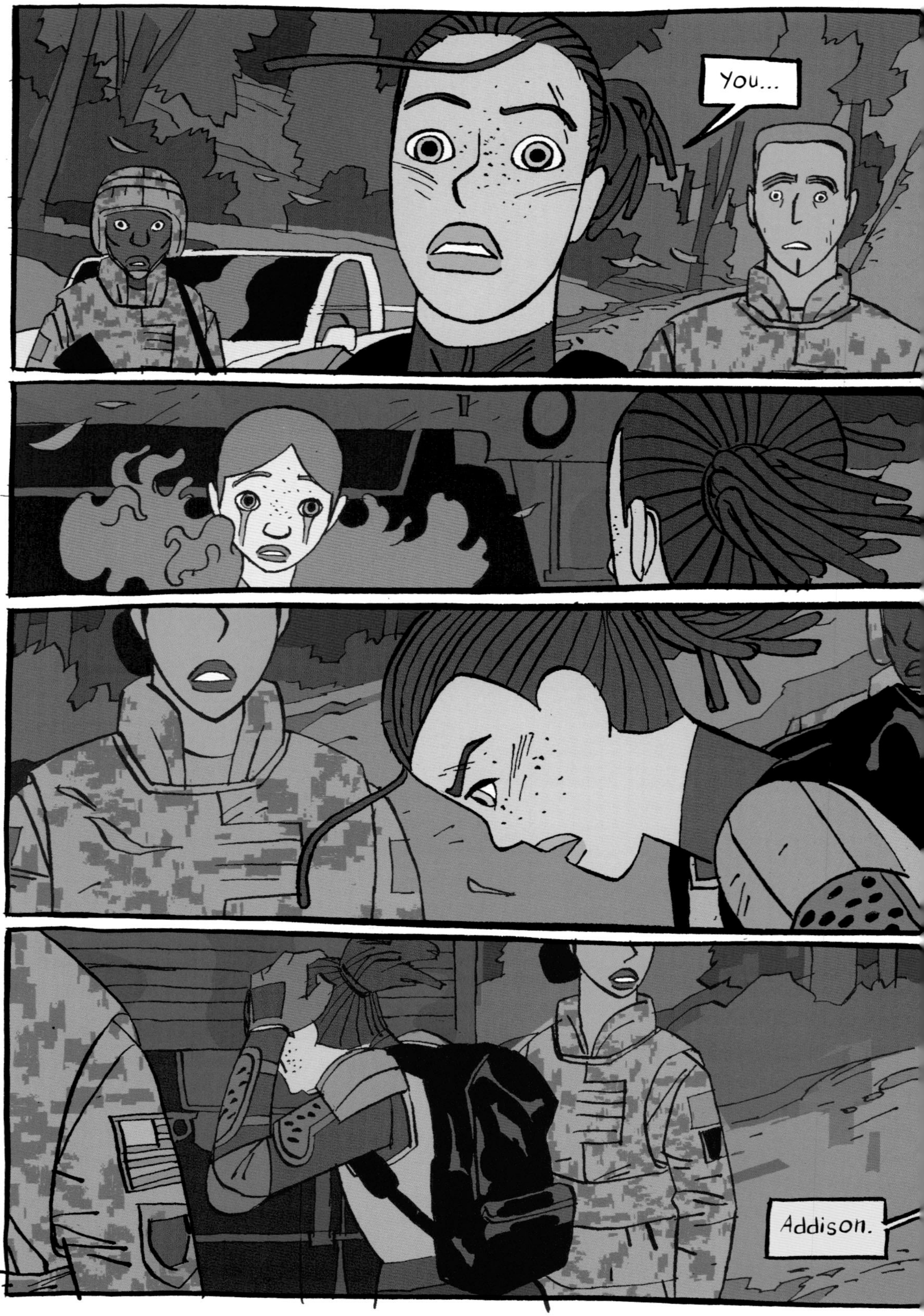
You...
Addison.

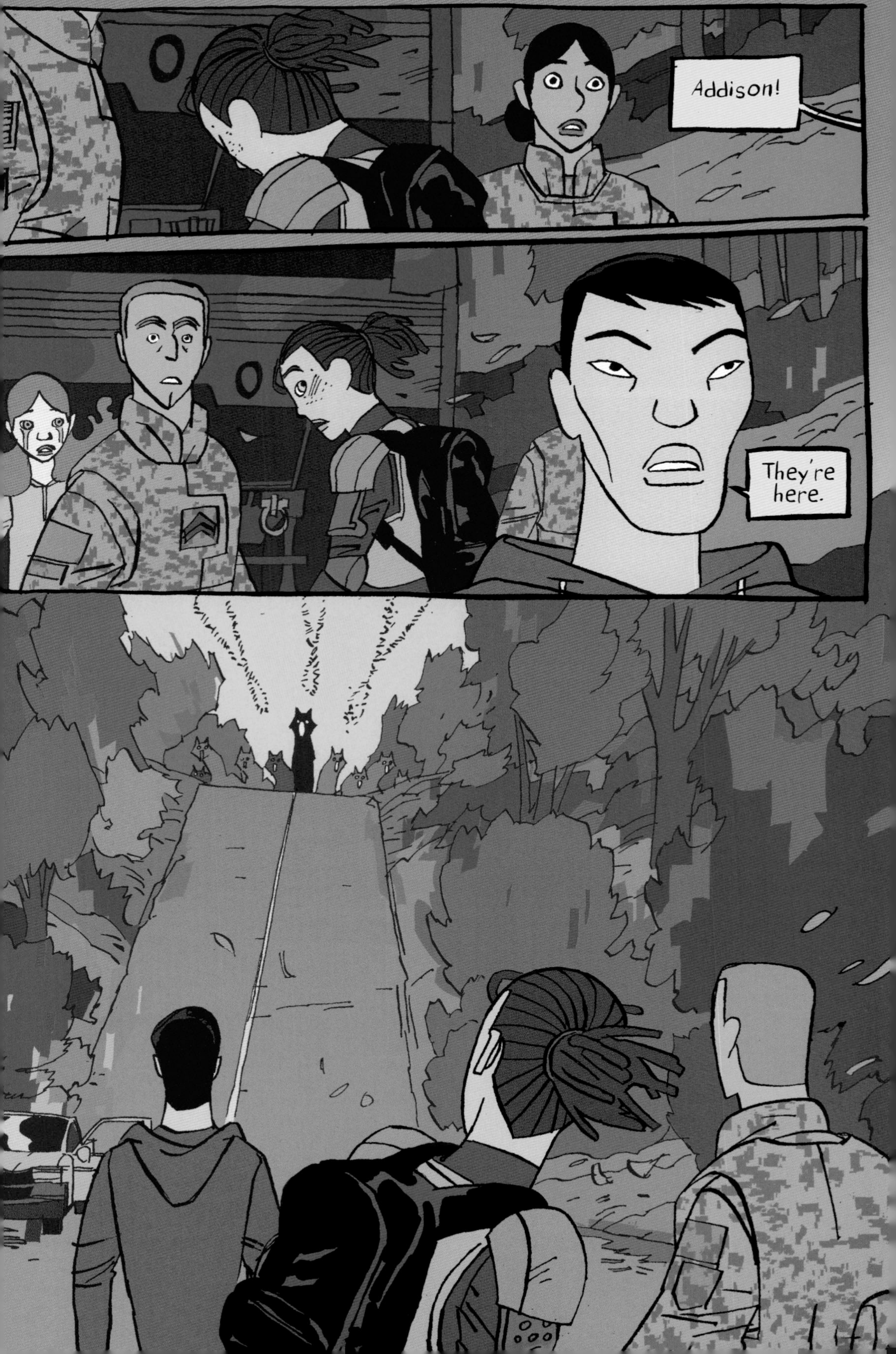
Addison!
They're here.

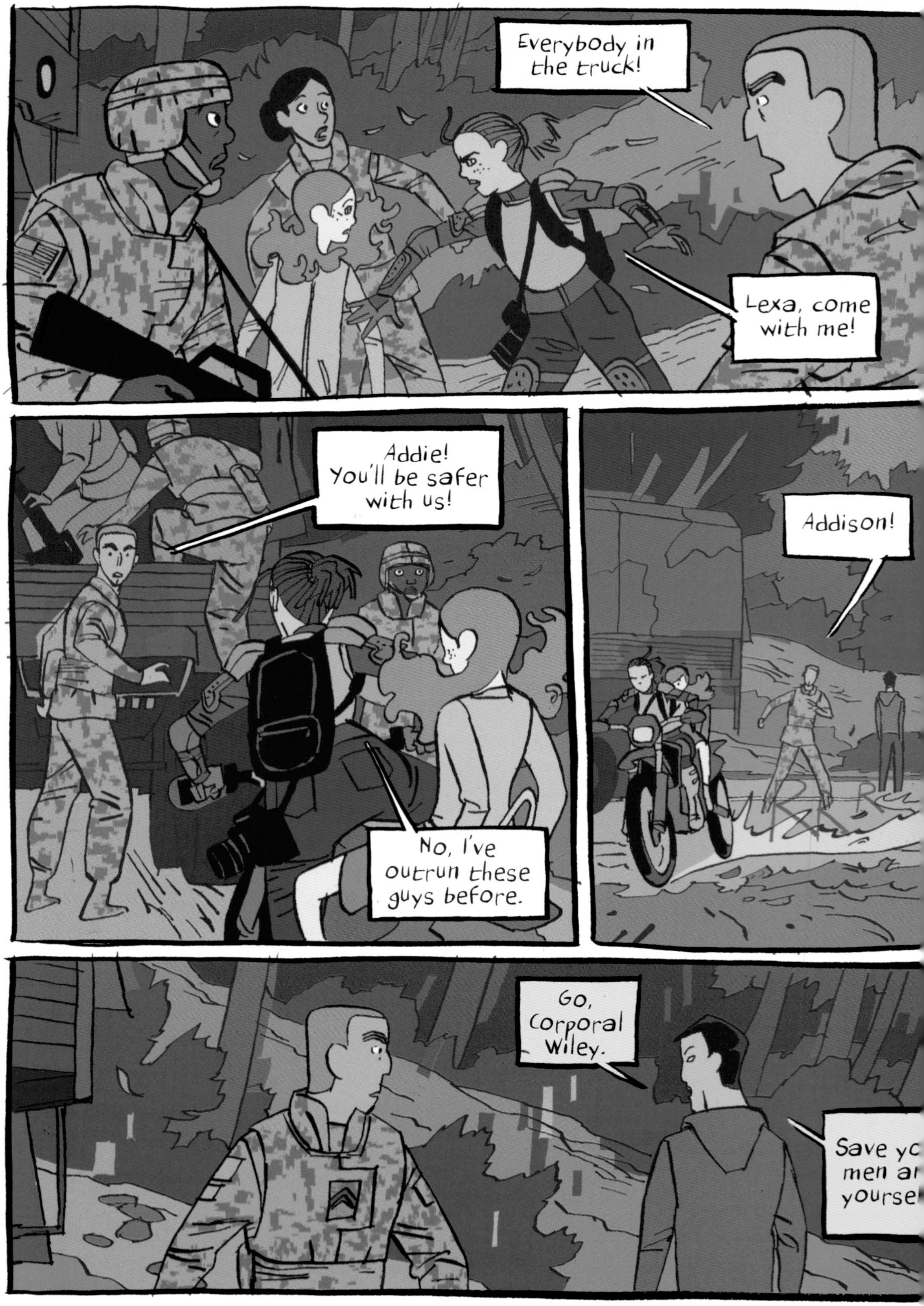
Everybody in the truck!
Lexa, come with me!
Addie! You'll be safer with us!
No, I've outrun these guys before.
Addison!
Go, Corporal Wiley.
Save
men

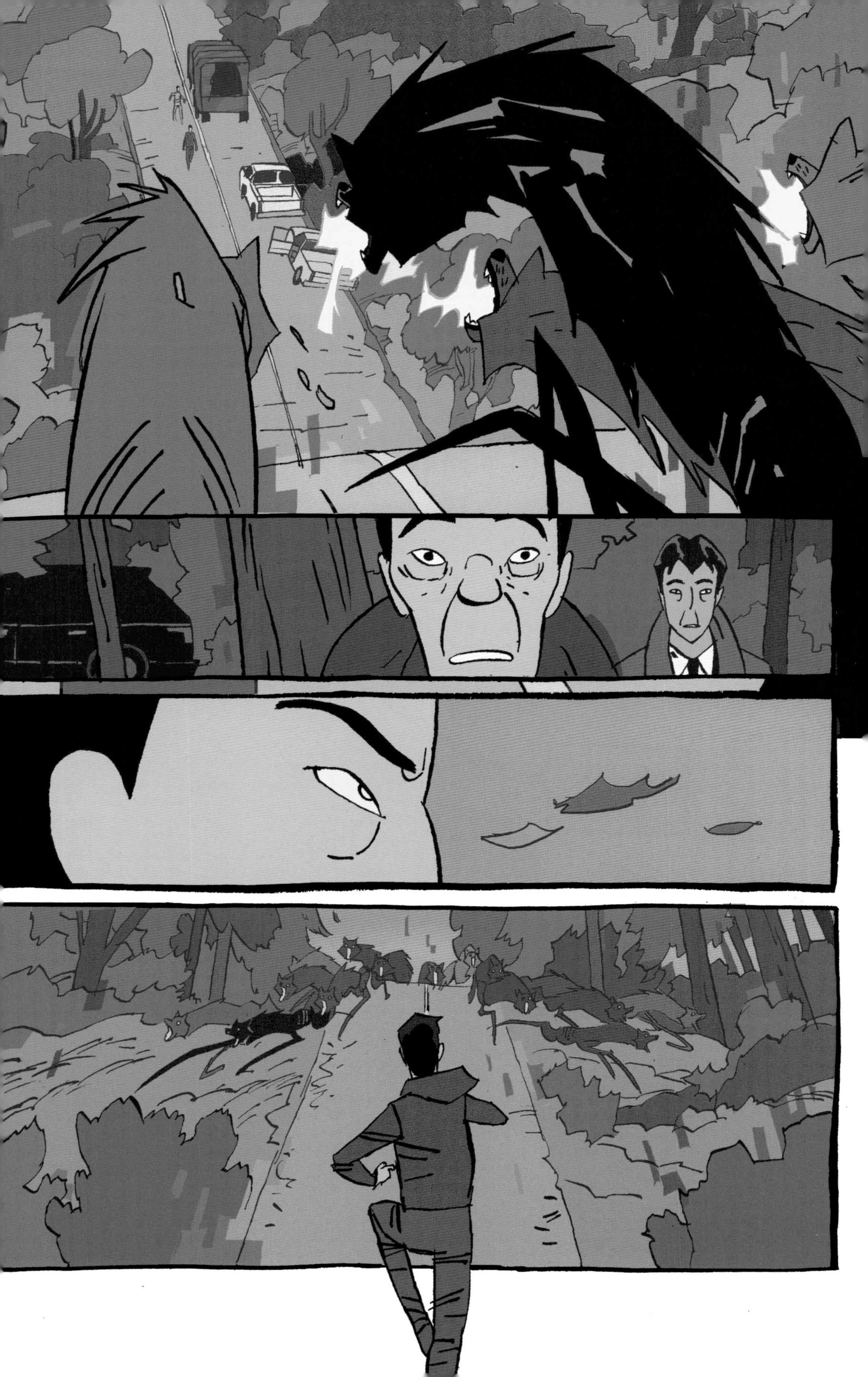

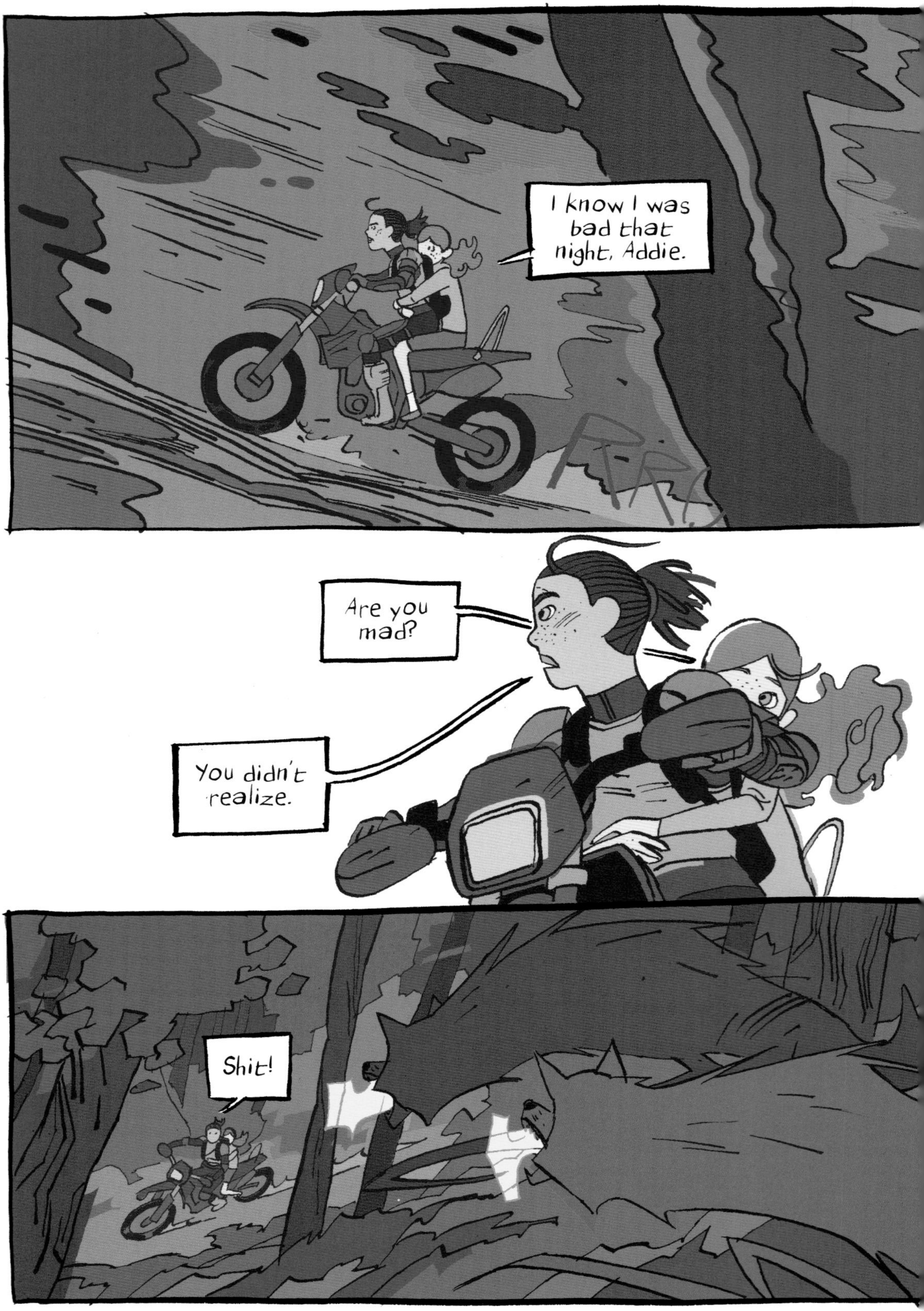
I know I was bad that night, Addie.
Are you mad?
You didn't realize.
Shit!

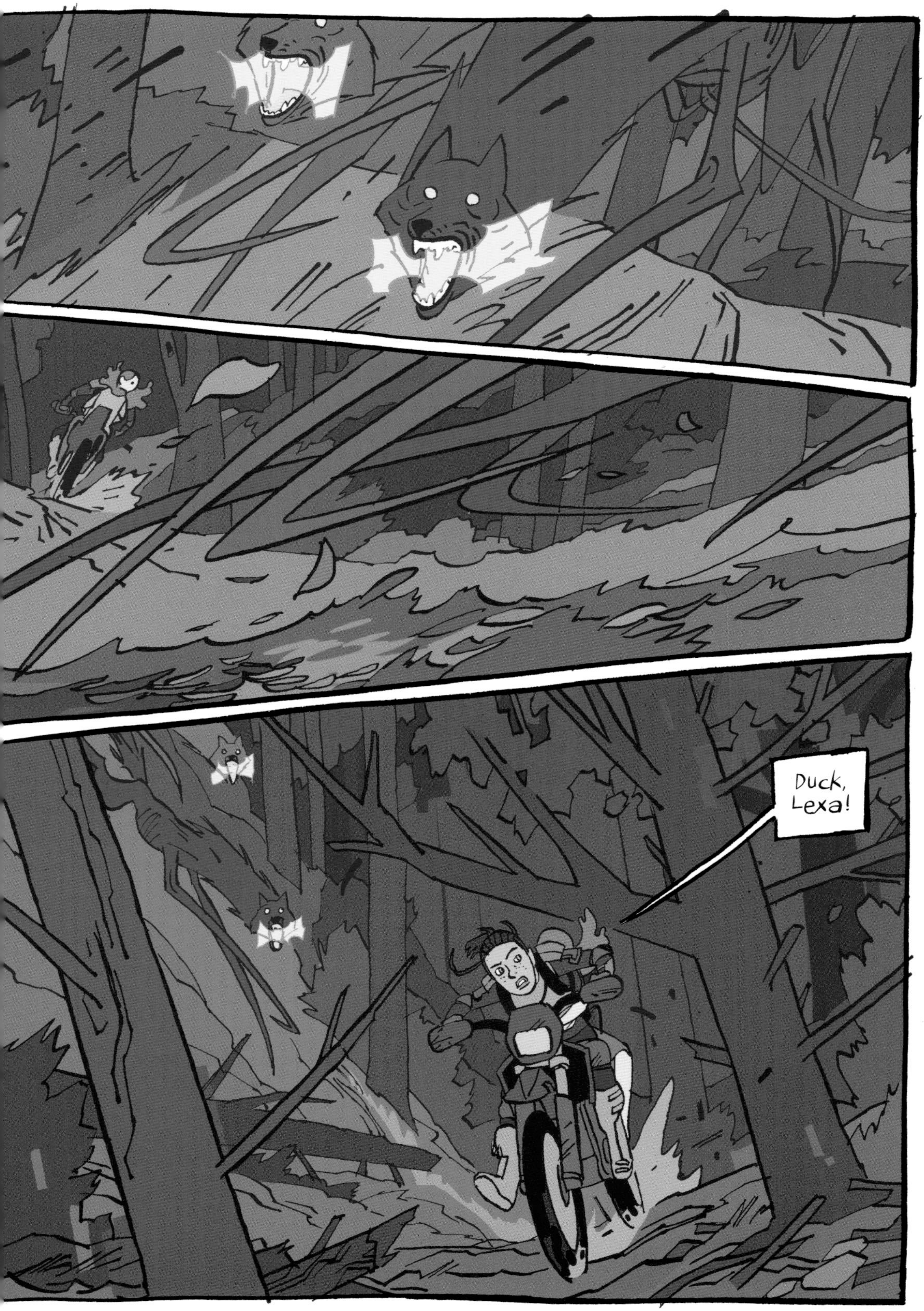
Duck, Lexa!

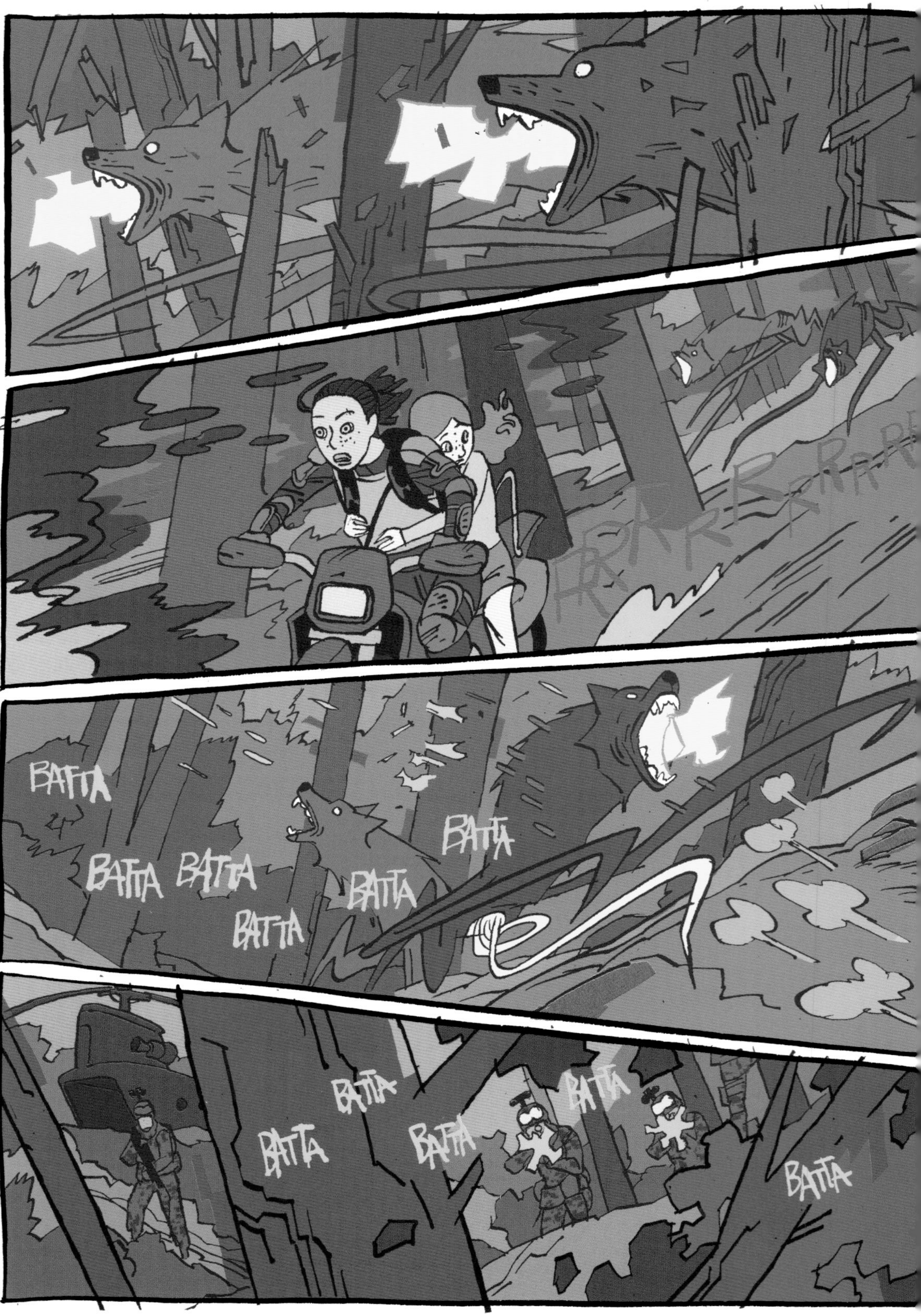
RRRRRRRRRR
BATTA
BATTA
BATTA
BATTA
BATTA
BATTA
BATTA
BATTA
BATTA
BATTA
BATTA

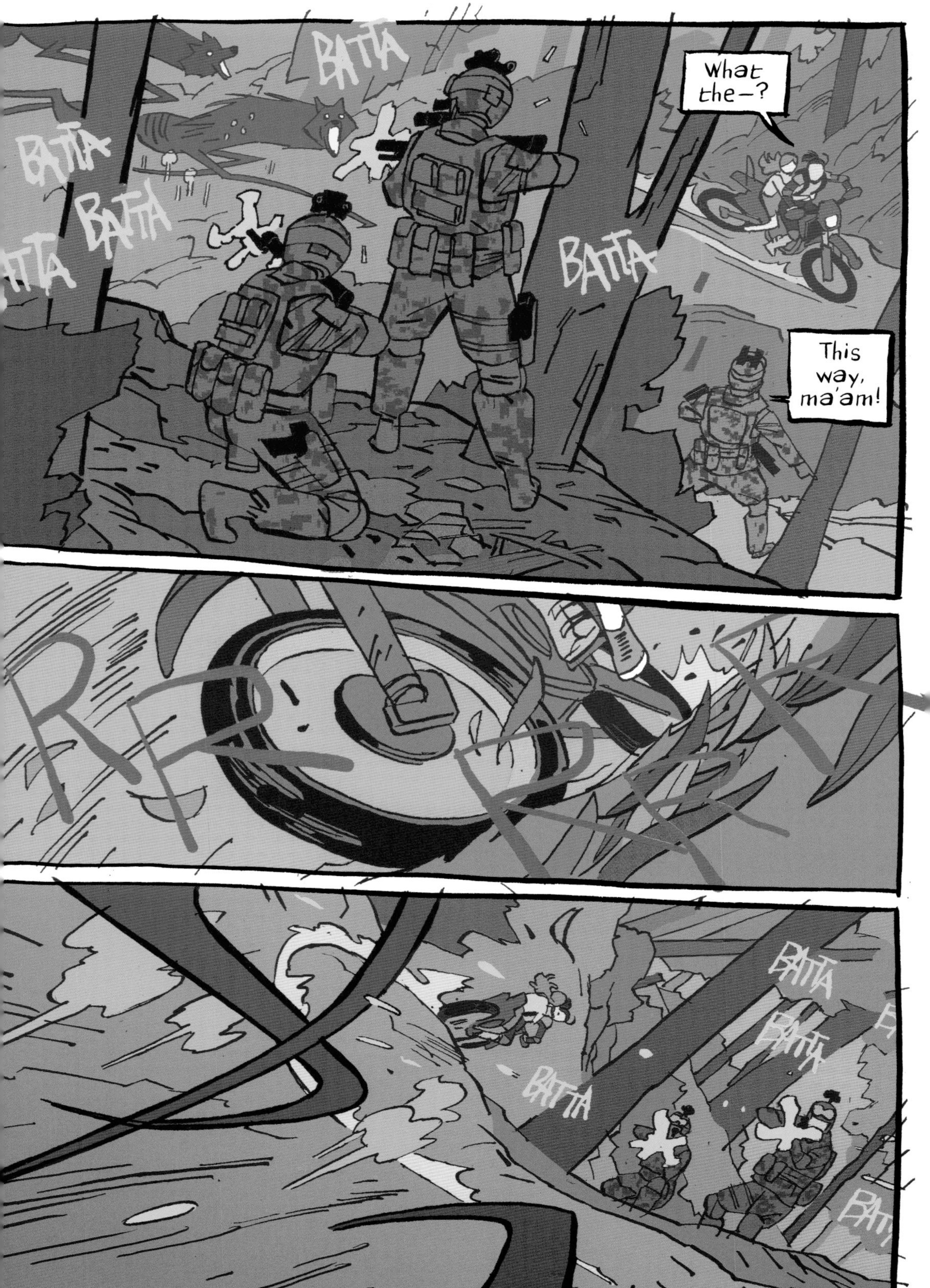
BATTA
BATTA
BATTA
BATTA
BATTA
What the—?
This way, ma'am!
BATTA
BATTA
BATTA
BATTA

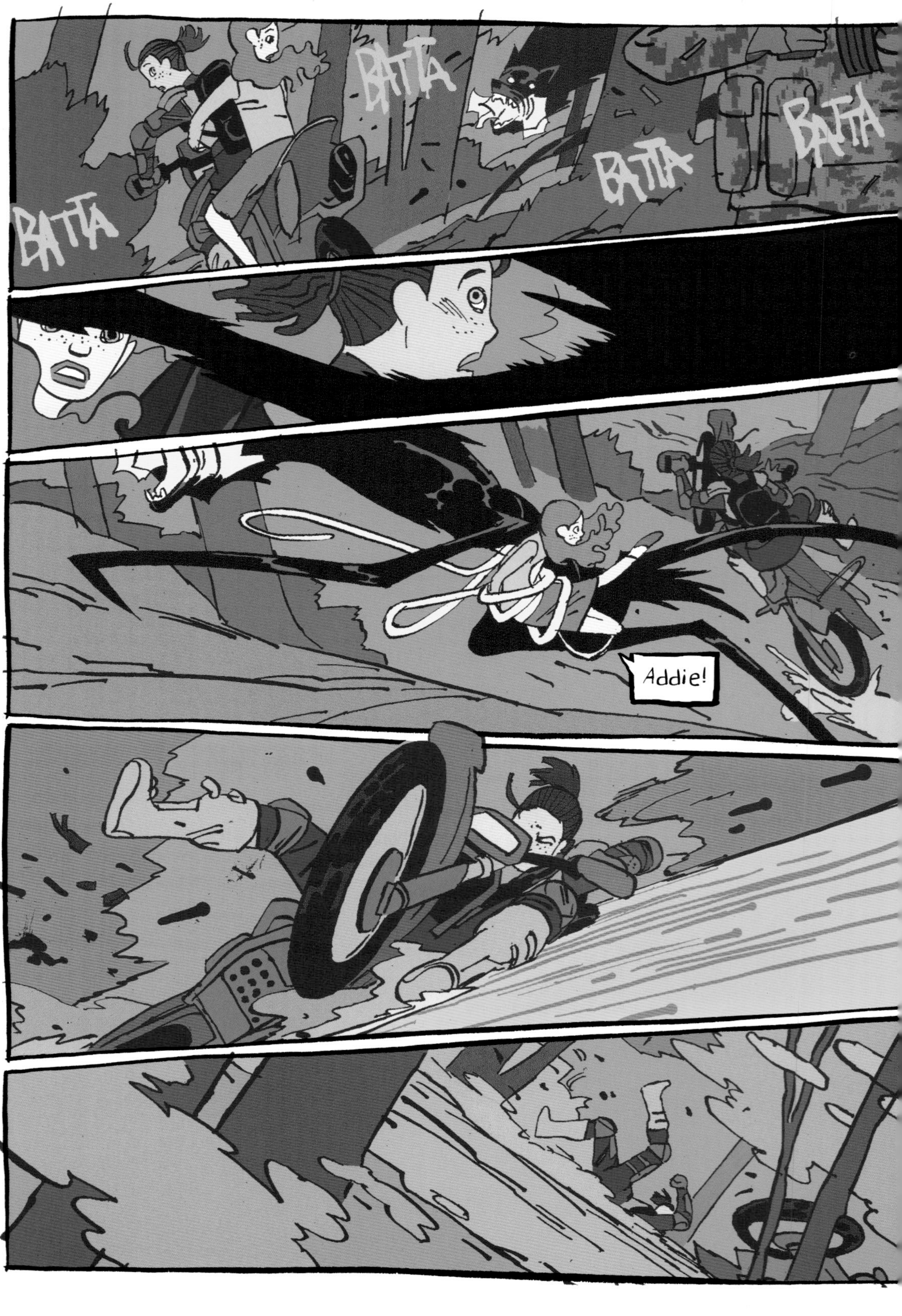
BATTA
BATTA
BATTA
BATTA
Addie!

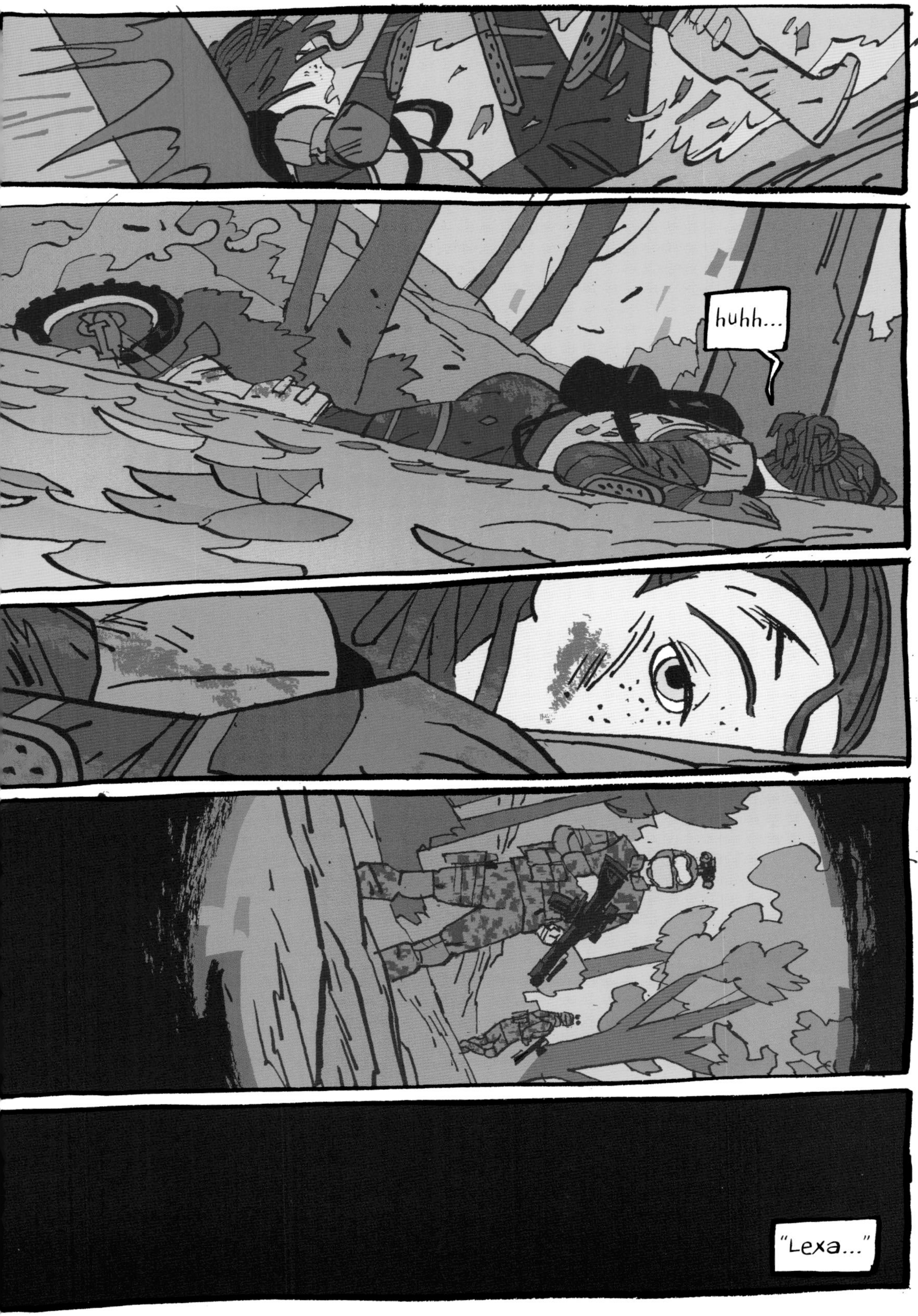
huhh...
"Lexa..."

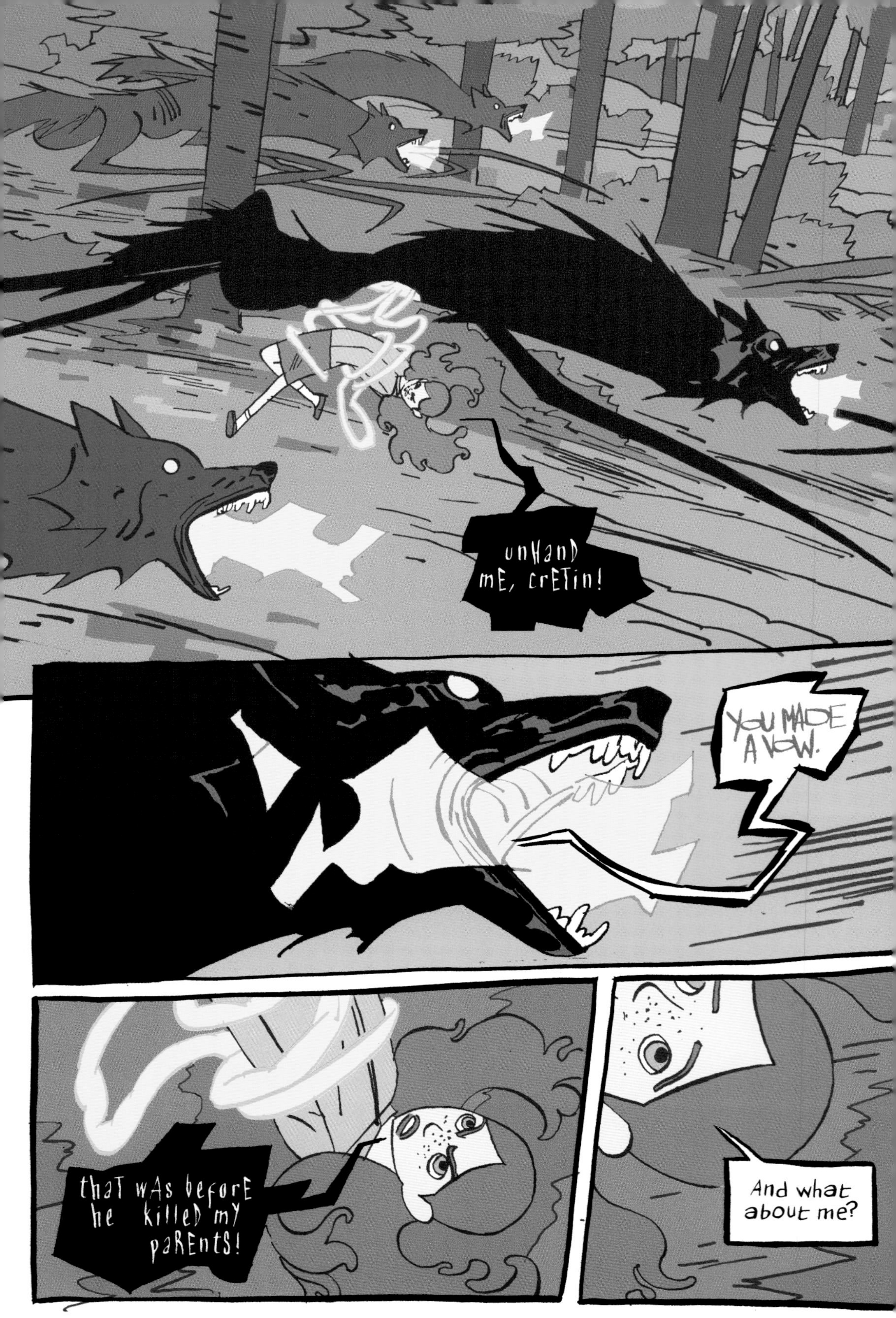
unHand mE, crEtin!
YOU MADE A VOW.
that wAs before he killed my parEnts!
And what about me?

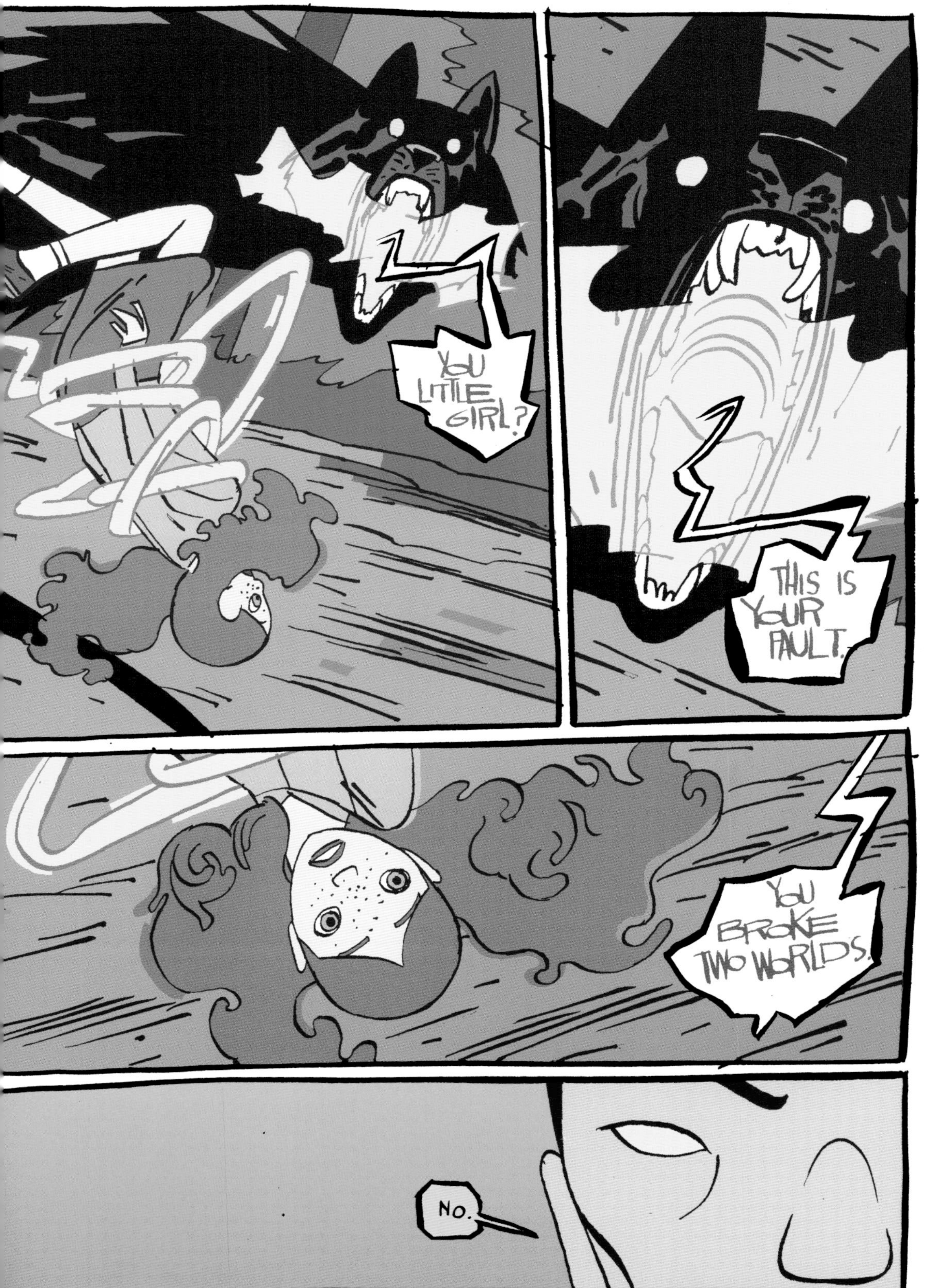
YOU LITTLE GIRL?
THIS IS YOUR FAULT.
YOU BROKE TWO WORLDS.
NO.

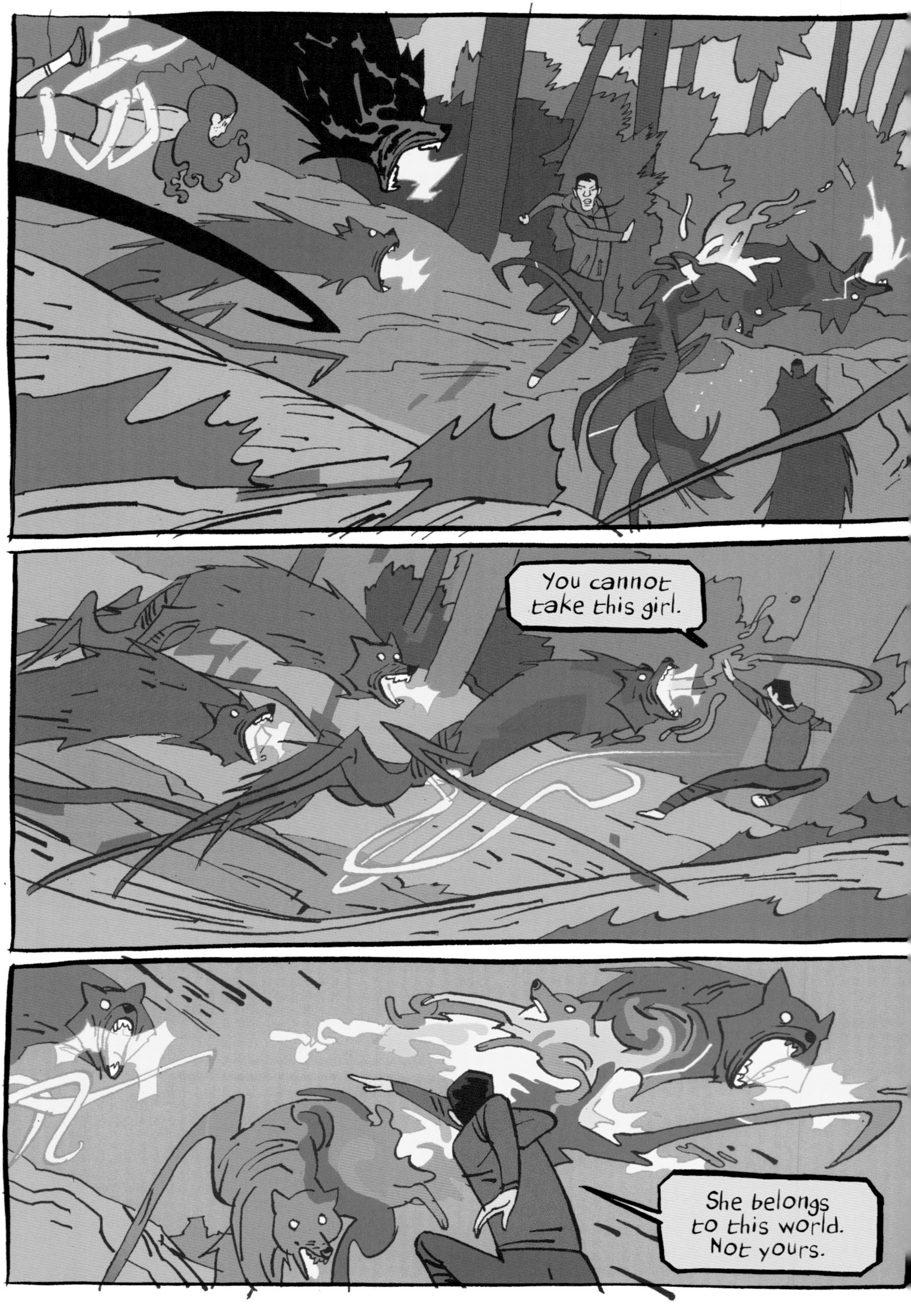
You cannot take this girl.
She belongs to this world. Not yours.

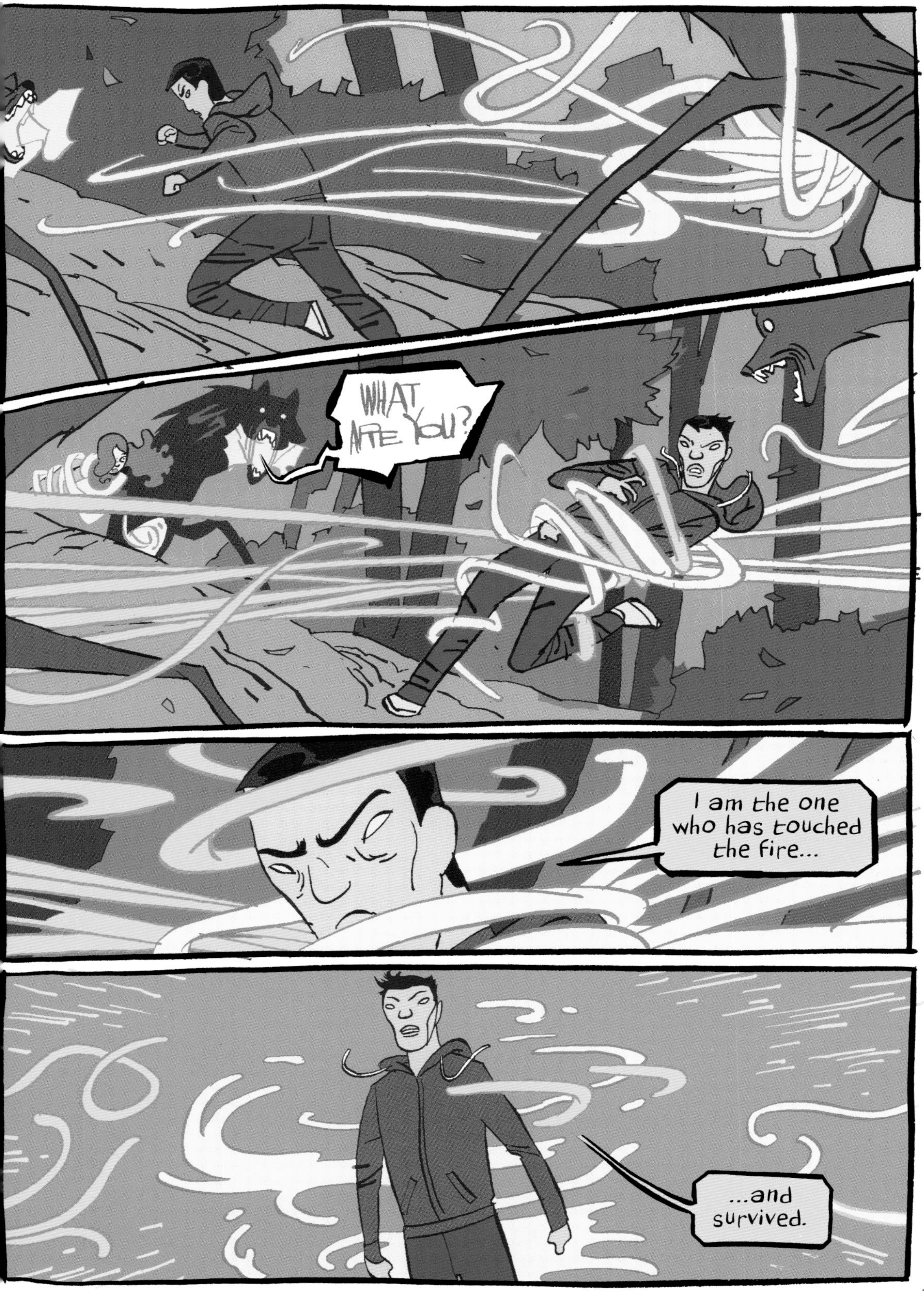
WHAT ARE YOU?
I am the one who has touched the fire...
...and survived.

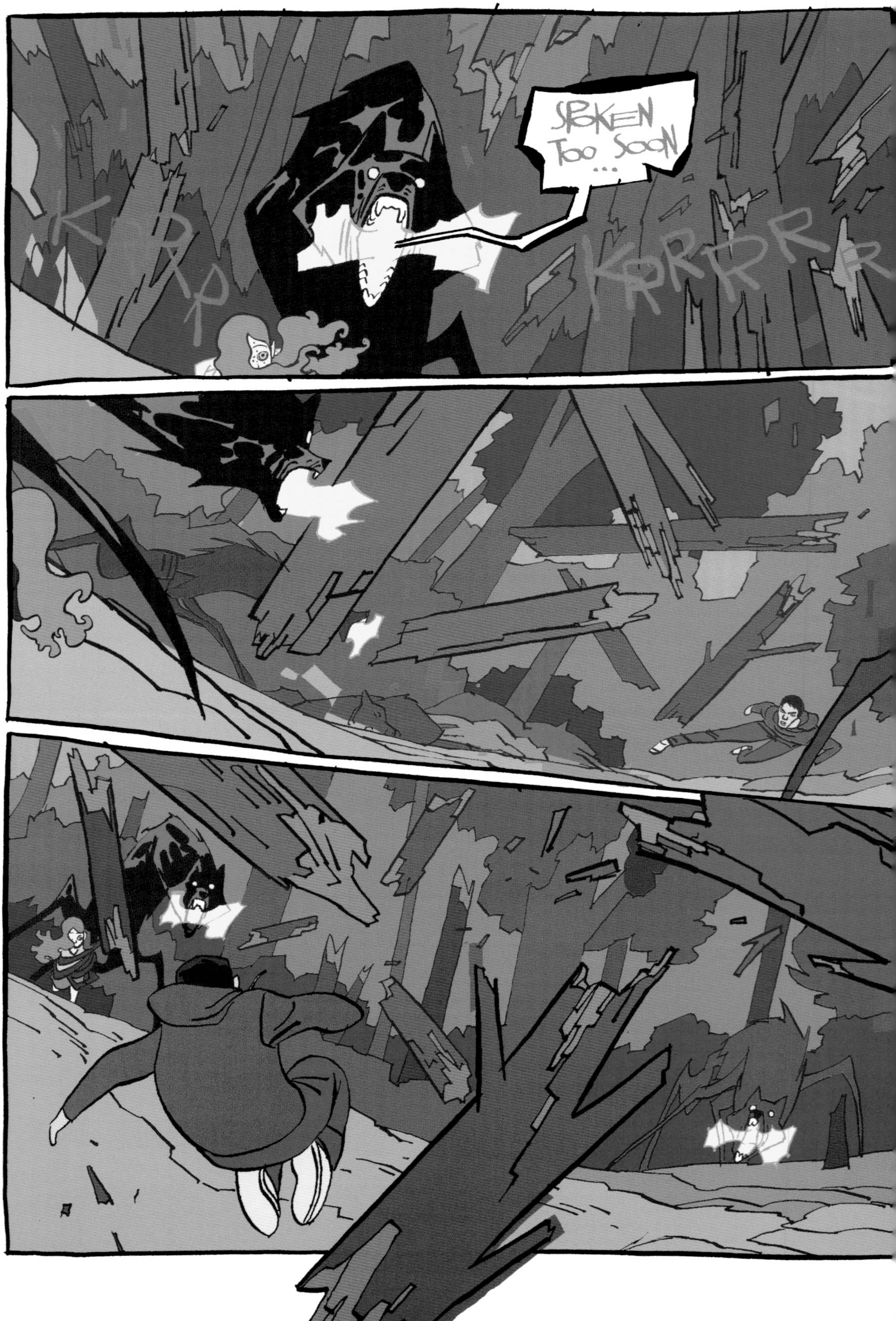
SPOKEN TOO SOON ...
KRRR
KRRRRRR

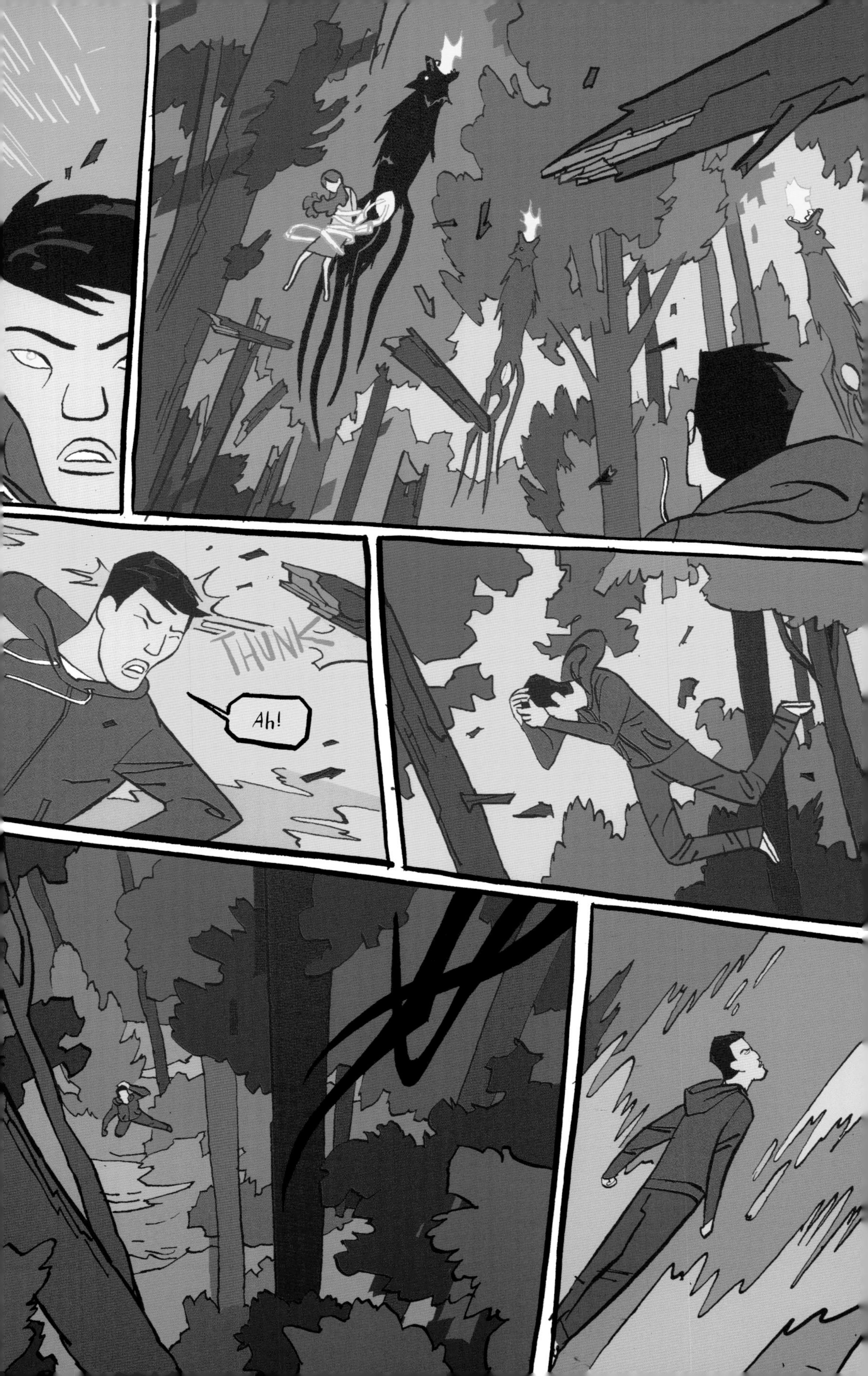
THUNK
Ah!

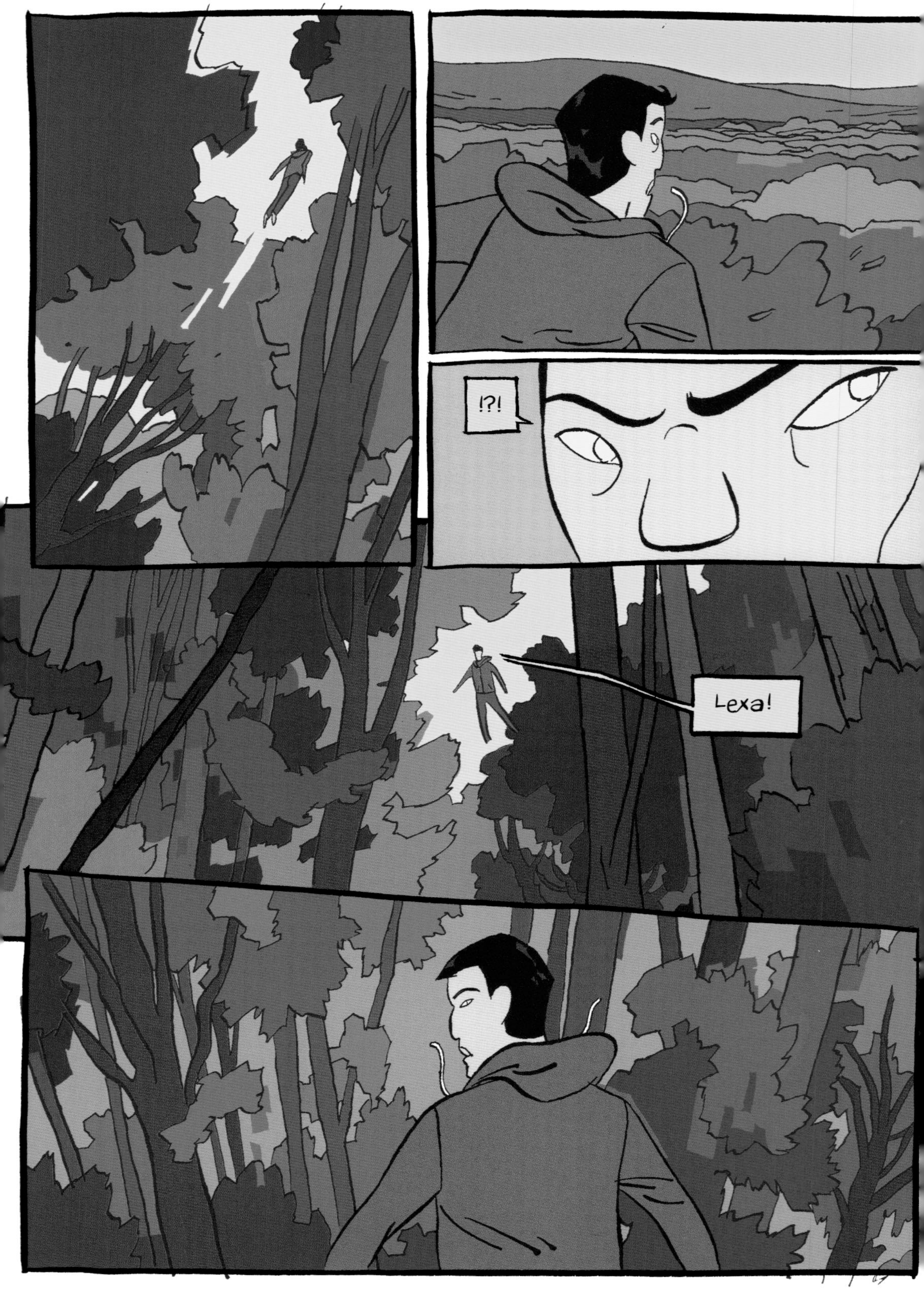
!?!
Lexa!

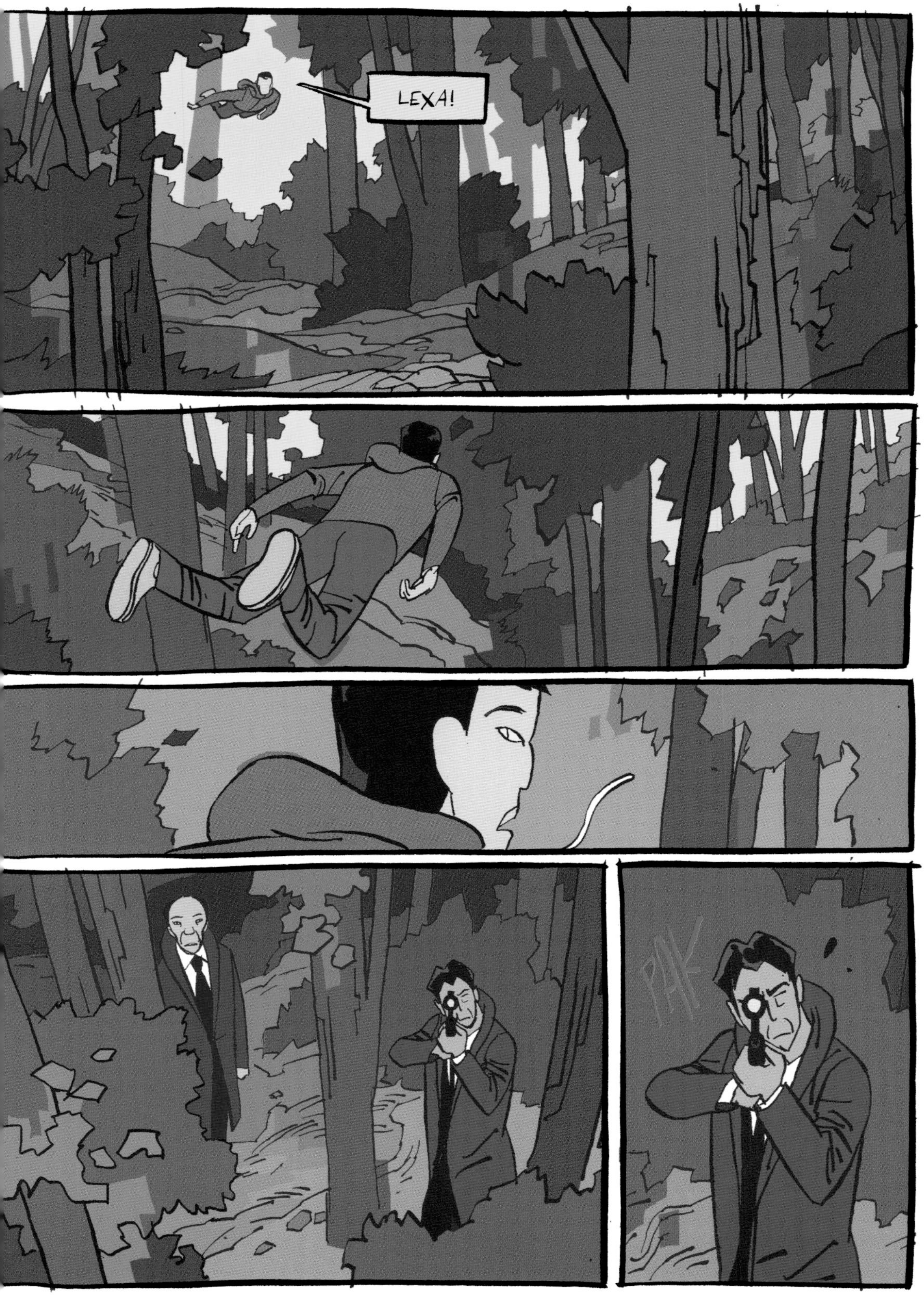
LEXA!
PAK

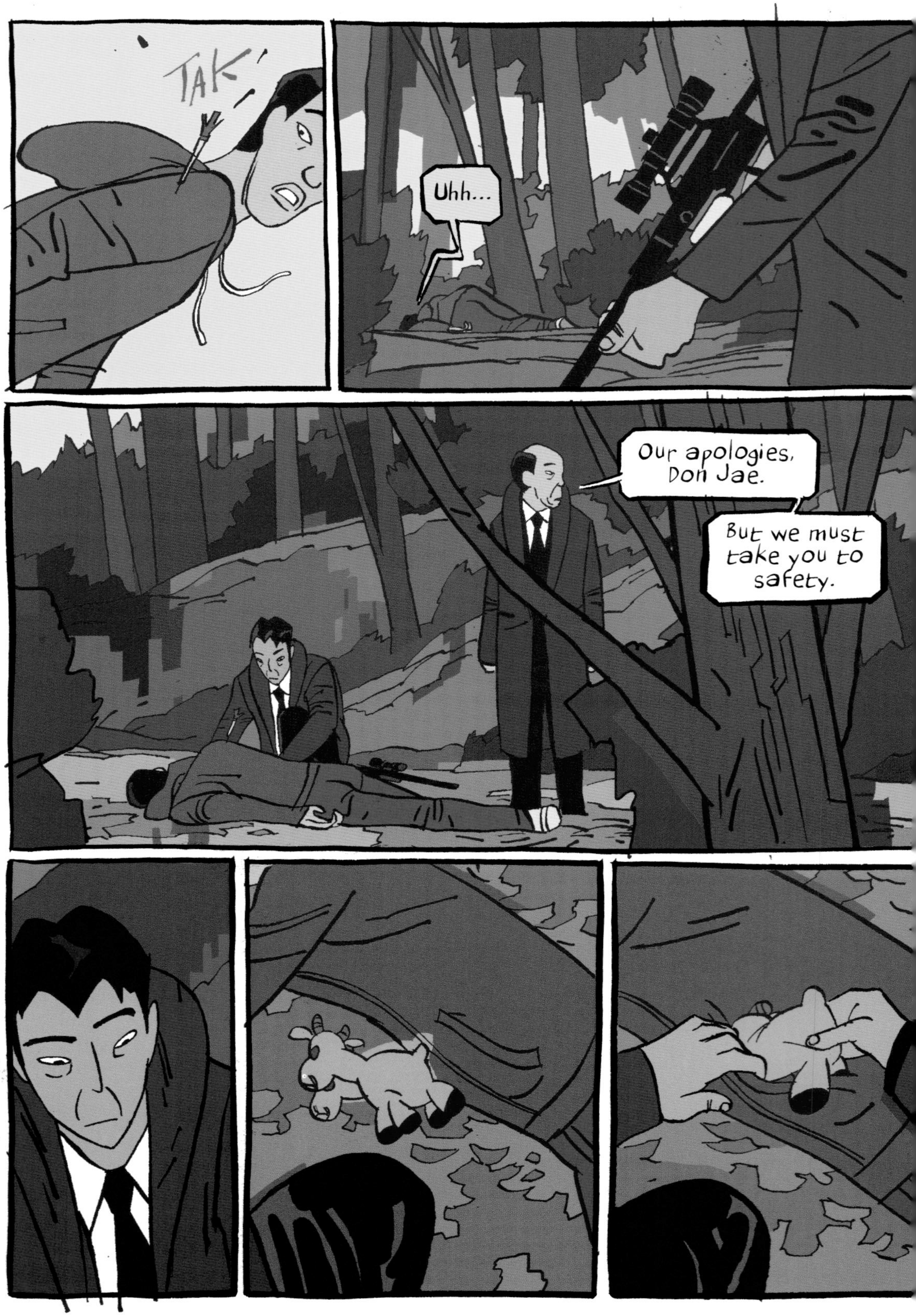
TAK
Uhh...
Our apologies, Don Jae.
But we must take you to safety.

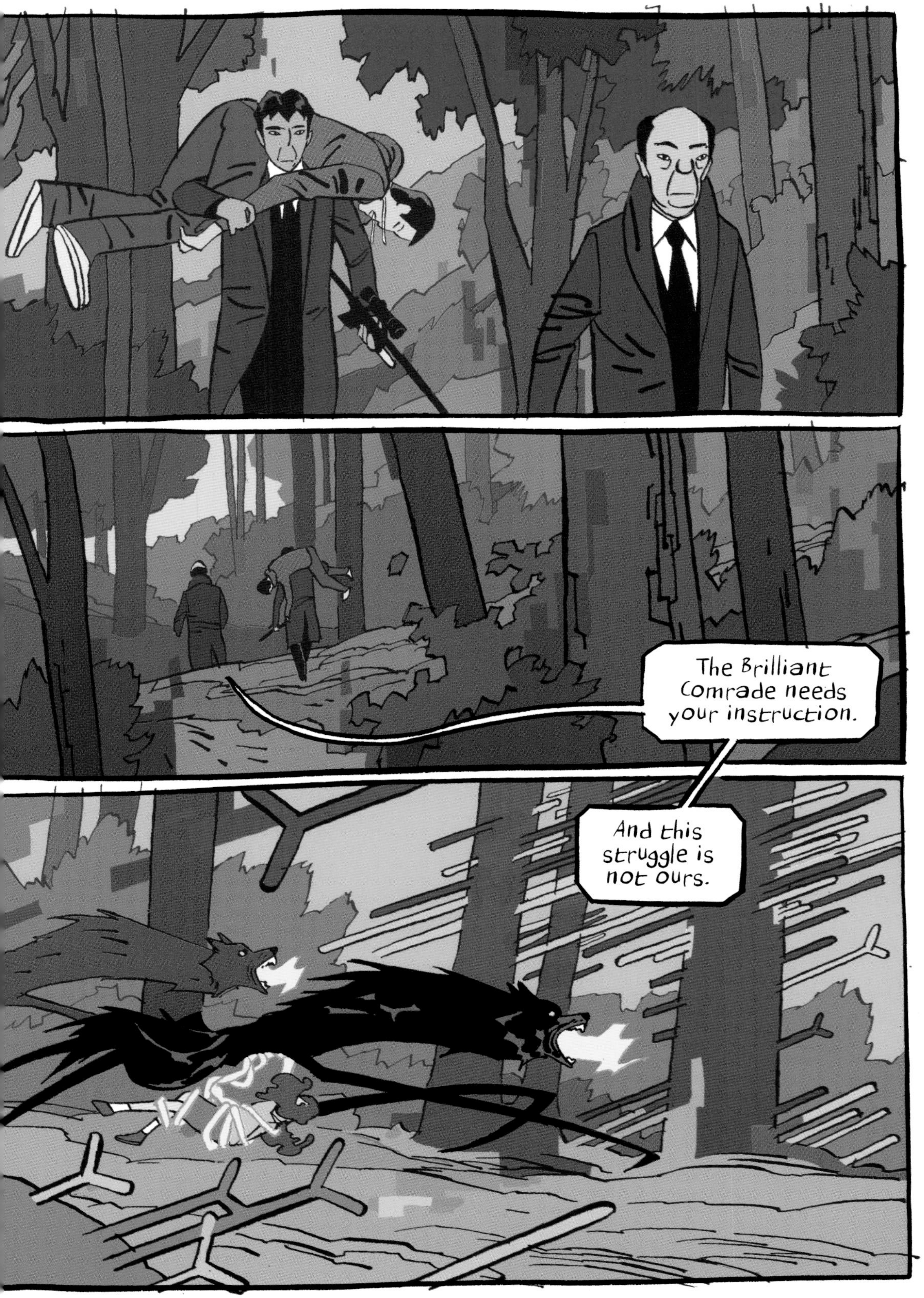
The Brilliant Comrade needs your instruction.
And this struggle is not ours.

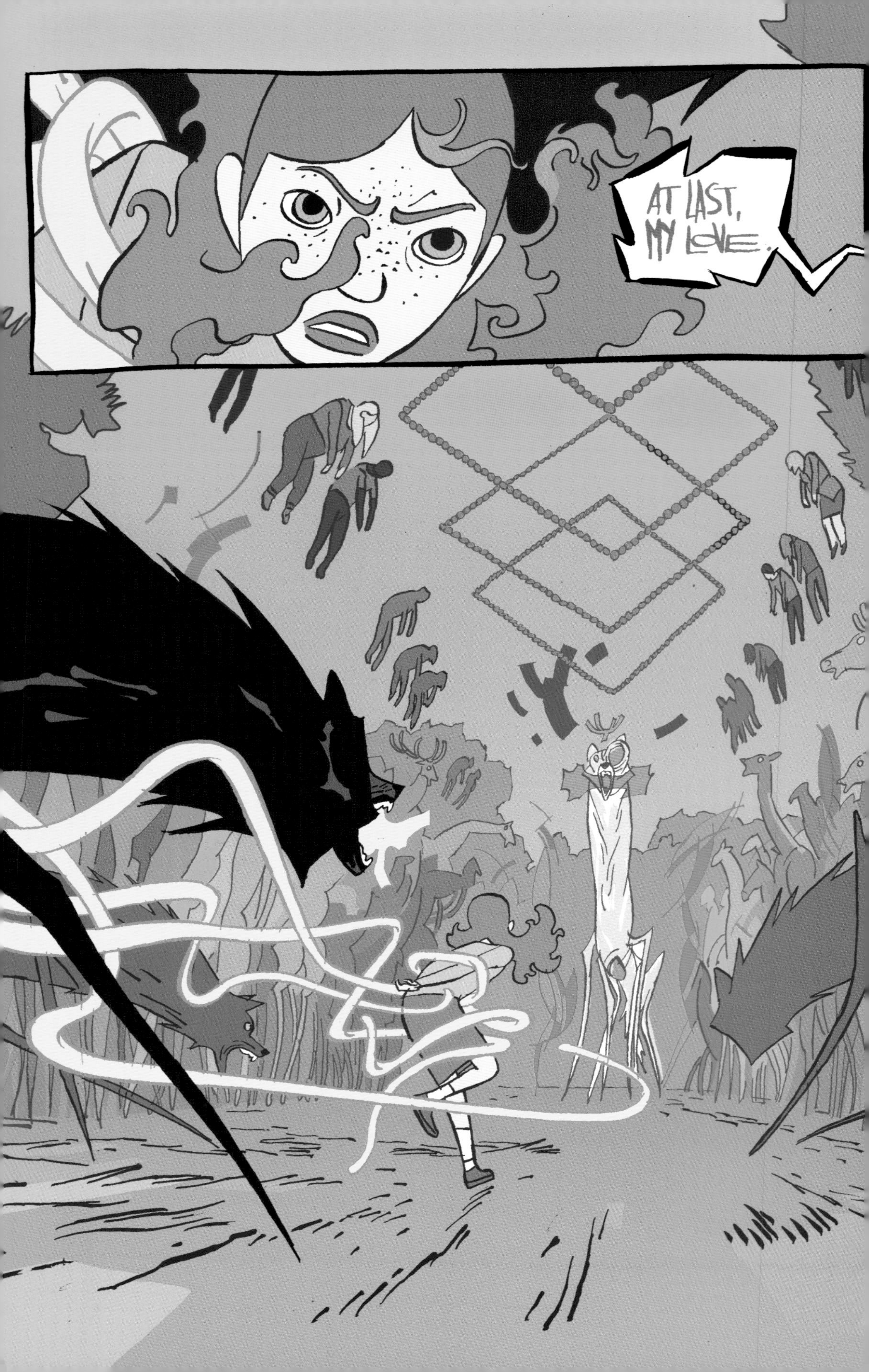
AT LAST, MY LOVE.

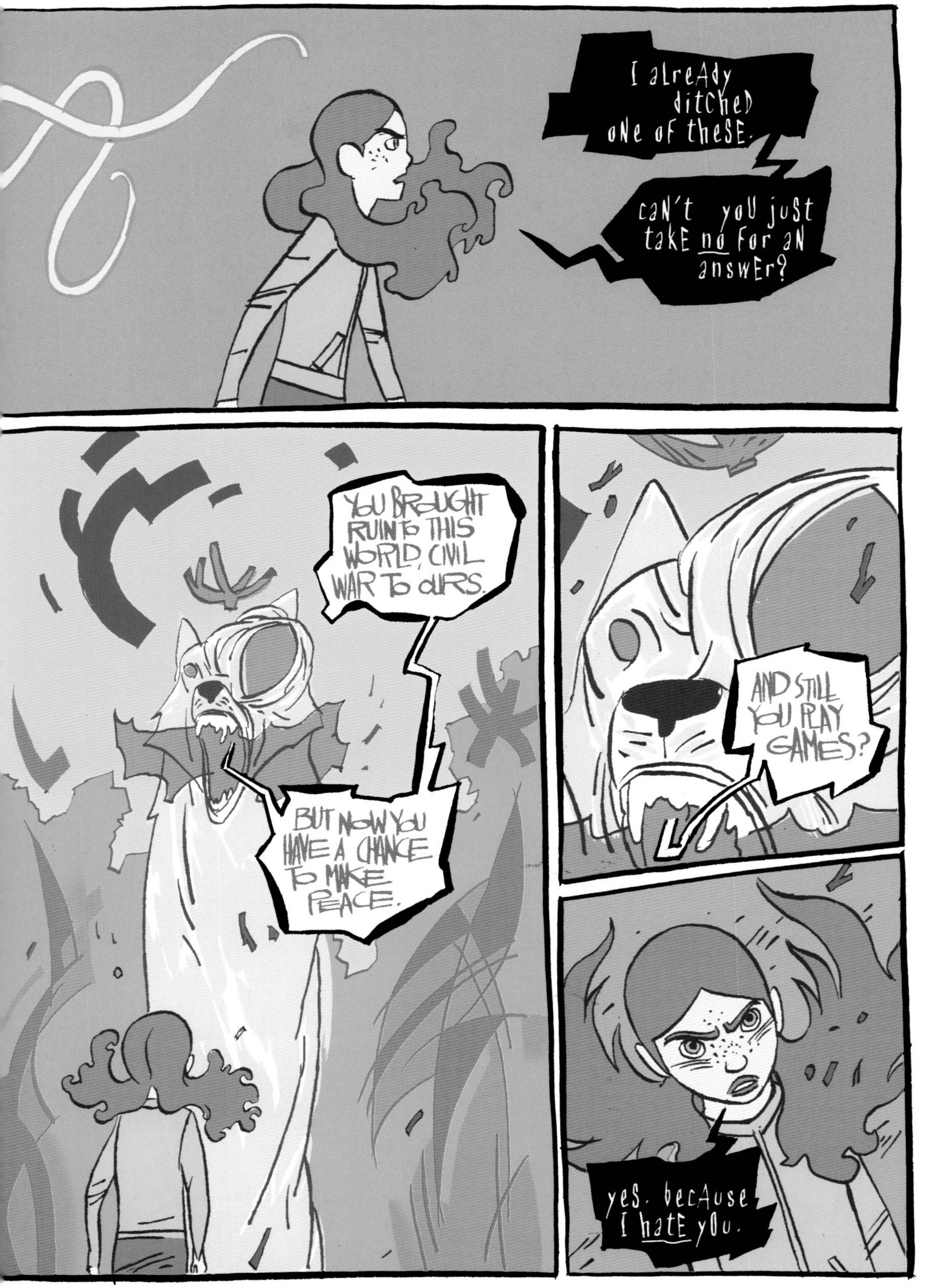
I already ditched one of these.
can't you just take no for an answer?
YOU BROUGHT RUIN TO THIS WORLD, CIVIL WAR TO OURS.
BUT NOW YOU HAVE A CHANCE TO MAKE PEACE.
AND STILL YOU PLAY GAMES?
yes. because I hate you.

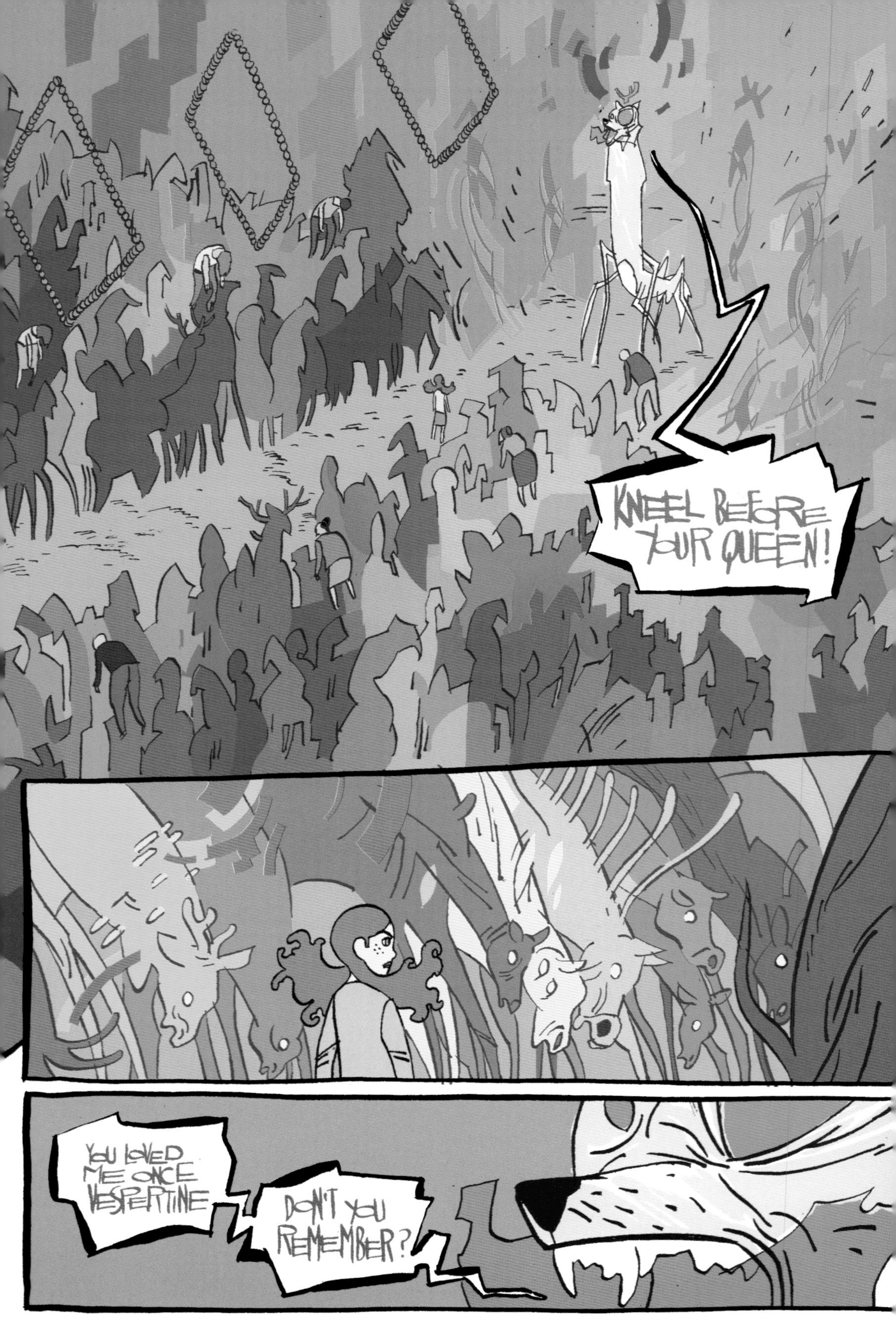

KNEEL BEFORE YOUR QUEEN!
YOU LOVED ME ONCE VESPERTINE
DON'T YOU REMEMBER?

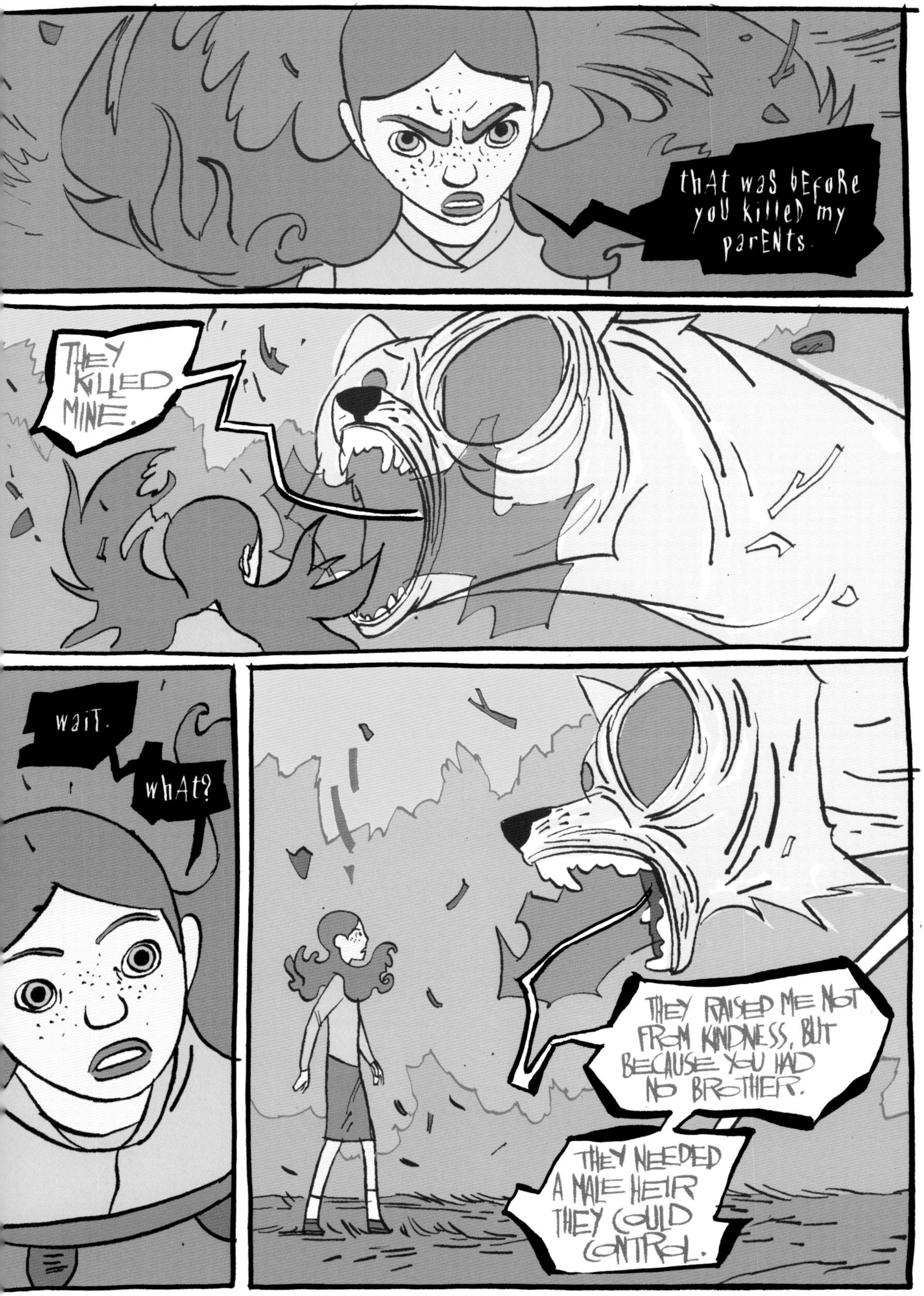
that was before you killed my parents.
THEY KILLED MINE.
wait.
what?
THEY RAISED ME NOT FROM KINDNESS, BUT BECAUSE YOU HAD NO BROTHER.
THEY NEEDED A MALE HEIR THEY COULD CONTROL.

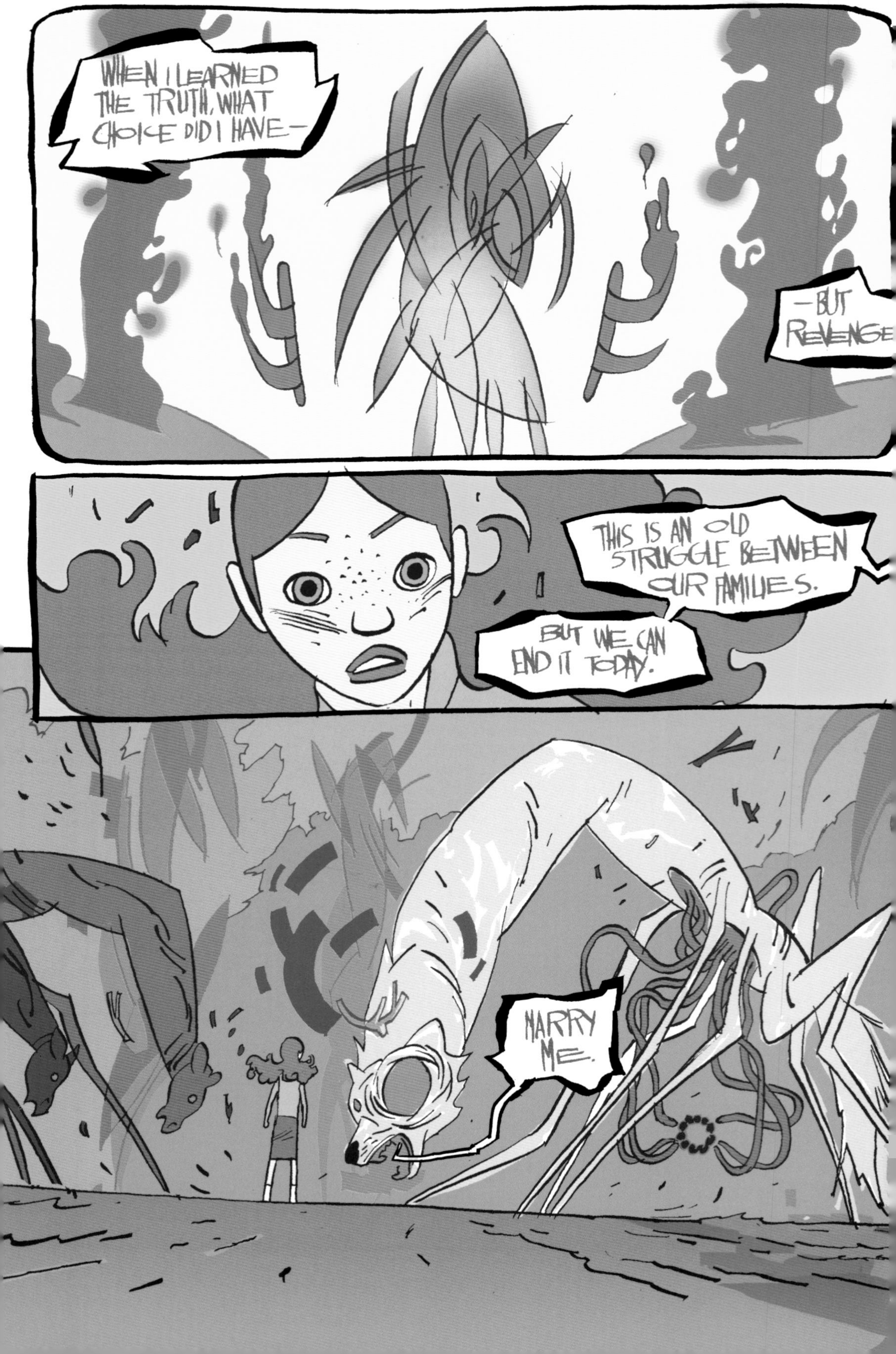
WHEN I LEARNED THE TRUTH, WHAT CHOICE DID I HAVE—
—BUT REVENGE
THIS IS AN OLD STRUGGLE BETWEEN OUR FAMILIES.
BUT WE CAN END IT TODAY.
MARRY ME.

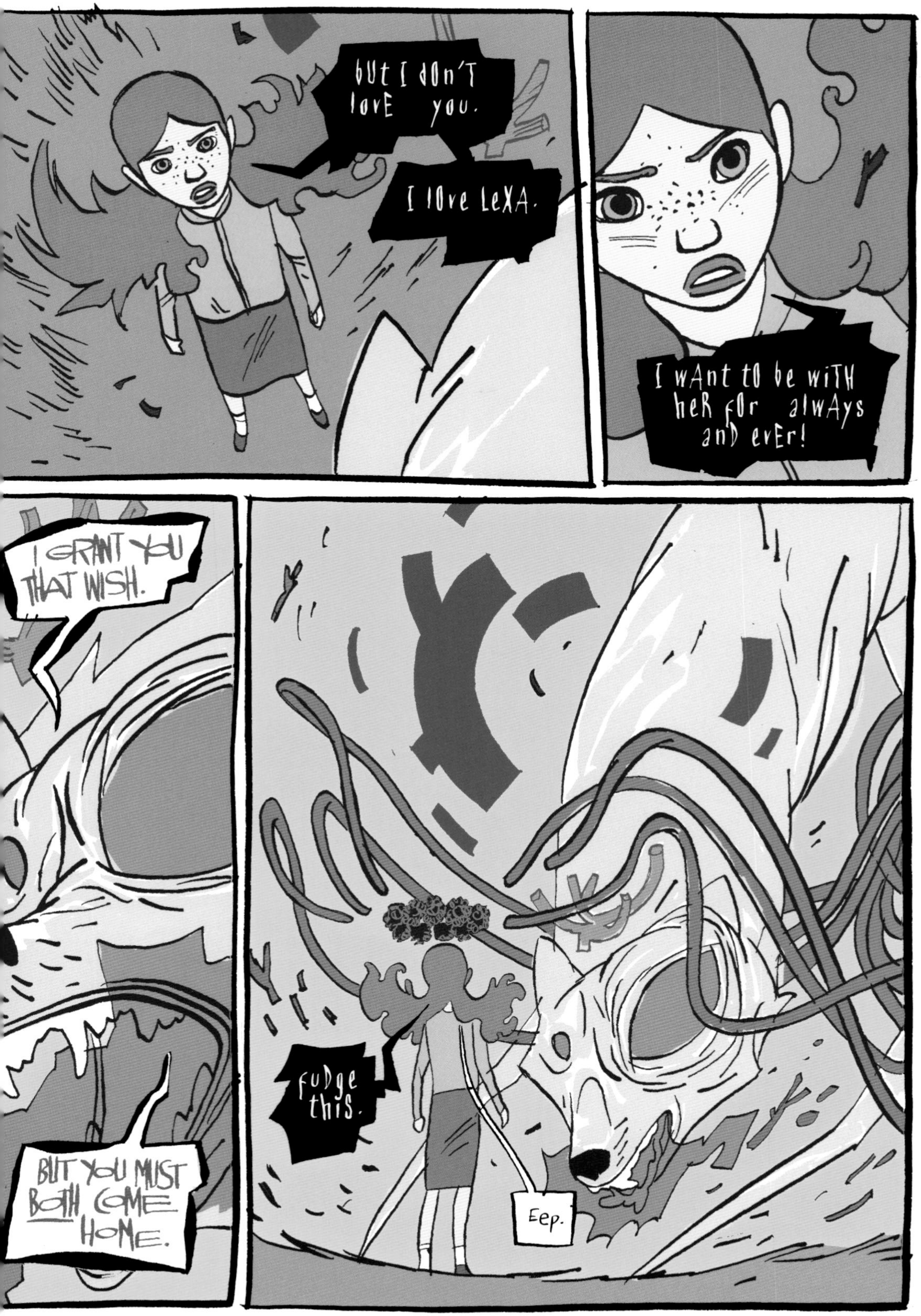
but I don't love you.
I love Lexa.
I want to be with her for always and ever!
I GRANT YOU THAT WISH.
BUT YOU MUST BOTH COME HOME.
Fudge this.
Eep.

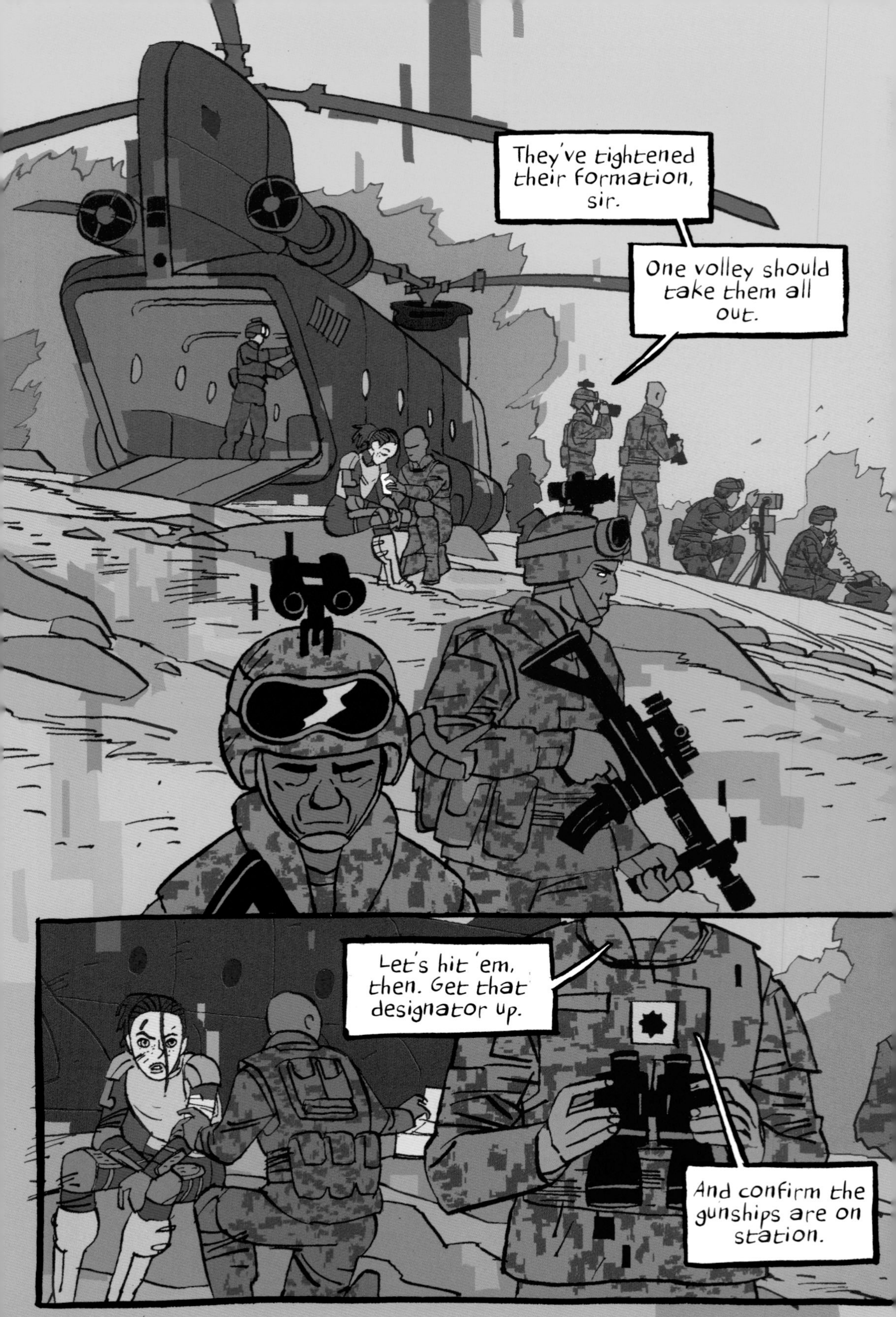
They've tightened their formation, sir.
One volley should take them all out.
Let's hit 'em, then. Get that designator up.
And confirm the gunships are on station.

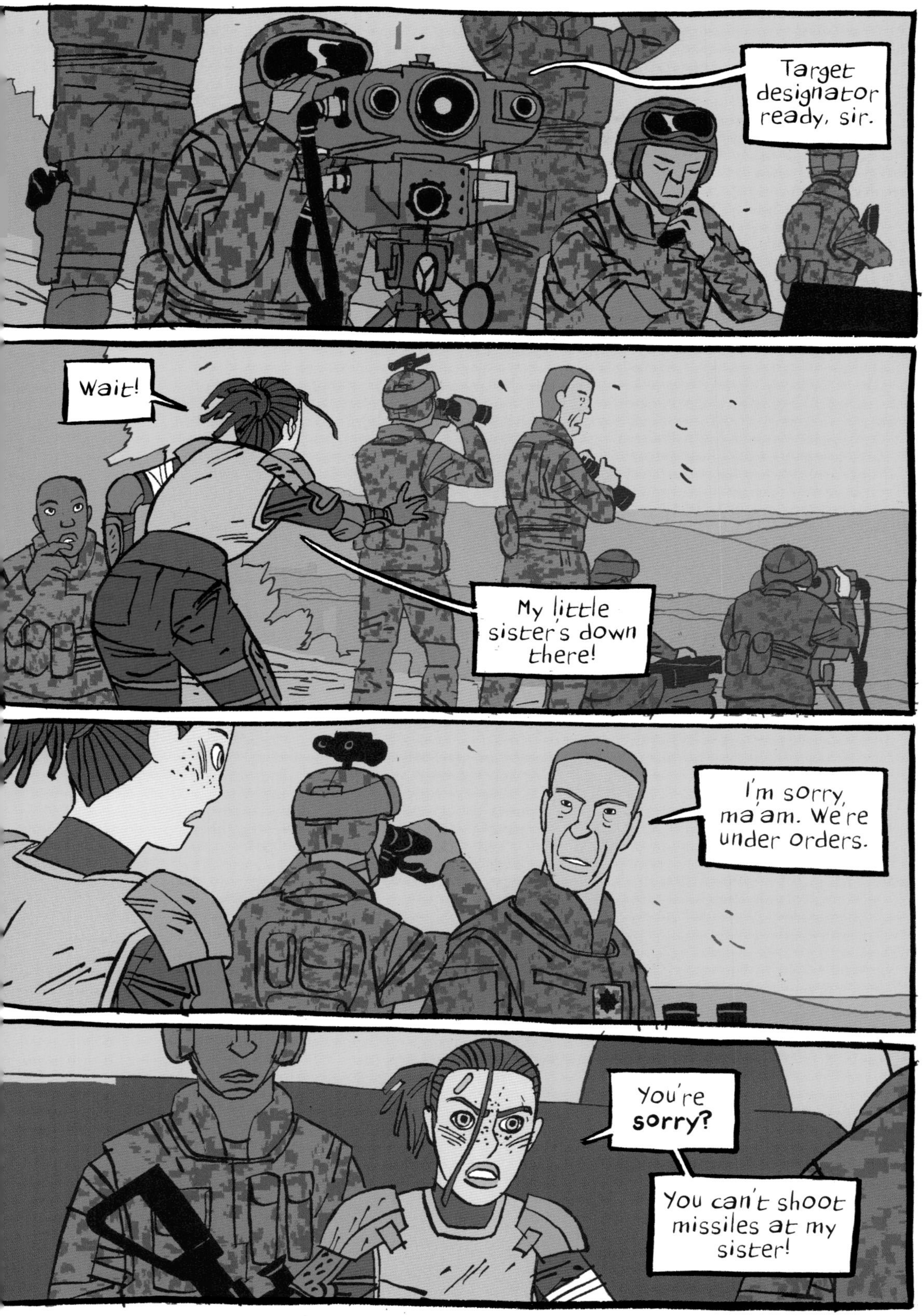

Target designator ready, sir.
Wait!
My little sister's down there!
I'm sorry, ma'am. We're under orders.
You're **sorry?**
You can't shoot missiles at my sister!

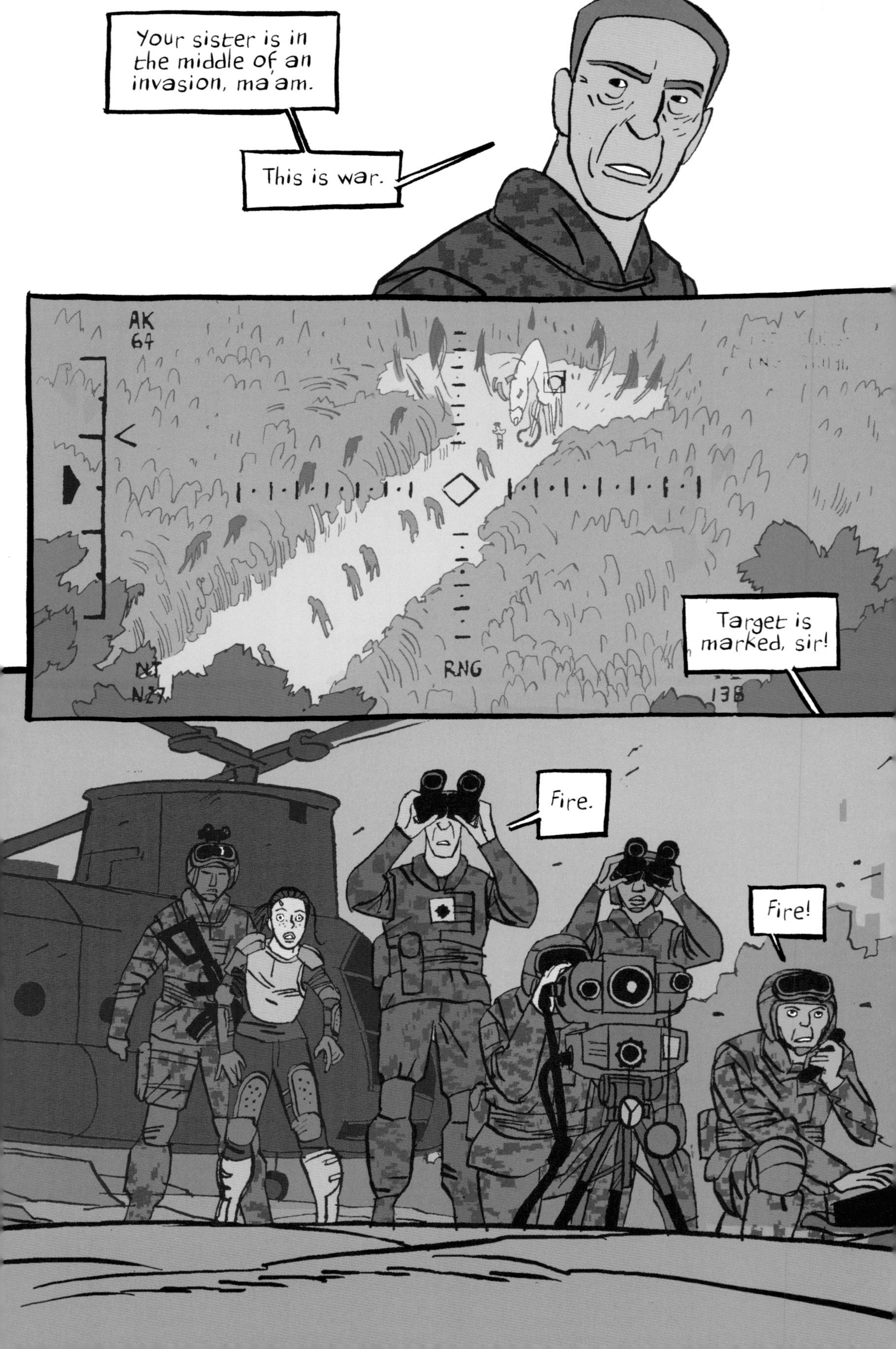
Your sister is in the middle of an invasion, ma'am.
This is war.
AK
64
RNG
138
Target is marked, sir!
Fire.
Fire!

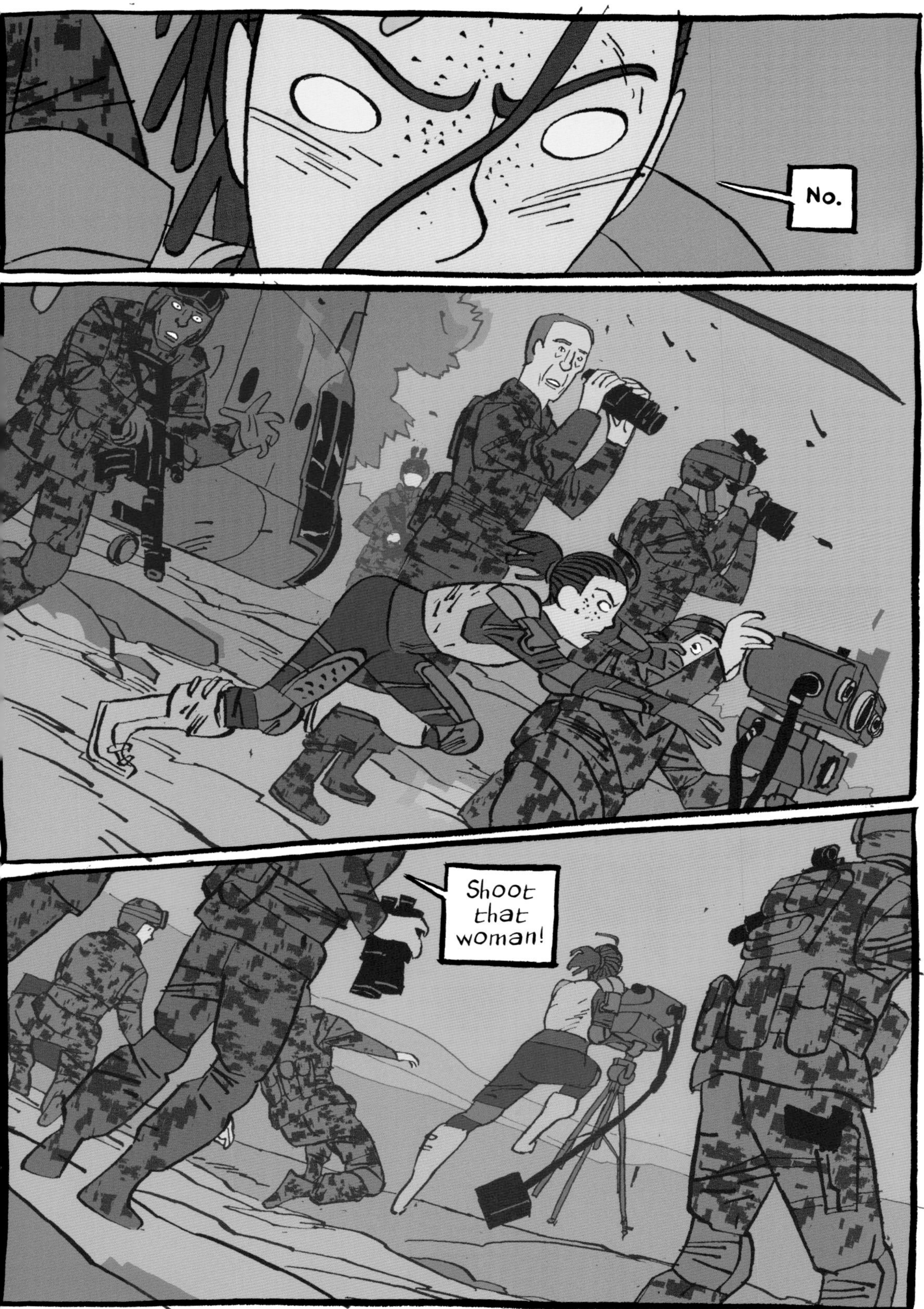
No.
Shoot that woman!

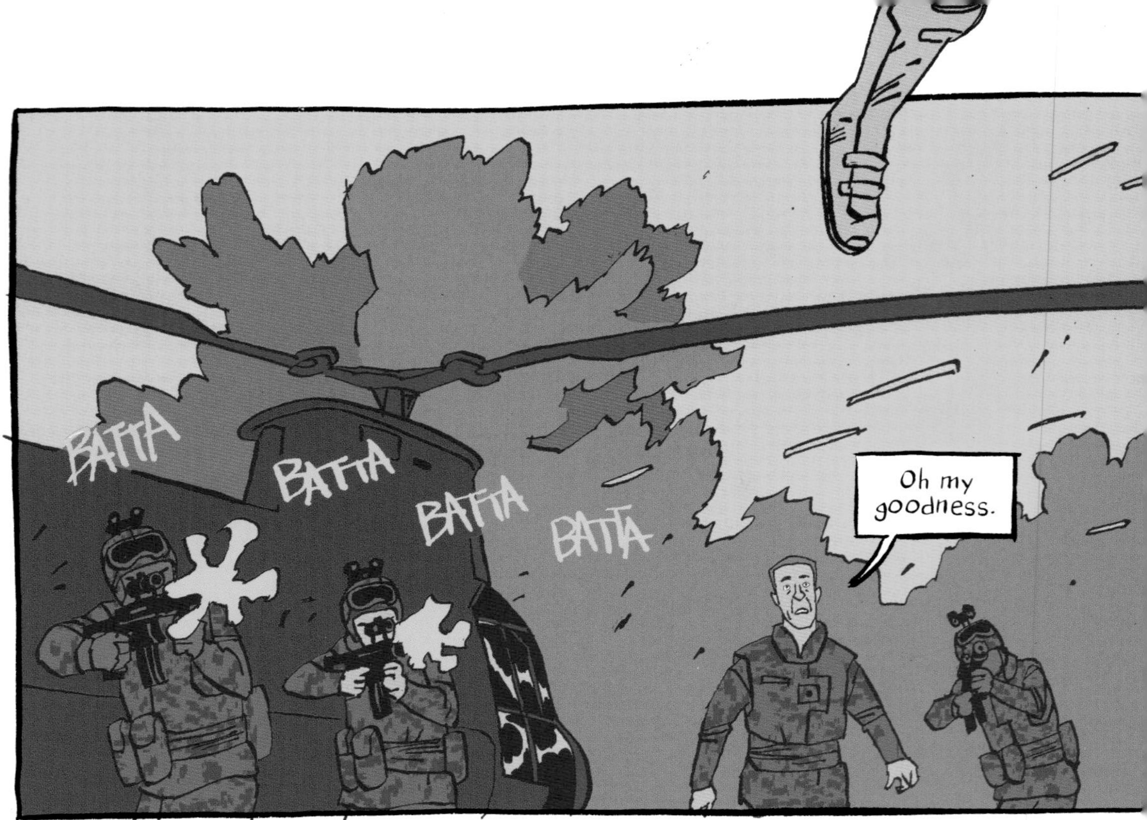
BATTA
BATTA
BATTA
BATTA
Oh my goodness.

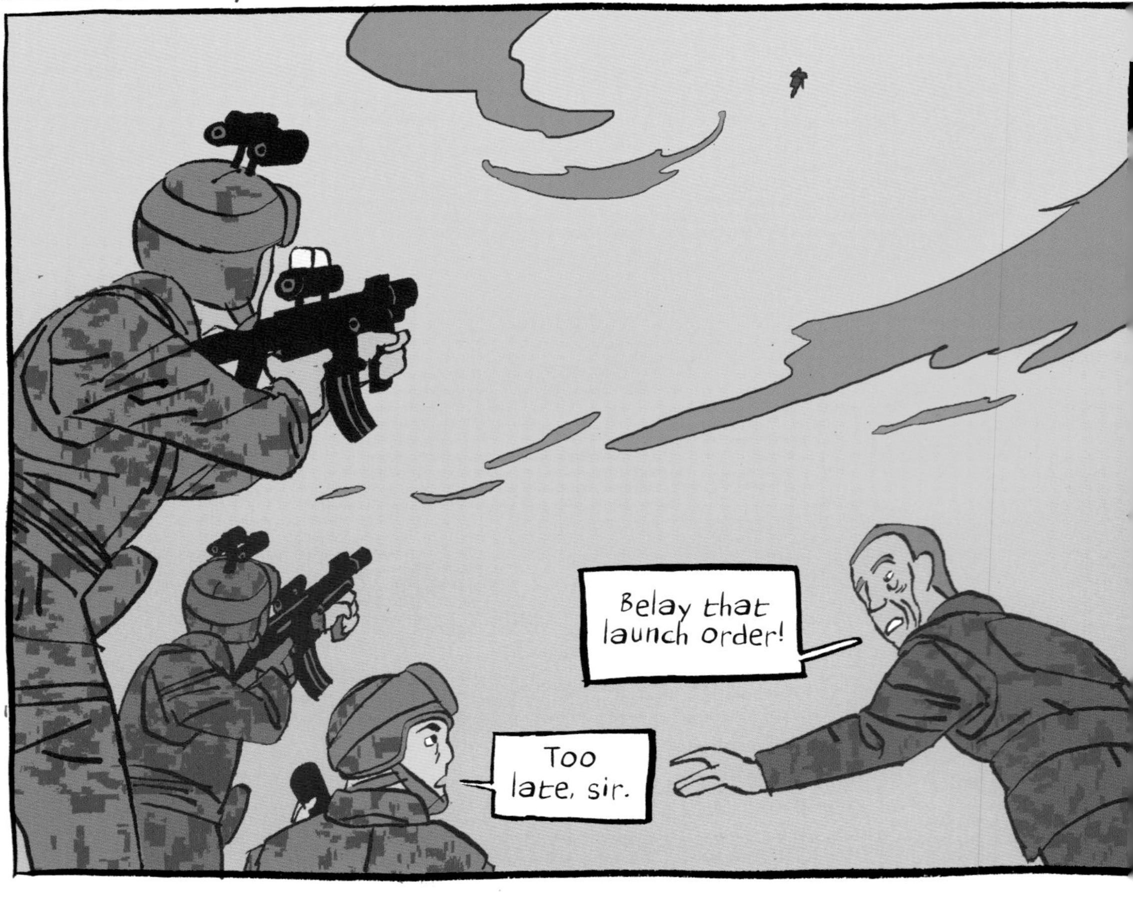
Belay that launch order!
Too late, sir.

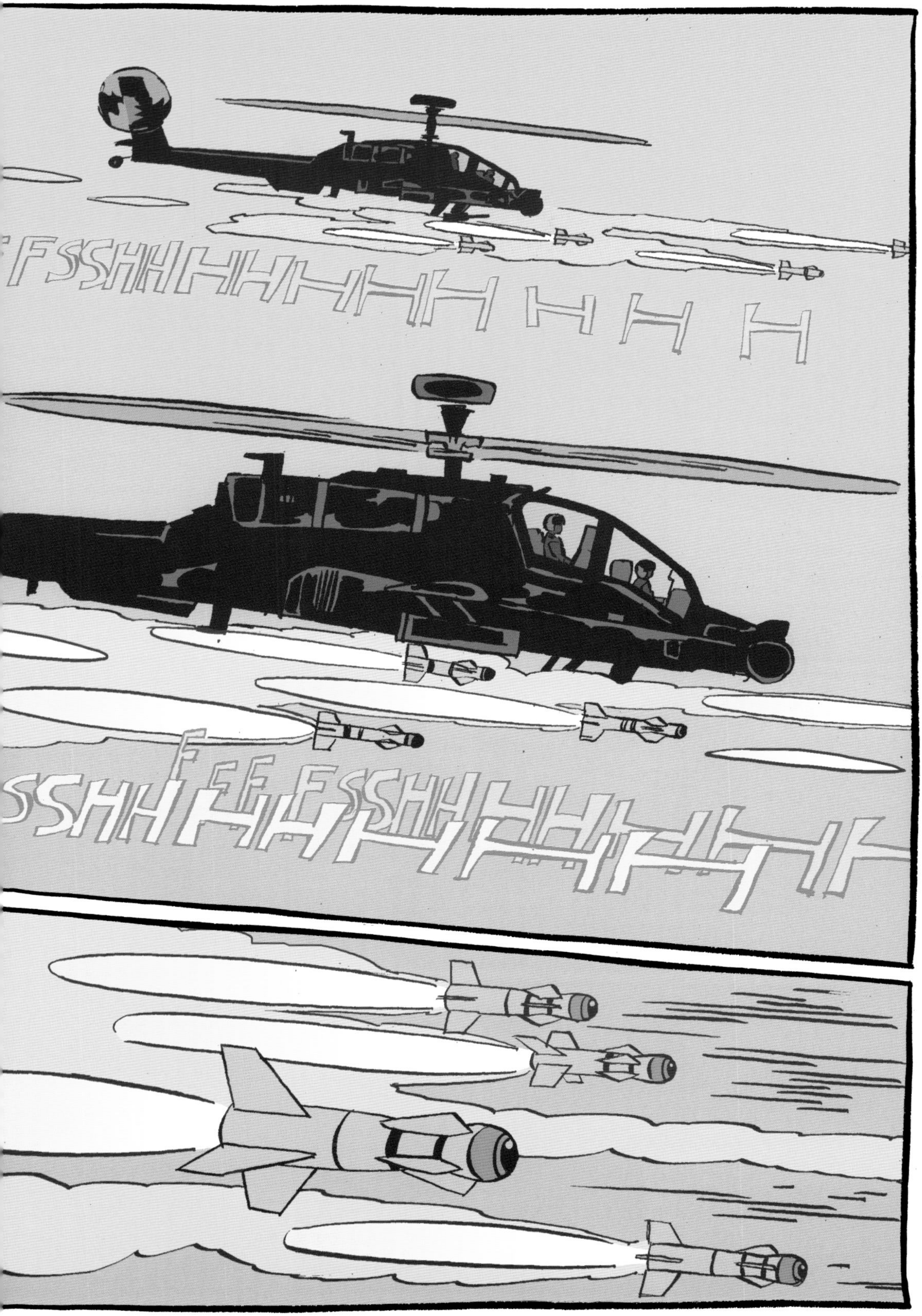
FSSHHHHHHHHHHH
SSHH FFF FSSHHHHHHHHHHHHH

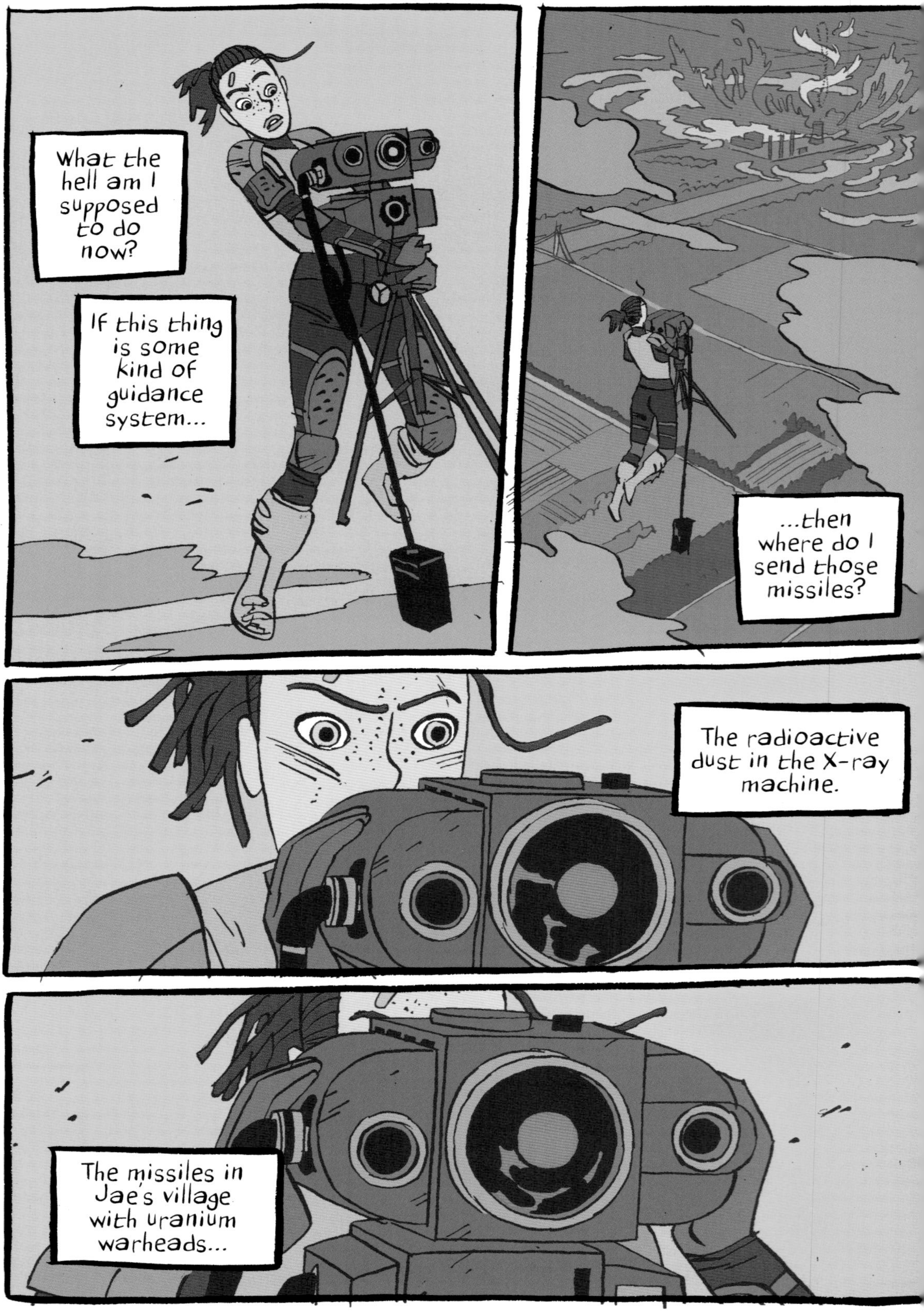
What the hell am I supposed to do now?
If this thing is some kind of guidance system...
...then where do I send those missiles?
The radioactive dust in the X-ray machine.
The missiles in Jae's village with uranium warheads...

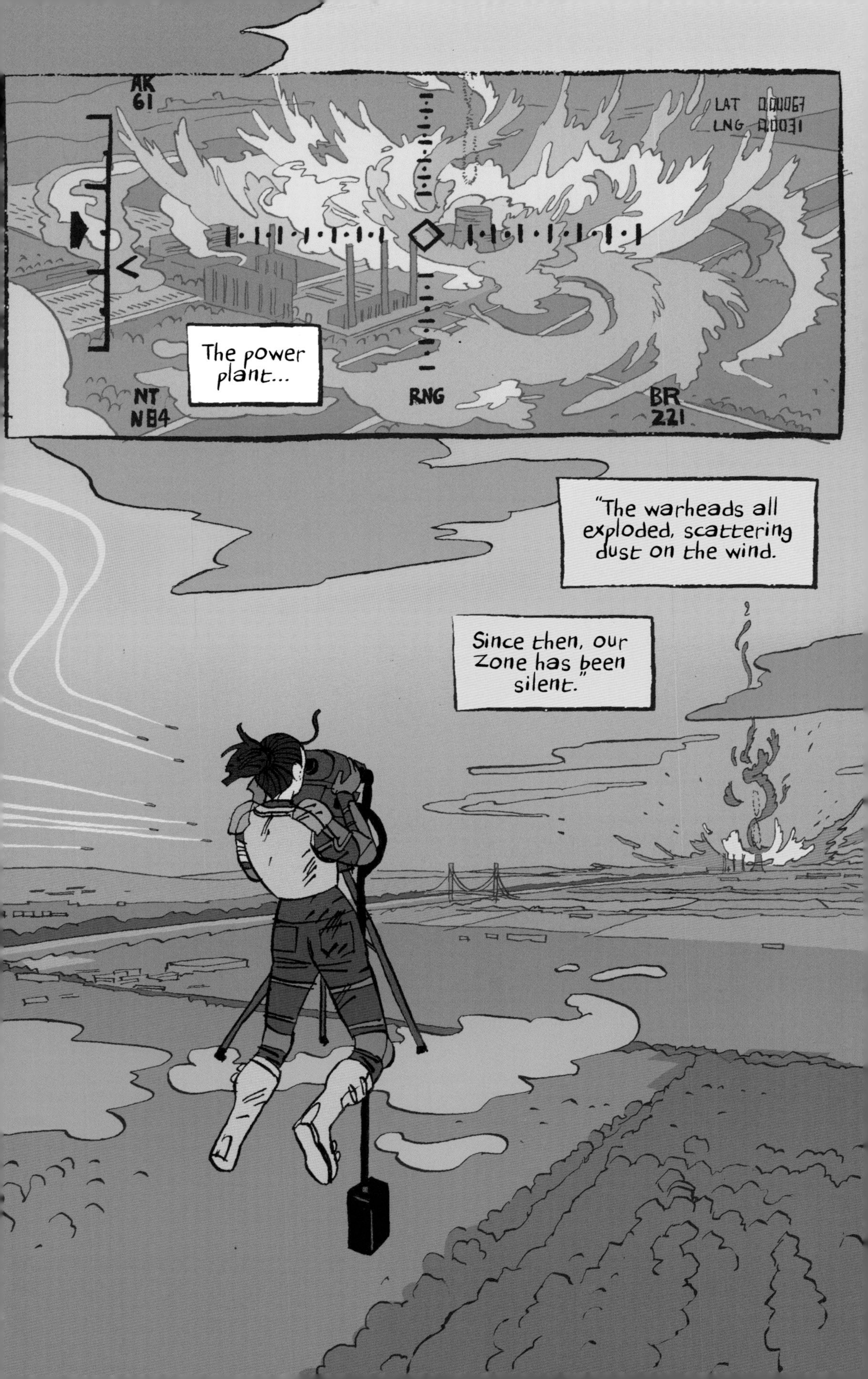

AR 61
LAT 0.0067
LNG 0.0031
The power plant...
NT N84
RNG
BR 221
"The warheads all exploded, scattering dust on the wind.
Since then, our Zone has been silent."

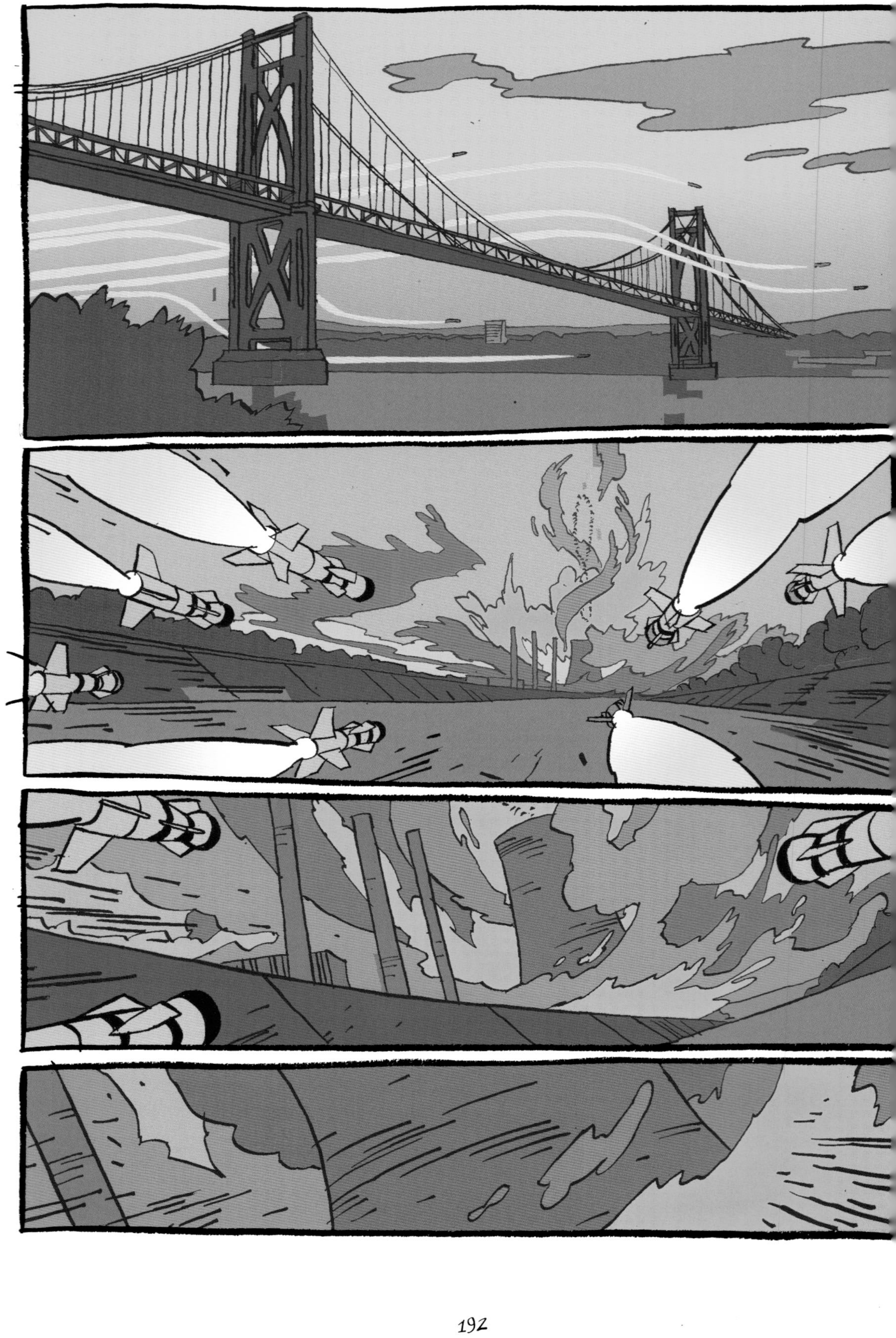

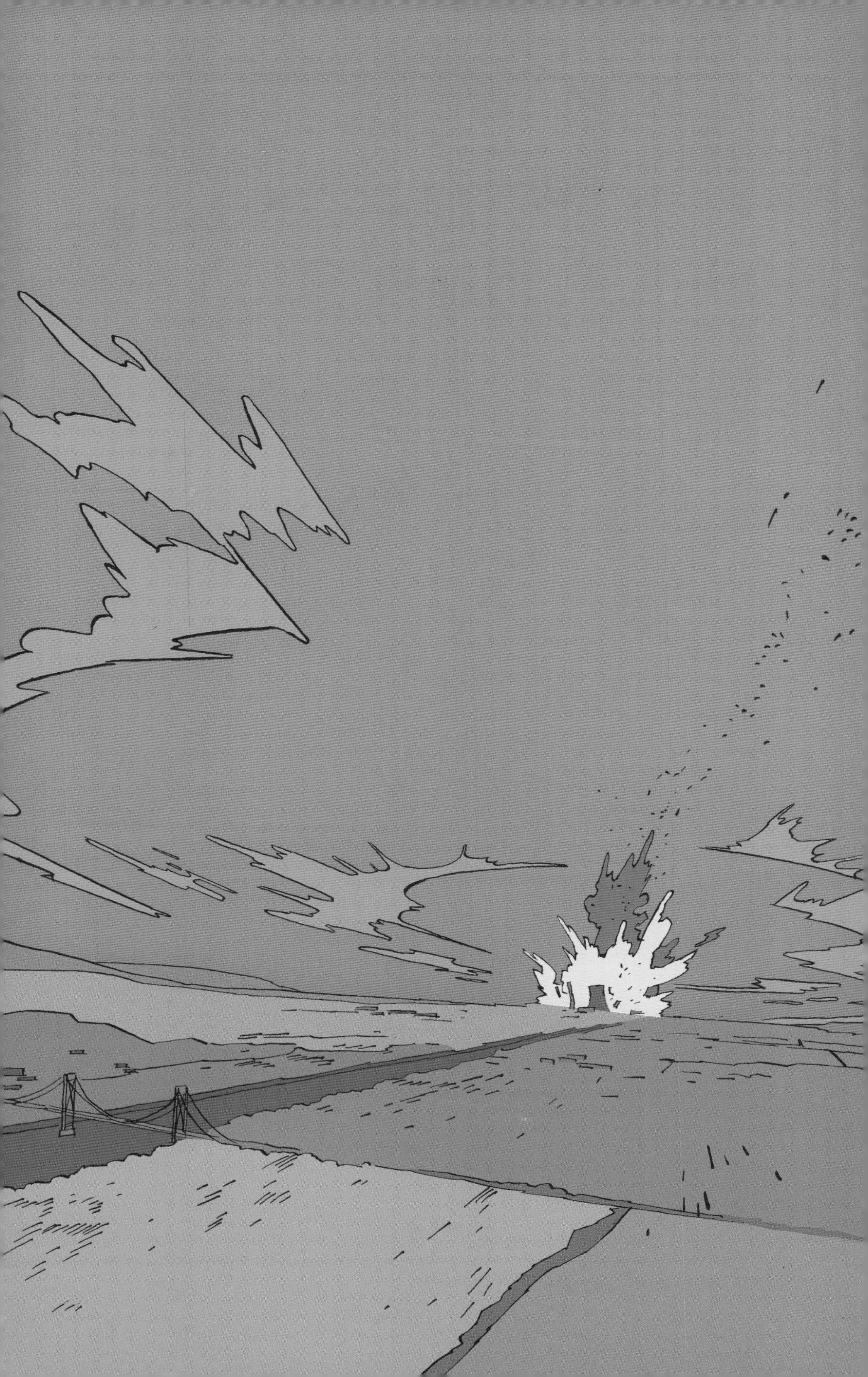

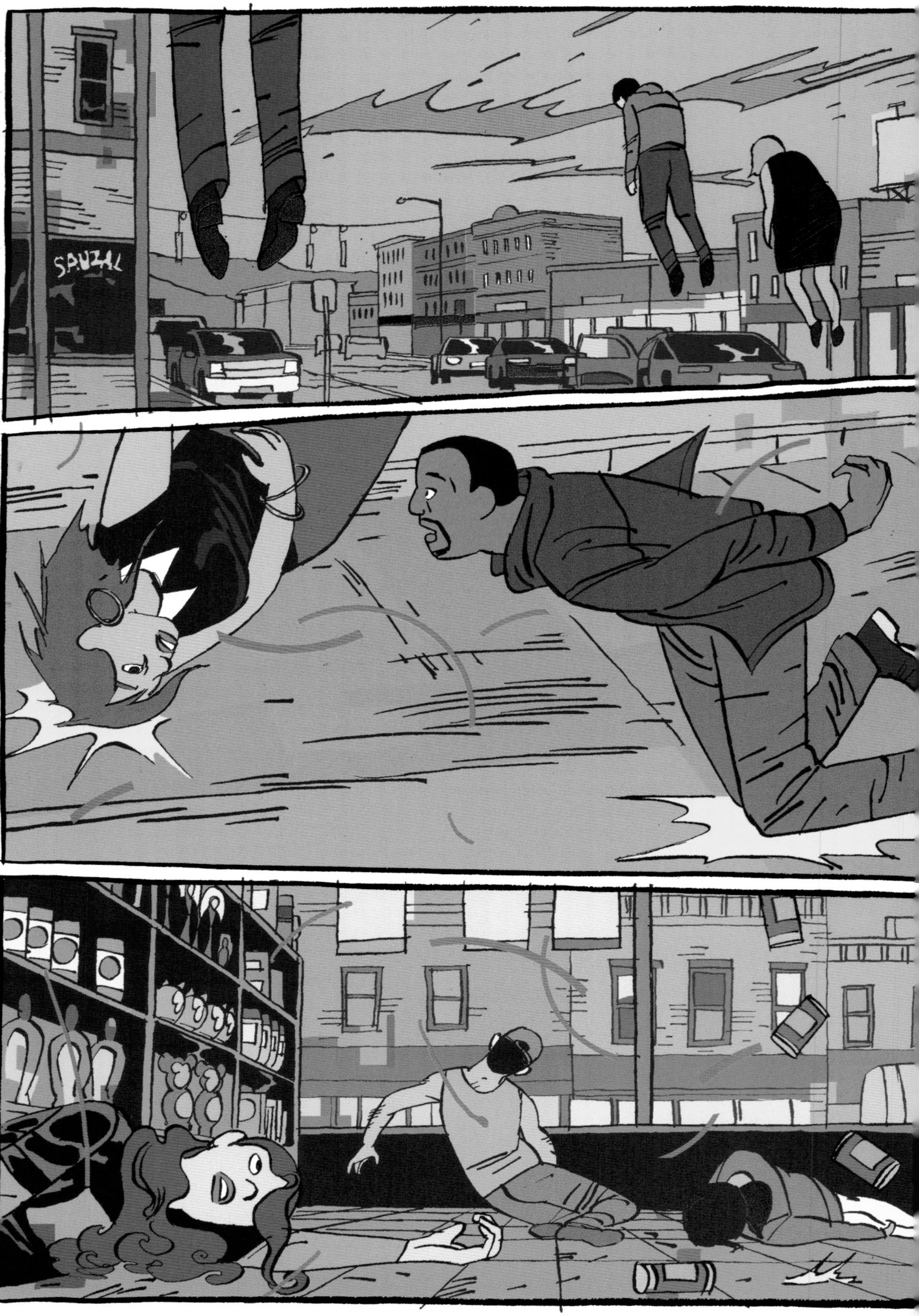
SAUZAL

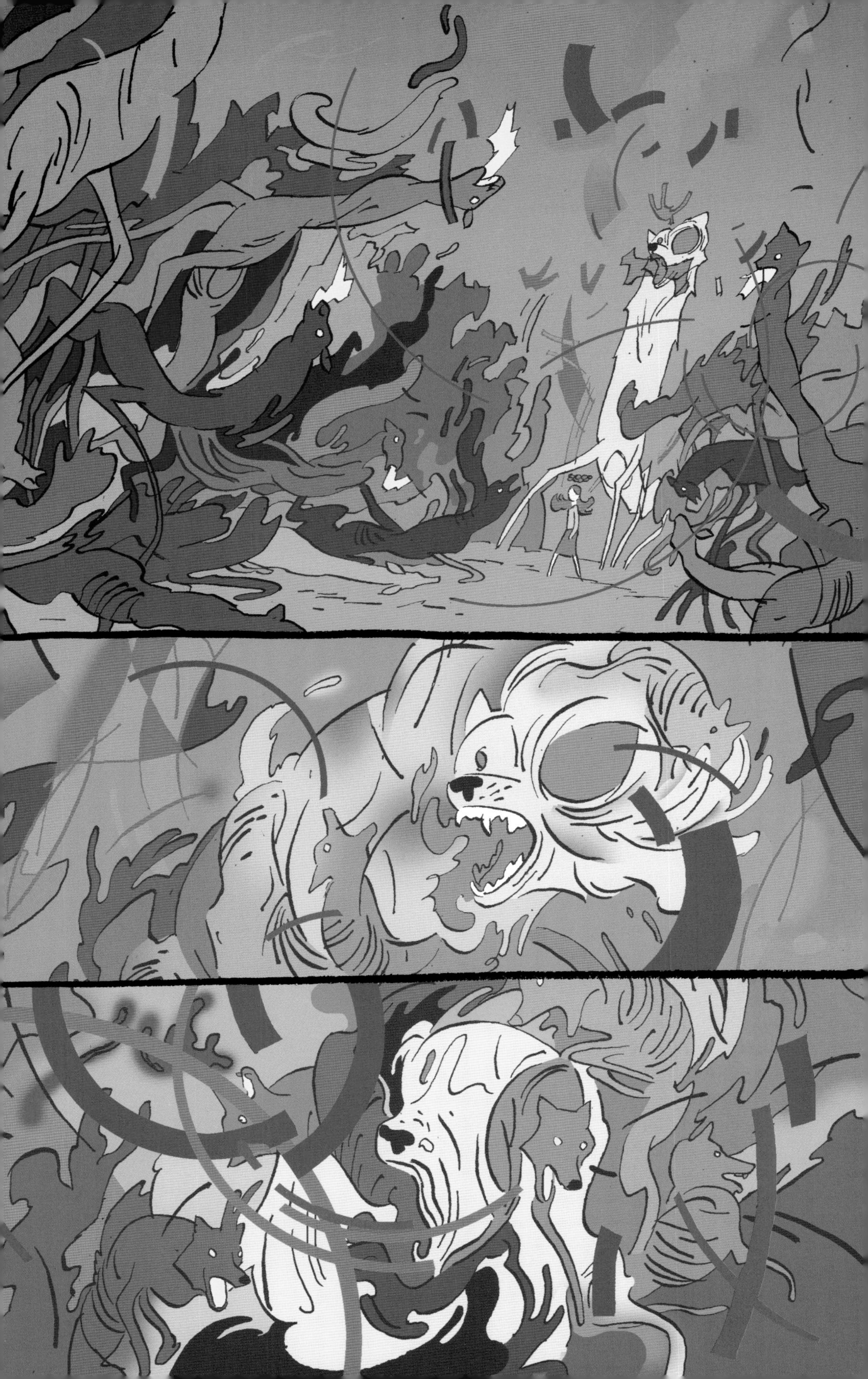

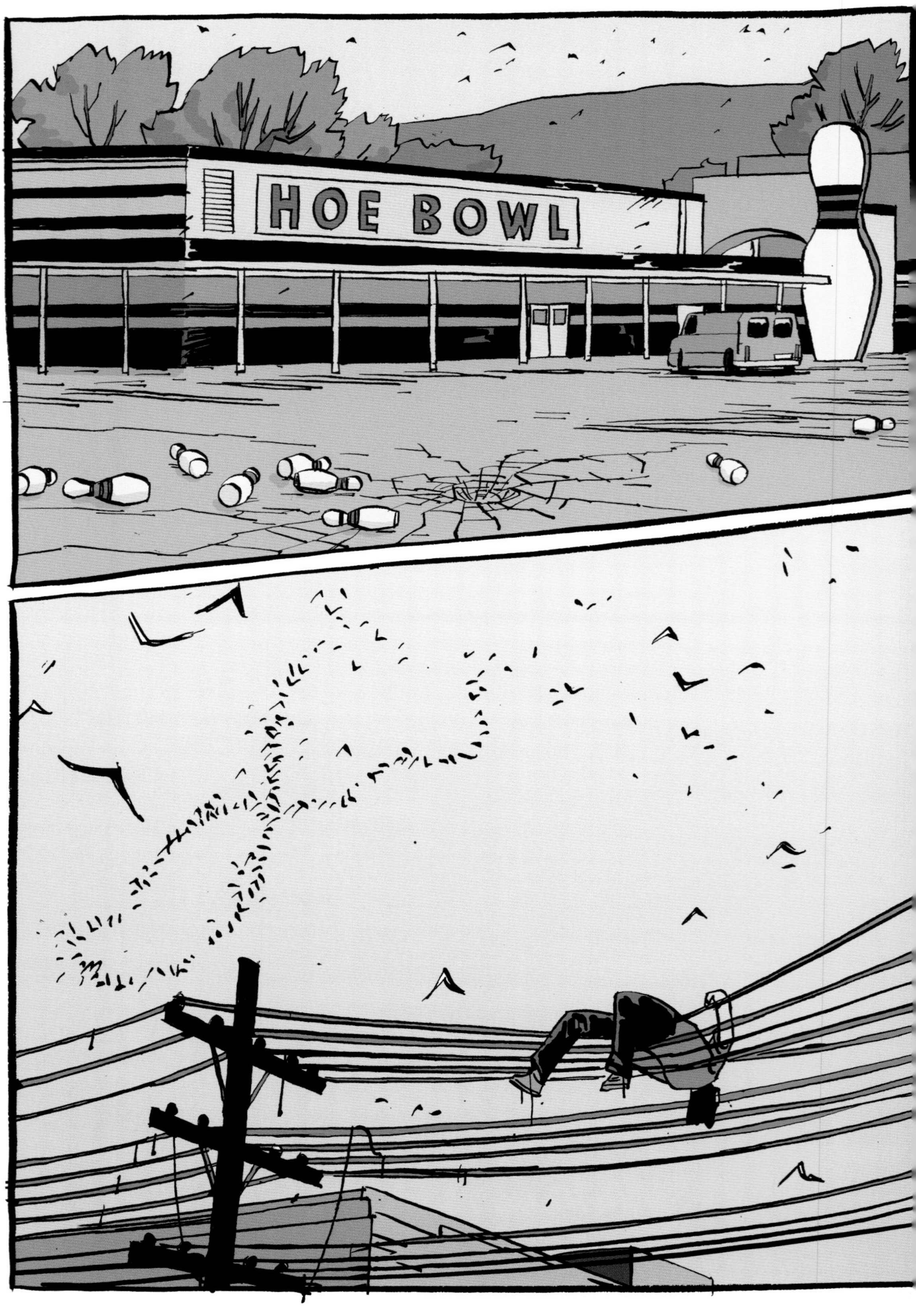
HOE BOWL

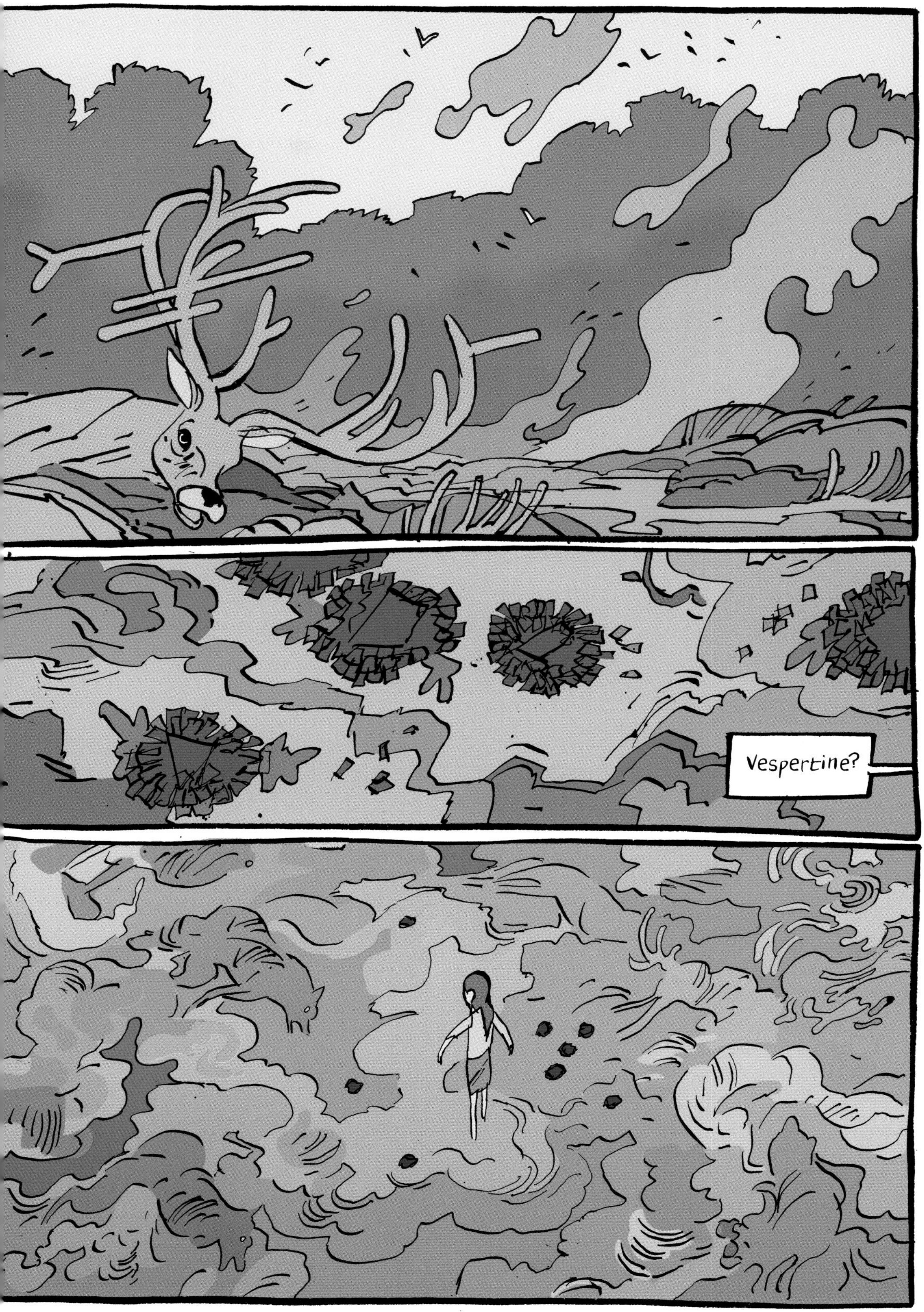
Vespertine?

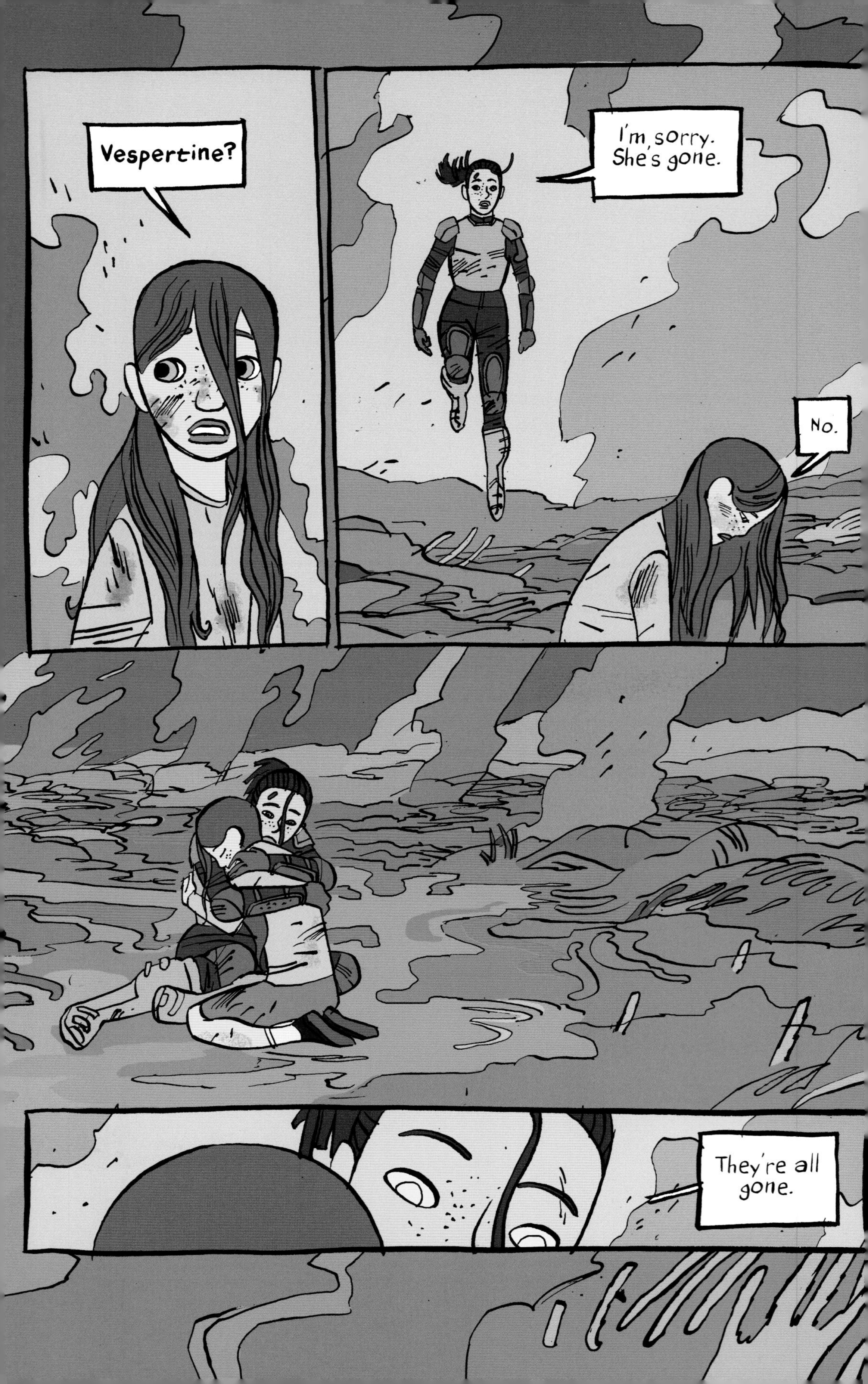
Vespertine?
I'm sorry. She's gone.
No.
They're all gone.

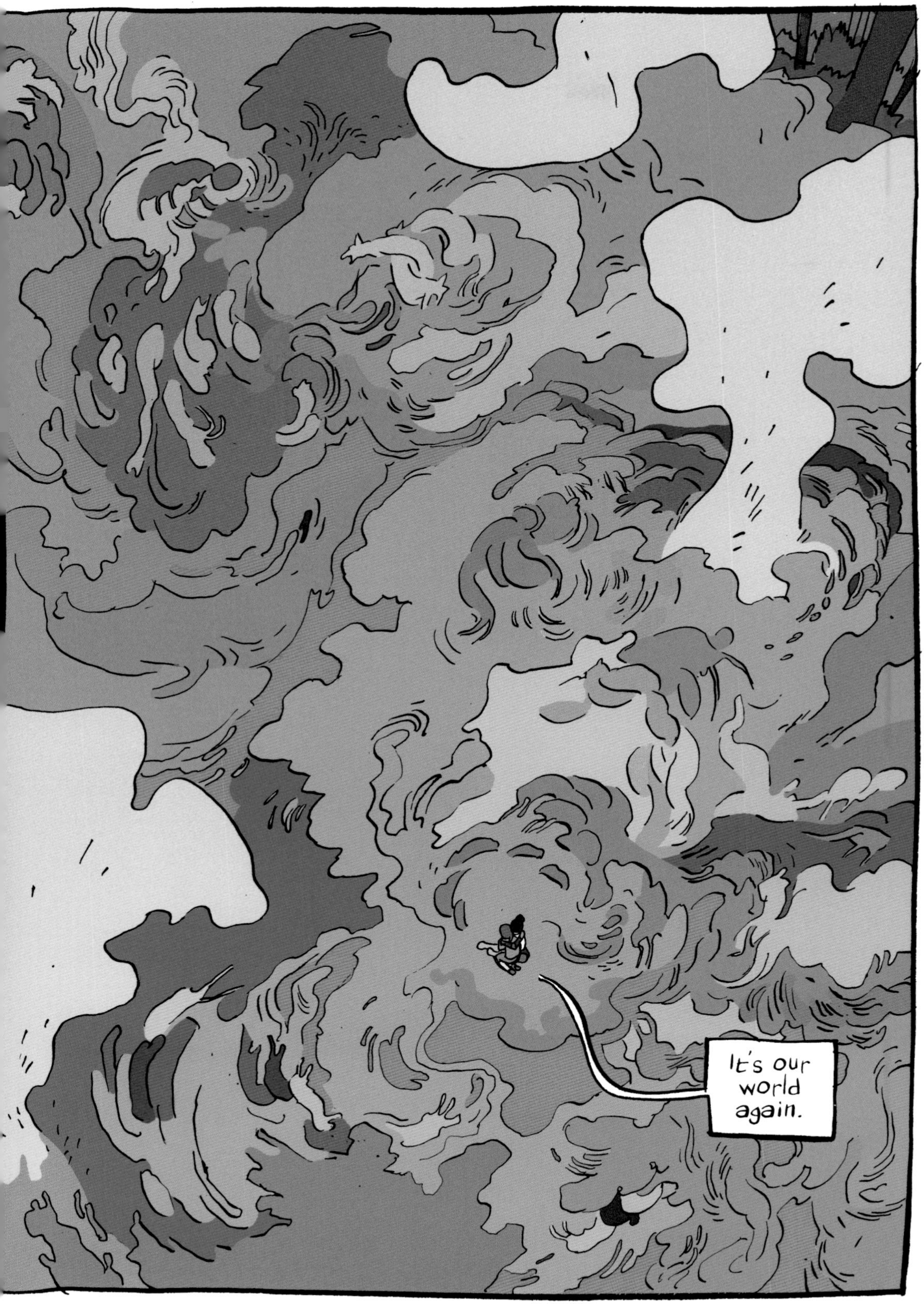
It's our world again.

3 YEARS LATER

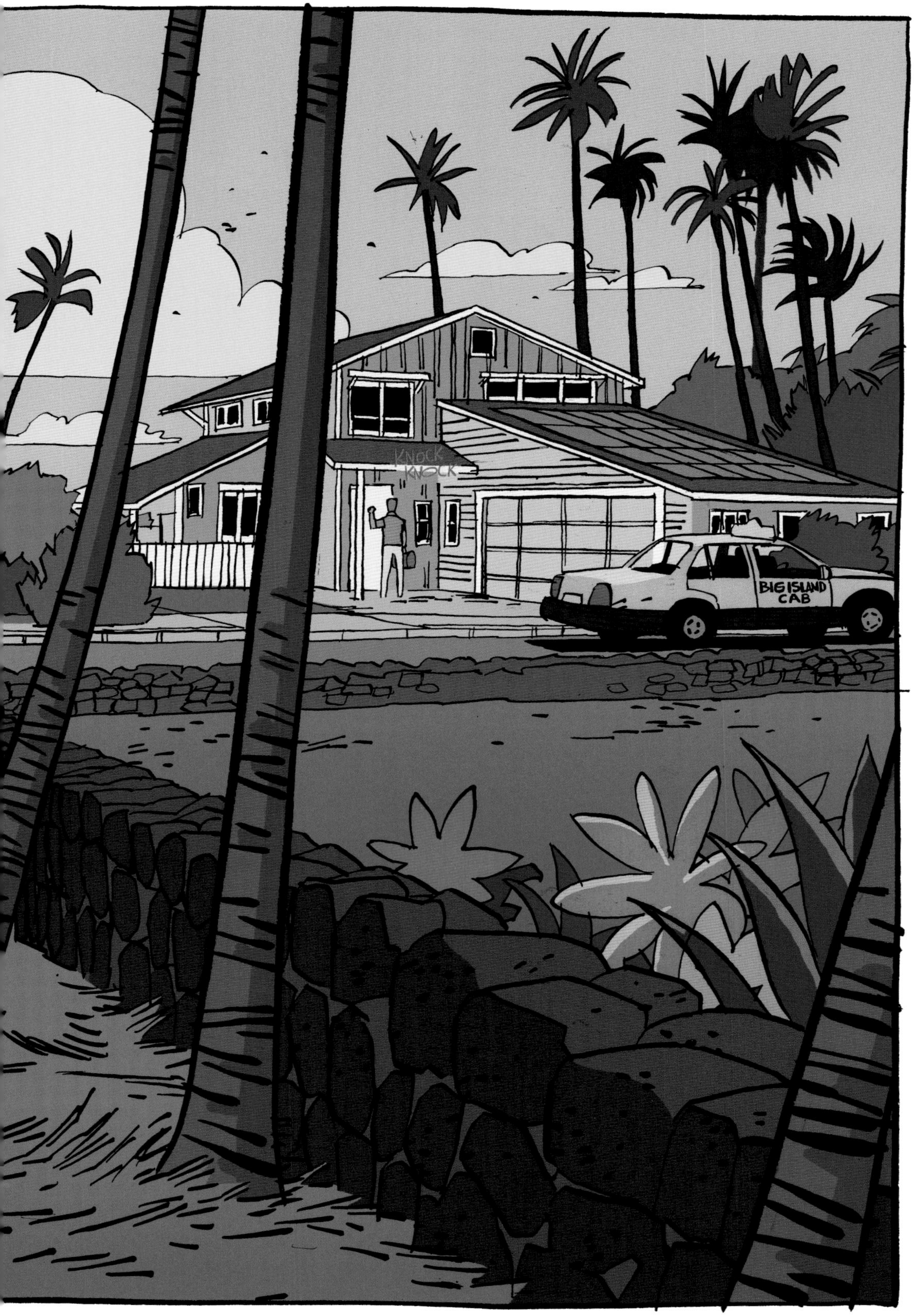
KNOCK
KNOCK
BIG ISLAND
CAB

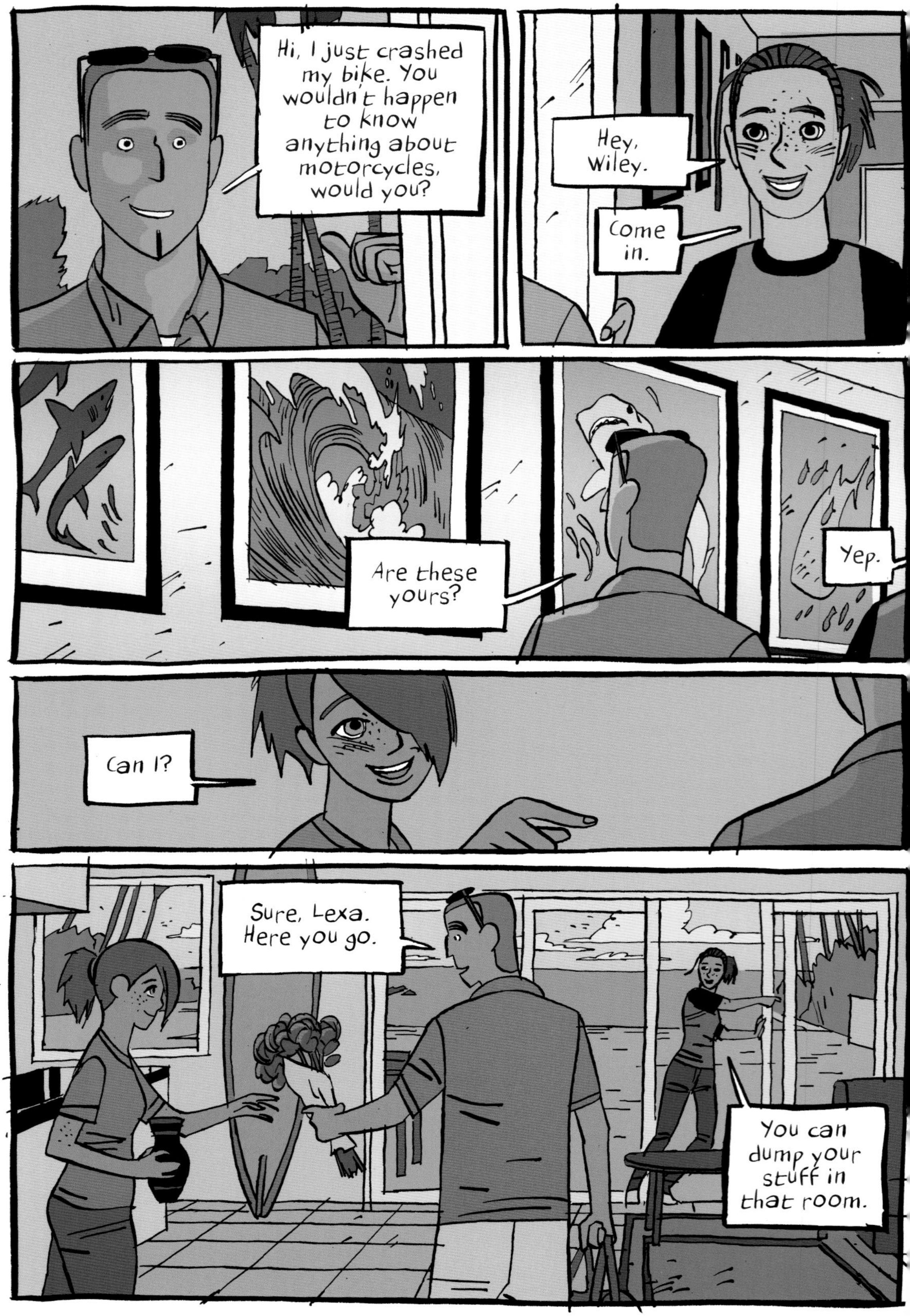
Hi, I just crashed my bike. You wouldn't happen to know anything about motorcycles, would you?
Hey, Wiley.
Come in.
Are these yours?
Yep.
Can I?
Sure, Lexa. Here you go.
You can dump your stuff in that room.

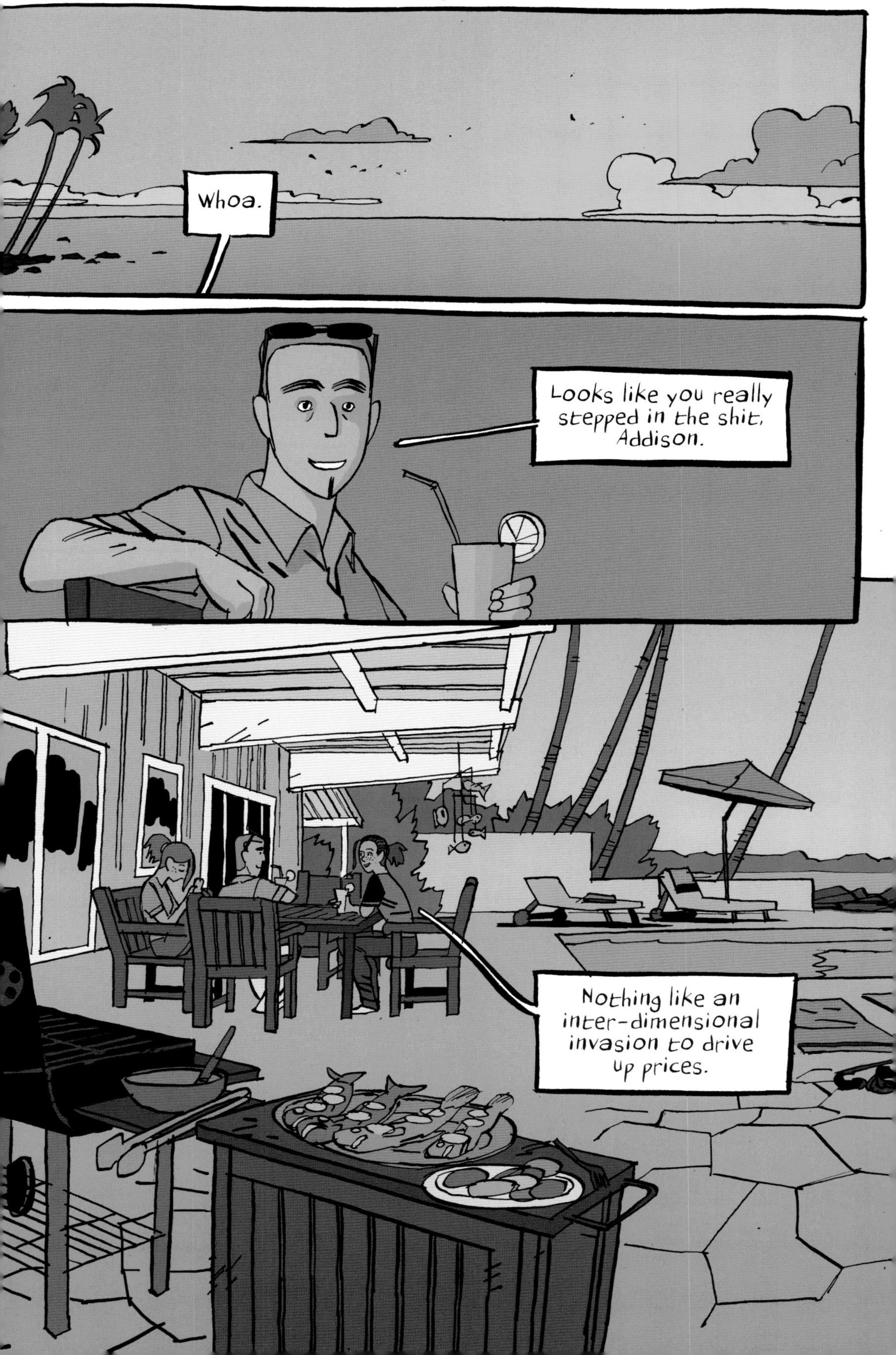
Whoa.
Looks like you really stepped in the shit, Addison.
Nothing like an inter-dimensional invasion to drive up prices.

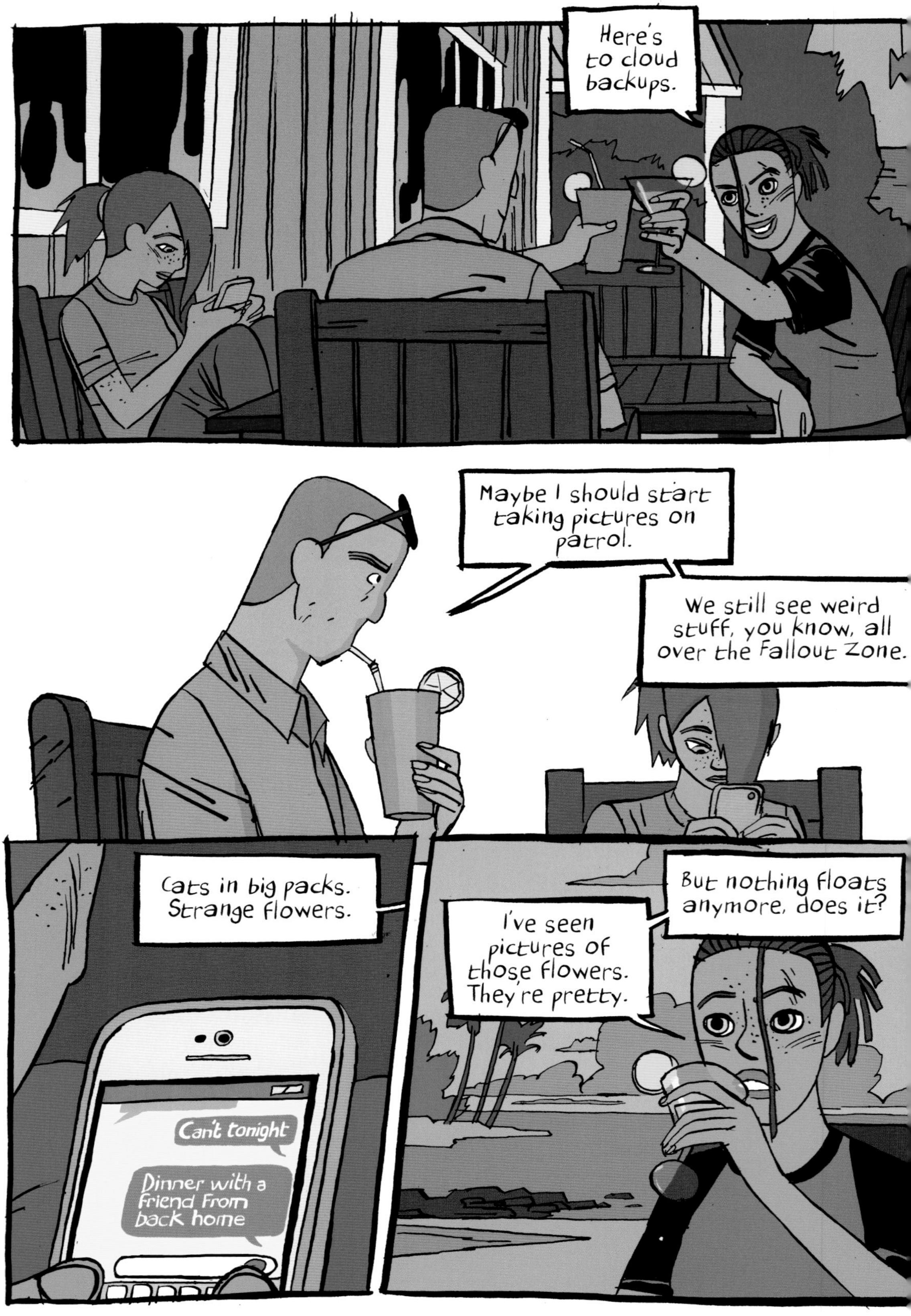
Here's to cloud backups.
Maybe I should start taking pictures on patrol.
We still see weird stuff, you know, all over the Fallout Zone.
Cats in big packs. Strange flowers.
Can't tonight
Dinner with a friend from back home
I've seen pictures of those flowers. They're pretty.
But nothing floats anymore, does it?

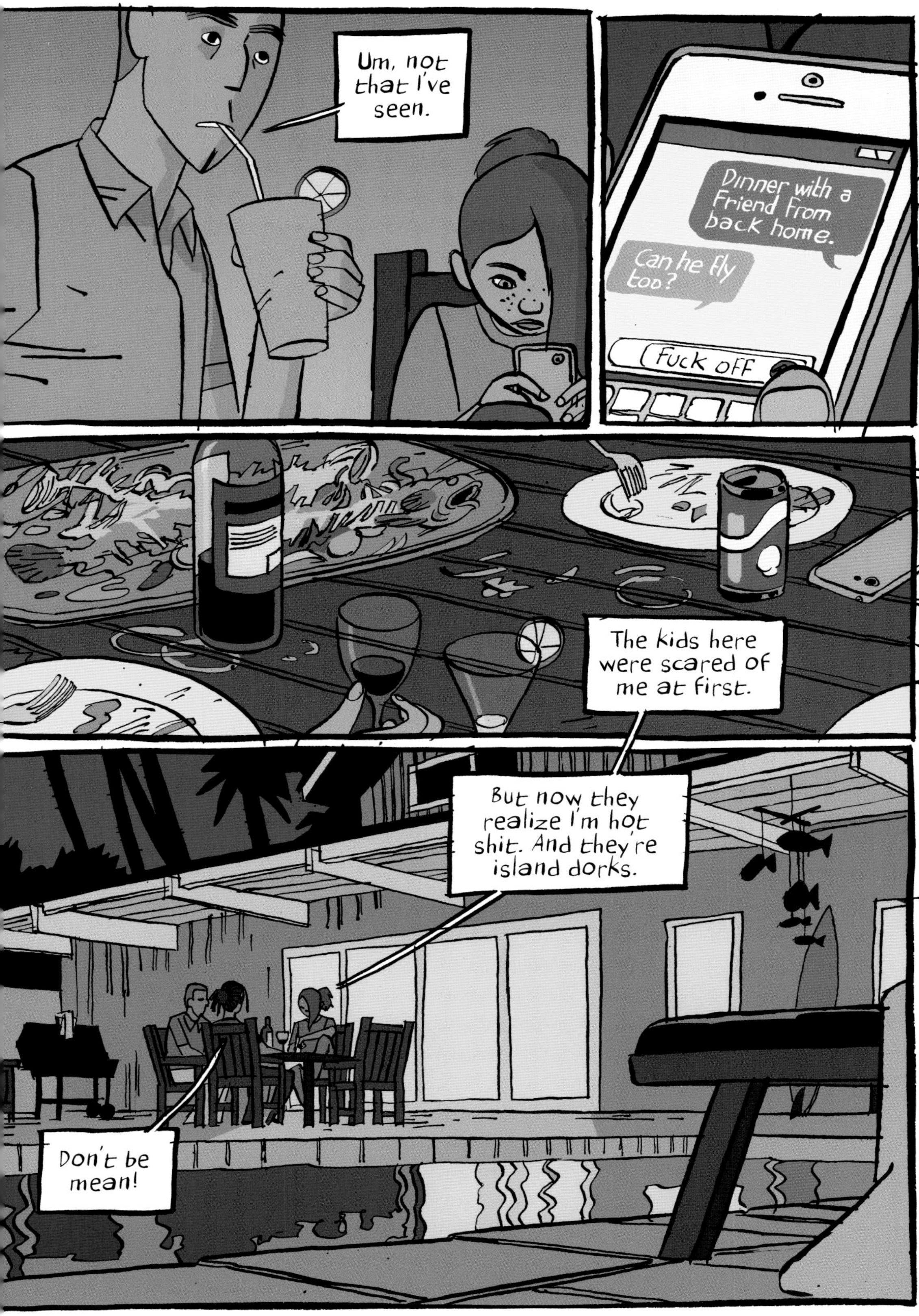
Um, not that I've seen.
Dinner with a Friend From back home.
Can he fly too?
Fuck off
The kids here were scared of me at first.
But now they realize I'm hot shit. And they're island dorks.
Don't be mean!

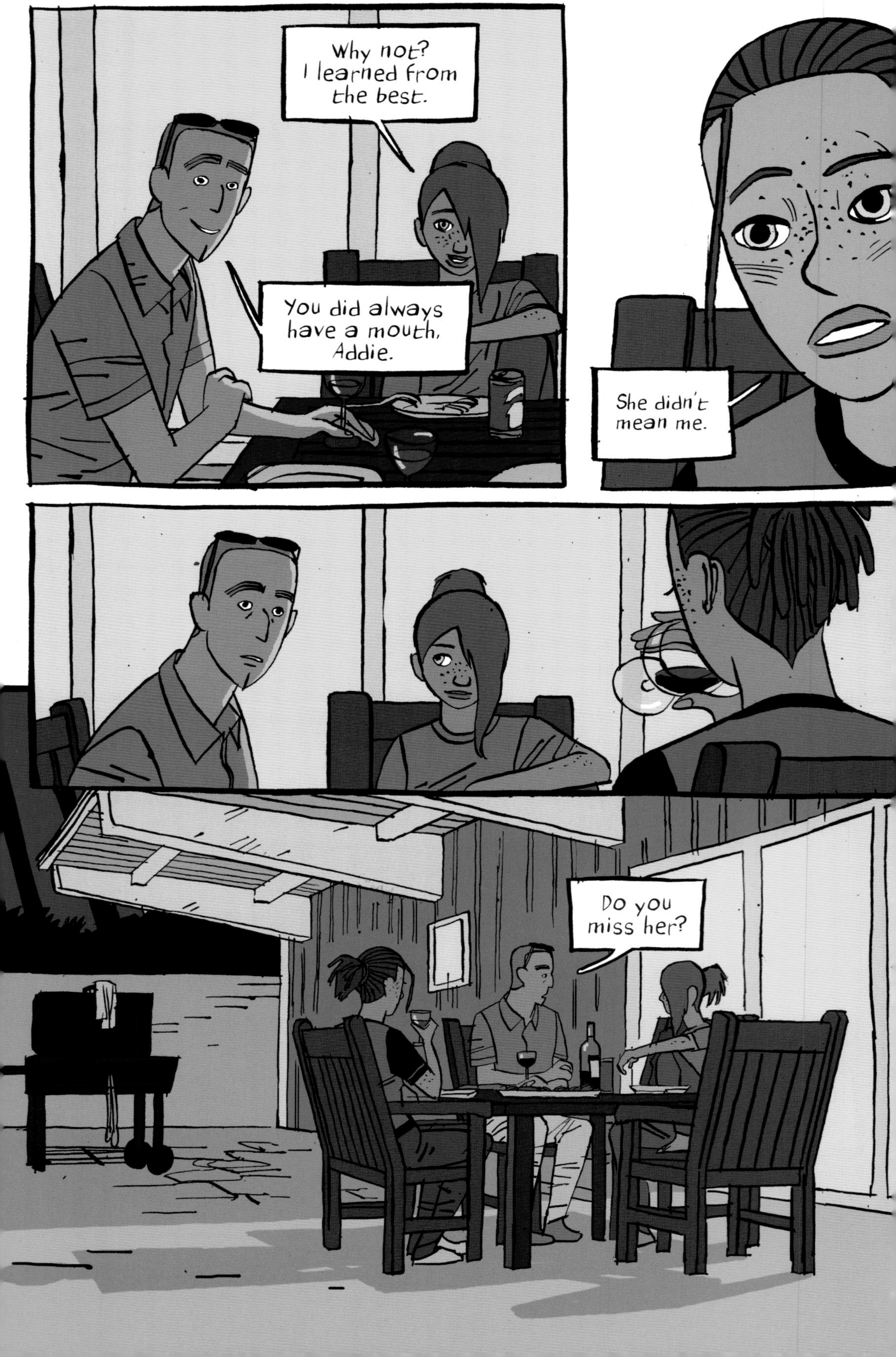
Why not? I learned from the best.
You did always have a mouth, Addie.
She didn't mean me.
Do you miss her?

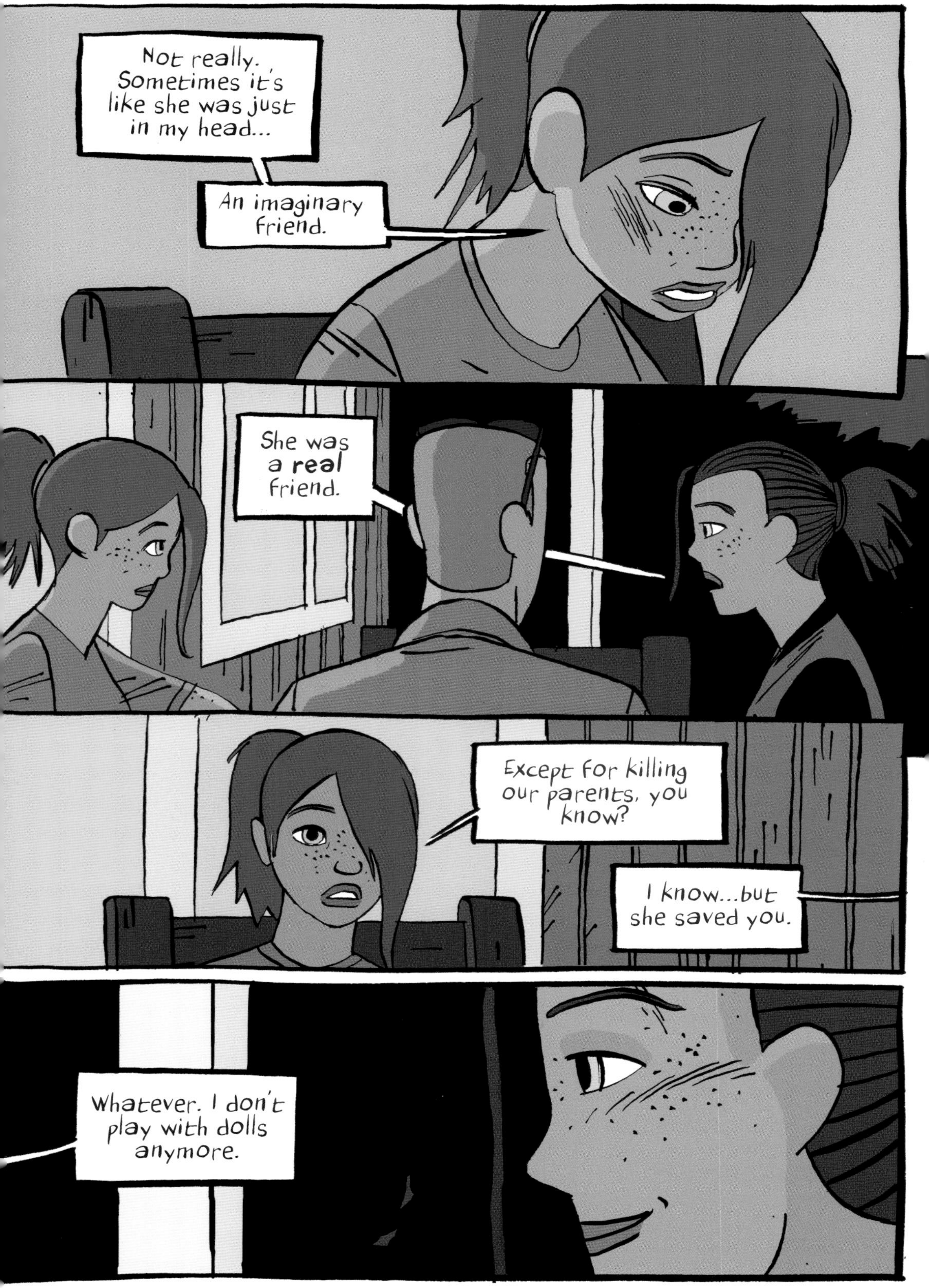
Not really. Sometimes it's like she was just in my head...
An imaginary friend.
She was a **real** friend.
Except for killing our parents, you know?
I know...but she saved you.
Whatever. I don't play with dolls anymore.

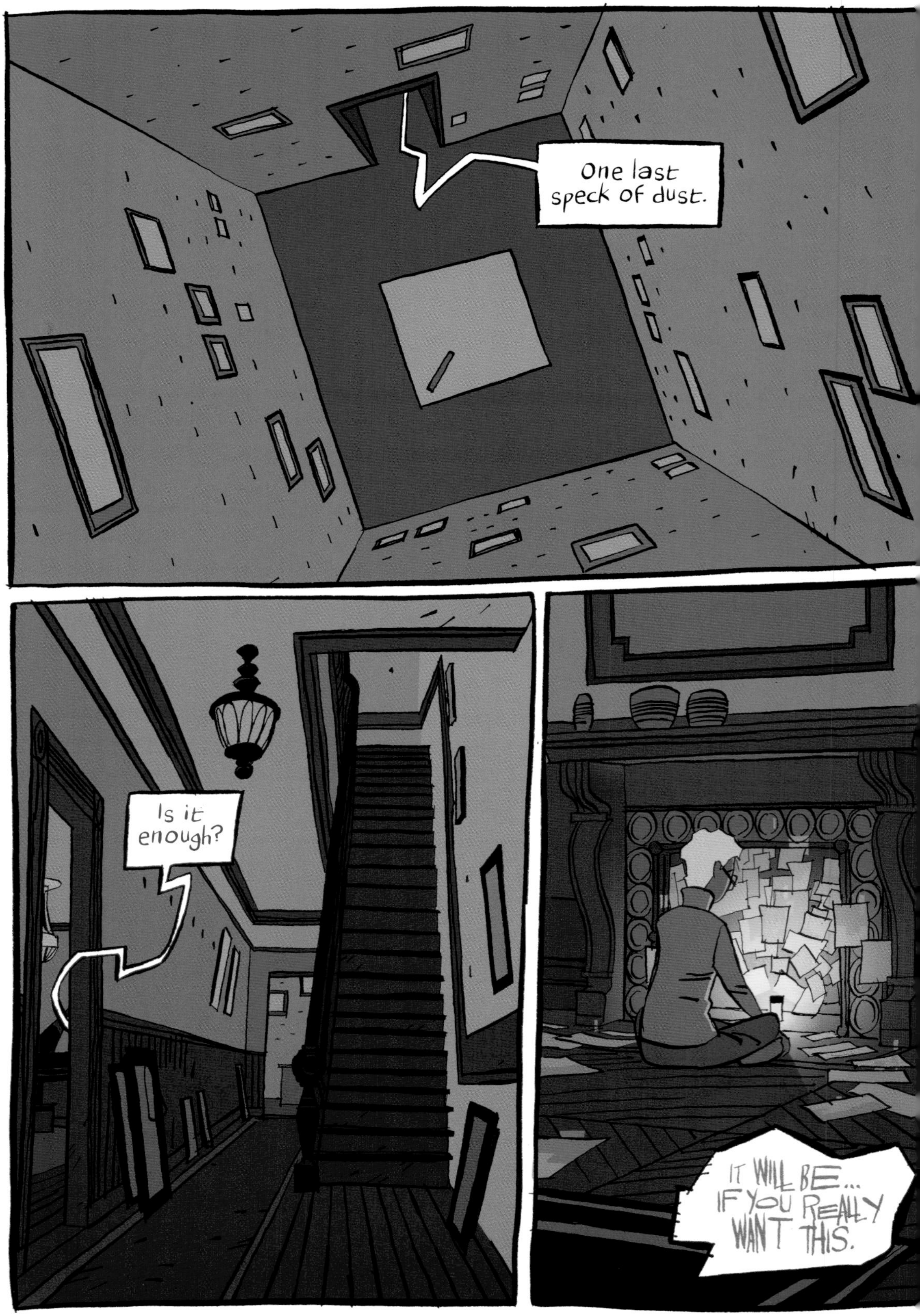
One last speck of dust.
Is it enough?
IT WILL BE... IF YOU REALLY WANT THIS.

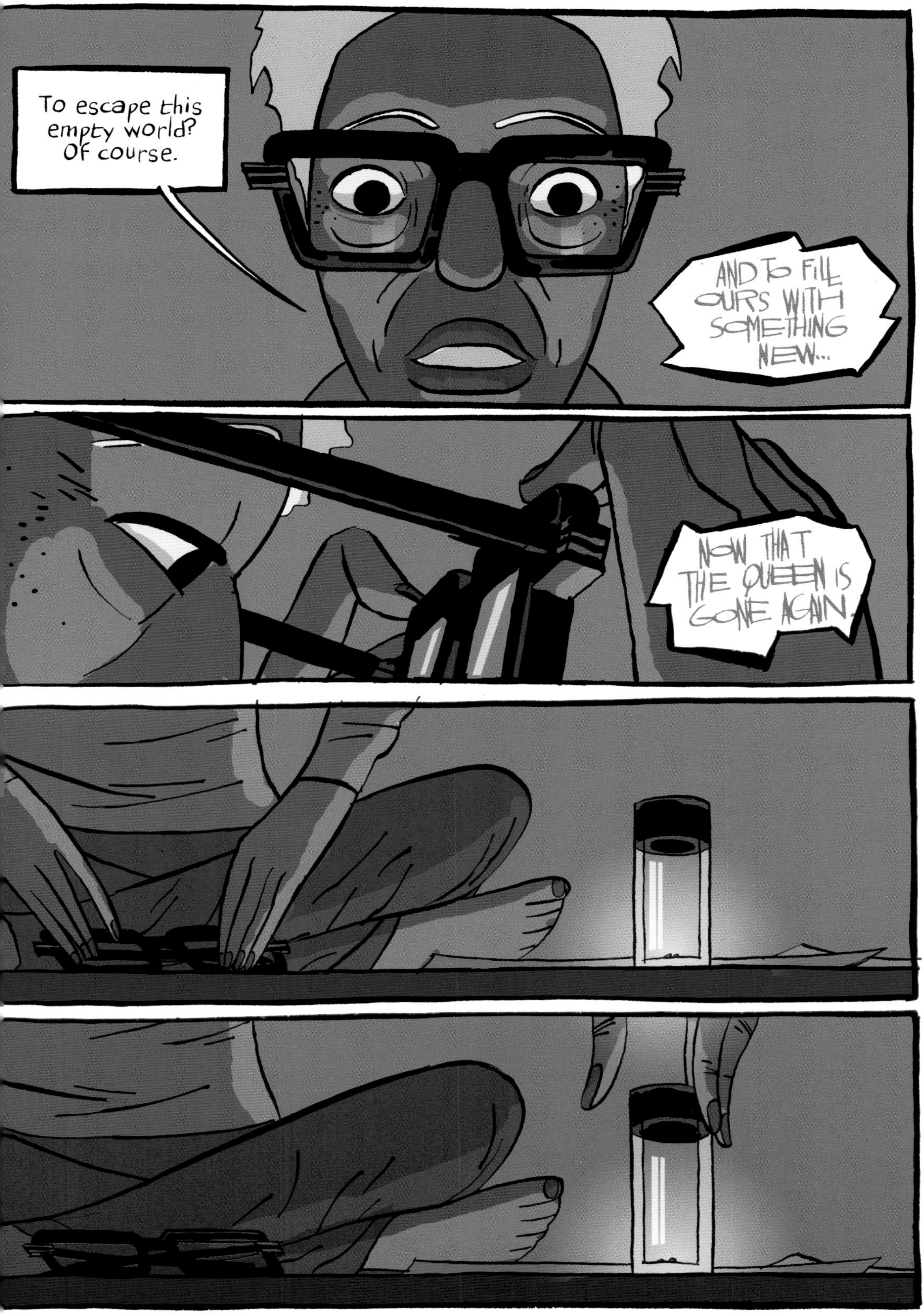
To escape this empty world? Of course.
AND TO FILL OURS WITH SOMETHING NEW...
NOW THAT THE QUEEN IS GONE AGAIN.

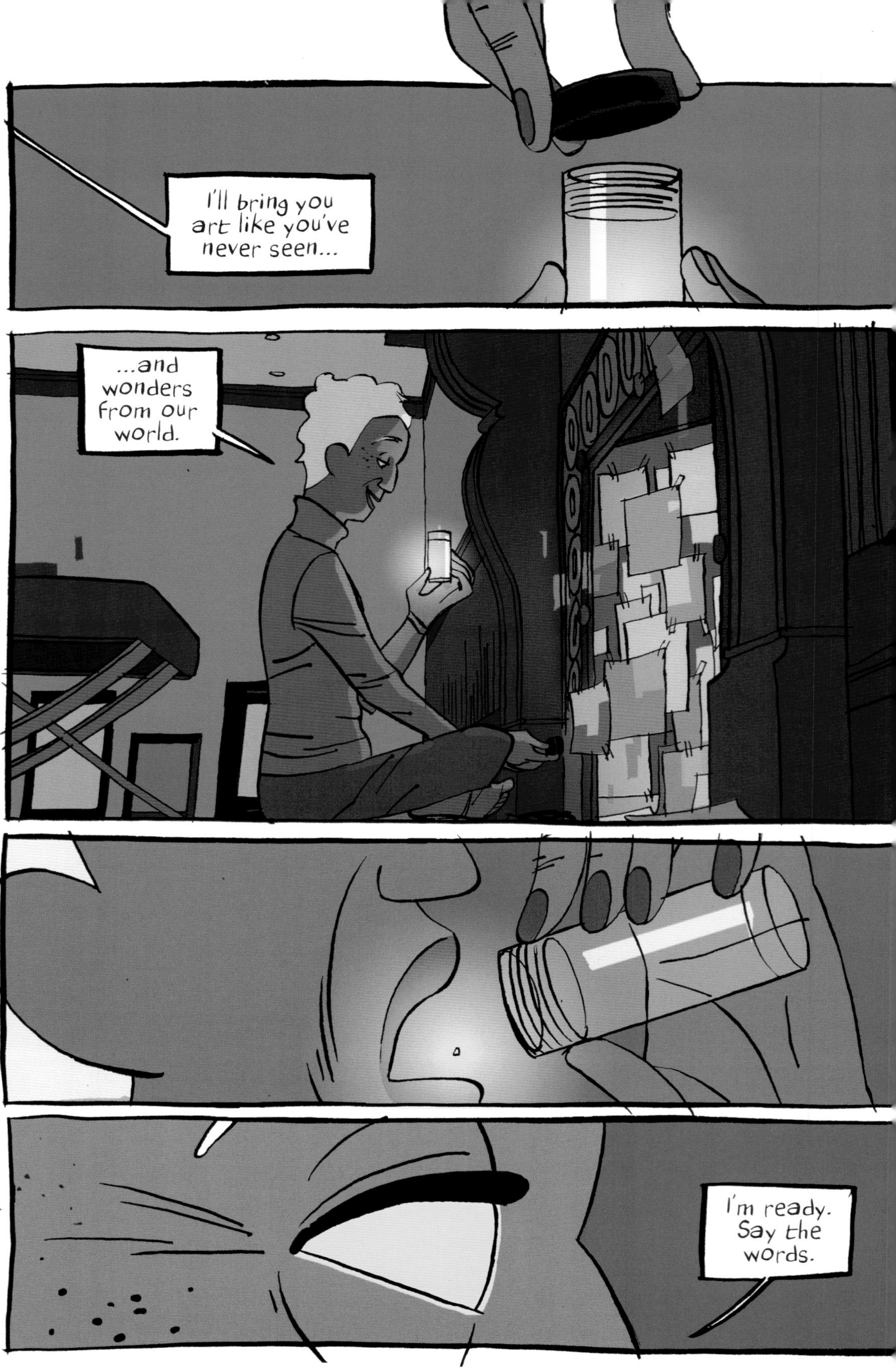
I'll bring you art like you've never seen...
...and wonders from our world.
I'm ready. Say the words.

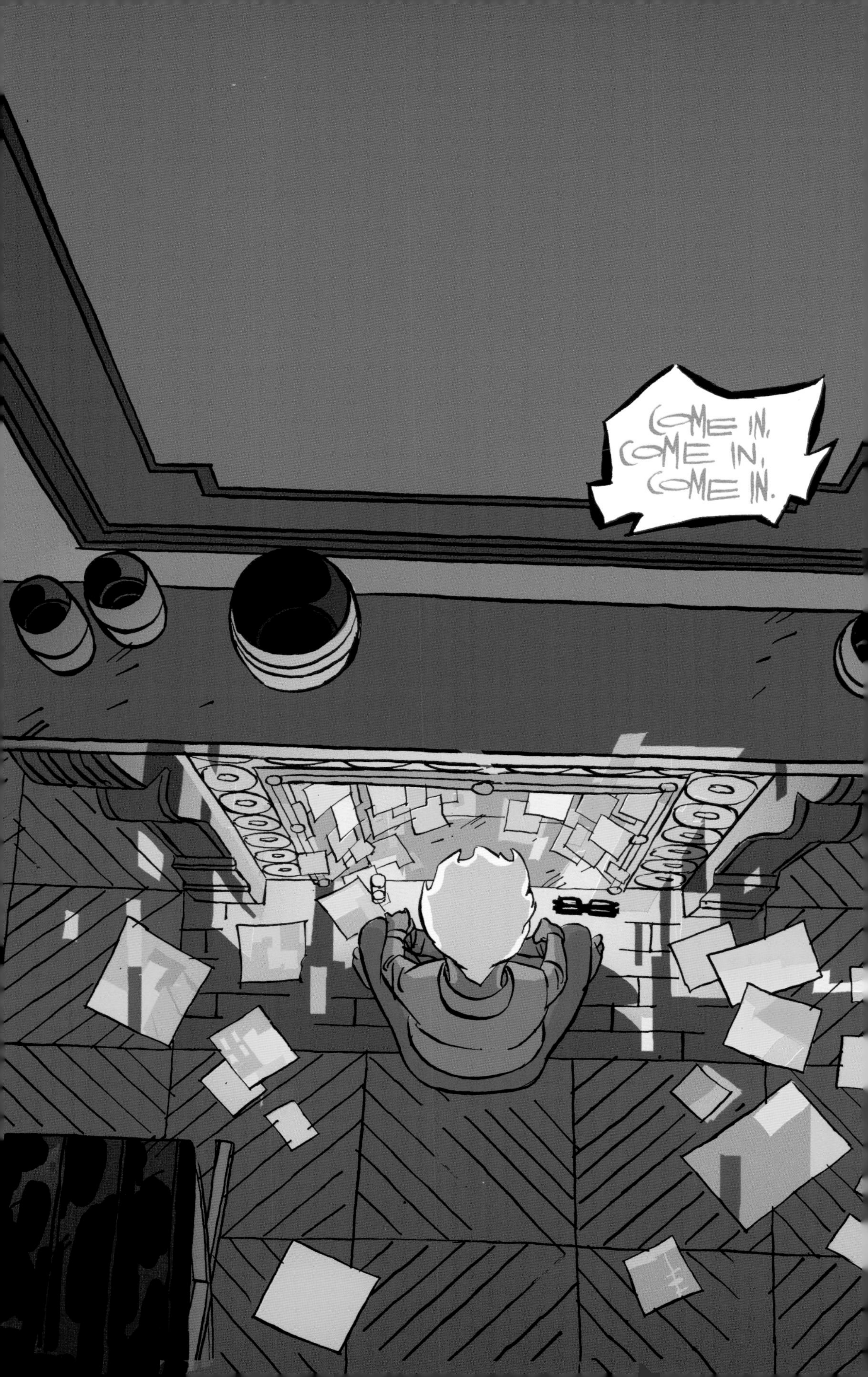
COME IN, COME IN, COME IN.

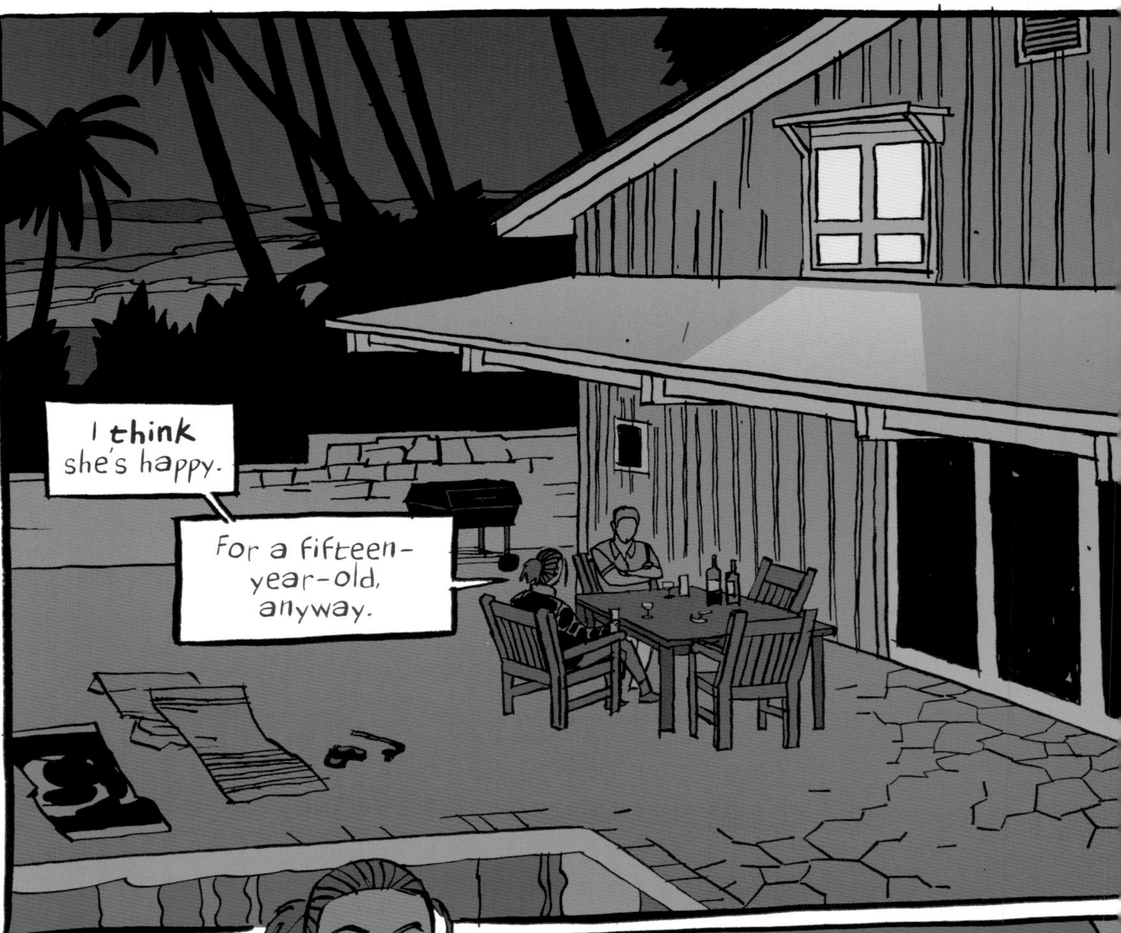
I think she's happy.
For a fifteen-year-old, anyway.

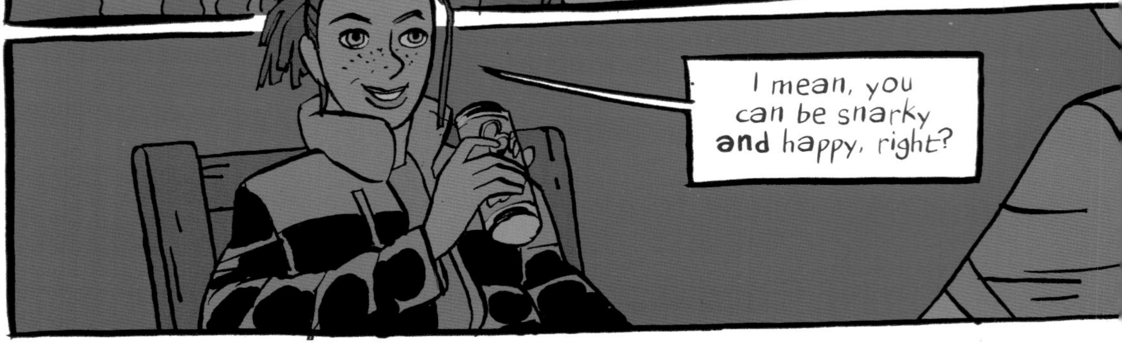
I mean, you can be snarky and happy, right?

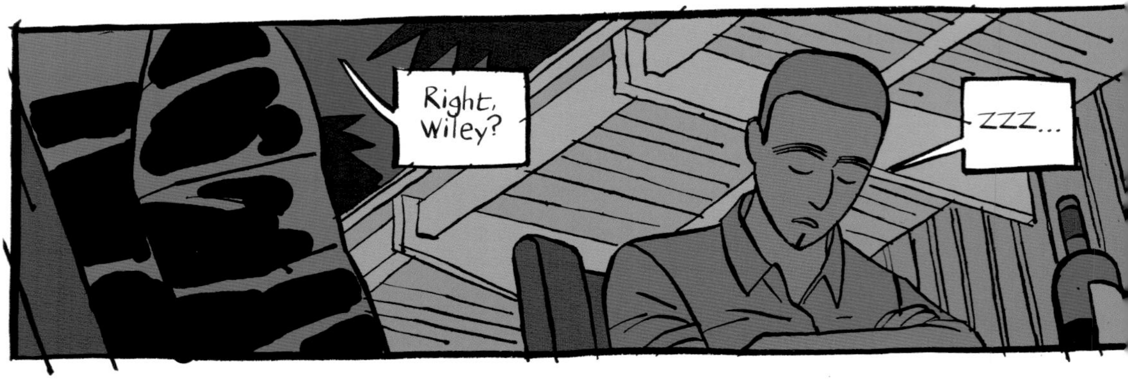
Right, Wiley?
ZZZ...

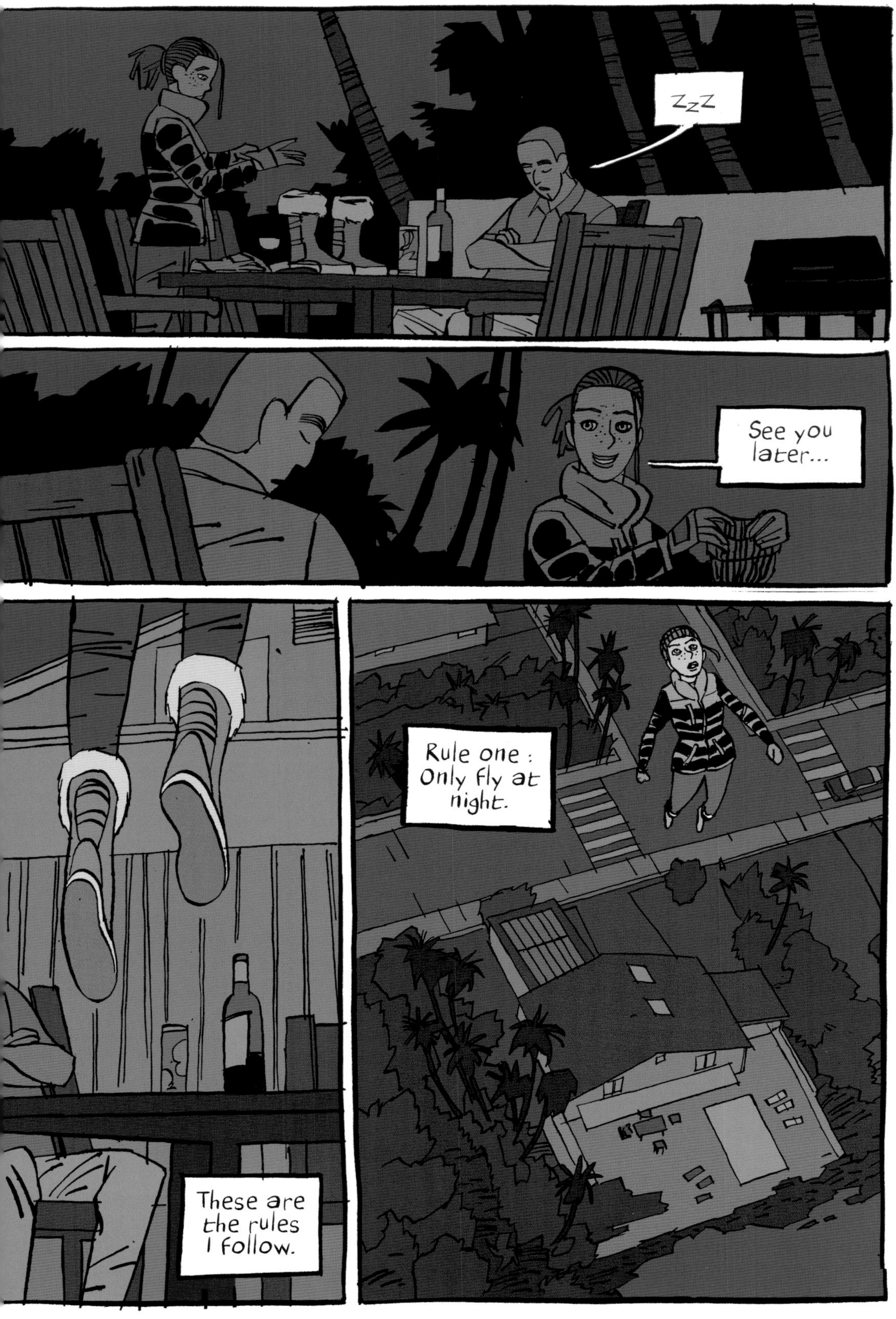
ZzZ
See you later...
These are the rules I follow.
Rule one: Only fly at night.

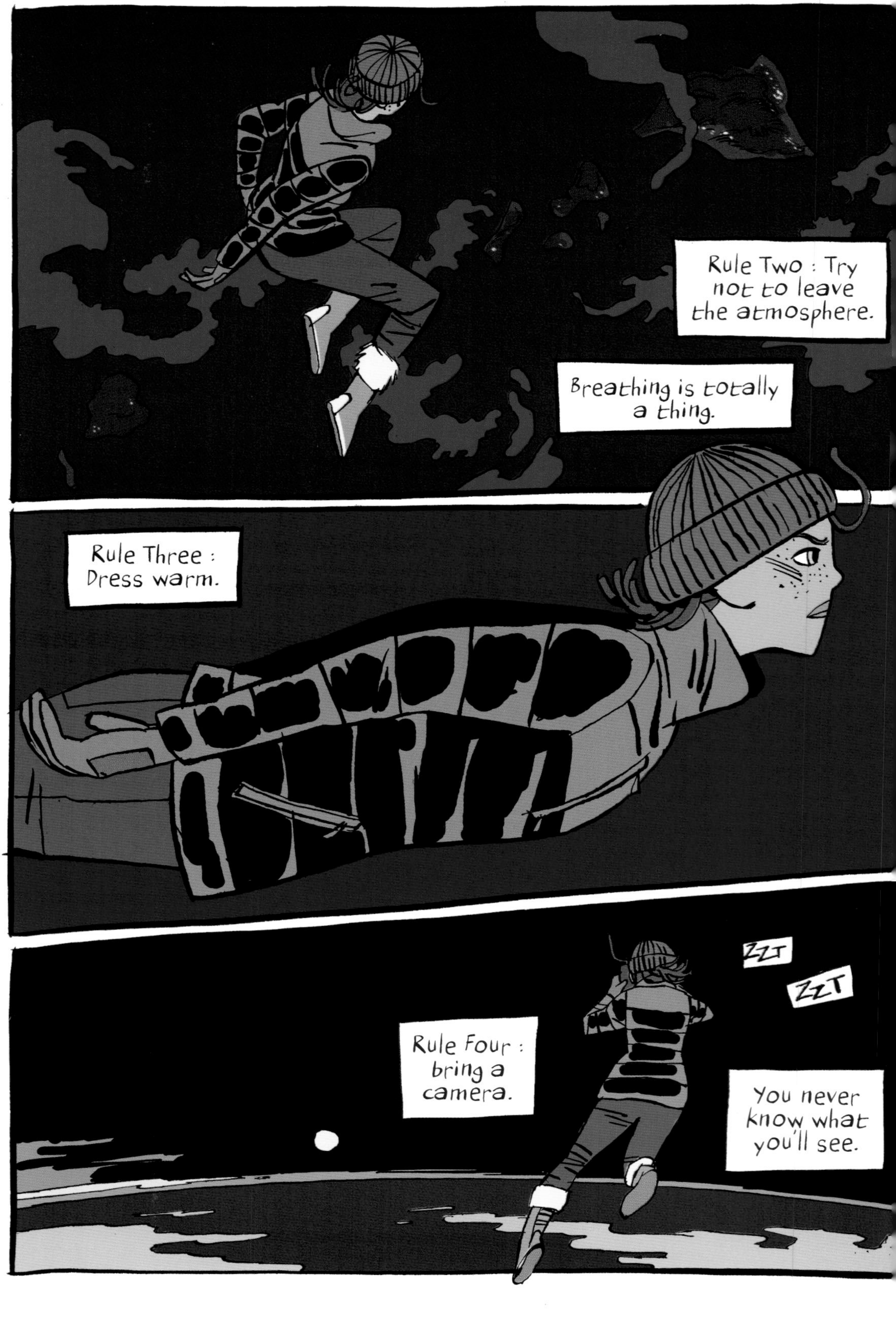
Rule Two : Try not to leave the atmosphere.
Breathing is totally a thing.
Rule Three : Dress warm.
ZZT
ZZT
Rule Four : bring a camera.
You never know what you'll see.

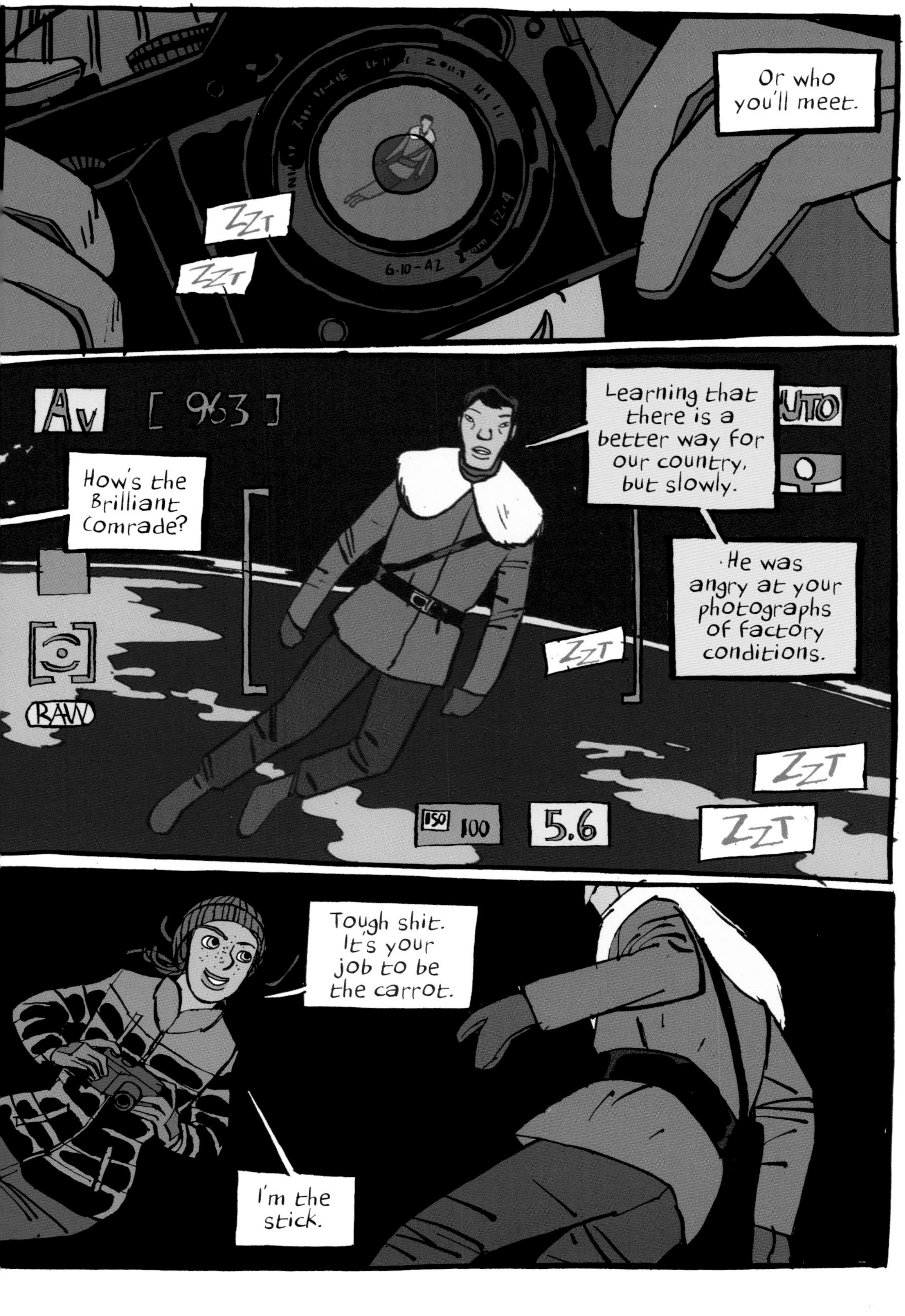

Or who you'll meet.
ZZT
ZZT
Av
[963]
How's the Brilliant Comrade?
Learning that there is a better way for our country, but slowly.
UTO
He was angry at your photographs of factory conditions.
ZZT
RAW
ZZT
100
5.6
ZZT
Tough shit. It's your job to be the carrot.
I'm the stick.

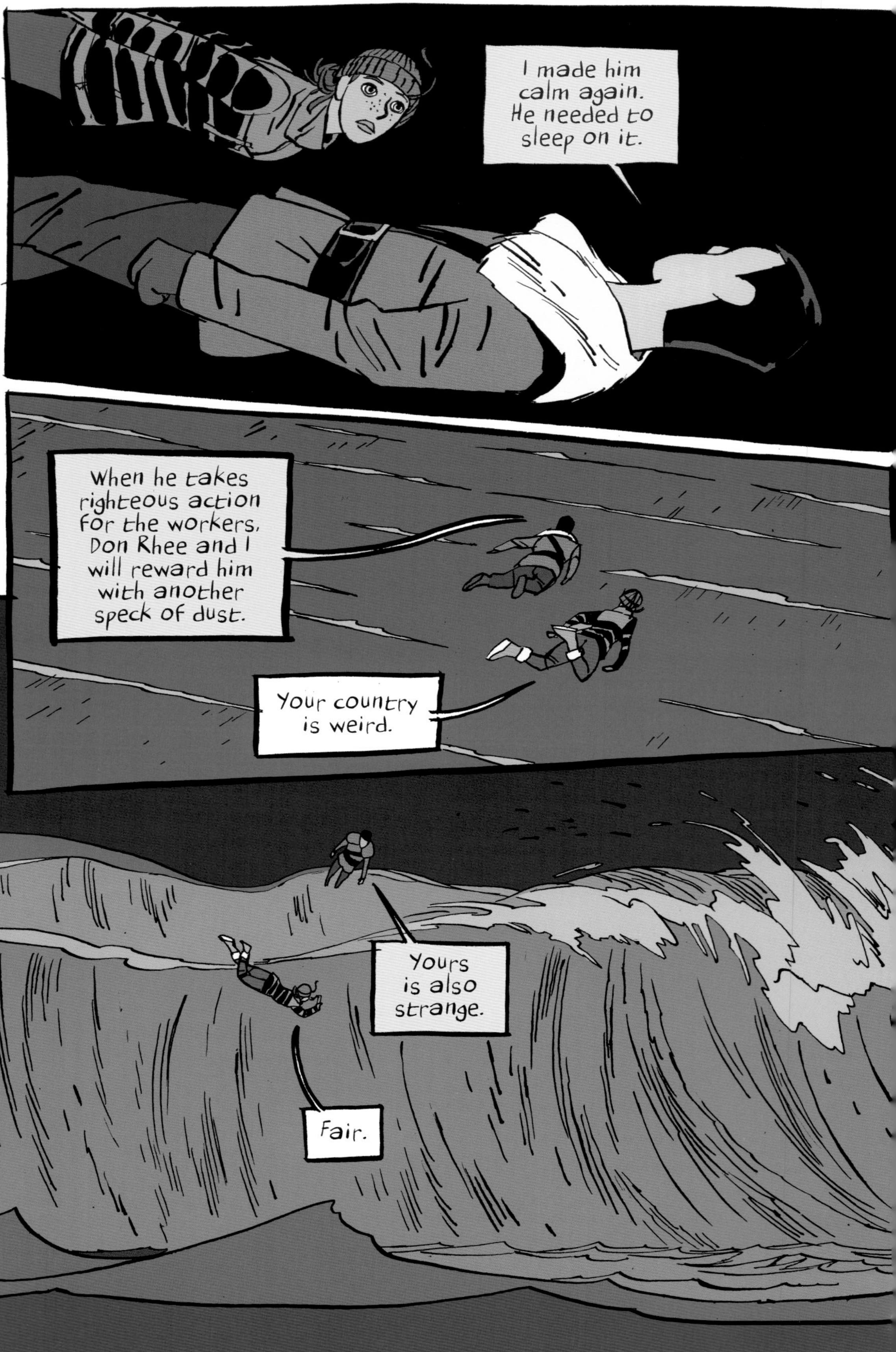
I made him calm again. He needed to sleep on it.
When he takes righteous action for the workers, Don Rhee and I will reward him with another speck of dust.
Your country is weird.
Yours is also strange.
Fair.

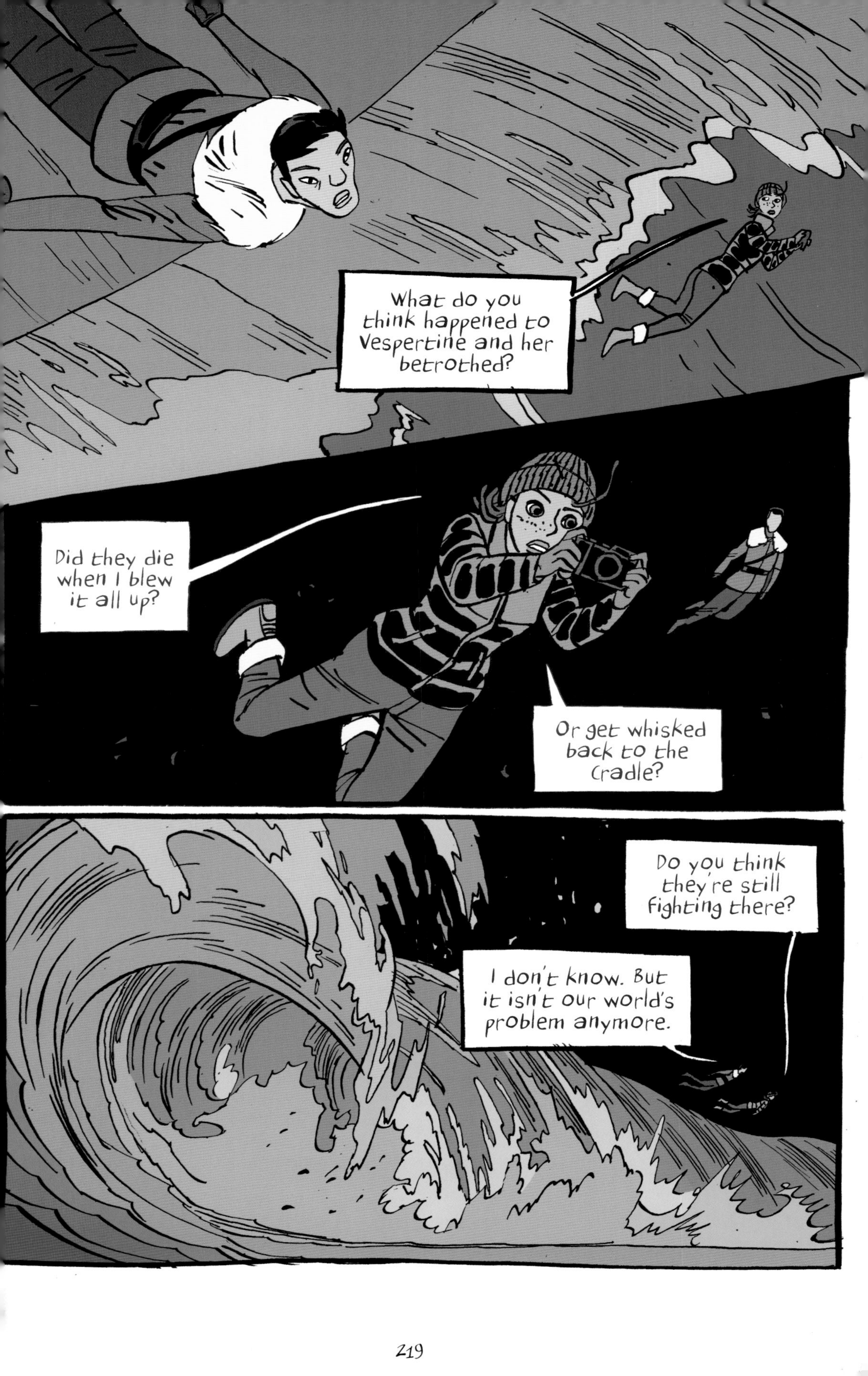
What do you think happened to Vespertine and her betrothed?
Did they die when I blew it all up?
Or get whisked back to the Cradle?
Do you think they're still fighting there?
I don't know. But it isn't our world's problem anymore.

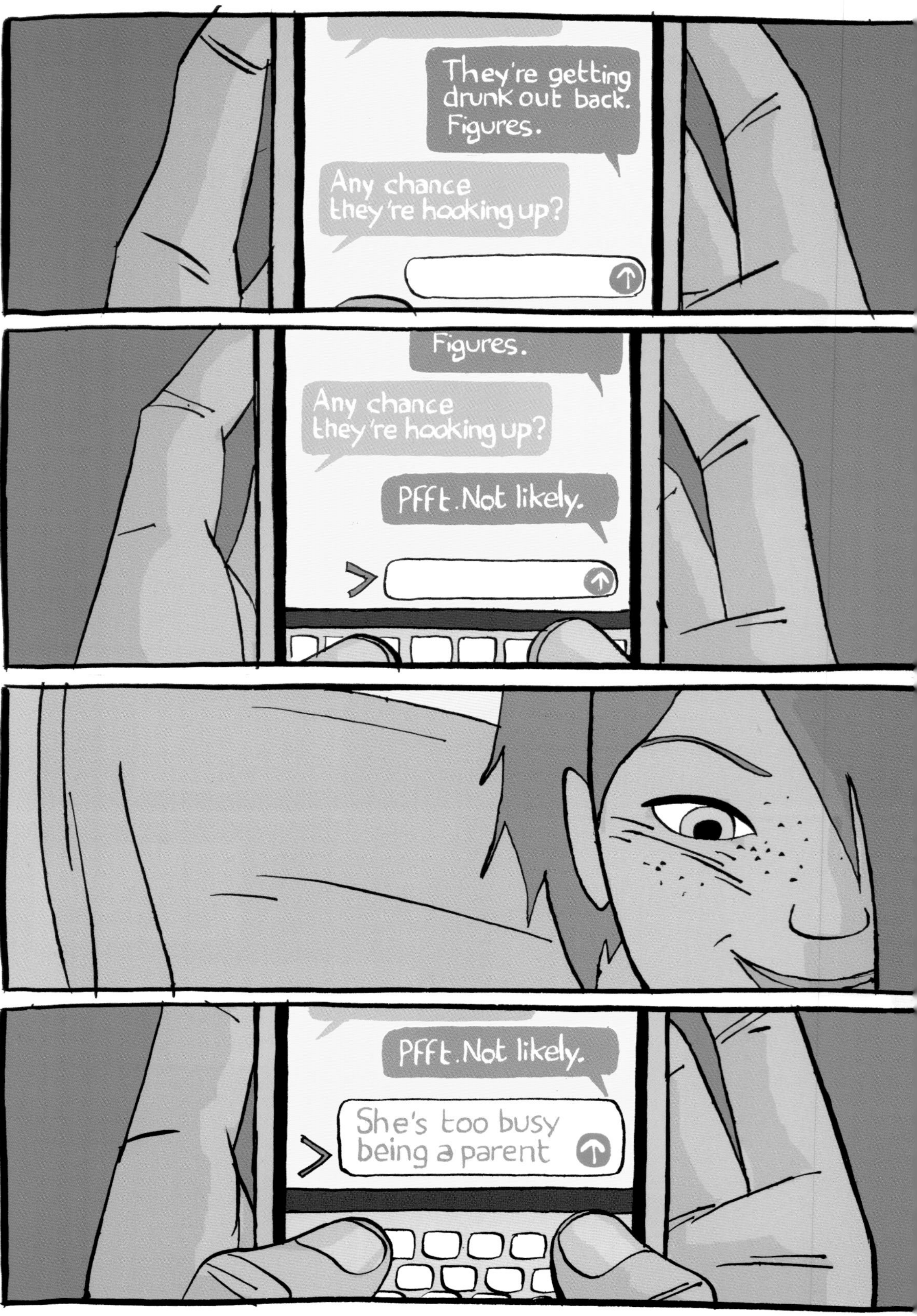
They're getting drunk out back. Figures.
Any chance they're hooking up?
Figures.
Any chance they're hooking up?
Pfft. Not likely.
Pfft. Not likely.
She's too busy being a parent

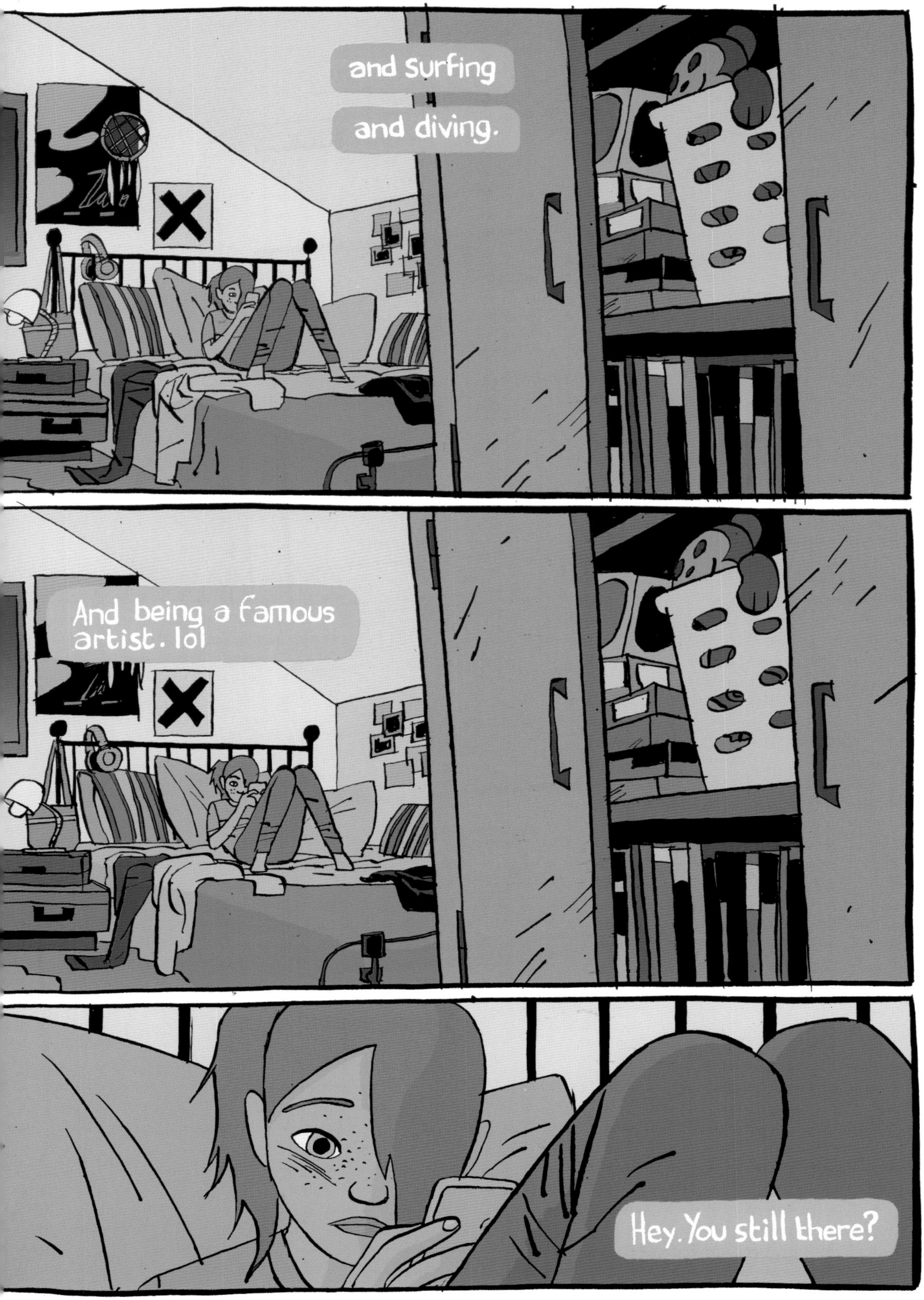
and surfing
and diving.
And being a famous artist. lol
Hey. You still there?

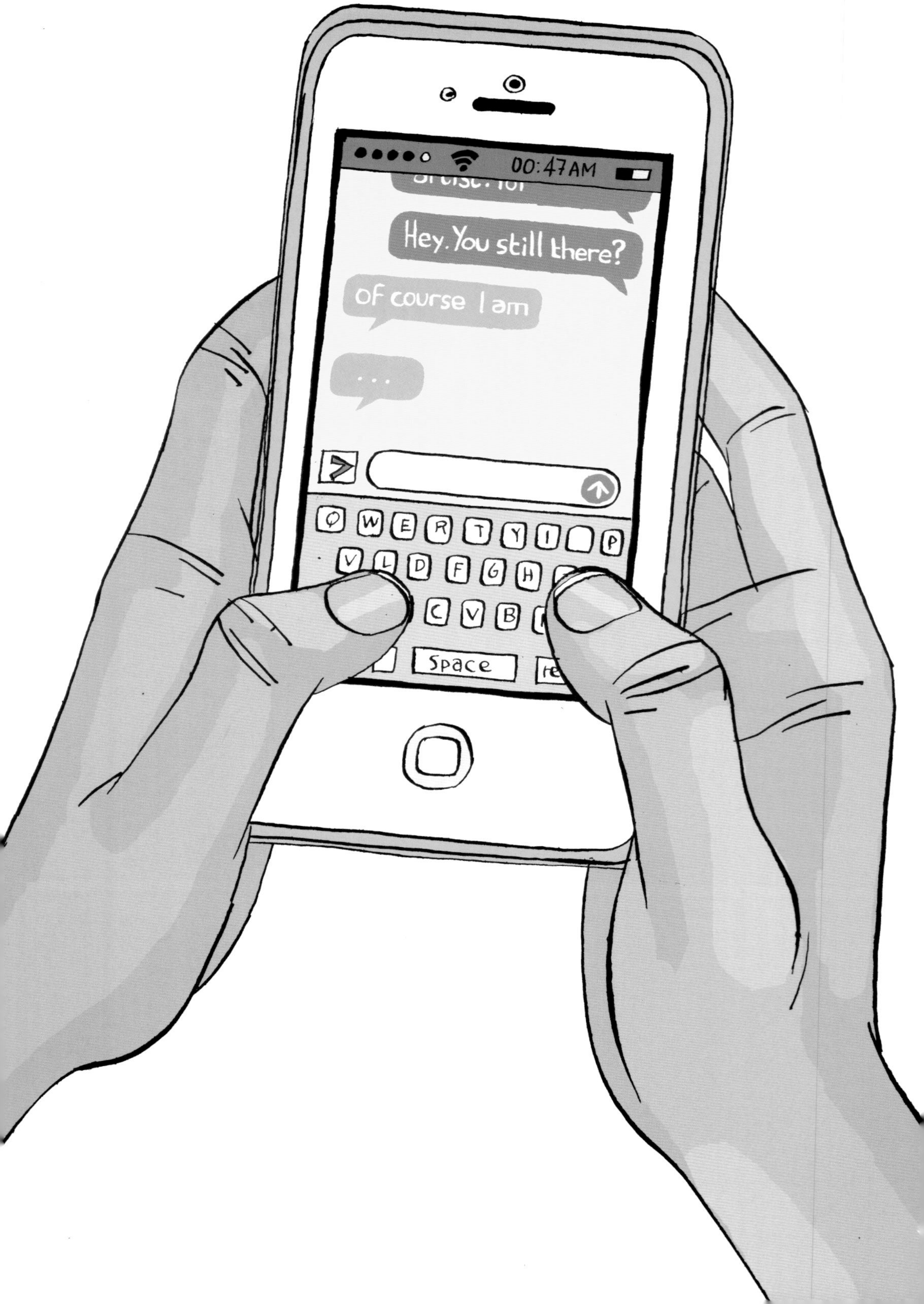

00:47AM
Hey. You still there?
of course I am
...
Space

For always and always kid.

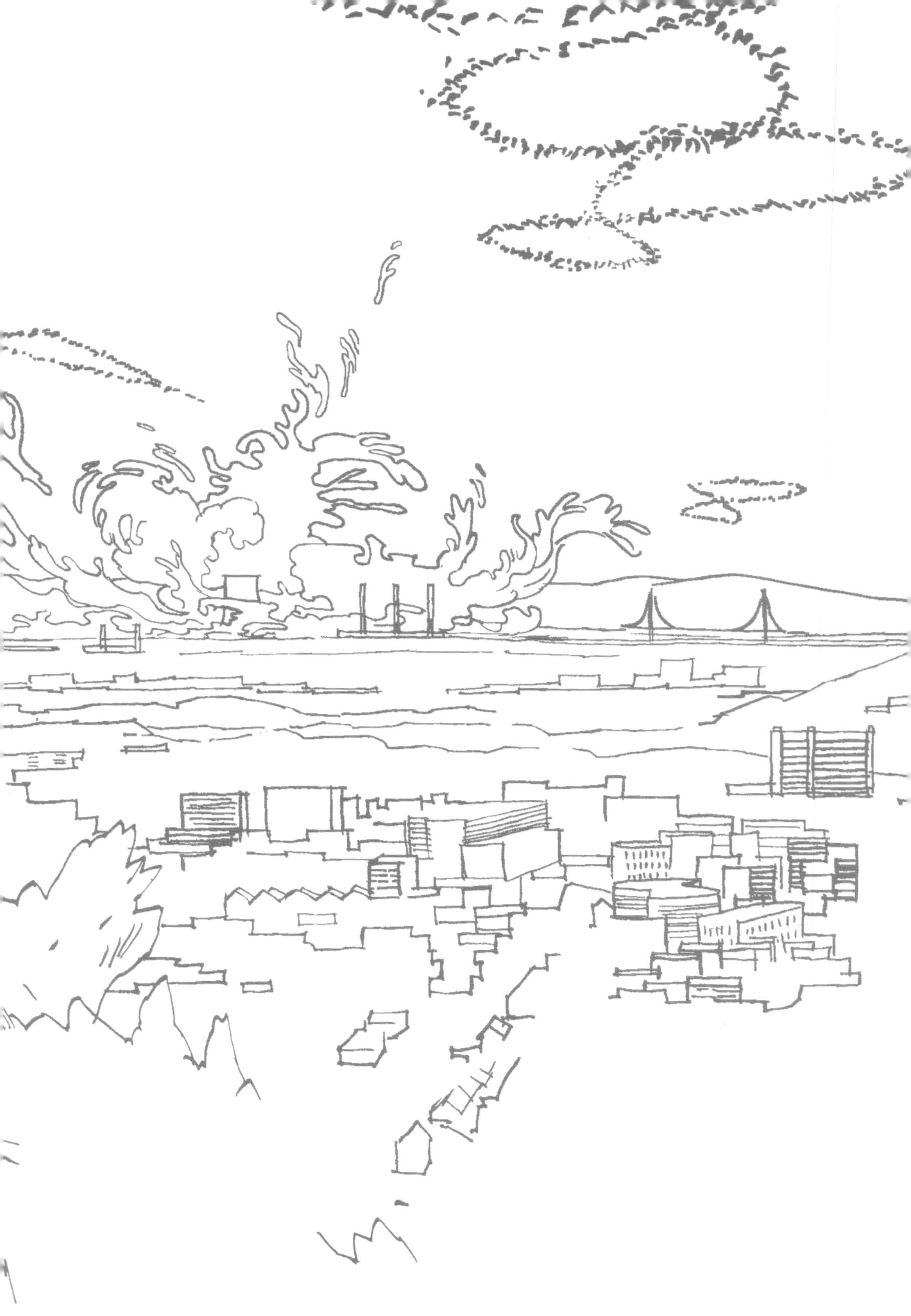

SPILL
ZONE

RESEARCH AND
DEVELOPMENT

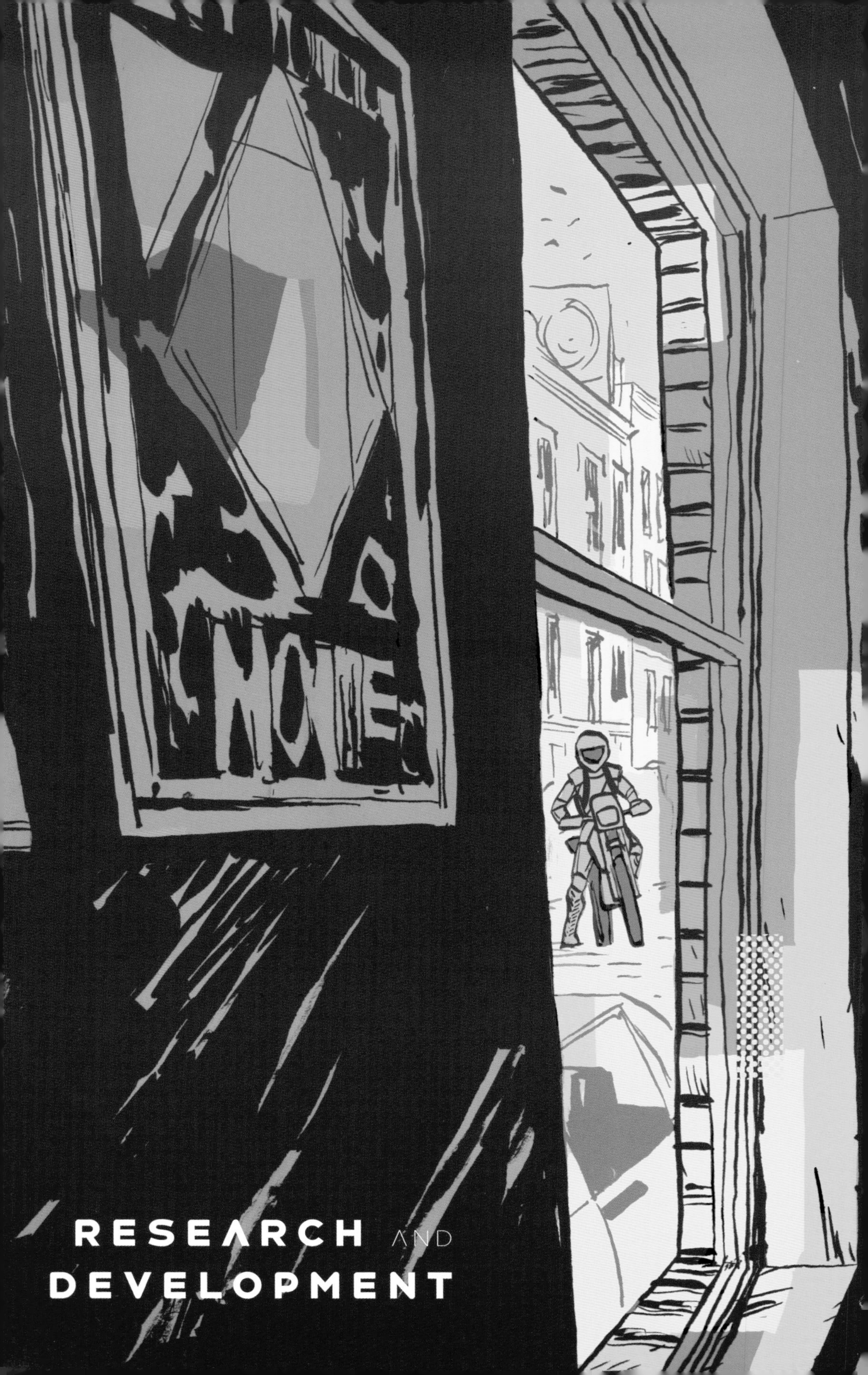

RESEARCH AND DEVELOPMENT

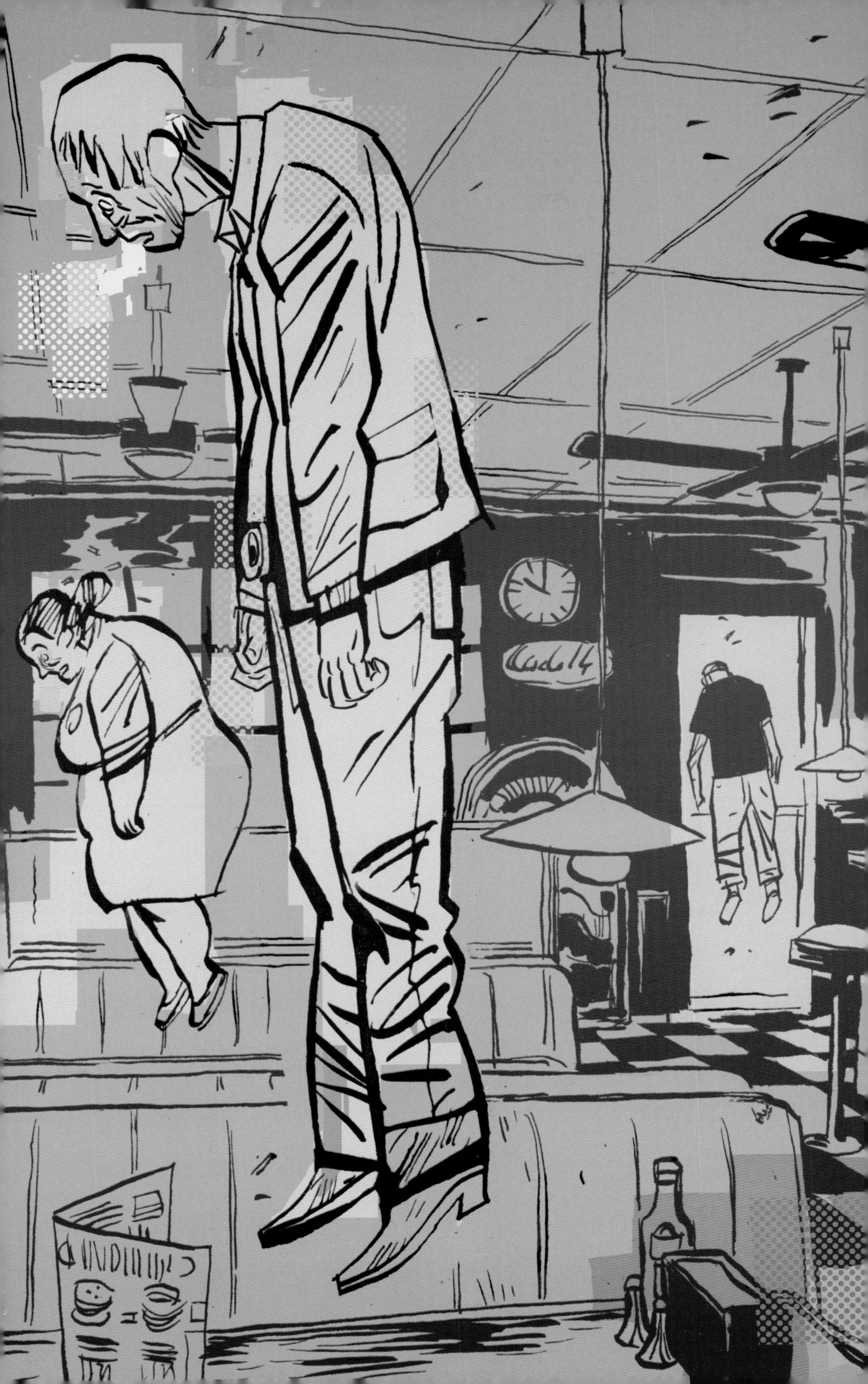

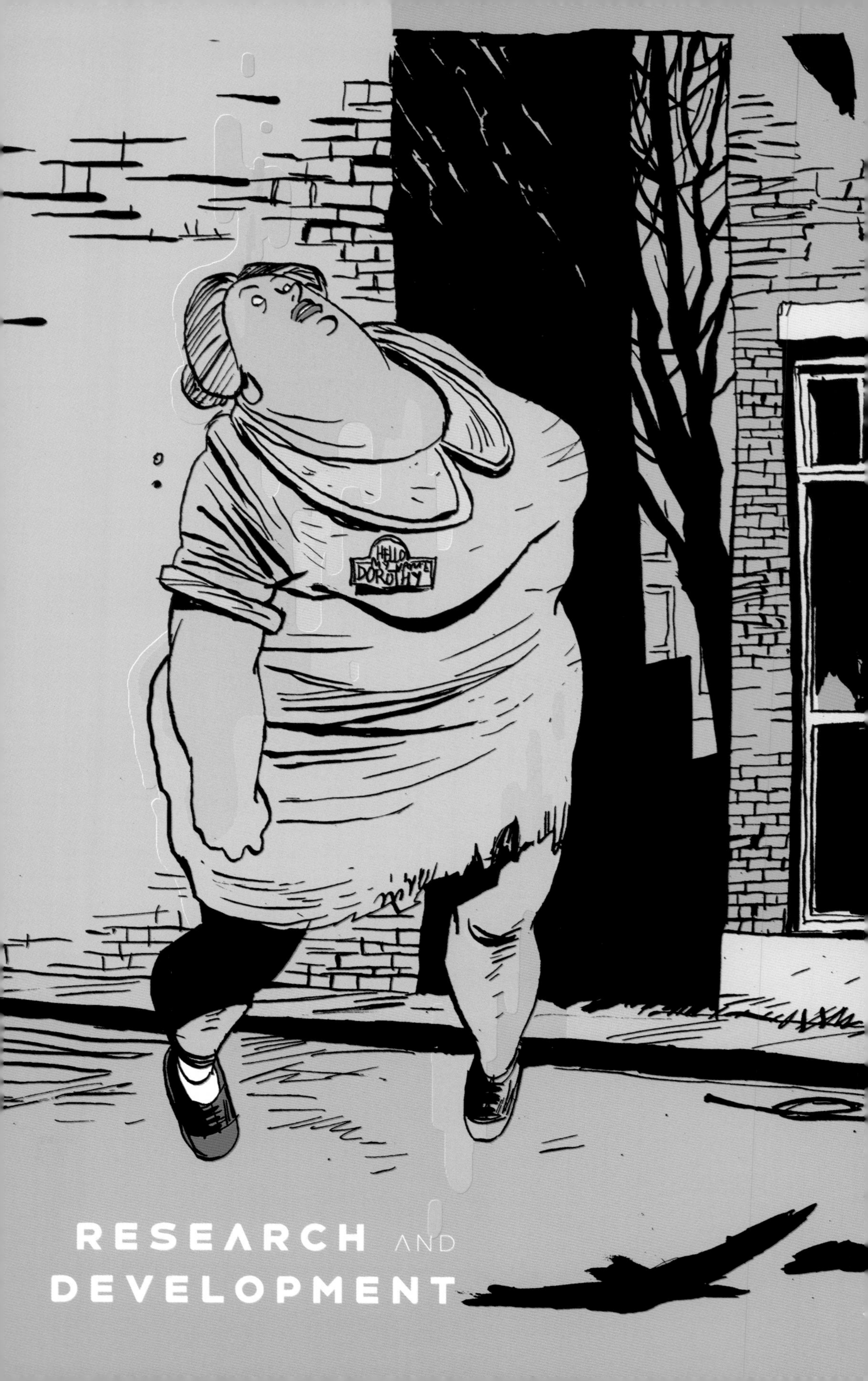
HELLO
DOROTHY
RESEARCH AND DEVELOPMENT

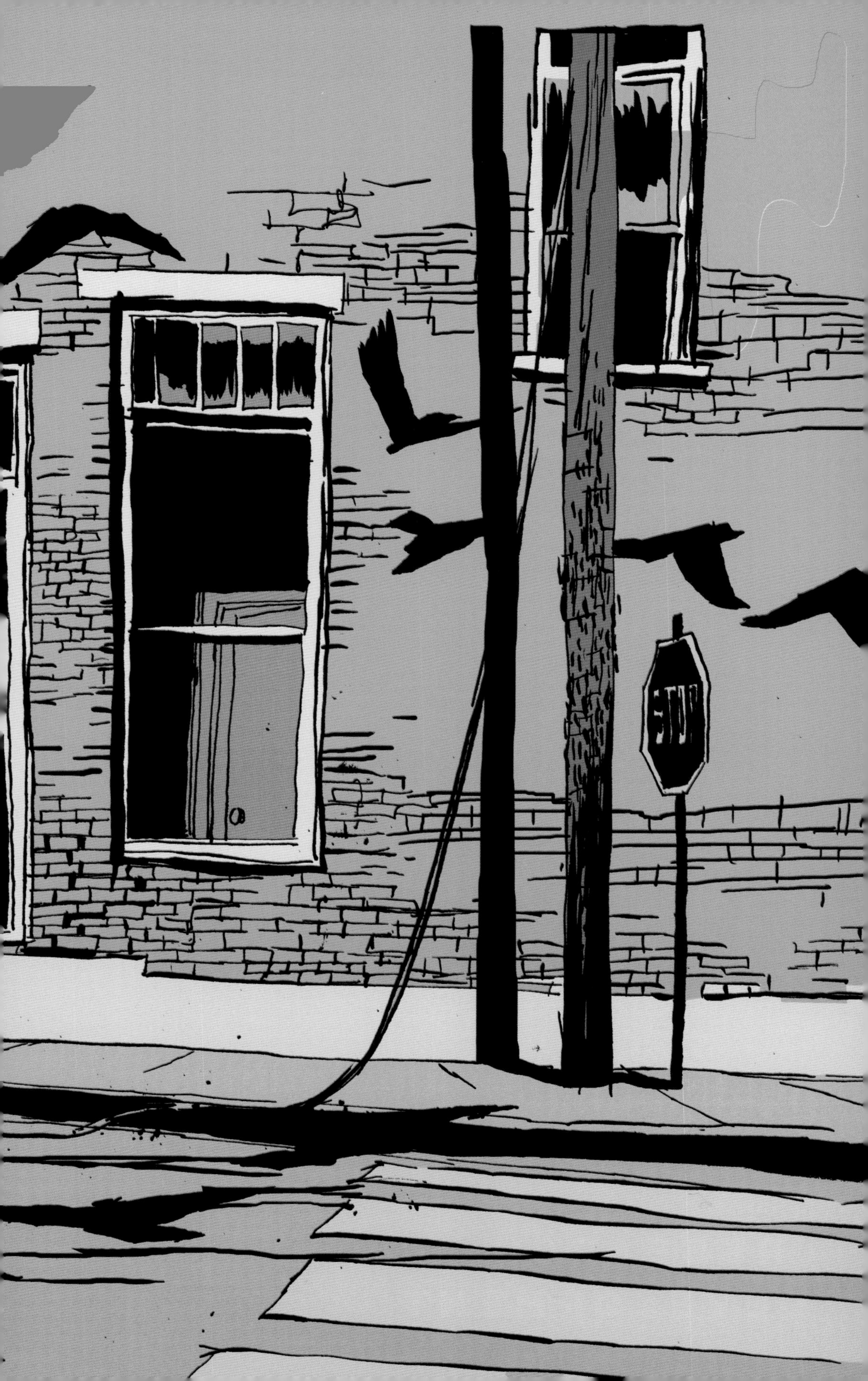

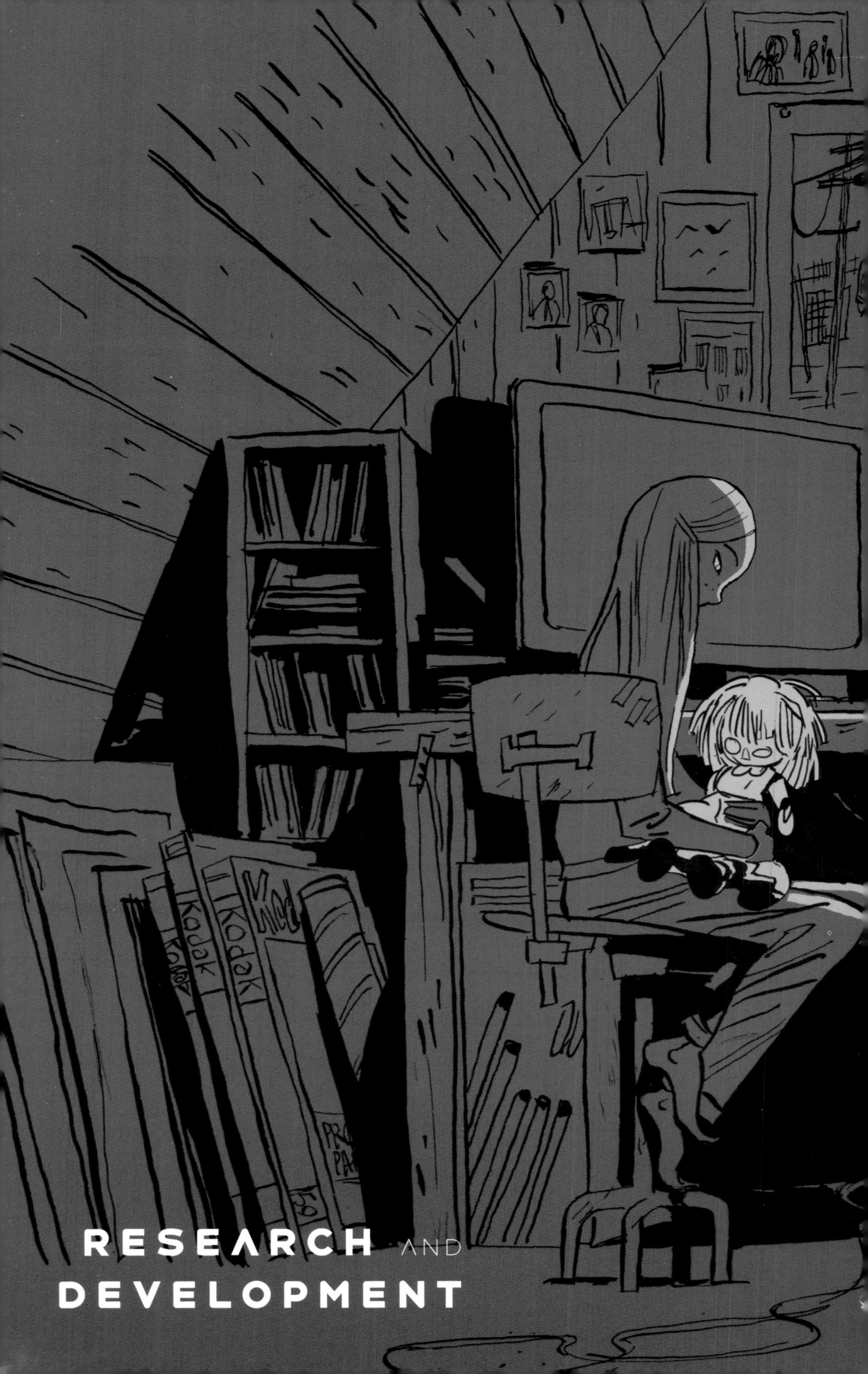
Kodak
Kodak

RESEARCH AND DEVELOPMENT

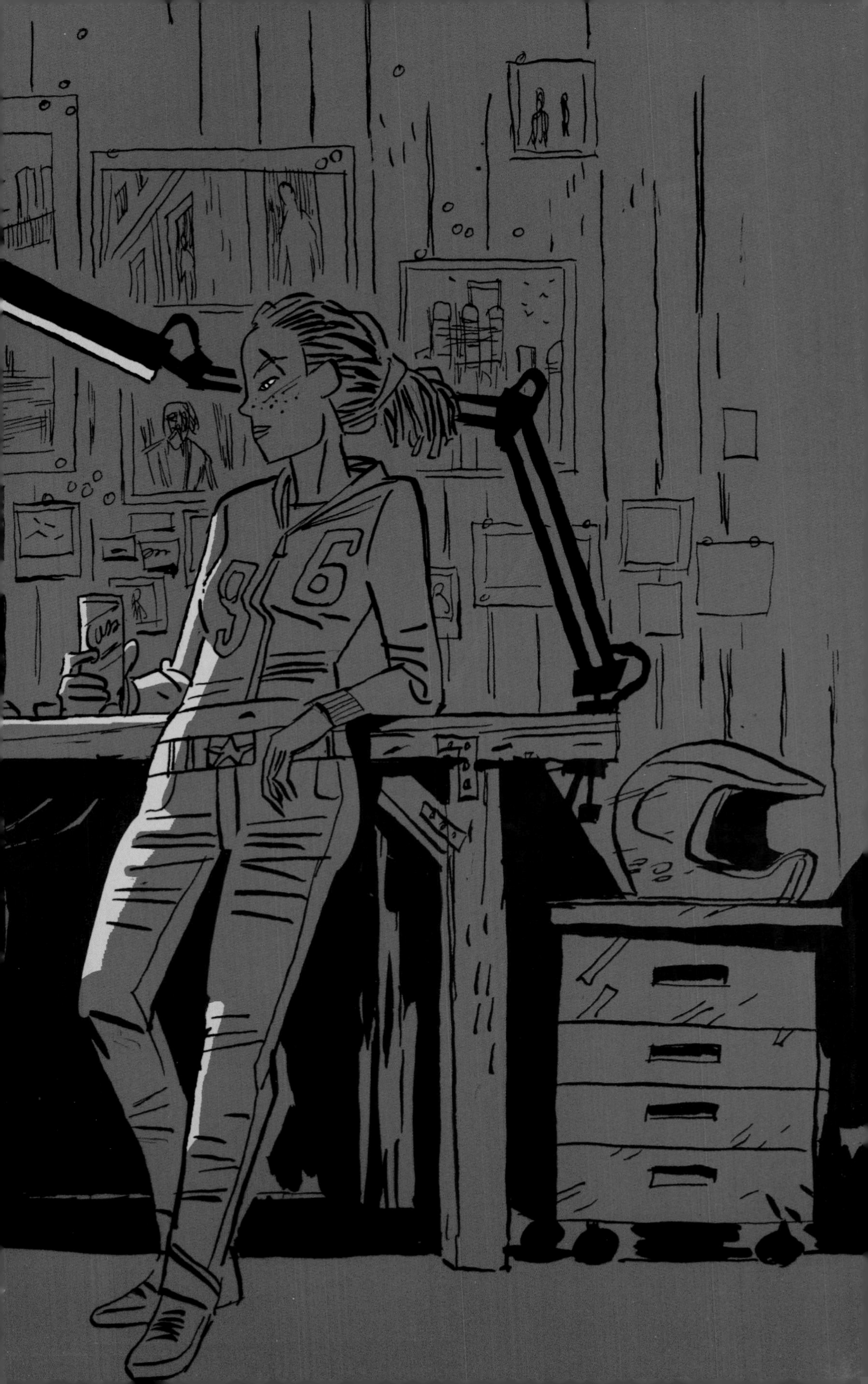
96

First Second
New York

Copyright © 2018 by Scott Westerfeld
Published by First Second
First Second is an imprint of Roaring Brook Press,
a division of Holtzbrinck Publishing Holdings Limited Partnership
120 Broadway, New York, NY 10271

Don't miss your next favorite book from First Second!
For the latest updates go to firstsecondnewsletter.com and sign up for our enewsletter.

Library of Congress Control Number: 2017946157

ISBN: 978-1-250-30942-6 (paperback)

Our books may be purchased in bulk for promotional, educational, or business use.
Please contact your local bookseller or the Macmillan Corporate and Premium Sales Department
at (800) 221-7945 ext. 5442 or by email at MacmillanSpecialMarkets@macmillan.com.

First edition, 2018
First paperback edition, 2019
Book design by Molly Johanson and Rob Steen
Printed in China by RR Donnelley Asia Printing Solutions Ltd., Dongguan City, Guangdong Province

1   3   5   7   9   10   8   6   4   2

Penciled and inked on regular copy paper
with a Speedball pen nib number 103 and a Pentel brush pen.
Colored digitally in Photoshop.